CW01270898

Planet Wrecker

(Doom Star 5)

by
Vaughn Heppner

Copyright © 2011 by the author.

This book is a work of fiction. Names, characters, places and incidents are either products of the author's imagination or used fictitiously. Any resemblance to actual events, locales or persons, living or dead, is entirely coincidental. All rights reserved. No part of this publication can be reproduced or transmitted in any form or by any means, without permission in writing from the author.

ISBN-13: 978-1496194213
ISBN-10: 1496194217
BISAC: Fiction / Science Fiction / Military

Junk drifted around Athena Station. Twisted girders, shell casings, asteroid rocks and dust, endless dust—it formed a black halo around the Jovian moon.

On the asteroid were shattered buildings, broken laser turrets and craters, many still hot and glowing red. In the tunnels, the underground storage facilities and now uninhabitable sleeping chambers were hundreds of Jovian corpses. Among them drifted cyborg bodies, most missing limbs or with smashed torsos. Deep in the station's core were the radioactive ruins of the former cyborg conversion unit. Jovian space marines had attempted capturing it intact. They'd paid a bitter price in lost soldiers when the last cyborgs had detonated the nuclear device. That had ended the battle for Athena Station.

The final patrol boat still on the moon ignited thrusters. It lifted off and began to thread its way through the endless debris orbiting the tiny planetoid.

The mass of debris blown off Athena Station dwarfed that blown off Carme fifteen months ago. Cyborg Gharlane, the prime unit in the Jupiter Assault, had ordered the extensive detonations for a reason. He now lay dead in a box that floated four hundred kilometers from the asteroid's surface. The box drifted among a field of rocks and fine particles of dust. Thick black-ice sheeted the box, which contained an AI, highly-advanced medical functions and battery power.

The box's power expenditure was minimal. With the ice-coating, it was low enough to have evaded Jovian sensor sweeps—at least so far. Lasers stabbed in the darkness, obliterating objects. The AI had run probability checks and concluded the Jovians weren't taking any chances. It appeared they were destroying anything with signs of life, anything with possible cyborg devices. It was only a matter a time before they beamed these rocks and ice as a precautionary measure.

Using a passive system, the AI monitored enemy communications. Then it used its intelligence to decipher the messages. One message met Gharlane's preconditions by seventy-three percent, enough to activate resuscitation.

Heaters warmed the dead bio-portions as energized blood began to pump through Gharlane. Needles entered his brainpan, injecting crystal-7, beginning the cryogenic de-thawing of his frozen tissues.

Gharlane had miscalculated on the speed of the Jovian counter-attack. Instead of two years, it had only taken fifteen months for them to retake much of their system. During these final weeks, he'd credited the speed and success of the enemy to Chief Strategist Tan. Within his minimal personality a hatred had grown for Strategist Tan which had transformed into a desire for revenge. Combined with the total silence of the Prime Web-Mind of Neptune, Gharlane had decided on a deception option. He'd sacrificed the last cyborgs in the Jovian System to cover his insertion into orbit.

The black-ice-coated box drifted through space, surrounded by the debris of battle. Around Gharlane's 'corpse', the medical devices began to hum at optimal levels.

In time, Gharlane opened his eyes: black plastic sockets with silver balls and red-lit pupils. His mouth twitched and he breathed shallowly, rapidly. Soon, the breathing deepened to a normal level.

He was cocooned and cushioned, with tubes sticking in his body. With an effort, he twisted his neck, moving his head until he faced a monitor. His titanium-reinforced fingers activated the box's passive sensors.

It took time, but he discovered three meteor-ships around Athena Station. They were at equidistant points, each more than one-thousand kilometers away from the asteroid. The searching, obliterating lasers stabbed out from these platforms.

Gharlane frowned. The AI should have—

A binary blip of data played in his head. He heard the message the AI had used to approve his revival.

Gharlane made a croaking sound, his first attempt at speech. He'd been right after all. The probabilities combined with the Jovians' noted parameters....

Powerful chemicals entered his bloodstream, cooling his elation. He would need cold calculation to achieve his last goal. The Chief Strategist had destroyed Athena Station, the last bastion of his life-function. Now he would exact a final penalty from her, and with it achieve a personal victory.

Gharlane turned his head the other way, and he began to issue directives. Stimulants granted him greater strength. New life surged with each additional dosage. He drained battery power into his booster-joints, magnifying his mechanical abilities.

Soon, the medical units whined as they began to retreat from him. Tubes popped out of his plasti-flesh. He slithered into a skintight garment and then crawled to a military vacc-suit. With painstaking care, he climbed into it and closed the seals. Then he attached primitive weapons to the belt. Enemy sensors would likely pick up higher-grade weaponry. Once finished, he uttered code words.

Darkness became complete as everything within the box shutdown. He waited.

...Ten seconds, nine, eight, seven—at zero, the locks snapped apart. The box split in two. That sent precise pressure against the outer ice. Cracks appeared in a zigzag line. From within the ruptured box, Gharlane exerted force. The lines in the ice crackled, and like a cocoon, the halves separated. The inner oxygen was a puff in the void. Then Gharlane appeared, climbing like a spiderling from its egg-sac.

The vacc-suit was black—coated with anti-radar. He crawled across the ice, and he pointed his helmet at the nearest meteor-ship. It would have been invisible to a human eye, but not to his enhanced orbs with teleoptic sight.

A patrol boat left the distant meteor-ship. The boat headed away from Athena Station. There was a high probability that the boat's occupants would rendezvous with the last Jovian

3

dreadnaught. The dreadnaught was two thousand kilometers away.

Gharlane gathered himself. He had the dreadnaught's coordinates, even though he couldn't see the vessel. He calculated its orbital drift. Mighty Jupiter hung in the darkness, but he ignored it and the giant storm known as the Red Spot. With cyborg precision, Gharlane leapt, propelling himself toward the dreadnaught's future location.

He was presently beyond the hot zone of laser strikes. More chemicals entered his bloodstream. His brain shut down as his body entered into hibernation. He drifted through space, heading toward his final destination.

Marten Kluge let the hot spray of the shower massage his tired muscles. That felt so good.

He had a lean, hard frame, with too many scars, tissue lumps and a purple bruise along the left side of his ribcage. A cyborg had almost killed him yesterday, using the stock of its laser carbine to butt his ribs. If they'd been fighting under regular gravity, he'd be dead now. Instead, he'd flown backward, cracking his helmeted head against a stanchion. The cyborg had been fast—they all were. Luckily, Marten's draw had been faster. As the cyborg had flown at him, he'd drawn his gyroc pistol, killing it before it had reached him.

The shower door opened then, causing the spray to cease automatically. Marten spun around, almost slipping on the wet tiles. A naked Nadia Pravda grinned at him. Then her eyes took in his purple bruise. She frowned.

"Marten—"

He grabbed a wrist and drew her into the tiny cubicle. He winced as she pressed against his ribs.

"I'm hurting you," she whispered.

He kissed her, and the hot spray began to jet against the two of them....

Lying on the bed afterward, Marten felt guilty about what he'd done. They weren't married yet. Nadia sat on the edge of the bed, combing her long hair. Her skin was so smooth, and her back—

"We should get married," he said.

Nadia turned her head, looking over her shoulder at him.

"You mean by a priest?"

"There are no priests among the Jovians," he said.

"How does one become married then?" she asked.

Marten groaned as he sat up. His ribs throbbed because of their lovemaking.

Worry filled her face. She set aside the brush and faced him. She had small, firm breasts, and her eyes were the most beautiful Marten had ever seen.

"The Jovians are killing you," she said.

Marten shook his head.

"Can't you see they're using you?" Nadia asked, anger entering her voice.

"I'm the best at this. It's what I do."

"No! They're merciless, and are squeezing every ounce of use from you before a cyborg puts a bullet in your brain."

"We finished the cyborgs."

"I don't believe that," she said.

"Athena Station was it," Marten said, "at least for the Jupiter System."

"That's another thing I don't understand," she said. "Why did Tan send space marines onto the station? Why didn't they just laser its offensive capabilities and annihilate it with nukes?"

"The cyborg conversion chamber—"

"Nearly got you and your men killed," Nadia said with heat. "The cyborgs detonated the thing before anyone could reach it."

"Did Omi tell you that?"

"It doesn't matter how I know. The Jovians are using you, and it nearly got you killed."

"I had to go down with my men."

"Why is it always you, Marten? Let others do the dirty work for once."

"Did Omi tell you we deactivated other nuclear devices? Without us there, *all* the space marines would have died."

"What?" Nadia asked, outraged.

Marten looked away. The Jovians were using him, he knew that. And it had been too close this time. Athena Station had been one giant booby-trap. The Force-Leader running the operation had told them it was vital they go down and salvage what they could. The Strategists needed clues concerning the cyborgs, some hint at what the Neptunian Web-Minds planned next.

Marten clenched his teeth as he rose up to his knees. He shuffled across the bed to Nadia. She was so beautiful. He put his hands on her bare shoulders and gently shook her.

She gave him a questioning look.

"I want you to be my wife, Nadia." He firmed his resolve, deciding to ask her straight out. That was the only way to be fair to her. "Will you marry me?" he asked, searching her eyes.

"Yes," she said, in a small voice.

Marten grinned, and his grip on her shoulders tightened. "Then before God, I declare you to be my wife."

"What does that mean?" Nadia whispered.

"It means that we're married. It means I'm your husband and you're my woman until death do us part."

"I don't want you to die, Marten."

"Neither do I," he said. "Now come here, wife." He drew her to him, and they lay down, beginning all over again.

An hour later, Marten entered a different cubicle. The dreadnaught's fusion engine made a soft thrum throughout the ship, and caused the bulkheads here to vibrate gently.

Omi sat on his cot as he cleaned his gun. It was similar to Marten's long-barreled slugthrower, which fired .38 caliber dum-dum bullets. A small piece of lead sat in the back of a bullet, in a tiny, domed-shaped cavity. When a dum-dum bullet struck an object, the lead in the cavity flew forward and caused the bullet to explode like a grenade. It made for murderous ammunition that caused ghastly wounds, a must against cyborgs.

"You ready?" Omi asked.

The Korean hadn't changed much since Carme. The only exception was his eyes. They were a little more haunted and there was a new line on his face.

"I married Nadia," Marten said.

Omi raised an eyebrow.

"You're supposed to congratulate me," Marten said.

Omi nodded slightly. Then he clipped the last part of his .38 back together and holstered it. "Chief Strategist Tan wants to speak with us."

"She's here?"

"Now that the war is over, the commander wants to inspect the front."

"I wonder what she's after?"

"You kidnapped her once, remember?"

"That was over a year ago."

"Do you think she's forgotten?" Omi asked.

"My kidnapping helped save her life."

"She might not remember it that way."

"No. If she feels that way about me, why hasn't she done something about it before now?"

Omi made a sour sound that might have been a laugh. "Are you kidding? You're the heart of their space marines, and you're the blood, too."

"They have others units beside ours."

"Those others died," Omi said, "or most of them died. We have the only unit that has survived contact with the enemy more than twice."

Marten crossed his arms. He could count the number of survivors on two hands—those that had made it through both Carme and Athena Station. When men faced cyborgs, the men died. He had a few theories now, some new tactics he wanted to try. The Battle for Jupiter was over, however, thank God.

"You think Tan's finished with us?" Marten asked.

"Didn't you notice the myrmidons when we came aboard, and the arbiter?"

Marten vaguely remembered. Then he had been too busy noticing Nadia. Now that Omi mentioned it...there had been changes these past few months aboard the military vessels. They were little things, or so he'd thought then.

"Arbiters and myrmidons," Marten said. "I wonder if she's going back to old Callisto methods."

Omi stood up. "My guess is we're about to find out."

Marten glanced at Omi's gun. Then he patted his own. "The arbiters don't have any nullifiers that will protect them from these."

"How long do you think they'll let us wear guns?" Omi asked.

Marten shrugged.

"She's a Strategist," Omi said, "and she's separated us from our men on the *Erasmus*. Our ship is more than two-thousand kilometers away. "

"...Yeah," Marten said, nodding. "Let's go find out the worst."

"Let's," Omi said.

The two of them headed for the door.

-4-

Marten forced himself to observe.

The corridors in the dreadnaught were narrow. At various intervals on the walls were stylistic syllogisms, pithy aphorisms and logical deductions. There was a golden statue in the middle of a nexus. It showed a bearded philosopher in a toga, with a stylus in one hand and a tightly-bound scroll in the other.

"I thought they'd removed all those," Marten whispered to Omi.

Omi was too busy glaring at the three myrmidons to answer. The myrmidons were from the gene-vats, and were a form of Jovian military police. None were as tall as Marten. Each was immensely broad of shoulder, with a deep chest and muscular arms that dangled like a gorilla's arms. The heads hunched low and beady eyes peered from beneath short-billed helmets. They wore uniforms with large epaulets on the shoulders, and carried an assortment of weaponry on their belts. The jangle of the weaponry mingled with the constant thrum of the fusion engine deep in the ship.

A white-haired arbiter preceded them. The arbiter wore a crisp white uniform with red tabs. He was as short as the myrmidons, but was aesthetically lean. At his belt was a palm-pistol. Whereas the myrmidons seemed bestial, the arbiter was refined. He possessed delicate features and a superior attitude, most notable by the distaste that twisted his mouth whenever he glanced at Marten or Omi.

"I thought they'd phased out arbiters," Marten whispered.

11

Omi nodded.

Marten had been busy these past fifteen months. He'd trained space marines using Highborn techniques. Osadar and Omi had helped him, and then they'd been his lieutenants in combat. The fifteen months had been a blur of activity and endless drills. Occasionally, he'd read a news site. The cyborgs had shattered the Jovian System. Slowly, the human survivors had jelled together, attempting to form a more perfect union.

Robot repair vessels had entered Jupiter's upper atmosphere, fixing those deuterium and helium-3-gathering floaters they could. New storage facilities on the Inner group moons arose. Europa and Ganymede launched defensive satellites. Survey teams probed a smoldering Io. People fled exposed asteroids and the smaller moons, emigrating to the larger Galilean moons.

Marten glanced at a golden triangle on the ceiling. A silver pyramid was in the center, with a lidless eye in the center of the pyramid. That had meaning in the old order of philosopher, guardian and mechanic. That order had died, however, when the cyborgs had destroyed ninety-seven percent of Callisto and its populace.

"Have you been reading the news sites much?" Marten whispered.

Omi grunted a negative.

Marten frowned. Osadar Di often tried to talk to him about the Jovian political situation. He'd paid scant attention to her, too worried about how to train his space marines so they could face cyborgs and survive, and maybe even win.

What had he read the other day? Osadar had scribed it to him. He deleted most of her messages unread. She wrote these long screeds on things, seemingly writing a book on each topic. It was too much for him even to try skimming. But he had read an interesting link the other day. It was concerning the growing triad of power in the Jupiter System.

There were the political leaders of Ganymede and Europa forming one side, the Helium-3 Barons forming another and the former Guardian Fleet personnel the third. According to the article, there had been a shift in fleet personnel during the fifteen months of war. The last survivors of Callisto—various station crewmembers, far-outpost personnel and monitors—had inexorably entered the fleet. There was no other place for them where they felt as comfortable. There were only a few military vessels left, and they were concentrated with the last people of Callisto. In effect, the old order had been resurrected in the remaining patrol boats, meteor-ships and the lone dreadnaught. The article had finished with a cry for civilian control of Jupiter and an end to the tyrannous rule of Chief Strategist Tan.

A cold feeling coiled in Marten's stomach. "Do you remember which units stormed onto Athena Station?" he whispered.

"You will cease with your infernal muttering," the arbiter said over his shoulder. Marten recalled the man had told them his name was Neon. He spoke with a nasal tone, with didactic authority.

Marten opened his mouth to reply, and he felt Omi's grip on his wrist. He glanced at Omi. The Korean minutely shook his head. The look said more than just 'stay quiet.' It said this wasn't the place for a showdown. It was better to wait.

Marten's nostrils flared, but he nodded minutely, and he kept his mouth shut.

The myrmidons had grown tense. They glanced at Neon. The lean arbiter sneered in his superior fashion, the way a highhanded teacher might before inferior students. Flicking his wrist, Neon indicated that they keep heading toward their destination.

Omi released Marten's wrist and the grip of his holstered pistol.

Marten found he'd been holding his breath. Anger surged through him. He stared hotly at the arbiter's back, wanting to clout the man across the back of the head. But the myrmidons would attack if he did that.

Then it hit Marten. Had that been staged? He scowled. If Chief Strategist Tan wanted him disarmed, she could order it. Yet maybe it wasn't that simple. The article had spoken about three keys to the Jovian power base.

Marten glanced around, and he spotted spy-sticks on the ceiling, recording devices. If Tan presented the controllers of Europa and Ganymede and the Helium-3 Barons with video of

13

him going berserk—

The cold feeling in Marten's stomach grew. He'd like to study the space marine manifests of the units that had stormed Athena Station. More importantly, he'd like to study the place of origin of the personnel. It was natural to put soldiers from Ganymede, say, into one unit. It was best to put men from the same town into a unit. Men fought harder with their friends around them and men fought more poorly amongst strangers. Which units had stormed Athena Station? Or asked another way, which units had remained out of the action and therefore had retained one hundred percent of its soldiers?

Chief Strategist Tan had fought a masterful campaign against the cyborgs. Would she simply relinquish power now, or might she have maneuvered these past fifteen months to retain authority? Her power rested on one thing: a preponderance of military personnel and hardware.

Marten rolled his shoulders, trying to ease the kinks out of them. It wasn't that he didn't care who ruled. He cared all right. But after Yakov's death fifteen months ago, he was more concerned with killing and defeating cyborgs.

Arbiter Neon halted, turned and raised his hand.

Marten noticed the arbiter glancing at the myrmidons, as if signaling them. Marten cleared his throat sharply and reached for his gun.

The myrmidons were fast. Each spun around with a shock rod in one hand and a stunner in the other. Maybe if they had fired that instant everything would have worked for them.

Omi had been a gunman once in a vicious drug gang in Sydney. Then he'd gone through Highborn training and had survived the Hell of the Japan Campaign. He caught the signal and clawed his long-barreled .38 free of its holster.

Marten drew even faster than Omi. While Omi aimed at the nearest myrmidon, Marten held his pitted barrel at Neon's forehead.

The arbiter's smug smile vanished as he stared at the ugly weapon. The color drained from his face, leaving it a pasty white. Then two bright dots appeared on his cheeks.

"Lower your weapons," Arbiter Neon whispered.

"Your myrmidons are fast," Marten said. There was steel in

14

his voice. "But I'm betting I can put a hole in your forehead and gun each of them down before they twitch a finger on their stunners."

Marten refrained from adding that Omi and he each wore a nullifier, won long ago on Yakov's meteor-ship.

"You are aboard the Chief Strategist's flagship," Neon said in a choked voice. "Her authority is supreme here. Any deviation from it is a breach of protocol."

Marten motioned Omi. The two of them took several steps back. The stunners might not affect them. The bony knuckles on the end of those dangling arms surely could, however. Marten had respect for the fighting prowess of the gene-warped warriors.

"The Dictates—" Neon began to say.

"Died with Callisto's passing," Marten said.

Neon stiffened. And that made the senior myrmidon growl menacingly.

"You spout inanities," Neon said harshly. "You—"

On the ceiling, a red light flashed near one of the spy-sticks. Neon's head twitched. He clamped a thin hand over his right ear. He must have had an implant there. He frowned, and he gave his head the slightest negative shake.

"New orders, eh?" asked Marten.

Neon opened his mouth. He never uttered his chosen phrase. A door swished open at the head of the corridor. Tan stood there.

She was a tiny woman, with smooth, bio-sculpted features. She was beautiful in an elfin way, with dark hair wound around her head. She wore a red robe, with red slippers and with red rings around her small fingers.

"Chief Strategist," Neon said.

"You and your myrmidons shall stand guard outside my door," Tan said. Her gaze flickered over Omi. "I didn't ask for your bodyguard."

"You asked to see both of us," Marten said.

Tan had dark eyes. They seemed to turn a shade darker as she stared at him. "Tell him to return to his quarters."

"She's separating us," Omi whispered.

"The Chief Strategist has given you instructions," Neon

15

said. "Instant obedience is expected, along with proper protocol. You will address her as—"

"What kind of protocol did you give the cyborgs on Athena Station?" Marten asked.

"What?" Neon said.

"Did you land with us?" asked Marten, sick of behind-the-lines policemen.

"I'm not an animal that grubs among the beasts," Neon said, outraged.

"Enough," said Tan.

"But Your Excellency—" Neon said, turning toward her.

"I have spoken," said Tan.

Neon stiffened, and the twin spots of color reappeared on his cheeks. After a half-second's delay, he flicked his right hand at the myrmidons. They spread out in the corridor and then crouched low, ready like defensive robots.

"Are you expecting trouble?" Marten asked.

"Order your bodyguard back to his quarters," said Tan. "Then tell him to disarm. You may give your sidearm to him as well."

"…Not just yet," Marten said.

Arbiter Neon's head swiveled toward him. The man placed his hand on his palm-pistol.

"I have given you an order," Tan said.

"We're still in a combat zone," Marten said. "Soldiers don't disarm under those conditions."

"You dare to engage me in a dialogue?" asked Tan.

"I'm a soldier and this is a combat zone. That means—"

"All the cyborgs are dead," said Tan. "You will obey me at once."

Marten didn't like the direction of the conversation. His only true friends had died or waited aboard the *Erasmus*, the handful of space marines that had endured two battles against the cyborgs with him. Maybe he should have paid more attention to what Osadar had been trying to tell him. He'd been too busy fighting a war to worry about the peace. That might have been a mistake.

"Chief Strategist," Marten said. "I request your permission to keep my sidearm. If you refuse, I will relinquish my command and return at once to the *Erasmus*."

"You are in no position to give me terms," Tan said.

Suddenly, Marten was weary of the bickering. It reminded him of Major Orlov, of Training Master Lycon and Arbiter Octagon, of everyone who'd tried to tell him what to think.

"I'm not giving you terms," Marten said. "I'm telling you what I'm going to do."

"You will adjust your tone while addressing me," said Tan.

Marten squinted at the small woman. She controlled the bulk of the military vessels in this planetary system. She was the de facto ruler. But Marten no longer cared. She was playing games he didn't understand, and through the arbiter, she'd just tried to disarm them.

"Did you wish to see me?" Marten asked.

Tan's mouth grew firm, and three seconds passed. "Your bodyguard will return to his room."

"And?" asked Marten.

"And you and I shall speak within," said Tan.

"Sure," Marten said, recognizing that she'd dropped any reference to his disarming, at least for now. He'd won this round. Now he'd have to make sure he walked out of her chamber a free man.

5

In Tan's chamber, a statue mused in a corner. The statue depicted a fawn of a woman with wisps of cloth heightening her semi-nudity. The statue stared into an unseen distance, as if thoughtfully concerned over the fate of the world. A golden lyre hung on a wall, as did several faint, brushstroke paintings. Brown and teal silk hung from the ceiling in a complex pattern of loops.

Tan knelt on a cushion before a low table. On the table was a small dispensary, with a silver chalice beside it. Smoothing her robe, Tan indicated that Marten should sit across from her. Then she picked up the chalice and pressed a button on the dispensary. A blue pill appeared. With tiny fingers, Tan slipped the pill onto her tongue, sipping it down with wine.

Feeling like a giant, Marten sat cross-legged on a cushion. He had to adjust his holster to do so. The table was metallic and smooth, with controls near Tan's hands. No doubt, she could project images on it.

"You leave me in a quandary," said Tan.

"I'm not sure I understand."

"It would trouble me if you did," said Tan, sipping more wine.

"I don't want to give you trouble," Marten said. "Look, you've just destroyed the last cyborgs in the system. You should be rejoicing. Then you should figure out how to take the fight to the enemy."

"Ah," she said, setting the chalice onto the table without making a sound. "You reached that conclusion even faster than

I'd expected you to do. But then, you are a monomaniac."

"What's that supposed to mean?"

"The obvious: that you're a single-minded soldier. I might add that you thrive on mayhem, on chaos and instability."

"You call fighting to stay alive mayhem?"

"I've studied you, Marten Kluge. You're more than a soldier. You are a killer, an atavistic throwback to man's earliest times. You would have done well in a suit of armor on a horse and with a sword."

"If this is about the kidnapping—"

"You once laid hands on my person," said Tan, with a trace of emotion. "Believe me, I haven't forgotten the event."

"Good. Then you'll also remember that you planned to go to Athena Station. If I hadn't stopped you, you would have unknowingly given yourself to the cyborgs."

Tan smiled indulgently. "You claim to have kidnapped me for my greater good?"

"Chief Strategist," said Marten.

Tan held up a small hand. "That day, your actions were beneficial to me. I concede you the point. No. This meeting has nothing to do with that. The cyborgs invaded our system, destroyed three-fourths of our society and then perished under our retaliatory strikes."

"I helped kill the cyborgs."

"Killing to you is as eating is to a glutton," said Tan.

Marten banged the table with a fist. "I resent that."

"Now your barbarism is on display."

"This is just great," said Marten. "Everywhere I go, people try to kill me or try to force me to accept their beliefs. They don't ever consider that I might want to run my own life."

"I'm sure every killer espouses a similar doctrine."

"I'm tired of you calling me a killer. You're the killer."

Tan smiled faintly. "Your dialogue lacks grace and wit. It is a sophomoric verbal assault. Undoubtedly, it's the reason you're so quick to resort to physical violence."

Marten's eyes narrowed. "You're the one using genetically-warped policemen. I thought you Jovians had stopped using myrmidons. When did that change?"

Tan's manner intensified as she stared at him.

19

It allowed Marten a good look at her eyes, at their dilatation. There was a glassy sheen to them, perhaps a side effect of the blue pill. It made him pause and wonder what it would be like orchestrating the war against the cyborgs. They were cunning, ruthless enemies. Yet Tan had made some brilliant guesses these past months, and she had outmaneuvered the guiding cyborg intelligence. Marten had never considered what that kind of high-level pressure might do to a person. He'd heard how the controllers of Europa and Ganymede constantly argued with Tan, and how the Helium-3 Barons tried to interfere with military matters.

"I congratulate you on your victory," Marten said abruptly.

Tan appeared not to hear.

"The cyborgs were clever," he added.

Leaning toward him, Tan clutched the table's edge. "Clever, you say. They were brilliant."

"Yet you beat them."

A line creased Tan's otherwise smooth forehead. It heightened her beauty. Then she eased back so she rested her butt on her heels. Turning her head, she looked at the golden lyre.

"They destroyed us," she whispered. "They killed the most superior form of life in the Solar System, and by that I mean the Dictates. Yes, I crushed them as one would a spider. As the last philosopher-queen of Callisto, it was my solemn duty to do so. Yet what have I achieved? Renewed life of the perfected form?" She shook her head slowly.

"The war was brutal," Marten said.

Tan stopped shaking her head to regard him. "Banality is your strong suit."

"I thought it was being a killer."

"A banal killer," she said with a soft shrug.

"What's wrong with you? You've just won a great victory. Now you sulk in your room and turn against your fellow soldiers."

Something flashed in her eyes. "You dare to equate me with yourself? I belong to the philosophers. You are at best a guardian who cannot understand his place in the hierarchy. There is no equality between us."

"Are you drunk?" asked Marten.

Tan made a sharp gesture. "I have enhanced my thinking. I see linkages between actions that are invisible to others."

"Yeah, I can see that," Marten said. He adjusted his holster. "You know what I think."

"Grace me with your wit," she said.

"I think you're trying to revive Callisto or these Dictates the only way possible now: through a military dictatorship. Which units landed on Athena Station? Did you hold back the ones with Callisto space marines?"

"How little you know."

"You're brilliant," Marten said. "You've fought a grueling war against aliens of human devising. The cyborgs are a nightmare, and they're merciless, more than willing to bring about our extinction. Your strategies checked them at every turn. I did some hard fighting, along with many others. Too many good men died implementing your orders."

"*The wisest should rule*," said Tan. "It is an axiom of inexorable truth."

"*Men should live free*," said Marten. "It's what makes life worth living."

"Ah, your quixotic belief," said Tan.

"I'm not sure what that word means, but your tone, the myrmidons outside—you want to revive the old Callisto order."

"Look around you, Marten Kluge."

Marten glanced at the paintings on the walls.

"No," she said. "That was a metaphorical phrase. How simple you really are, how direct and…barbaric."

"What happened to you?" Marten asked. "You've changed."

The glassy look to Tan's eyes had grown. "I peered into the abyss, barbarian, into the future. I saw the cyborgs staring back at me—and no humans existed in that future."

"We beat the cyborgs."

"We defeated a small penetration raid into our system."

"How do you know it was just a raid?" asked Marten.

"It is self-evident," whispered Tan. She picked up the chalice, staring into the depths of the cup. "How does one face

21

certain doom?" She shook her head. "I realized many months ago that I must retain full control of the Jovian moons, as only I possessed the insights, the sheer brain-power to counter cyborg brilliance. Strategically, there was only one manner in which I could do so."

"You're wrong," Marten said.

Tan looked up, blinking. She seemed surprised to see him. "Wrong?" she said, as if tasting the word.

"You're trying to re-forge the chains that bound the Jovians in servitude. Don't you remember Force-Leader Yakov? He sacrificed his life so we could defeat the cyborgs on Carme. He didn't sacrifice it so proud philosophers from Callisto could lord it over the people of Ganymede."

"You poor barbarian, you're too ignorant to appreciate the glory of the superior life."

"Do you think I've fought these past months in order to let you handcuff me?"

"You are a virus, Marten Kluge. You spout your inanities about freedom and find eager listeners, I know. By freedom, however, you mean license for the glutton to gorge himself with food and the sex fiend to rut like an animal with any willing partner. Humans need guidance. They need purpose. The philosopher does what I've done: giving this guidance for the furtherance of the whole. Your freedom would dissolve human associations into chaos. Then the cyborgs would defeat us with even greater ease."

"Yakov fought to free Ganymede from your philosophic oppression."

"Yakov, Yakov, I grow weary of hearing his name. He is dead. Let him remain so."

Marten leaned across the table. "Yakov gave his life because he saw how precious freedom was. He'd tasted it, as I've tasted it. The cyborgs sought to enslave us in nightmarish servitude. Yakov gave his life to defeat them and stop such a bitter future."

"Yakov was a soldier, a guardian, a man of spirit. It was his nature to do as you've described. You shouldn't try to give his act more grace than it deserves."

"I see," Marten said. He found that he was breathing hard.

He struggled to control himself. "You're under the illusion that it was your generalship that gave us victory."

"Your emotionalism has confused you," said Tan. "First you entered my chamber, praising my guidance. Now you reverse course. Which is it, because you cannot logically say both?"

"Your generalship would have been useless without hard-fighting soldiers."

"Ah," said Tan, "therein lays your ignorance. Like most fighters, you overvalue yourself. The sword is nothing without the brain that guides it."

"Fancy footwork stops when a laser burns you down," Marten said.

"Is that a threat?" Tan asked softly.

Marten banged the table with his fist, and this time, Tan flinched.

"Forget about that," he said. "The truth is I don't care who rules here. It's such a little thing that it makes me angry I'm even arguing about it."

"You are amazingly illogical and sporadic. I'm beginning to wonder if your chaotic thought-patterns act as a protective shielding. It's almost impossible for a high-grade logician such as me to predict your course or understand your thinking."

"Listen to me," Marten said. "I've thought a lot about how to defeat the cyborgs."

"You are a monomaniac, as I've said." Tan fingered one of her rings. Its signet was the Greek letter *omega*. "Has your single-mindedness unhinged you? The cyborgs *are* defeated."

"I'm talking about killing every one of them in the Solar System," Marten said. "I've actually met them on the battlefield, not just theorized about them in the quietness of my study. I know how incredibly deadly they are."

"...The people of Callisto knew that too," Tan said softly. "My cousin Su-Shan knew that."

"That's why you should be listening to me, instead of insulting me," Marten said. "You've seen the devastation caused by these aliens. You must know like me that the Jovians cannot defeat them on their own."

Tan lowered the chalice with a clunk. She frowned at

Marten.

"We have to unite against them," he said.

"We?" asked Tan.

"Every human in the Solar System," Marten said. "The Jovian moons, Mars, Earth, Venus, maybe even the Highborn. The Praetor gave his life to kill cyborgs. Maybe the other Highborn—"

"The Highborn are too arrogant," Tan said. "It would be like taking orders from myrmidons. That would be worse than foolishness."

"Okay, forget about the Highborn then," Marten said. "The point is we should be joining forces to take out the cyborgs."

"Join Social Unity?" asked Tan. "They obliterated the Jovian expeditionary fleet many years ago."

"No, I'm not taking about *joining* Social Unity. I fled from them, remember?"

"What do I care about your past actions? You must make your meanings clear, barbarian."

"Bah!" Marten said. "You're drugged. Why am I even bothering with you?"

"I possess the superior intellect. I have trained my entire life so I can control my emotions and think logically."

"Yeah, sure," Marten said. He scowled, and he pressed both palms onto the metal table. "You said it earlier. You looked into the future, and no humans looked back at you. That tells me we have to bury our differences and band together. Every human left in the Solar System needs to unite, just as the various Jovians united here."

"I cannot believe that Social Unity rulers would agree to abide under the Dictates."

"They won't. But they might agree to fight together against the cyborgs. Use that superior intellect of yours and think about what I'm saying."

Tan pursed her lips. She opened her mouth, but before she uttered any words, a klaxon began to wail.

6

Gharlane withdrew his blade from the warm carcass. It collapsed in a seemingly boneless fashion at his feet. Kneeling, Gharlane plucked the hammer-gun from the corpse's belt. He searched and found extra ammo magazines.

Gharlane had drifted through space for endless hours, submerged in a coma. His life-readings had been underneath the threshold of any sensors that had scanned his region of space. After a precise length of time, an internal chronometer had clicked and he'd been injected with vigorous stims. Upon waking, he'd discovered that his calculations had been off by point zero-zero-two percent. As he'd floated in space, he'd fired a spring-loaded spear gun. It had shot a barb with monofilament fiber over a kilometer, attaching to the dreadnaught's particle-shield. Gharlane had reeled himself to the dreadnaught, crawled between two particle-shields and gained entry into the ship.

"Override," he now whispered in the ship, adding a sequence of binary numbers. He overrode the calming chemicals in his bloodstream and gave himself combat-enhancing injections. His existence would end during the next few minutes. The achievement of his goal—that was primary.

The ship corridor was narrow, and there was a trace of oil in the atmosphere indicating working mechanisms and recycled air. The nearly imperceptibly-vibrating deckplates showed that the fusion engine was online.

Gharlane surged forward, colliding into a bio-form that came fast around the corner. Over three times its weight,

Gharlane knocked the bio-form backward and off its feet. Its head snapped back hard against a deckplate, almost rendering the female unconscious. A precise kick of his vacc-suited foot against the female's head killed it. A quick inspection of its torso added another hammer-gun to his growing collection.

Klaxons wailed as Gharlane trotted down the corridors—the ship was under centrifugal-gravity. He repeatedly emptied his hammer-guns, killing over two dozen humans, the last group obviously sent to intercept him. These were inferior specimens compared to the space marines that had stormed onto Athena Station. For a moment, he wondered if he could reach the fusion core and blow the entire ship.

No. The core would be protected. Every human captain had learned to guard it after the destruction of a Doom Star during the Martian Campaign. None of that mattered now, however.

Gharlane slammed a magazine into one of the hammer-guns. The other had malfunctioned. He'd sacrificed his last cyborgs so he could achieve this location. Chief Strategist Tan—she was a first level intellect that had used the Jovian military with canny ability. Web-Mind analysis of the Homo sapiens indicated the rarity of such unmodified first-level intellects. As primary targets, such rare individuals were to be expunged with extreme prejudice.

I will cease to exist soon. But I will take the first level intellect into the darkness with me.

The death of such a militarily important target was, according to a Web-Mind's parameters, worth the deletion of a planetary system's controlling cyborg.

Gharlane jumped around a corner into a fusillade of shots. They'd been waiting for him. A hammer-bolt smashed against his chest-plate. Another caromed off his titanium-reinforced skull. Instead of falling onto his back, Gharlane bent onto one knee. Smoothly, he snapped off three shots before another hammer-bolt clipped his hip, spinning him.

Painkillers already flooded his bodily system. Boosters accelerated his reactions. From his kneeling position, he leaped at the nexus-node, firing with cyborg precision.

A blue-uniformed woman tumbled back, her forehead a gory ruin. Three other ship-guardians were already twisted into bleeding heaps, their weapons clattering across the deckplates.

"Die, you freak!" a guardian shouted. He had a pulse rifle poked around a corner. A red pulse ejected from the tube. It missed by a fraction, blowing a hole into the wall of the corridor and producing a metallic-smelling gout of black smoke.

Gharlane fired. The man's throat became a red ruin as he cartwheeled away from the corner. Before the pulse rifle could hit the deckplates, Gharlane snatched it out of the air.

He moved like a giant insect in a blur of motion. Black blood dripped from several of his wounds. Gouged titanium showed in places. His vacc-suit was useless now, torn in a dozen spots.

One sobbing guardian tried to run away. Gharlane hurled his expended hammer-gun, catching the slow-moving creature in the neck. With a howl, the man flew off his feet and hit the flooring with his chest. Gharlane cracked his left elbow into the last guardian's face, breaking bones. A punch into the thing's throat finished it.

Turning into the corridor with the prone guardian, Gharlane charged down it toward the commander's cubicle. He connected with his steel-toed boot, caving in the guardian's forehead. Then he moved his legs like pistons, firing from the hip as he sprinted through the ship.

He was at eighty-three percent capacity, the enemy shots having taken a toll of his efficiency. He was a master unit cyborg: heavier, and constructed of more durable materials than the combat models.

I will die soon. I will cease. Chief Strategist Tan defeated me. She cannot be allowed life. I must end her existence.

A growl alerted Gharlane. His lips drew back into a platinum smile. He spun around the last corner, firing the pulse rifle, adjusting as the pulse ejected from the tube.

A myrmidon sprang. The red pulse blew it backward, leaving a gaping hole in its thick chest.

Two others charged. There was no finesse to their attack. Stun impulses struck Gharlane's body. It felt like steel balls slamming against him. The stun-shots would have dropped a Homo sapien and would have forced a Highborn to his knees.

The stuns disoriented Gharlane. Then pain-rejecters momentarily numbed his nerve endings.

He fired the pulse rifle, and clipped a myrmidon's shoulder. The attacking creatures snarled, and each stroked his body with their shock rods. Gharlane punched the pulse rifle's tube into a myrmidon's gut, achieving penetration. The thing howled, and it clawed his face. The other myrmidon must have recognized that its shock rod was having minimal effect. It dropped the rod and attacked barehanded.

Gharlane freed his blade, burying it in a myrmidon's chest. The creature possessed amazing vitality, however. It kept attacking. So did the other, and it was damaging him. His efficiency had dropped to seventy-nine percent, and was dropping several percentage points each second of combat.

Yanking the blade free, Gharlane slashed and stabbed with cyborg speed and strength. If the myrmidons had held combat knives, it might have ended differently. But they didn't.

Gharlane drew a ragged breath as he hurled the gene-warped creatures from him. Black blood soaked his vacc-suit, mingling with red myrmidon blood. Graphite-strengthened bones showed in places.

One myrmidon flopped on the deckplates, twitching in death. The other mewled with rage, attempting to crawl back into combat. But its back was broken and it made minimal progress.

Gharlane bent down to retrieve his pulse rifle.

The door to the commander's chamber swished open. Gharlane didn't waste time looking up. With blurring speed, he grabbed the rifle and hurled himself forward. While airborne, he lifted the rifle and paused a fraction of a second. He'd expected more charging myrmidons or humans leaning out of the door. He didn't expect to see a man standing in the doorway, aiming a long-barreled slugthrower, tracking him.

Gharlane's finger twitched. Maybe it was the sixty-eight percent efficiency. Maybe the man was just fast. He beat Gharlane to the trigger. The slugthrower bucked in his hands, and a dum-dum bullet exploded the pulse rifle, causing the pulse-shot to fizzle.

Landing on the deckplates, Gharlane scrambled fast,

charging the human. If the human had hidden behind the door, shown even a margin of timidity—

The man with the slugthrower snapped off shots. Each dum-dum bullet blew off chunks of flesh and graphite-bones and twisted titanium-reinforcement. The kinetic force of the shots also slowed Gharlane. The man's firm stance, his deliberate tracking and near perfect shots—each one telling effectively—caused Gharlane to smash against a bulkhead instead of taking out the human.

The man's hands blurred as he slammed in a fresh clip. Gharlane lifted his torso, and he gathered himself for a final assault. If he could get into the room, he would detonate himself. Maybe he should detonate himself now and hope the blast reached Tan. She had to be in the room.

The man fired, aiming at the brainpan. Dum-dum bullets jarred the casing.

Explode, Gharlane thought. It was his last.

The final fusillade of bullets mashed enough brain tissue to garble the neuron impulses. The explode sequence never reached the explosives.

The man with the gun killed the master unit cyborg.

7

Marten sat across from Chief Strategist Tan.

It was a day after the cyborg had died in the corridor. After-battle analysis had proven it was a unique cyborg, unlike the skeletal kind. Further analysis had been impossible. The team examining the cyborg had died in the blast that had obliterated it.

Tan knelt on a cushion. The pill dispensary was gone, although the silver chalice was still there. She pushed a twin chalice toward Marten before lifting a decanter and pouring him white wine.

Marten accepted by lifting the chalice and sipping. It was a dry wine, with a hint of peach flavoring. He wore a black Force-Leader uniform. Today, there had been no argument about his having a sidearm.

"Your dialogue yesterday was persuasive," said Tan.

Marten nodded, but kept silent. Yesterday, the two of them had watched on her embedded table-screen as the cyborg advanced through the corridors. Marten had urged her to flee while there was time. She'd sat frozen, fixated on the death machine. Finally, Marten had decided to use the spy-sticks, to time his entry into the battle at the perfect moment. Even so, it had been a near thing.

"I had thought earlier...." Tan bit her lower lip. She frowned, and she glanced to her right. It was where the dispensary had been. Her right hand seemed to twitch involuntarily, as if wanting to press a switch to gain a blue pill.

"My thoughts yesterday were selfish," Tan said. "I believed

it was possible to rebuild our system as the cyborgs invaded Social Unity planets or other Outer Planets."

"We can rebuild," Marten said.

"I thought it would be possible to arm ourselves with enough satellites and warships to defeat any cyborg armada." Tan shook her head. "The way the cyborg moved yesterday—it slew the myrmidons with ease."

"Cyborgs are deadly," Marten agreed.

Tan's brow furrowed. "I ordered space marines to go down onto Athena Station and face them. Seeing that thing yesterday—I ordered those space marines to their deaths."

Marten nodded as he tried to gauge the Chief Strategist. Did she feel real sorrow, or was this an act? Could someone as certain and arrogant as she'd been yesterday change her opinion so quickly? He didn't know. Maybe she didn't know.

"Tomorrow," Tan said, "I plan to open negotiations with Mars, with the Planetary Union leaders. Then I will speak with the leaders of Social Unity."

"What do the controllers of Europa and Ganymede have to say about that?" Marten asked.

She looked up at him. "I showed the controllers a video of the cyborg's assault. I told them it detonated itself during examination. How it managed to get onboard.... Why did scientists develop such things?"

"Why did eugenicists create the Highborn?" Marten asked.

"We must unite," Tan said. "The Solar System must band together to destroy these things. You were right in telling me that."

Marten wondered about that. He and Omi had talked last evening. Usually Omi didn't say much. He did point out that he remembered a vicious gang leader in Sydney that the other members had hated more than feared. The leader had kept power by involving them in a deadly and ongoing turf-war. Everyone had recognized the leader's gift at street fighting, and had been content to follow him as long as they were engaged against a tougher gang. Was Tan like that leader?

"Yesterday cleared my mind," Tan said.

"Yeah," Marten said. It had cleared his too.

"The cyborgs devastated our system," Tan said. "Now we

31

must rebuild before the next fleet arrives. The cyborg yesterday showed me that they will never stop attacking until they're dead or we're dead."

"That seems obvious," Marten said.

Tan frowned. "This is difficult for me. You—" By a seeming effort of will, she smoothed her features. "You must not taunt me. Instead, you must allow me grace."

"Granted," said Marten.

Tan gave him a level stare. It was calculating and hard, and belied her elfin beauty.

"You are more than you seem, Marten Kluge. You walked out to face the death machine. Then you proceeded to shoot it apart."

"It wasn't a machine, but a cyborg, which made it partly human."

"Do not lecture me," Tan said.

Marten waited.

She flicked her hand. "No. I shouldn't have said that. Just now, I spoke with hyperbole and you stated fact." Sighing, Tan leaned her elbows on the table and massaged her forehead. "Do you know the kind of pressures that have battered me this past year? One wrong misstep and I could have lost us everything. Yet everyday, the controllers and the industrial barons complained or demanded I meet another of their imaginary needs."

"The war grinds us down," Marten said.

She lowered her hands and straightened her back. "We've lost too many warships. Our fleet—it could not withstand a full-blown cyborg invasion now. You do recognize that, don't you?"

Marten waited for her point.

"Yet it's madness to simply sit and rebuild," Tan said. "We must strike back and destroy their industrial capacity. But how can we do that with any hope of success?"

"Are you asking me?"

"How polite you've become," said Tan, with an edge to her voice. "Please, grace me with your thoughts. It's one of the reasons you're here."

"I'm a ground fighter," Marten said, "not a grand

strategist."

It was Tan's turn to wait, to say nothing.

"Okay," Marten said. "You asked. So I'll tell you what I think. This is a war to the death. It's either them or us. So we should gather the biggest fleet we can, go to Neptune and burn them out with nukes."

"And this can be achieved how?"

"Talk to Social Unity. Talk to the Highborn. Convince them to unite their ships into one invincible fleet."

"The Highborn are too arrogant to listen," said Tan.

"They're arrogant," Marten agreed. "But I don't know if they're too arrogant not to fight with us. The Praetor gave his life to kill cyborgs. That ought to prove something."

"They will want tactical control," Tan said.

"If it gives us victory, give them that control."

Tan's eyes narrowed. "You are like most people, I'm afraid. You see what's in front of you, but you cannot conceive of what's behind that. Of what use is it to defeat the cyborgs, only to fall victim to the Highborn?"

"The cyborgs are aliens and attempt to convert all of us into their likeness. The Highborn are still human after a fashion. But you have a point. I don't want to live under the Highborn. Therefore, I suggest you keep doing what you've been doing."

"Which is?"

Marten laughed sourly. "I didn't understand it yesterday when I came to see you. But I understand it now. You've been maneuvering this past year to beat the cyborgs but also to keep control. Do the same thing with the Highborn and with Social Unity."

"You presume much, Marten Kluge."

"Look, Chief Strategist. I've been doing a lot of thinking since yesterday. One thing that struck me was that the lone cyborg had a goal. He fought to reach this room. He didn't fight to reach the fusion core. That tells me the cyborgs think you're critical."

"Go on," said Tan.

"If they think you're critical, well, then I guess I do too. I don't like the Dictates. In fact, I loathe them. But I'll back you until the cyborgs are dead. If my choice is the cyborgs, the

Highborn, Social Unity or the Dictates—" Marten blew out his cheeks. "Social Unity or the Dictates, I don't know which is worse."

"You insult us. The Dictates are the greatest form of human—"

"Yeah, yeah," Marten said, waving his hands at her. "You told me yesterday that it's greater than sludge waste. Now let me tell you how I see it. Social Unity let a psychopath put me in a glass tube to pump for my life. The Dictates allowed a sadist to put a collar on me and shock me to his delight. You'll excuse me if I don't see the benefit of either system."

"No system is perfect."

Marten snorted. "Look. What I'm trying to say is that I won't interfere with your political maneuvering. At least, I won't interfere if you're working to destroy the cyborgs."

"You are not in a position to thwart me."

"I killed the cyborg for you, remember."

"Yes. I am grateful."

"I've trained Jovians to kill cyborgs. I may be more use to you than you realize."

"...Yes," Tan said softly. "I'm beginning to see that. And that surprises me."

"That's the trick," Marten said. "To always have one more surprise up your sleeve."

Tan toyed with her chalice. She frowned, and she took a deep breath. Then she let it out slowly and looked up at Marten.

"You have confirmed my decision," she said.

"Oh."

"The controllers and helium barons believe the emergency has ended. They are quite wrong."

"Yeah?" asked Marten.

"We have scoured our system and destroyed the cyborg infestation. Now we must toil even harder, rebuilding our infrastructure. But we cannot rebuild civilian comforts. No. That would be a strategic mistake. We must launch more floaters into Jupiter's upper atmosphere. We must construct moon-based lasers and point-defense satellites. Most importantly, we must launch three to four times the number of meteor-ships and dreadnaughts and train new crews."

"Keep the Jovians scared, eh?" asked Marten.

"I am frightened of the future, aren't you?"

"Yakov showed me the way," Marten said.

"You are chaotic," Tan said. "Your thinking—well, we discussed that yesterday. Are you saying now that you plan to sacrifice yourself for the greater good?"

"I remember some Social Unity battle-slogans," Marten said. "The exact sayings escape me, but it was something along the line of dying for your society in order to save Earth from the Highborn, that was the highest calling." Marten scratched at the metal tabletop. "The Highborn had a counter-saying for those of us in the Free Earth Corps: *Make the enemy* die *for his society.*"

"Yakov followed Social Unity's dictum," said Tan.

"Yakov had learned to stand his ground," Marten said. "He helped me see that sometimes if you're a man and want to live free that you have to take a stand. Before that, I'd been doing a lot of running away. I'm through running, though."

"I fail to grasp how Yakov's sacrifice—"

Marten made a fist and set it on the table. "That's the first part of it," he said. "Standing. We did that here. So did Yakov. Now we have to do the second part. Attacking. We have to enter the enemy's territory to burn him out and make sure he can never hurt us again."

"Your vision and zeal has confirmed my decision," said Tan. "And you are familiar not only with Mars, but also with Earth and the Highborn. I cannot conceive of a better spokesman than you."

"Eh?" said Marten.

"There is a derelict meteor-ship floating in orbit around Callisto. I have already sent repair boats full of technicians and mechanics to it. I cannot afford at this time to diminish our defenses. The cyborgs could even now be in the void with another invasion force. Yet you are right in saying that to win, we must attack. And we must attack in conjunction with everyone else. You, Marten Kluge, will head to Inner Planets as the Jovian spokesman. You will go with a major warship and a full complement of space marines."

"I'll be in charge of the space marines?"

"Are you not listening?" asked Tan. "You will be the Force-Leader of the meteor-ship. Put whoever you desire in charge of the soldiers."

Marten blinked at Tan. His own warship, not just a shuttle? Then it hit him. He'd be returning to Social Unity, returning to the Highborn. He sat back and wished he were sitting in a chair, not on this lousy cushion.

"Naturally," said Tan, "I shall begin negotiations through laser-communications, and I shall retain full authority over anything concerning Jupiter."

That brought Marten up short. "Who will crew the ship?"

"I shall amalgamate the decimated units who stormed Athena Station," said Tan. "You will therefore possess veteran soldiers."

"Who will crew the warship?"

"There are some highly decorated veterans—"

"Their moon of origin?" asked Marten.

"Why does that matter?"

"From Ganymede?" asked Marten.

"As a matter of fact, yes," said Tan. "Does that concern you?"

Marten could have told her that he clearly saw what she was doing: getting rid of the non-Callisto space marines and warship crews. At least, she would be getting rid of the most independent-minded ones. In her terms, she would likely think she was getting rid of the worst ones. Yet he'd already told her that he wouldn't interfere with her political maneuverings.

Shaking his head, Marten wondered if that would be mankind's failing, the inability to unite totally, that someone would always try to achieve his own selfish aim. He made a face. Maybe that made man, man. Cyborgs united perfectly, but they were no longer completely human.

"I'll do it," Marten said.

"Excellent," said Tan, lifting her chalice.

Marten lifted his and they clinked cups, sipping wine afterward.

"You have given me a vision of the future," Tan said. "You have given me hope. If we can unite humanity...."

"It's going to be a big 'if'," said Marten.

"Things worth doing are seldom easy."

"Yeah," Marten said, sipping his wine again, wishing it was beer. He was going to be a warship captain. And he was returning to the Inner Planets. Life was strange, and he wondered what the future held for him, and what it held for the Solar System.

8

"I don't recommend this, sir," Captain Mune said for the fifth time this hour.

Supreme Commander Hawthorne understood Captain Mune's concerns. And he silently agreed with the captain's reasoning. Coming here was…penitence maybe. Or maybe he was a glutton for pain, or maybe he needed to feel the fear in his belly.

He'd always hated the generals in what the ancients had called World War One. Those generals and field marshals had lived and dined in French chateaus as their soldiers had died in the mud and on the wire by the tens of thousands. Soft hands had moved pins on a map or pushed little blocks of wood representing a battalion of terrified soldiers, wet from the constant rain. If the generals and field marshals had slogged through the trenches with their men, they might not have continued the senseless butchery for years on end. Those generals might have striven for a way to win without fields of corpses.

Hawthorne sighed, and he tied the laces of his hood. He wore a green tunic with a hood covering his head. He was taller than the security people around him, but he was no longer thinner. His eyes felt gritty and he knew there were discolored bags under them. There had been too many sleepless nights lately.

"Be careful who you're touching," said Captain Mune. He jostled a security woman's arm, shaking a chemsniffer out of her grip. She'd been using it on Hawthorne. The chemsniffer clattered on the pavement as the woman gasped with pain.

Other brown-clad security people turned, facing Mune.

The captain was a bionic soldier, and today he was Hawthorne's sole bodyguard. The captain's arm made soft whining sounds as he produced a card, handing it to the chief of lift security. The whining noise came from Mune's mechanized joints.

The chief of lift security, who wore dark glasses and badly needed a shave, glanced at the plastic card and then at Mune.

Like the Supreme Commander, the captain wore a tunic, and like Hawthorne, Mune was incognito today. He was nearly as tall as Hawthorne, but thicker and more than five times as strong. That thickness now made Mune noticeable, made him stand out among the thin security people in their baggy uniforms.

Hawthorne knew that Mune had a heavy-duty gyroc pistol hidden on him. The gyroc fired rocket-propelled, fin-stabilized shells, an unlikely weapon down here in the lower levels of New Baghdad, the capital of Social Unity on Earth.

"What is this about?" asked the chief. His unshaven chin had plenty of white hairs among the black ones.

"Sure you really want to know?" asked Mune.

Hawthorne glanced at the captain. Mune spoke in a menacing tone.

"It's your life," said the chief, who had grown pale. "Just to let you know—"

"Don't," said Mune.

The chief nodded, backing away. It seemed he worked to keep his face neutral. He motioned to the other security people, who gripped well-used shock rods.

Mune stepped beside Hawthorne and said in a low tone, "I recommend you go back to your office and watch videos of the latest bread riots, sir. This is too risky."

"Do videos carry the stench of despair?" Hawthorne asked. He moved past the security cordon, his shoes echoing on the pavement. They were on Level Fifty-Three, a low-card district. Some of the lamps on the ceiling were broken. Across the wide veranda were five-story offices, human welfare buildings. Some had smashed windows on the lower stories. There was burn damage as well.

"It's quiet," said Mune.

Hawthorne listened to his shoes click as he set out in a fast stride. Several blocks later, he crunched over broken glass. The cleanup crews hadn't made it very far, and he wondered why not. There were green apartment barracks on the next street. All the shrubs and synthi-trees there had long ago been torn out. People boiled bark, leaves and roots. According to reports, some had ground up the wood and eaten that too. He spied a group of children listlessly sitting on steps. The best off were rail-thin. Several lacked shirts and had the bloated, distended bellies of the truly starving.

"Has it really gotten that bad in the capital?" whispered Hawthorne.

Mune had glanced at the children before passing on to study the surroundings. "We're being watched, sir."

"Hmm," said Hawthorne.

It had been nearly three years since he'd sent the reinforcement fleet to Mars. To ensure the fleet's passage past the Doom Stars, he'd attacked from several farm habitats orbiting Earth. Those habitats had helped feed the planet's billions—no longer. Because of the attack, the Highborn had retaliated, destroying some habitats and conquering the others. It had been a bitter decision, but Hawthorne had ordered Space Command to begin targeting enemy-controlled habitats. Merculite missiles and proton beams—

Few habitats in Earth orbit existed as farms now. Most were drifting hulks. A few of them had degraded orbits, and might have fallen like meteors onto the planet. Proton beams had sliced them into manageable chunks. The atmosphere had burned ninety-eight percent of the chunks. The last two percent had hit the surface, most of those plunking into the oceans. A tiny percentage had struck land, doing damage, but nothing to affect the outcome of the war.

"There, sir," said Mune.

Hawthorne stopped, and looked where the captain pointed. Three scarecrow-thin men walked toward them. They wore threadbare shirts and worn shoes.

"I don't see any others," said Mune. "But that doesn't mean

40

anything."

"Is this level fully populated?" asked Hawthorne.

"The block-leader reports said yes."

"Could those reports have been fabricated?"

Captain Mune glanced at him.

Hawthorne gripped his belt with both hands and watched the approaching men. The loss of the habitats had hit food production hard, as had lost landmasses. There was growing starvation throughout the Earth. That it occurred here in the lower levels of New Baghdad, the very capital—what must it be like in other cities?

"Sir," Mune said.

Hawthorne saw them, another group of men. This group was ten strong. Like the first three men, the second group headed toward them.

"I've read reports of cannibalism," said Mune.

"No," Hawthorne said, feeling ill. "It couldn't have gotten that bad." How could he have remained so ignorant of the situation? Were his people shielding him?

"The riots several days ago, sir—" Mune ripped the gyroc from under his tunic. Then he jumped at Hawthorne, grabbing the Supreme Commander's shoulder. He jerked hard, almost dislocating the bone from the socket.

Hawthorne grunted as pain blossomed in his shoulder. He went down, and he heard the crack of a fired rifle. Then he heard the whine as a slug passed near and a ricochet as the bullet *spanged* off pavement.

"Sniper," said Mune. The gyroc clicked. A shell popped out as its thruster-packet almost immediately ignited. With a whoosh, it sped up at a fourth-story window. There was a shattering of glass, an explosion and seconds later the sound of masonry as bits showered on the paving below.

One of the scarecrow-thin men shouted. The rest panted eerily as they came on faster. Some produced knives. Others brandished clubs. More than twenty men came at them now. They came from three different directions. Their clothes were tatters at best. The look in the men's eyes—they were full of desperation.

"Halt!" Hawthorne shouted, raising his hands as if he could

push them back.

Mune manually ejected the shells in his gyroc. He inserted others with red tips. "Fragmentation rounds, sir," the captain explained.

"I didn't realize it had gotten this bad," Hawthorne whispered. There was a gun in his hand. He didn't remember drawing it. "It's murder just shooting them down."

"Murdering them is better than dying, sir."

"I order you to halt!" Hawthorne shouted.

One man did. Two others shouted at the man. That one jumped as if poked with fire, and he sprinted after the others.

Mune fired. A shell sped at the ten-man clump. Hawthorne witnessed the red burn of the rocket-shell's exhaust. Then a proximity fuse must have sensed the targets. The shell exploded. Shrapnel tore into half of them, knocking down several, making too many scream and shriek.

Those still standing turned and sprinted for safety. Some of the fallen jumped up and ran after the others. The screams of the wounded continued.

Mune snarled a curse, and he aimed at a distant barrack. Two shells popped out of the gyroc. Then he leaped before Hawthorne, and Mune staggered as something thudded against him.

"You're hit," said Hawthorne.

"Yes, sir," Mune said, wheezing heavily. "Now run while I shield you." Without waiting for confirmation, the captain shoved Hawthorne, propelling him toward the lift. Another slug tore into his back, and the captain's left arm abruptly sagged. Mune whirled around, lifted his gyroc and fired one second after another rifle cracked. A bullet chipped pavement near Hawthorne's foot.

The Supreme Commander's belly curled with fear. *Snipers are trying to kill me.* He ran. Something whined past his ear. A spark against a metal post and another ricochet—Hawthorne roared with frustration.

"Go that way, sir."

Hawthorne heard the voice, and he felt pressure move him rightward. He ran toward the human welfare buildings. Beyond them was one of three operable lifts to this level. Political

Harmony Corps had blocked the stairwells two weeks ago, while the other elevators had been dynamited by lift security.

The reports he'd read said the food riots down here had been suppressed. Emergency supplies and riot control squads were supposed to have dampened things. He'd wanted to see a lower level himself, assess things with his own eyes and ears. This had been a surprise inspection. The snipers, they implied that someone in the higher government echelons had smuggled rifles down here.

Have the security people been compromised?

Mune groaned. Hawthorne glanced at him. Pain creased the captain's heavy features. Blood welled from holes in his tunic. One arm hung limply. The other held the gyroc.

"Hang on," Hawthorne wheezed. "We're almost to the lift."

The muscles on the captain's face bunched tight. He gave an imperceptible nod.

They rounded the last corner of the welfare buildings, with the wide veranda before them and then the lift.

Hawthorne uttered a single-word curse. The lift was shut and the security people were gone. In twenty seconds, he passed the temporary barriers, ran a little farther and slapped his hand against the call button.

"Sir," Mune said.

Hawthorne turned as the captain's heavy body crumpled onto the flooring. Blood welled from Mune's back where he'd taken several sniper slugs.

At that moment, the elevator door opened, and half-a-dozen bionic men tumbled out. They wore combat armor and cradled machineguns.

"Sir," said their leader.

"Where did you—?" Hawthorne tried to ask.

"Captain Mune sent us a signal, sir," said the leader.

One of the bionic bodyguards knelt beside Mune. He pulled out a medkit and pressed it against the captain's neck.

"Where are the lift people?" asked Hawthorne.

"In custody, sir," said the leader.

Hawthorne nodded. It was time to leave.

9

Two days later, James Hawthorne paced before his desk in his office on the Third Level of New Baghdad. The city had sixty levels all told, one of the deepest in the Eurasian landmass. New Baghdad contained more than fifty-seven million inhabitants, the majority of them government workers.

Old-style books lined the shelves beside him. The shelves were filled with military history texts. Hawthorne clasped his hands behind his back as he paced. He'd worn a path in his carpet. More than once, he'd debated putting in wood flooring but had never gotten around to giving the order.

The more he thought about the episode in the Fifty-third Level, the more it troubled him.

Hawthorne stopped and scowled at his military history books. Reading was his greatest comfort. History and military history in particular had always been his passion. Earth was like the Chin Empire that had once faced Genghis Khan and his Mongols. Genghis Khan had fielded a single host of nomadic horse-archers. The Chin had possessed hundreds of thousands of solid soldiers, as well as owning the Great Wall of China and countless cities of teeming millions with vast protective walls. As important, the nomads had lacked siege equipment to breach those walls.

Yet Genghis Khan's nomads were warrior's born and bred. The windswept steppes and vicious tribal warfare had hardened the nomads into the most brutally efficient warriors of the medieval world. Genghis Khan had been arguably the greatest warlord of history. The combination had proven too much for the Chin, for the Sung, the Turks, Arabs, Russians, Poles and Hungarians. The Mongols had swept the medieval world in a relentless tide of conquest. Their march hadn't been merely measured in miles, but in degrees of latitude and longitude across the globe.

The Highborn were the Mongols of today. Few in number compared to Earth's masses, they outfought and outgeneraled Social Unity's armies.

A ping sounded at the door. Hawthorne turned in surprise. He'd left orders that no one disturb him. Because of what had occurred two days ago, he now became queasy. Had someone corrupted his bodyguards? Three strides brought him behind his desk. He opened a drawer and placed a hand on his gun, the same gun he'd used down in Level Fifty-Three.

"Enter," he said.

The door opened and Captain Mune's wheelchair rolled in.

"What are you doing up?" Hawthorne asked.

"Reporting for duty, sir," Mune said. He had a bandage on his cheek and a crease on his forehead that quickheal hadn't been able to erase yet.

Hawthorne released his gun and closed the drawer. "You should still be in the hospital."

It was a heavily-built wheelchair, made to take Mune's weight. His chest looked bulkier than normal, making the fabric of his uniform strain against his buttons. Bandages likely caused that. His gyroc was slung in a holster, dangling from his right armrest.

"The bullets caused a lot of bleeding, but little internal damage, sir."

"I've read the report, Captain. You're belittling your injuries."

"I'm supposed to keep off my feet. I can do that sitting here, sir. In case of another emergency, I'm quite capable of standing and doing what's necessary."

"Your health is necessary to me."

"Thank you, sir. I'm sure—"

"Now listen here, Captain Mune. You've saved my life on more occasions than I care to count. You're.... Damnit, man, you're making this harder that it should be."

45

"I'm sorry, sir. And thank you for what you did."

"What are you thanking me for?" asked Hawthorne.

"You saved my life, sir."

Hawthorne shook his head. "That was a terrible experience. Every time I close my eyes, I see those poor souls falling to the cement. I killed them. I shot down the very people I'm supposed to be protecting. I don't know, Captain. This war...."

"If you can't win it, sir, no one can."

"That's propagandist crap."

"No, sir, it's the truth. It's one of the reasons...." Mune looked away, appearing uncomfortable.

Hawthorne also looked troubled as he cleared his throat. After a moment, he pulled out his chair, plopping into it. He turned on his desk-screen. The truth was that Captain Mune had become his best friend. The thought of Mune dying—

Hawthorne cleared his throat again. He brought up a map of Earth. The red parts were Highborn-controlled. Now that meant all the islands of Earth, which included Antarctica Sector, Australian Sector and even Old Britain Sector. The Highborn had taken South America, driven through Central America and now fought a continent-wide campaign in North America. Projections indicated a total defeat there in another five months.

Hawthorne had debated with a warlord policy in North American Sector. The Highborn controlled everything above the stratosphere, making shipping impossible. Even quick jet flights were questionable. North American Sector was on its own. It wasn't really a question of stopping the Highborn there, but a matter of how long it would take the Highborn to pacify the continent to their satisfaction. If he gave independent authority to hard-bitten, ambitious people—warlords—might they hang on longer than if they were mere Social Unity functionaries?

There was no way he could convince the other members of the Politburo.

Mune's chair made noise as the captain wheeled himself into a corner. "With your permission, sir?"

Hawthorne nodded absently. It was good to see Mune, good to have him around again. The captain was the one man

46

he knew he could trust. Hawthorne turned back to the large desk-screen.

Social Unity on Earth was Eurasia, Africa and parts of North America. It was the last battlefleet orbiting Mars, with a friendless understanding between them and the Planetary Union there. Neither side on Mars shot at the other. Neither side completely trusted the other.

Hawthorne stared at the green-colored areas of Earth, Social Unity territory. The algae tanks could only feed so many people. Highborn laser platforms had destroyed the many fishing fleets and the oceanic fisheries. That left traditional agriculture. Even with strict rationing....

"We're starving to death," Hawthorne said.

Mune looked up.

Even as he said that, Hawthorne knew he hadn't stated the problem accurately. If he was going to start lying to himself, it was time to step down. The rationing system was rational, at least in terms of fighting the Highborn. Soldiers, production workers, PHC personnel, block leaders and the like received the highest calorie count. People who lived in the lower levels—those who served no warfare-useful purpose—they received much less.

"If I may be so bold, sir," Mune said, as he tucked away a cell phone.

"Eh?" said Hawthorne, looking up.

"Have you discovered how rifles managed to appear in Level Fifty-Three?"

Hawthorne frowned.

"I didn't think so, sir. I therefore request permission to begin an internal investigation."

"You'd better explain that," Hawthorne said.

"The lift security people fled their posts."

"I'm aware of that."

"They've been discovered, sir. Each of them has been shot in the back of the head."

"Why wasn't I informed before this?" Hawthorne asked.

"Yes, sir, that's what I'd like to know."

The cold feeling Hawthorne had felt as the food rioters had charged him returned. "My own people have been corrupted?"

he whispered.

"Chief Yezhov is a cunning opponent, sir."

"What evidence compels you to suspect him?" Hawthorne asked.

"I don't consciously think about it as I shoot my gyroc, sir. I simply fire, relying on hundreds of hours of practice to guide me."

"And your point?" asked Hawthorne.

"I'm a bodyguard, sir. I suspect those my instincts tells me are guilty. What happened down in the lower level—it smacks to me of the Chief of Political Harmony Corps."

"Maybe we should give him a visit."

"Let me visit him, sir. Meanwhile, perhaps you could turn your military insights into uncovering the moles in your organization."

Hawthorne frowned at his desk-screen. The green areas of Earth versus the red areas—he needed to do something to change the course of the war. If he couldn't, maybe it was time to let someone else try. Was Chief Yezhov the candidate for the job? Hmm. He doubted that. The Chief had strengths. They were shadowy powers like intrigue, sabotage, assassination and double-dealing. They were useful, certainly, but unlikely to win a war against the Highborn.

Looking up, Hawthorne said, "I'm a military man, Captain. I wield the sword better than anyone else does in Social Unity. But there's an ancient saying about swords. You can do many things with them, but you can't sit on them."

"Sir?" asked Mune.

"Swords make a poor throne."

"I'm not sure I follow you, sir."

"Direct action, the bolder the better, that's the way to wield a sword. You said I have moles."

"The facts indicate that, sir."

"I can't beat Yezhov his way. My counter-intelligence teams simply lack PHC guile and secret police ruthlessness. What happened two days ago, we don't know for certain that Yezhov had a hand in it."

"Who else would, sir?"

"That's a cogent question. Yes...." Hawthorne tapped his

48

desk with his fingertips. "We're at the verge of the precipice, staring down into the abyss of defeat and Highborn domination. Social Unity is crumbling. The strain is too much for us. I'm at the top and I'm in charge of the bitterest defeat ever faced by men. I can no longer survive by the old methods."

"Sir?"

"There was a ruler in the Twentieth Century, the Shah of Iran. Someone named the Ayatollah Khomeini had horribly weakened the Shah's grip on his country. There was a Muslim rebellion against the monarchy, and agitators had caused the people to march in the streets against him. The Shah had an Imperial Guard. He should have used them."

"Used them how, sir?"

Hawthorne smiled bleakly. "If you'll allow me a further example, I'll tell you. His name was Napoleon Bonaparte."

"I've heard of him."

"He was one of the greatest military leaders in history. Before his rise to power, however, he was one general among many. He happened to be in Paris when the mobs rose up and marched in the streets against the Directorate. The five men of the Directorate ran revolutionary France. The five rulers froze at the uprising, terrified of the Parisian mob. Napoleon was made of sterner stuff. He gathered some tough soldiers and rolled cannons into the streets. Then he set a line in the streets. The mob surged across the line, and Napoleon ordered his artillerists to open fire. They shot canisters of grapeshot."

"What was that, sir?"

"The cannons acted like giant shotguns. The grapeshot tore into the mob, blowing down many. The mob broke in terror, fleeing to their homes. Napoleon then sent his soldiers into Paris to arrest the worst ringleaders. Afterward, Napoleon said he'd solved the insurrection with a *whiff of grapeshot*."

"You plan to use grapeshot, sir?"

"The Shah of Iran should have sent his Imperial Guard into the streets, set up machineguns and blown away the mobs in his capital. He could have saved his life and his country from the Islamic Revolution that caused grave havoc to the world for countless decades afterward. He could have sent his soldiers to arrest and then execute the Ayatollah Khomeini."

"Did they have food riots back then, sir?" Mune asked.

Hawthorne blinked, and he shook his head. "The lesson for us is similar but not identical. I have a sword, and now I need the willpower to use it. Someone practiced deceit against me. The likeliest candidate is Chief Yezhov, but I'll probably never find the proof. Well, maybe I don't need proof, not if I'm willing to use the sword. Or in my case, the cybertanks and soldiers in New Baghdad."

"What are your orders, sir?"

"Call out your men, Captain. We're going to go pay Chief Yezhov a visit."

-10-

Hawthorne frowned as he stood in an underground room in Political Harmony Corps Headquarters. The video shots he watched were grainy, with occasional white-line wavers. Then everything fuzzed horribly, and the technicians at the boards adjusted controls.

The room was dark except for the wide-screen on the wall. Besides Hawthorne and the PHC technicians, there was Captain Mune in his wheelchair and Chief Yezhov of PHC.

The Chief wore a red uniform with black straps. He was a medium-sized man with round, un-athletic shoulders, pale skin, a weak chin and washed-out blue eyes. He nervously glanced at Hawthorne.

"This is quite normal, I assure you," Yezhov said.

Hawthorne noted dryly to himself that Yezhov had been doing a lot of assuring the past six hours. The Chief had good reason to be terrified. A little more than seven hours ago, massive cybertanks had smashed through the front barriers. Into the rubble had swarmed bionic soldiers. Sixteen PHC guards had died in the ensuing gun-battle before the rest of the guards had thrown down their weapons, surrendering.

Hawthorne's counter-intelligence people now combed through PHC computers. He doubted they would find anything damning against Political Harmony Corps. Yezhov had likely set up the real PHC operational headquarters elsewhere, leaving the headquarters in New Baghdad as a shell. The howl against what he'd done would soon begin. He'd have to decide whether he was going to initiate a bloodbath to maintain his authority or if he could continue along old lines but with upgrades.

"How long can the operative beam these images?" Hawthorne asked.

Yezhov cast him another nervous glance. "Perhaps I wasn't clear enough. The...*operative* doesn't know she's beaming the information."

"What form of transmitter does she use?" Hawthorne asked.

"It's a retinal scan," Yezhov said.

"Explain that."

"One of her eyes was surgically removed. A bio-replacement was inserted along with a cerebral power-pack. You're watching what she's seeing."

Hawthorne stared at Yezhov. It seemed the Chief of PHC carefully kept his gaze on the screen in order to keep from looking at him. Finally, Hawthorne turned back to the picture.

The grainy images showed war-torn streets: rubble, blasted buildings and overturned vehicles. People moved quickly, usually with their heads bent and shoulders hunched. A soldier stood on a street corner. He wore a Free Earth Corps uniform.

"Where is this again?" Hawthorne asked.

"New Orleans, in Louisiana Sector of North America," Yezhov said.

"That's far behind enemy lines."

"Ah," Yezhov said. "If you would watch this...."

Hawthorne became absorbed as a giant strode into view. The Highborn wore combat armor, but without the customary helmet. He strode closer, until he filled the screen. His mouth moved as he talked to the operative. The Highborn had pallid skin, and the intensity of his eyes was overwhelming.

"We've studied their preferences," Yezhov said. "They prefer tall women, at least tall in our terms. They enjoy big firm breasts and wide hips. The last no doubt is to absorb their...ah...vigorous ways."

"She's a volunteer?" asked Hawthorne.

"...Not as you might conceive of it," Yezhov finally said.

"Explain," said Hawthorne, who found that he was frowning.

"She believes herself an infiltration operative. For morale reasons, her true mission is kept from her."

Hawthorne felt nauseous. It was one thing to send soldiers into desperate situations. But this—it was monstrous. Yet he found that he couldn't tear his gaze from the screen. In morbid fascination, he continued to watch.

"Skip to the end sequence," Yezhov told a technician.

One of the women at the controls made adjustments. The grainy image vanished, replaced by another. It was a shot of a ceiling. Then a door panned into view. Through it walked a nude Highborn. The man's musculature was amazing, as was his other endowments.

"This is obscene," whispered Hawthorne.

"War is vicious," Yezhov said, without any inflection.

The next few moments were like a bad porn video. The Highborn's face took on an animalist cast. Then everything went red on the screen. Suddenly, there was a white flash. The grainy image vanished, and the screen remained white.

"End of sequence," a technician said.

Hawthorne blinked as a growing foulness filled him. This was inhuman. He said in a choking voice, "She didn't know what would happen?"

"Few would volunteer if they did," Yezhov said.

"What method did you use?" Hawthorne whispered.

"A cortex bomb," Yezhov said. "The Highborn implant them in certain personnel of their suicide squadrons. You shouldn't be troubled. We're merely paying them back in like coin."

"They're not murdering their own people to kill our soldiers," Hawthorne said.

"With respect, Supreme Commander, this is no different than your ordering soldiers to stand and fight the Highborn. My method is in the end more merciful."

"Do you actually believe that?"

For the first time, Yezhov faced Hawthorne. "What have you said before? We could lose a million civilians to kill one Highborn. I have lost a single human and killed one Highborn. I doubt even your elite units have a better kill ratio than that."

"You sacrificed her without her consent."

"Do you ask permission when you send your soldiers into places that will get them killed?"

"That isn't the same thing!" Hawthorne shouted.

"...I agree," Yezhov said after a moment. "The military slaughters far more of its operatives than PHC does theirs."

Hawthorne found that his right hand was trembling. He gripped it so the others wouldn't see. Now if he could only grip his growing anger.... "We don't send soldiers to their certain death," he said.

"Come now," said Yezhov. "That's mere semantics. You must realize that when a battalion goes into battle that few of its soldiers shall survive contact with the Highborn. I sent a lone operative—"

"You altered her."

Yezhov silently indicated Captain Mune.

Hawthorne shook his head, but he couldn't muster further arguments. He could hardly think. It was true that Yezhov killed Highborn. But this was nasty work, low, foul and un-soldierly. *But economical of lives,* said his coldly logical half. The Highborn were winning, and it was extremely hard to inflict kills on the super soldiers. They were very good at using FEC soldiers as fodder. Could this vile method help turn the tide of the war? No. It wouldn't bring victory, but it might help in an attritional way.

"World War One," Hawthorne muttered.

"Is that a historical reference?" Yezhov asked.

"Captain Mune," Hawthorne said.

"Sir?"

"Alert the team outside," Hawthorne said. "Tell them to put these technicians into protective custody." He felt soiled having witnessed this. Yet that wasn't logical. Yezhov was right. It could be argued that he'd ordered much worse.

"These are my best people," Yezhov was saying. "I'll need them to keep my operations running smoothly."

"You'll need my good will to keep running smoothly," Hawthorne said, his voice rising.

Yezhov looked away. His fingers twitched.

Hawthorne glanced at the technicians. They had stood, and at Mune's orders, they filed for the door.

"Kill them," Hawthorne said.

"What?" Yezhov said, turning around.

A gun barked in Mune's hands. One by one and in quick succession, the technicians thumped against the walls. The woman who had spoken before slid down to the floor in a growing pool of blood.

Yezhov stared open-mouthed at Hawthorne.

The door burst open and three bionic soldiers fanned out with drawn weapons.

"Check the dead," Mune said from his wheelchair.

One soldier pulled out a chemsniffer. Another had an electro-scanner. The last kept his gun trained on Yezhov. The soldiers waved their wands over the dead. The electro-scanner beeped. In moments, a soldier peeled a tiny device from a technician's breast.

"What did your finger-twitch signal?" Hawthorne asked, with his voice under tight control. He had to grip his right hand. It was badly trembling. Was this his nerves, an old wound?

"You're mad," said Yezhov.

"Begging your pardon, sir," said Mune. "He'll never admit his guilt. I recommend you allow my men to drag him outside to be shot."

"You're already in control," said Yezhov. "So this can't be a coup. Is this a personal vendetta against me?"

"What did you signal, Chief?" Hawthorne shouted. "I saw your fingers twitch. My file on you says nothing about nervous mannerisms. It says you have the emotions of a lizard."

Yezhov turned to the bionic soldiers, addressing them in a grave voice. "The episode two days ago has unhinged our Supreme Commander. You can see for yourselves that he is no longer fit for command."

"Yezhov," Hawthorne warned.

"I used to admire him," Yezhov said, continuing in his grave manner. "Yes, he has fought hard, but the truth is that the Highborn are winning the war. It saddens me to say this. But for the good of Social Unity you must relieve him of duty as you once relieved Lord Director Enkov."

"Good try," Hawthorne said. He didn't like the way the

three bionic soldiers listened to Yezhov. Their faces were like masks. "But your chatter only shows your desperation. Your life is now being measured in seconds."

"I've served the Supreme Commander, and look how he rewards me," Yezhov said. "In his growing madness, how will he reward you?"

From his wheelchair, Mune made a sharp motion.

The bodyguard with the gun trained on Yezhov holstered it and took two heavy strides to the Chief. The bodyguard put a hand on one of Yezhov's shoulders, and squeezed with bionic strength.

Yezhov cried out in pain, twisting as a small boy in the grip of an angry father.

"Killing your technicians just now was ugly and brutal," Hawthorne said. "I despise myself for ordering it. I wonder if another person could fight this war better than I. I do not wonder, however, if having you in charge would be better for humanity. Someone on Earth still has contact with the cyborgs, the same cyborgs that turned on us at Mars."

"Not guilty!" Yezhov shouted.

Hawthorne shook his head. "Speak honestly, Chief, and you will live. Continue with your present tactics and you will lie on the floor of this room, dead."

Yezhov opened his mouth.

"Think carefully before you utter another word," said Hawthorne. "And know that I've decided on ruthlessness. I believe it's the only counter I possess against your secret-police guile. The incident on Level Fifty-Three—" Hawthorne shook his head. "The decision to practice ruthlessness is difficult. But be assured of this. Killing you will not prove difficult."

Bent over in pain, with the bionic bodyguard gripping his shoulder, Yezhov looked about wildly. His eyes finally showed fear and approaching terror. He tried to squirm free. It only made the guard squeeze harder. Yezhov's hands flew to the iron fingers as he desperately tried to pry them free—to no avail.

"Yes, yes," Yezhov said. "I signaled the technicians. Tell him to let me go."

"What did you signal?"

Yezhov panted. "It hurts! He's so horribly strong! Tell him to stop!"

Hawthorne was disgusted with himself. This wasn't his way. The fact that he'd doubted his bodyguards showed how shaken he was. Yet now was the moment. He could choose to be like the Shah of Iran, who ran away and allowed the wolves to devour his country. Or he could be like Napoleon Bonaparte and roll out the cannons, with the will to use them on anyone who stood against Social Unity. Hawthorne hardened his resolve.

"Be glad that you're still able to feel pain," he told Yezhov.

"No," Yezhov groaned.

"No more evasion," Hawthorne said. "Begin talking, or my men will beat you to death with their fists."

Bent over, with the bionic man squeezing his flesh, Yezhov craned his neck and looked up at Hawthorne.

James Hawthorne forced himself to look down steely-eyed at the PHC Chief.

Yezhov shut his eyes, and he whispered, "I signaled them to begin Operation Inversion."

Hawthorne motioned the bodyguard as he told Yezhov, "Explain."

Yezhov cried out in relief, stumbling away from the bodyguard. He rubbed his shoulder, and bumped against one of the technicians' chairs. With a groan, Yezhov sagged onto it. He looked up at Hawthorne. Rat-like, survivor's cunning was visible on his face.

"Why should I speak?" Yezhov asked in a cracked voice. "You'll have me shot anyway."

In that moment, Hawthorne decided to maintain one facet of his old life. He would do what was necessary to hold power so he could save humanity. But he would keep one part of himself pure.

"You have my word of honor, Chief, that I will not shoot you."

"How can I trust your word?"

Hawthorne forced himself to stare at Yezhov, to stare at the monster who planted bombs in pretty women's brains. Then he sent those women into enemy territory, to seduce Highborn and blow both her and her lover to death. What other horrors had this monster committed? He must never become like Yezhov. He must never sink into depravity. Maybe the only dike against that would be to keep his word.

"My solemn word is all I have left," Hawthorne said.

While crouched in his chair, Yezhov sneered.

Hawthorne almost drew his gun and fired. To have this worm doubt him....

"Your days of power are over," Hawthorne said, and he was surprised at his calmness. "But I want your expertise. You shall become one of my advisors. You will receive a double ration of food and full privileges. But you will be in confinement in my headquarters. I want to know everything you've been doing, Chief. You must hold nothing back."

Yezhov gingerly massaged his shoulder. "The Directors won't stand for your highhandedness."

"My reading of history indicates otherwise. If those with the guns are willing to use them ruthlessly, then a small group can with terror effectively control nations."

"You'll use PHC methods?" asked Yezhov.

"We're on the brink of the abyss. Will humanity hold together through good will? I doubt it. We need fierce ruthlessness now."

"Your way has failed us," Yezhov said.

Speaking with this filth was wearying, but Hawthorne clamped down on his revulsion. He needed the Chief's knowledge. If he would practice ruthlessness, he would also practice it against himself.

"We're still holding territory," Hawthorne said, "and that's due to my way, my control of the military."

"Your years at the helm have changed you," Yezhov said. "Or don't you recognize that in yourself? Each year, you've become increasingly dictatorial."

It was probably true. Wars brutalized soldiers, people and the commanders. Long wars only intensified the process. Even so, Hawthorne doubted he could keep listening to Yezhov. The desire to kill the monster was nearly overwhelming now.

"Each year, I become increasingly desperate," Hawthorne

said. "You now have five seconds to answer me."

Yezhov glanced right and left, and stared at the dead technicians. Three seconds passed as his gaze froze on them. Then sweat bathed his face. He jerked upward. Maybe he realized he'd been immobile. Maybe he didn't know for how long he'd stared.

"I'll talk!" he screamed. "I'll tell you everything."

Hawthorne found that his heart was beating with heavy thumps. In a thick voice, he said, "That's too bad, Chief. I wanted to kill you." He took a deep breath, tried to make it a calming one. His heart kept thumping, and he didn't know why. "My word is my word. Now start talking."

"Where should I begin?" Yezhov asked.

Hawthorne took a second deep breath, and finally his heart-rate began to return to normal. That was a good question. Then he knew the answer.

"What do you think will make me the angriest? Start there."

-11-

Hawthorne paced before a one-way mirror. In the other room was an operating chamber. Former Chief Yezhov lay strapped down on a gurney, with a metal band around his shaved head.

Three doctors stood in green gowns around him, with surgical masks covering their faces. Medical equipment filled with room, with banks of computers, imagining holographs and mind-scanners.

Yezhov squirmed as a doctor inserted a tube into his left arm. Turning toward the one-way mirror, Yezhov shouted, "You're breaking your word, Supreme Commander!"

Captain Mune stood to the side. He glanced at Hawthorne. "The man's a liar, sir. He's been lying for months."

It had been five-and-half weeks since the raid on PHC Headquarters. Since then, Hawthorne's most trusted soldiers had arrested the top echelon of Political Harmony Corps and sixty percent of the under-chiefs and ranking secretaries. Eleven of those secretive men and women had been shot. Twenty-three more faced Director-controlled Tribunals. Unfortunately, three Directors were discovered attempting to initiate a coup. They'd used a hidden fraternity of PHC personnel, together with altered people in various security services.

"You gave me your word!" Yezhov shouted.

Hawthorne bared his teeth in a grimace. The altered people—they had been proto-cyborgs, with the same brainwave patterns that Commodore Blackstone had transmitted from the Mars Battlefleet. The cyborgs had altered certain fleet personnel there during the Battle for Mars.

What do cyborgs have to do with Chief Yezhov? Hawthorne dearly wanted to know.

"You've kept your word, sir," Mune said.

Hawthorne shook his head. The captain had left his wheelchair nine days ago. He still moved gingerly, but he said he felt as fit as ever.

"Supreme Commander!" Yezhov howled. "Let me out of here!"

The three doctors looked up, turning toward the one-way mirror. It was made of ballistic glass.

"Tell them to proceed," Hawthorne whispered.

Mune pressed a button and said just that.

"No!" Yezhov shouted, trying to squirm free.

The three doctors returned their attention to him. One pressed a hypo against his arm. Soon, Yezhov's struggles slowed and then ceased altogether.

The hospital room was part of Political Harmony Corps, this one in the former headquarters. In this very chamber, the three doctors working on Yezhov had operated on the women sent into enemy territory.

"You never could have trusted him," Mune said.

Hawthorne knew that to be true. These past weeks, Yezhov had proved himself a masterful liar. If the art of deception were one of the martial practices, Yezhov would be a ninth-degree black belt.

"You *must* mind-scan him," Mune said.

"The scanning burns out the brain," Hawthorne whispered.

"He brought this on himself, sir. Your word implied that he would cooperate."

Hawthorne squinted at Yezhov. These past five-and-half weeks had been murder on his conscience. His bionic teams had turned into death squads. He was becoming no better than Stalin or Mao of the Twentieth Century. Soon, he'd be no different from Lord Director Enkov. Social Unity was disintegrating under the crushing pressure of the Highborn conquest. In his gut, Hawthorne knew he had to do these things. But he wasn't the right man for it. Each morning it was becoming harder to look in a mirror.

And that made little sense. He'd originated the frightful idea of blowing the deep-core mines and blaming the Highborn for it. He'd sent hundreds of thousands of soldiers to their doom. This political infighting, though, it felt different. Maybe it was the striving to stay on top, and the brutal killing to do it, that hammered at him. Maybe years at the top had worn him down. A colonel or general could only last so long in combat. Then he had to be rotated out of the field and into a quiet place to recuperate.

When do I get to recuperate? When do I get to rest?

Yezhov lay limply on the gurney. The doctors began to move the mind-scanning equipment into position.

Hawthorne's chest began to thump. He put his hand over his heart. It raced. His mouth was dry.

"Wait," he croaked.

"Sir?" asked Mune.

Hawthorne strode to the one-way mirror. He pressed a call button and said in a dry voice, "Wait."

The three doctors looked up.

"Don't operate," Hawthorne said.

"No mind-scan?" asked a doctor.

"I gave him my word," Hawthorne said.

"His death isn't certain," a doctor said. "If you wish, we can perform a third level interrogation." The doctor's head twitched as if he saw something. Then he sharply turned toward one of the other doctors. "What are you doing?" he asked.

The questioned doctor never answered, but pressed a hypo against Yezhov's arm.

"I asked you what you're doing?" the first doctor said.

The questioned doctor yanked down his mask. He grinned wildly, with drool leaking from his lips. Then he exploded. Pieces of flesh and blood, and plastic, smacked against the ballistic glass of the one-way mirror. Smoke drifted in the chamber, and from somewhere, a klaxon began to wail. The other two doctors and Yezhov, their bodies were torn and bleeding.

Hawthorne stared at the wreckage. Then he felt Mune's

hands on him, turning him, propelling him toward the exit. Two things kept drumming in Hawthorne's mind. He'd tried to keep his word. He would have let Yezhov live. The other thing beating in his brain was that there was a hidden enemy among them.

12

Yezhov's death leaked out, and that infuriated Hawthorne.

"It's possible there's a traitor among the bionic soldiers?" he told Mune, a week after the incident.

They walked in a botanical garden in New Baghdad, on the Fifth Level. The lamps overhead shined brightly and with heat. It caused Hawthorne's shirt underneath his uniform to stick to his sweaty skin. A glance at Mune showed an undisturbed captain.

Hawthorne wondered if Mune resented what the surgeons had done to him. The captain had artificial muscles, his bones were laced with titanium reinforcements and his nerves ran through plastic tubes instead of their natural sheaths. Added glands secreted various drugs, giving him heightened reflexes, strength and the ability to heal more quickly than a normal man could. It surprised Hawthorne that he'd never questioned Mune about it. He'd taken so much for granted with the captain. Did Mune feel sympathy for the cyborgs or a connection to the Highborn? If Mune did not, might not some of the other bionic soldiers question why they continued to fight for the losing side?

"I've considered the possibility of traitors, sir," Mune said.

Hawthorne frowned, noticing movement in the distance. Moving a frond, he spied a gleam of metal several hundred meters away.

Mune turned that way. "It's a cybertank, sir."

"I'm aware of what a cybertank looks like, Captain. Why is it here?"

64

"Security, sir."

"Is this your doing?" asked Hawthorne.

Mune inclined his head. "I approved Specialist Cone's suggestion, sir. You said she had first-rate clearance and that I had full authority concerning your security."

"You're correct on both counts," Hawthorne said. "But a cybertank—this is the garden level. It's almost seems obscene to have the cybertank's treads clanking among the experimental plants."

Mune glanced toward the cybertank, but kept any opinions to himself.

"Hmm," said Hawthorne. "Cone's right. I must maintain tighter security. I just hope all these extra guards doesn't smack of cowardice on my part."

"Begging your pardon, sir, but I wish you would show cowardice sometimes."

"Captain?"

"It would make my task much easier, sir. You're far too likely to enter a combat zone. Level Fifty-Three would be a good example of that, and your insertion into the assault on PHC Headquarters."

"I must keep my hand on the pulse, and sometimes that entails risk."

"If you say so, sir."

Hawthorne opened the top button and pulled at his uniform, trying to let some of his body-heat escape. "Have you taken any measures among your men?"

"Loyalty tests, sir?"

"We're not PHC," Hawthorne said.

"I've made discrete inquires," Mune said. "And I'm handpicking a group for you, sir."

"What kind of group?"

"You need a guard team, sir."

"I already have that."

"When you enter a combat zone you have such a team, or usually when you enter one. My suggestion is that you maintain such a team at all times, giving them license to shot down anyone suspicious."

"Hmm. Such a team can quickly turn into my jailors. I

prefer you around me, Captain, and leave it at that."

"I'm honored, sir. But the truth is that I might not be enough now. The ongoing campaign against PHC has turned ugly and desperate."

Hawthorne turned away from Mune. Craning his neck, he looked up at the sunlamps. The heat felt good, even if it did cause his clothes to stick to him. He had acted too precipitously, he saw that now.

"We're being squeezed," Hawthorne said, as he let the sunlamp's heat beat against his face. "Years of losing ground, as the Highborn tighten a noose around our collective throats—"

Hawthorne faced Mune. "I'm out of ideas."

"I'm not sure I believe that, sir."

Hawthorne looked back up at the sunlamp. "I'm not talking about tactical battlefield surprises, but original ideas that approach this from a new angle. Yezhov had ideas. He killed Highborn in a degenerate fashion, but it was new and frankly, inventive. As for me—we fought the Highborn to a standstill at Mars. It changed nothing. Earlier, we struck at the Sun-Works Factory, to little effect. My grand plans have delayed the enemy, but I've done nothing to reverse the direction of the war."

"The Highborn have problems, too, sir," Mune said. "We just don't know what they are."

"Don't use my own words against me. That's too depressing today."

"You've implemented plans that have contested every inch of ground," Mune said. "The emergency construction of more proton beams and the mass merculite missile sites were entirely your ideas, sir. Without you—"

"We must beat them *back*," Hawthorne said. "I don't know how to beat them back. Now everything threatens to unravel because I've started an underground war with PHC. I don't dare let up or they'll devour me on the rebound. The military will lose morale if I retreat. No. It's them or me, and I intend to come out victorious."

"I've thought about the attack on Yezhov, sir. Why would PHC personnel kill their chief?"

"He was going to tell me everything he knew, or the mind-scanner would have revealed it."

"Begging your pardon, sir, but you'd just countermanded the order. The doctor injected him then."

"The doctor might have injected Yezhov during the operation to ensure his silence. Since he thought the chance had passed, the doctor attacked when he did."

"You saw the doctor's face, sir. In my opinion, he was no longer rational."

Hawthorne began to unbutton his uniform before he had a heatstroke. There was rot in Social Unity and it was growing. Maybe there had always been the rot, and maybe there was in any human organization. Now the endless defeats versus the Highborn and the growing pressure made the rot more noticeable. Somehow, he had to burn out the gangrene and then find a way to stiffen North American Sector.

Don't lie to yourself, James.

He had to drive the Highborn from Earth orbit. That was the only true way to win the war. Yet how could he achieve such a miracle? The strongest SU Battlefleet remained in Mars orbit. Yet those remaining warships dared not travel here and face the Doom Stars a second time.

What were the cyborgs doing in Neptune? Had they attacked the Saturn System as some reports indicated? The cyborgs had attacked the Jovian System, but failed to take it. That was interesting for several reasons.

The cyborgs...there were altered people on Earth—proto-cyborgs. The proto-cyborgs had similar brainwave patterns as found in the SU Battlefleet after the Highborn retreated. Who had altered these people on Earth? The evidence pointed to PHC. The evidence was also mounting that cyborgs were here, and they were always dangerous to human life.

After wiping sweat from his face, Hawthorne fanned himself. He'd struck at Political Harmony Corps and found it to be like the hydra that Hercules of the Greek myths had battled. Each time Hercules had cut off a hydra head, another two had grown in its place. If he couldn't kill PHC, he had to call a truce with them. Which was the better decision?

"I need to call a meeting," Hawthorne said.

"The Directors are clamoring for one."

"I'll talk with Danzig and Juba-Ryder, but none of the others."

"The others will take that as a slight, sir."

"Didn't I tell you not to repeat my own words to me?"

"You did, sir. You also told me to always tell you the truth—that you trusted truth-tellers more than you did yes-men."

"I wouldn't mind a few yes-men now and again," Hawthorne said.

"You would hate them, sir, and they would weaken your position."

"Danzig and Juba-Ryder, call the two old Directors. I want Specialist Cone there, Crowfoot—" Hawthorne asked, "What's the situation on Director Danzig?"

"Extremely comprising," said Mune.

Hawthorne shook his head. "I'm getting slow and forgetful. Hmm. I'll give you the rest of the names in an hour, and then I'll see them tomorrow. Today...." Hawthorne stared up at a sunlamp. He needed ideas, but he was fresh out of them. Maybe the meeting tomorrow would jog something in him, but he doubted it. He dreaded the possibility that all initiative had left Social Unity for good. He dreaded the nearly certain truth that all he could look forward too was the relentless grind of defeat as he bitterly hung on for as long as he could.

13

Sharply at 6:13 A.M. the next morning, the meeting began on Level Three of New Baghdad. It was held in the Supreme Commander's quarters. Director Danzig of China Sector and Director Juba-Ryder of Egyptian Sector joined Air Marshal Crowfoot of Earth-Air Defense, Security Specialist Cone and Field Marshal Mead of Missile Defense.

Two years ago in order to dilute the power of the Directorate, Hawthorne had shrunk each Director's area of authority. Danzig used to run Eurasia and Juba-Ryder Africa. As the area under Social Unity control shrank, the number of Directors had risen to three times the former size.

Captain Mune attended, sitting in back. Outside waited three more bionic soldiers, part of Hawthorne's new personal security team.

***

From the Supreme Commander's biocomp transcriptions, File #3:

The meeting opened with a long, detailed report by Cone on the conflict between Hawthorne's security teams and renegade PHC murder-squads. Next, Crowfoot spoke about the impossibility of airlifting critical reinforcements to North American Sector. Hawthorne made few comments on these reports. Army Chief of Staff Engel entered and reported on Eurasian and African readiness for Highborn invasions. He then took his leave, and the Supreme Commander began to comment.

HAWTHORNE: The situation is grim. Everywhere we are on the defensive. Yet we have certain strengths remaining, as pointed out by the Army Chief of Staff. We hold Eurasia and Africa in a fierce grip. It is the majority of the landmass on Earth, and Earth is by far the most important planet of the Solar System. We, therefore, continue to hold the critical real estate. Earth is heavily armed with proton beams, merculite missiles and point-defense cannons. We also have more trained soldiers than at the beginning of the hostilities.

MEAD: We have twenty times the number of missiles now.

HAWTHORNE: Yes, an excellent point. Unfortunately, it is also true that in order to win a war, one must do more than defend. One must attack. We last attacked at Mars, which happened much too long ago.

DANZIG: I'd like to comment on that, if I may.

HAWTHORNE: This is an open meeting.

DANZIG: We took a gamble then. It resulted in the destruction of a Doom Star. Yet it also resulted in the loss of the farm habitats. Mass starvation has badly shaken Social Unity. I wonder if here is the source of the hostility between PHC and yourself.

CONE: Hostility? It is an urban campaign fought in our cities like a civil war. We cannot afford it. (To Hawthorne) I suggest we call out the military instead of just using the security teams.

DANZIG: No! The tenants of Social Unity are clear. The military must never turn on the society or the society's guardians.

CONE: PHC no longer guards Social Unity. They attacked the Supreme Commander, thereby attacking the chief representative of the people and abrogating their responsibilities.

DANZIG: When did this attack occur?

CONE: (To Hawthorne) With your permission, sir.

HAWTHORNE: (Nods affirmatively).

CONE: They attempted assassination through proxies on New Baghdad's Fifty-third Level, during the Supreme

Commander's surprise inspection.

DANZIG: I was not aware of this.

CONE: Internal security has demanded a need-to-know basis.

DANZIG: But we're talking about dismantling one of the critical pillars of Social Unity. We know the creed. The Party, PHC and the Military are the tripod that upholds the State. If we lose one leg, the State totters. Sir, I highly respect you. But now isn't the time for a military dictatorship.

HAWTHORNE: I quite agree, Director. Social Unity is the glue that binds our society together. We need that glue more than ever. In the past, PHC has been the watchdog of our hearts. Unfortunately, an insidious infiltration has occurred in Political Harmony Corps. The infiltration began during the Battle for Mars. Each of you is aware of the cyborg treachery there. During the battle, the cyborgs gained mental dominance of key Fleet personnel.

DANZIG: What form of mental dominance?

CONE: Cybernetic implants.

DANZIG: Do you expect us to believe such—

HAWTHORNE: Director, please, I am aware that your security teams have gained access to secret files on the Mars battle. I am also aware that you have sent two family members to *Star Chamber* meetings with other disgruntled directors.

DANZIG: (A three-second hesitation ensues) I have the minutes of those meetings, sir. Tomorrow, at the latest, I was going to turn those minutes over to Specialist Cone. Their actions were and are deplorable. I sent two…family members in order to monitor their treachery. They are cunning people, and extremely paranoid. I believe they have infiltrated your communications net. I feared to alert you too soon, lest I lose access to their inner councils.

HAWTHORNE: You misunderstood me, Director. It's true I desire knowledge concerning their thoughts, but not as a loyalty test to me.

DANZIG: You are too trusting, sir. Their words bordered on treachery. I recommend you send your bionic squads to their residences.

HAWTHORNE: You surprise me. I should arrest them?

71

DANZIG: Several of the stated directors wish to make common cause with Political Harmony Corps, and have sent high-level envoys to them.

HAWTHORNE: Which squads do you suggest I employ against them?

DANZIG: These directors have quietly strengthened their bodyguard services. It's possible you'll need maximum force to arrest them.

HAWTHORNE: You've given me excellent advice. Captain Mune, would you alert your teams and await my go-word.

MUNE: (Rises and leaves the room).

HAWTHORNE: I have—yes, Director Juba-Ryder?

JUBA-RYDER: I do not trust him, sir. (Pointing at Danzig).

HAWTHORNE: While I most certainly do.

JUBA-RYDER: If I could have a word in private with you, sir?

HAWTHORNE: (Shakes head) I have called this meeting for several reasons. We have discussed one of them. The second item is the Highborn. Specifically, how can we tear the initiative out of their hands? They have relentlessly continued their assault on Social Unity. While it is true that Eurasia and Africa can hold out indefinitely, if we are to win the war, we must go on the offensive. Through the years, I have initiated several offensives. I would now like to open the floor to any novel ideas any of you might have.

DANZIG: These are military matters, outside our scope.

HAWTHORNE: You are incorrect, Director. The Party supplies the leadership to the State. Leaders must decide grand strategy. It is then the Military's function to proceed with the plans using the best means possible.

DANZIG: I stand corrected.

CROWFOOT: We must gain mastery of orbital space. Without it, we shall never be able to launch sustained land offensives.

JUBA-RYDER: (To Hawthorne) Since you will not meet privately with me, sir, I most openly declare my distrust of Director Danzig.

DANZIG: (To Juba-Ryder) I wasn't aware you had a vendetta against me.

JUBA-RYDER: I do not. But my security services have uncovered high-level communications between you and the Planetary Union bosses on Mars.

HAWTHORNE: (To Juba-Ryder) Come now, Director. This is unwarranted.

DANZIG: (to Juba-Ryder) You forget that I was the spokesman for Social Unity to the Martians.

JUBA-RYDER: Do you still hold this post?

DANZIG: I don't understand what you're trying to—

JUBA-RYDER: I lost three good operatives gaining this information. The reason is that you zealously guarded such knowledge. I want to know why these communications are so important to you.

DANZIG: You admit to spying on me?

JUBA-RYDER: We all spy on each other.

HAWTHORNE: (To Danzig) What is the Director talking about?

DANZIG: I assure you it is nothing, sir.

HAWTHORNE: Amuse us then with this nothing.

DANZIG: The Jovians, sir, they—ah, look, your captain has returned.

MUNE: (Reenters the chamber and nods crisply to the Supreme Commander).

HAWTHORNE: You have sent the order, Captain?

MUNE: I have followed your orders, sir.

HAWTHORNE: (to Danzig) You were saying, Director?

DANZIG: Your captain has ordered the attacks on the questionable Directors?

HAWTHORNE: That isn't your concern, but mine. Now please, you were saying?

DANZIG: I'm feeling ill, sir. Do you mind if I consult with my physician?

HAWTHORNE: Do you need refreshments?

DANZIG: It's a heart complaint, sir. I brought my personal physician with me. If I could consult her for a few minutes…?

HAWTHORNE: Naturally, I wish you to remain in full health. Before you go, however, I'd like to hear of this Jovian communication.

DANZIG: The Jovians are a stealthy people, sir. I consider them completely untrustworthy.

HAWTHORNE: So there has been communication between Mars and Jupiter?

DANZIG: If one could call it that. They've sent questionable queries to the Martians. If you'll recall, the Jovians had an alliance with Mars over a decade ago.

HAWTHORNE: You've aroused my curiosity. What was this query?

DANZIG: (A long pause) The Jovians claim to be seeking an understanding with Social Unity.

HAWTHORNE: The Planetary Union bosses passed this on to you, did they?

DANZIG: It is nothing, sir. I understood it as a ploy. (Puts hand over his heart) I fear I must see my doctor. (Rises) With your permission—

HAWTHORNE: Captain Mune, will you assist the Director to a holding cell. Then take a team and arrest this so-called doctor of his.

DANZIG: (Turns pale) Have I offended you, sir? If so, I gravely apologize.

HAWTHORNE: You've offended me on two counts. One, you attempted to trick me into sending my bionic squads into certain ambushes. I did nothing of the kind, but gave the order to see what you would do. Now, you've kept secret a possibly critical diplomatic opening with the Jovians. I'd hoped to continue using you as a link with the disgruntled directors. Now I see they plan a coup, possibly in conjunction with what remains of PHC. You've chosen the wrong side, Danzig.

DANZIG: Please, sir! Let me make amends. I've served you well in the past.

HAWTHORNE: (Signals Mune) I want a full confession. And I want all the information he has on the Jovians.

DANZIG: Yes, yes, you'll have it. I guarantee it.

MUNE: (Takes hold of Director Danzig and marches him out of the chamber).

HAWTHORNE: (To the others) Let us continue. In the African Sector....

74

End of File #3

14

A week after Hawthorne had Director Danzig arrested, far out in the Jupiter System, Marten Kluge still had trouble believing that he'd become the Force-Leader of a capital ship.

"Get ready," Osadar said. "I'm about to begin docking procedures."

Marten sat beside her in a shuttle half the size of the former *Mayflower*. They were in mid-orbit around Callisto. Far below against the Galilean moon shined a bright orange light. It was a giant booster-ship making a landing, bringing badly needed supplies to a stranded cleanup crew. The Jovian System was like a kicked-over ant colony. Everyone left alive was busy trying to repair the horrible damage created by the cyborg assault.

Using his screen, Marten glanced at the nearing cargo vessel: the *Thaliana*. It was a huge teardrop-shaped spaceship and belonged to Meta-mines Incorporated. Meta-mines was a consortium with quarter shares by several of the most powerful Helium-3 Barons. Her survival of the war with the cyborgs was attributable to her clever captain. The captain had kept a strict visual of any suspicious vessel that approached too closely. Then she had promptly put the cargo ship behind a planetary body, shielding them from the intruder. The *Thaliana* was the third cargo ship this month to dock by Marten's warship, and brought critical supplies.

Marten clicked a toggle. In spite of himself, he grinned as he witnessed his meteor-ship yet again. It was a battered warship, and had belonged to the cyborgs. Despite the brutal pounding it had taken on the original attack against Callisto, the meteor-ship had retained its basic shape. It was a rock, a hollowed-out asteroid packed with a repaired fusion engine, compartments, supplies, living quarters, coils, missiles and laser generators.

Through the screen, Marten noted that his ship looked as if it had passed through a floating junkyard. Tubes, oddly-shaped polygons, girders, patrol boats, antennae and trailing lines were attached in a seemingly random fashion. The warship still needed a lot of work to turn it into the combat-vessel it had been. But the warship could move under its own power now, and it could accommodate its crew. Maybe in another month, it would be ready to head for Earth.

"Initiating docking procedures," Osadar said, clicking a switch.

The shuttle thrummed with power and thrust. Marten sank against his seat, and they eased toward one of the *Thaliana's* docking tubes....

15

"What?" Marten asked. The meeting was only seven minutes old, and he was getting angrier by the moment.

He sat in the *Thaliana's* wardroom, a cramped space with a kidney-shaped metal table taking up most of the area. Riveted stools around the table provided seating. Marten and Osadar had both squeezed around the table and to their present spot.

The cargo-ship's captain was here. She was short like most Jovians, lacked hair and wore a crumpled brown uniform. She had large eyes, reminding Marten of Nadia. Those eyes the captain carefully kept downcast. She was obviously a cautious woman, a characteristic which had likely won her the position and had certainly allowed her to keep it throughout the cyborg assault.

"No," Marten said, shaking his head. "I think that's a bad idea."

Another Jovian sat on a stool. She was small, although not as small as Chief Strategist Tan. As Tan often did, the Jovian woman wore a sheer silk gown. It revealed a gymnast's body underneath—small firm breasts, a tight belly and smooth limbs. She had dark curls and an aloof attitude. Affixed to her forehead was a jet-black stone.

Osadar had informed Marten about the stone's significance. On Callisto and under the Dictates, it had meant an Ur-philosopher of the Third Rank.

"*Ur*—that means she's greater than a regular philosopher?" Marten had asked as they'd first entered the chamber.

"No," Osadar had whispered back. "She is, or was, a

philosopher-in-training, likely groomed for the highest level of governance."

Marten's anger had begun then, and in these few minutes, it had been steadily getting worse. Tan was changing the game on him. Maybe as bad, he hated dealing with anyone remotely connected to Callisto's philosophers. Their arrogance approached that of the Highborn, although it was less physically oriented and more cerebral.

The gowned Jovian—her name was Circe—presently clicked her fingernails on the metal table.

Three myrmidons flanked her on each side. At the clicking, the six gene-warped warriors stiffened, and their dark eyes seemed to become wet with anticipation. It was an intimidating experience, and the room was too close and confining. Marten might draw fast enough to shoot two of them, but that was no guarantee he'd kill those two. Osadar was a cyborg, but he doubted she could tear apart the remaining four before the myrmidons finished the two of them.

Their uniforms were a bright orange color. They lacked stunners and had knives and knuckle-mounts instead of shock rods. These six seemed more animalistic than the other myrmidons he'd seen. Marten had yet to hear any of them speak even the most rudimentary speech. It seemed like a crime against humanity to mutate Homo sapiens like this. If he could, he'd outlaw such practices. Maybe the one good thing the cyborg attack had achieved was the destruction of such gene-tampering centers on Callisto.

"This matter is far beyond your scope, Force-Leader," Circe was telling him. "I have a directive from the highest level. Nothing can stop its implementation, certainly not your displeasure."

"Tan gave you this directive?" Marten asked.

Circe's mouth tightened. She had full lips, sensuous lips. It seemed to Marten that such lips were unsuited for an Ur-philosopher.

"I insist you act with decorum," Circe said. "The one you speak about is the Chief Strategist. You sully her position and the importance of her rank by bandying her name with such indifference. I will not tolerate it."

"She gave me my captaincy and made me the ambassador," Marten said.

"If by that you mean you are the meteor-ship's Force-Leader, why yes, you have accurately stated the situation. I fail to see, however, how your comment affects my statement."

"I mean that Tan—her name—is, ah, important to me." Marten rubbed the bridge of his nose. Trying to talk with an Ur-philosopher, so she could understand him, was giving him a headache.

Circe seemed faintly amused. "Do not attempt to dialogue with me, Force-Leader. I am many times your intellectual superior."

"Listen. I'm not interested in your IQ."

"Yes," she said. "That is another indictor of barbarism."

Marten slapped the table with an open palm. "*Tan* gave *me* the position of ambassador. Now you're trying to tell me she lied?"

"Your manner is unseemly and vulgar. And I find it distressing that you would resort to such brutish tactics."

"Lady, I have no idea what you're talking about."

Once more, Circe clicked her fingernails on the table. "The Chief Strategist assured me your veneer of barbarism was something akin to a disguise. She assured me you knew your place in the hierarchy. Now I'm beginning to wonder if that's so."

Osadar leaned minutely forward, and she said in her strange voice, "The Dictates no longer run the Jovian System."

A half-second passed before Circe answered. "Your statement lacks precision," she said, without looking at Osadar. "The Guardian Fleet practices the mandates, even if the system as a whole has sunk into unrestrained emotionalism."

Marten silently counted to ten. If ever there was a time to watch his speech, this was it. He had a warship to run. He'd already received the majority of his crew and the surviving space marines from the storming of Athena Station. Omi was in charge of training the marines, and even now ran them through an exercise. It was wise to keep combat troops busy.

"If I am a barbarian," Marten said, "know that I fought hard to defeat the cyborgs."

"Your prowess in such matters has been noted," Circe said. "Perhaps that is the reason why the Chief Strategist employs you in such an important mission."

Marten glanced at Osadar.

Osadar never turned to face him. The cyborg had changed outwardly. She wore a senso-mask now, giving her the illusion of a human face. A beret covered her head, and she wore a heavy spylo-jacket and gloves. Everything helped maintain the human illusion, except for her manner of speech and the occasional electronic whines of her limbs when she moved or shifted.

"You don't approve of my…uh…Force-Leader status?" Marten asked, trying to talk like a Jovian.

"My approval was not sought," Circe said.

"I'm surprised," Marten said. "If we're to work together—"

"A moment," Circe said, raising a slender hand.

The myrmidons as a group grew tense. Their knotted hands dropped to their knives, some slipped fingers into knuckle-mounts.

Marten felt their hostility and the intensity of their eyes. He leaned back until his shoulders bumped against the wall behind him. The wardroom was much too small for this table. His hand dropped onto the butt of his holstered slugthrower. Maybe it was time to use a short-barreled weapon. He hardly had room to draw his .38 long-barrel.

"We will not *work together*, as you put it," said Circe. "I am now the ranking member of the expedition. I am the Jovian voice. Your task is to maintain ship discipline and to ensure our arrival in the Martian System."

"I thought we were headed for Earth."

"I'm sure I was clear," Circe said. "There has been a new directive."

"Can you tell me what changed Tan's mind?" Marten asked.

"Force-Leader Kluge, I have already spoken to you concerning the use of the Chief Strategist's name. Because of the present lack of arbiters, I will soon instruct my myrmidons to instill discipline in you if you cannot control your tongue. From this moment on, you will refrain from using the Chief

Strategist's name."

"What arbiters?" Marten asked.

Circe looked away, and she clicked her fingernails on the table. "I am unused to barbarians, even tamed ones such as you. Your endless barrage of queries wearies me. I insist that you compose yourself to receive orders."

She was irritating him, even if the body under that sheer gown was nearly perfect. The idea of spending months on the same ship with this Ur-philosopher....

"The Solar System beyond Jupiter is filled with barbarians," Marten said. "If you can't handle talking to me, how will you handle negotiations with Martians and Earthlings?"

"I am of the Third Rank. I—" Circe's eyes narrowed as she glanced at Osadar and then focused on Marten. "I'm beginning to see. Yes, the Chief Strategist holds the highest rank for rational reasons. You and I shall speak throughout the trip. That communication will accustom me to barbarian crudeness. The Chief Strategist was wise to let you keep what is for you an exalted station."

Marten thrust forward until his elbows rested on the table. "What's really going on, eh? What game are you playing? The Dictates died with Callisto. Now...the Chief Strategist is trying to pull this?"

Circe glanced at the *Thaliana's* captain. The captain lifted the palms of her hands in a Jovian shrug.

"To begin with," Circe said, "your questions lack precision."

"Yeah?" asked Marten. "Then let me put it like this: I was in charge of the mission until you showed up. Now suddenly Tan—oh, pardon me, the Chief Strategist—ships you out here. You're given nominal control of the warship—"

"I will have full control," Circe said.

"Sure. You have six myrmidons, a new set of orders—"

"More are coming, Force-Leader."

"More orders or more myrmidons?" asked Marten.

"Your tone has become insulting. Alter it at once or my myrmidons shall take matters in hand. You will not enjoy the consequences."

"Maybe you'd better alter your tone," Marten said, glancing at Osadar. "She is a cyborg, which trumps your pack of myrmidons."

"How dare you threaten my person," Circe whispered.

"Now it's you who lack precision," Marten said. "I didn't say anything about you, but your myrmidons."

"The creatures belong to my suite. They represent—"

"Listen," Marten said. "The Chief Strategist has filled my ship with former dissenters, with those who hated Callisto's dictatorial rule. The Chief Strategist obviously wants them out of the Jovian System. Now she thinks you can reinstall the Dictates by waving a new directive?"

"These conjectures are far beyond your scope," said Circe. "Your behavior here, I suspect you are presuming greater leeway for yourself because of your valorous act."

"You mean killing the cyborg or surviving Athena Station?"

Circe shook her head. "I will not tolerate this. I will not subject myself to continuous queries or listen to your barbaric tones. I hold a directive from the Chief Strategist. It shall be implemented and you shall learn to comport yourself properly in my presence."

Marten struggled to hold his tongue, barely winning in the effort. Maybe he should try a different tactic.

"It's obvious I lack your grace," he said. "Seeing as I'm a barbarian, I lack your training in the Dictates. What I understand is fighting."

"Just like a myrmidon," Circe murmured.

"Yeah, I'm a fighting animal."

"Do not let emotionalism taint your thinking," said Circe. "As a barbarian, you are far above an animal."

"Thank you...I think."

Circe inclined her head.

Marten kept himself from glancing at Osadar. Ur-philosophers seemed to lack a sense of humor. He'd have to remember that.

"What has transpired to change the mission?" Marten asked.

"The mission remains identical to its original parameters.

83

We attempt to forge an alliance with the Planetary Union and with Social Unity. As a particle of our good will, we are sending a warship to help against the Highborn."

This time, Marten glanced at Osadar.

"If we're to help against the Highborn," Osadar said, "that implies we've already reached a decision with Social Unity."

Several of the myrmidons made low-throated growls at Osadar.

"Such matters are beyond your jurisdiction," Circe said coldly.

Marten decided on a change of tack. "Yes," he said.

"Excuse me?" asked Circe, who looked confused for the first time.

"Tell the Chief Strategist we will follow the new mandate to the letter," Marten said.

"That was taken as a given," said Circe. "Therefore, I will need to tell her nothing."

"Was there anything else you wished to tell me?" Marten asked.

"Indeed," said Circe. She revealed a scroll-pad. "Item two on the agenda is…."

16

Several hours later, Circe entered her quarters on the *Thaliana*. It was a spacious room, decorated with silk and works of Jovian art. She instructed the pack-leader of her myrmidons to allow no entry into her chamber until further notice. Then she retreated to her communication's net, attempting a laser lightguide link with the Chief Strategist. After a brief delay, a link was established. Circe thereupon put on a neural-helmet and reclined in her com-bed.

***

CIRCE: The barbarian is clever and less direct than I had anticipated. He swallowed his anger and attempted subterfuge.

TAN: Kluge is quick-witted. Do not underestimate him.

CIRCE: He has defeated cyborgs on more than two occasions. That implies fighting prowess of an unusual degree. I view him as a killer virus.

TAN: That is an apt analogy. The virus in his instance is not direct, but rather the ideas he propagates.

CIRCE: My myrmidons are immune to such ideas.

TAN: The barbarian lacks Jovian mores. If he believes himself threatened, he will kill the myrmidons without hesitation.

CIRCE: Whatever he is, he is male.

TAN: That is why I sent you. Hmm. I could almost pity him.

CIRCE: You say he has a lover.

TAN: Her name is Nadia Pravda. She escaped from the

Sun-Works Factory. I believe he has taken to calling her his wife.

CIRCE: They are married?

TAN: I believe he preformed the rite himself.

CIRCE: This is interesting. Where?

TAN: I do not know. Is it important?

CIRCE: As I'm sure you're aware, I have perfected the Cleopatra grip. He is a fighting male, filled with testosterone, and I have already initiated a strong response in him. Among my myrmidons, I find that is an irresistible combination.

TAN: You...engage in *liaisons* with your myrmidons?

CIRCE: Like many of the martial arts, the Cleopatra grip demands constant practice in order to maintain a high level of competency. It also reinforces their loyalty to me.

TAN: But with an animal....

CIRCE: They are theoretically human. They have a heightened musculature, vigorous responses and a therapeutic effect upon me.

TAN: Doesn't it produce emotionalism in you?

CIRCE: We are philosophers, and we have learned to subdue the proto-urges. During the act, I redirect the pleasure sensations and practice isometric exercises. It helps me maintain perfect body tone.

TAN: You risk become a sensualist.

CIRCE: The bodily arts demand risk. Yet you have a point. I believe some of my practices have delayed my ascension into the highest ranks.

TAN: Hmm, undoubtedly. On a tangential note, I wish you to realize that this will be a difficult assignment. Despite his barbarism, Kluge has accurately stated the situation. His ship contains the worst dissenters and agitators.

CIRCE: My own reading of the data has led me to a similar conclusion. I therefore suggest a redirection of effort. As the meteor-ship heads for Mars, send a flock of ship-killing missiles after it.

TAN: That is a logical thought. I have considered it for some time. Three factors have rendered it moot. One, Jovians hostile to the Dictates might well witness the meteor-ship's destruction and correctly conclude I ordered the act. Two,

Marten Kluge is a dangerous man. He might discover a way to thwart the flock of ship-killers. Who knows what his response would be after that? Three, our Solar System faces a hideous threat in the form of the cyborgs. We need every warship possible. Therefore, it is illogical to destroy the meteor-ship.

CIRCE: Kill Marten Kluge.

TAN: Again, that would be a difficult act.

CIRCE: My myrmidons could easily achieve it.

TAN: Difficult to achieve successfully in the dark, I mean. As an official act, it would be simplicity itself. But that would harm my Chief Strategist position and force my political enemies to unite against me. No. You are my answer, Circe. You must practice the Cleopatra grip on him and control the barbarian through your sexuality.

CIRCE: His...*wife* might already have a fierce grip on him. I note they practice the olden custom. That implies she has some form of dominance over him. Why otherwise would he agree to such an antiquated practice?

TAN: That is beyond my area of expertise.

CIRCE: To achieve your mandate, I may have to eliminate her.

TAN: Do what is necessary to gain control of Marten Kluge. The mission is too important to leave to random factors. He is a barbarian and therefore unaware of our philosophic ruthlessness and purity. We seek to achieve the highest good for the greatest number. Nothing will be allowed to stand in our way.

CIRCE: I consider him little more than an intelligent barbarian.

TAN: I caution you against underestimating him.

CIRCE: Noted.

TAN: I feel I must also warn you against letting him or anyone else aboard the vessel knowing about your liaisons among the myrmidons.

CIRCE: Perceptions are critical. I am aware of that.

TAN: Hmm, yes. I do not mean to imply that you do not. As a side note, this taking of a wife...I find that troubling.

CIRCE: Wife or not, I shall subdue him. He is only a man after all. What about the cyborg?

TAN: When the time comes, kill it. No one will mourn its loss. In this purpose, I am determined: the eradication of the cyborg infestation. With their passing, the Dictates will flourish, in time, throughout the entire Solar System.

CIRCE: Long live the Dictates.

TAN: May they guide us forever. Chief Strategist Tan signing off.

17

Eight days later between Luna and Earth, an orbital fighter zoomed out of a bay in the *Julius Caesar*. It was one of two Doom Stars in the Earth System. The other presently hid behind the Moon.

The orbital fighter was an ugly craft, triangular-shaped and squat, with cannon ports and extra fuel tanks. It was a single-seater, and it held the Grand Admiral of the Highborn, Cassius. He wore a battleoid-suit. Behind his visor, he ground his teeth in anger.

The *Julius Caesar* was much nearer Earth than Luna. Cassius had brought the Doom Star into near-orbit as a threat against Eurasia. He had been doing this for the last three months. There was a reason for it, historical in nature.

Despite his rage, Cassius worked out ship-vectors, rates of laser-fire, proton-beam pumping and prismatic chaff levels. Eurasia and Africa had become bristling fortresses. The Supreme Commander down there was good, too good for a preman. Storming North America was still taking much too long. Cassius attributed it to Hawthorne.

The nine-foot Grand Admiral shrugged within his battleoid-suit. Because he wore it, it was badly cramped within the orbital fighter. He looked around at the stars. They shined brightly. To his side was the great blue-green ball of Earth. There were drifting clouds above Mexico, where he was headed, toward Mexico City specifically.

Cassius had been moving the two Doom Stars near Earth and over Eurasia in imitation of Alexander the Great.

Alexander was arguably the greatest warlord the premen had ever produced or likely ever would produce. Naturally, Cassius knew he could have easily outfought and outgeneraled Alexander. Maybe the reason the young Macedonian held such fascination for him was that Cassius believed he was the Highborn Alexander. He was the greatest military genius among the greatest military soldiers the Solar System had ever seen. The truth of that was obvious.

With his big hands, Cassius shifted the fighter's controls. The squat craft plunged toward the stratosphere. Almost immediately, the heat-shield began to glow as the fighter began to rattle and shake.

The ploy with the Doom Stars was just like Alexander's maneuvers before the Hydaspes River. It had tactically been Alexander's most brilliant large-scale battle. Alexander had marched, for him, to the ends of the Earth—in reality, India. There King Porous had waited with an army of chariots, archers and elephants. Porous had spread out his army, covering the various fords over the Hydaspes River. Alexander had marched back and forth on his side, accustoming Porous' soldiers to his presence. Finally, the day came where Alexander's phalanxes did as they always had. Elsewhere, however, a picked company of cavalry crossed the river, making it because the enemy had grown lax.

Cassius was accustoming the soldiers of Social Unity to the near presence of the Doom Stars. It was risky, because at any time, Hawthorne might order a vast barrage of proton beams, merculite missiles and whatever orbital fighters they had been secretly constructing to attack the *Julius Caesar* and its sister ship.

Despite the heat-shield, the fighter's solid construction and the battleoid-suit, Cassius heard the howling wind outside his craft. He dropped at combat speed toward Mexico City.

The radio crackled, and a FEC lieutenant came online, asking for identification.

Cassius was surprised. *Have we stretched ourselves so thinly that premen run sectors of air-defense?*

The FEC soldier could easily activate the air-defense over the city and region. With a single finger, the preman could achieve what many SU soldiers had been unable to do—kill the commander of the Highborn.

There were loyalty tests, to be certain. The lieutenant manning the air-defense-net had a stake in the Highborn victory. Still....

Cassius punched in the fighter's code.

"Acknowledged, SA-12," the FEC lieutenant said over the radio. "You are cleared for a scanning pass."

Cassius grimaced. He'd do more than that. Before he was through, high-ranking Highborn would be on the air-defense-net. Maybe it would be a lesson to them all. But he was more concerned that the young cockerel bearing his chromosomes would realize the foolishness of his action. Yes, Felix was about to discover that with such a grand genetic heritage as he possessed came responsibilities.

Gripping the controls, Cassius kicked in the afterburners. Time was critical. He might already be too late. With a lurch, he slammed deeper into the cushions, his fighter screaming down toward the surface level of Mexico City.

-18-

The orbital fighter gushed licking flames as it landed on a Mexico City street. Around him, GEVs ground to a halt. In the distance, a siren wailed. The few premen on the streets had uniformly stopped, staring at his orbital in shock.

His hatch popped open as a ladder extended down from the canopy to the pavement fifteen feet below. Grand Admiral Cassius stood up. He gleamed in his silvery battleoid-suit. The camouflage unit was turned off. He looked like a giant robot of the action vids, with a mirrored visor. On his right arm was a rotating hand-cannon.

Climbing out of the cockpit and onto the stubby nosecone, Cassius leaped to the ground. The battleoid-suit had a powered exoskeleton. Twin Titan-5000s motors energized it. They purred, allowing him to make one hundred meter jumps.

Cassius landed heavily, the pavement under his shock-absorbers cracking and splintering. It had been some time since he'd worn a battleoid-suit. But it was just like being a jet-jockey, something you never forgot how to do.

Premen scrambled to get out of his way. A woman screamed. A young one, a child, staggered against the side of a building and began to cry.

Cassius snorted in disbelief. How could such weaklings as these stand against the Highborn? It was inconceivable. Only their mind-numbing numbers gave them long-term resistance.

Checking his HUD, locating the brothel—three streets over to the north—Cassius jumped two more times and then began to run. He moved like a magnetic train, picking up speed as he ran. He'd forgotten the joy of a battleoid-suit. Maybe he should do this more often.

"Is he present?" asked Cassius, using the suit's radio.

"Yes, Grand Admiral," a Highborn replied.

"Did you delay him as ordered?"

"Sir—"

"Answer my question!" Cassius thundered.

"Yes, sir," the Highborn said. The soldier sounded truculent, but that didn't concern Cassius. If the Highborn had whined, he'd have been surprised and concerned. It wasn't in the nature of a Highborn to show fear. Even one caught in a flagrantly prohibited act would show courage to the end.

"Release the girl," Cassius said.

"Sir, are you sure this is—"

"Release the girl!" Cassius roared. "And if he dies, you will die under SU agonizers."

"Understood, sir," the Highborn said. "Tech Sergeant Gaius out."

Tech Sergeant, that meant he was from one of the newer batches. Yes, this was beginning to make better sense now. This demonstration was more needed than ever.

A four-story building rose up before him. It was red-colored on his HUD. Cassius grinned like a feral wolf, and he charged, activating the buffers.

He crashed through the main door of synthi-oak. Scantily-clad women screamed. Several FEC soldiers raised guns, most quickly lowering them. The inner area possessed red couches and thick shag rugs. A shot rang out. A bullet hit the battleoid-suit, and bounced off.

Cassius grunted. Then he fired a single round from his rotating hand-cannon. That took trained fire-control. The offender flew off his feet and against a wall, his chest a gory ruin. His gun tumbled over a shag rug until it struck a woman's leg. She crumpled and began to wail in agony.

Ignoring them all, Cassius leapt, landing on an upper level. Wood groaned and a lamp shattered into pieces. The display on his HUD changed, showing him the building's layout. He wondered if Felix had heard any of this.

Growling, the Grand Admiral of the Highborn crashed

93

down the hall. He chin-clicked a sensor. The girl had entered Felix's room. Yes, this was nearly perfect timing. That would add to the retelling of the tale.

Four seconds later, Cassius smashed through the door to Felix's room. Unaccountably, the fool had heard nothing or even worse, he'd ignored it.

Felix was a big Highborn fresh from the Training Academy. He had blond hair, a wide face and a god-like physique. He lay on a huge bed and he was naked, with his arms behind his head. A woman with a towel around her waist stood ten feet from his bed. She might have been dancing for him, as dance music played in the room.

Felix scowled as he sat up. He looked like a clone of Cassius, just many years younger. There was a reason for that. The same chromosomes had been used in the birth tubes.

"Who are you?" Felix demanded.

Cassius raised his battleoid arm, aiming the hand-cannon at the woman. She was pretty, extremely so. Her eyes became wide.

"There is a proscription against prostitution," Cassius said over his suit's speakers.

"She's clean," Felix said. "I've used her before."

"The premen have operatives among us. They might have kidnapped her between sessions and inserted a cortex bomb."

"I don't see how—" Felix started to say.

Cassius opened fire, letting the hand-cannons rotate as he shredded the woman into bloody chunks.

"No!" Felix howled. He rolled out of bed and charged Cassius.

The hand-cannons stopped as smoke drifted out of the barrels. The woman was a ruin of flesh, and blood smeared the wall as if someone had hurled a bucketful at it.

This mindless attack galled Cassius more than Felix's taking of prostitutes. The youthful fool leaped at him. With contemptuous ease and exoskeleton strength, Cassius swatted him, batting the Highborn onto the floor and into unconsciousness.

94

19

Cassius returned to the *Julius Caesar*. Three days later, he took the Doom Star into its nearest orbital pass yet across the Eurasian landmass. He sat in his command shell, tense and expectant.

The crew went about their tasks quietly and efficiently. They monitored the battered hulks of the drifting farm habitats. A few months earlier, SU ships had launched from Earth and tried to slip commandoes and supplies into the old habitats. They'd attempted to install field-grade weaponry there. It was unlikely there had been other secret attempts, yet Cassius suspected the worst. Supreme Commander Hawthorne had surprised him once too often on other occasions. The man was a miracle-worker.

"Launch a squadron of fighters," Cassius ordered. "They are to use a random, C-targeting sequence on any habitat within a thousand-kilometer radius of the ship."

"With their cannons, Grand Admiral?" asked Scipio. He was an uncommonly tall Highborn, a full ten feet. Scipio had a prosthetic hand, covered by a white glove. Replacement therapy had never taken on him. Some Highborn believed it had made him overly cautious, but Cassius had never complained.

"As preparatory fire, yes," Cassius said. He used a knob, rotating holoimages before him.

The farm habitats were uniformly vast cylindrical satellites. The satellites spun to create centrifugal-gravity. They used mirrors to reflect light into the interior. Once, each habitat had been filled with algae tanks heated by the Sun to a bubbling temperature and a strange organic soup from bacteria that formed a protein-rich jelly. Drop membranes with giant dura-chutes had floated the produce to the planet. Now most of the cylinders were vacuum-filled and devoid of life. Countless farm workers had died during the launching of the SU Mars supply fleet. More satellites had been destroyed during the ensuing months as Highborn space commandoes had stormed onto them. The last useful habitat had been gutted nearly a year later by proton beams and Earth-launched merculite missiles. Now only lifeless habitat hulks drifted around the planet.

Cassius understood perfectly. If Social Unity couldn't have them, no one would. Hawthorne and his SU directors cared nothing about the conquered territories or feeding the billions of Highborn-dominated premen.

For a variety of reasons, there were endless food riots in the conquered territories, the worst in South America. Cassius had ordered many Free Earth Corps formations there to reestablish discipline. That had soon caused dissension in the FEC units. The dissension had surprised some Highborn commanders.

"You forget," Cassius remembered telling them. "The premen are weak willed and often tender-hearted. Too many are squeamish at the sight of blood and become conscience-stricken. Cold-blooded killing—such as firing into chanting mobs—heightens this process in them. This produces alcoholism, heavier drug-usage and in some cases sedition among our troops. Therefore, we will comb the FEC units, searching for psychotic and sadistic individuals. These we'll train into riot-control battalions, helping to restore order in the worst territories."

The riot-control battalions had been trained and deployed. Now they were stretched thin. It had surprised Cassius how few sadistic or psychotic individuals there were. Therefore, he had reluctantly begun using hypnotically-drugged police units. The percentage of mental breakdowns had meant a high level of wastage among the personnel. Sometimes, he wondered if simply letting mass starvation do its work to thin out the billions of useless mouths would be the wisest course. His psychological profilers had told him that would give added impetus to the SU propagandists. So for now, he tried to keep the billions alive on their starvation diets, gunning down the most unruly.

"The fighter squadron has launched," said Scipio.

The Grand Admiral adjusted his controls. Tiny yellow lights sped toward the various holographic cylinders.

"Launch a squadron of heavy orbitals," Cassius said. He made a quick calculation. "Launch Squadron Seven."

"Squadron Five is in rotation, sir," Scipio said.

Cassius's features tightened, the only indication that he'd heard the officer.

"Squadron Seven, sir," the tall Highborn said after a moment.

Cassius watched his holoimages. A few minutes later, red lights began to zoom among the wrecked habitats. He had transferred Felix from Ground Command and into orbital duty. The cockerel would be acting as a weapons officer aboard one of the heavy orbitals. They were two-seaters. There was a growing belief among High Command that two-seater orbitals were wasteful of Highborn. Some suggested a phase-out of the heavy orbitals. A few wanted to train premen as weapons operators.

A warning horn blared on the bridge.

Cassius swiveled around.

"Powerful SU sensor sweeps are coming out of stations in Ukraine Sector," Scipio said.

Cassius showed his teeth in a grin. "They're awake down there. Good."

Several Highborn chuckled.

"Let's give them something to target," Cassius said. He checked his holoimages, noted the location of Felix's heavy orbital. With a click of a button, numbers appeared under the various cylinders. "Destroy Targets A-13 and R-11."

"Both satellites are deep in the gravity-well, sir," said Scipio.

"Exactly."

"Their decaying orbit means that some debris will head straight down, sir. The SU operators might think we've launched missiles."

"I don't think they're that stupid," Cassius said. "But let's find out."

"Shall I order the beginning of a prismatic-shield, sir, or begin spraying aerosol gels?"

"We are the Highborn," said Cassius, who watched his command crew sidelong.

Tall Scipio frowned as his white-gloved hand hovered over his control-board. The Highborn glanced at him, meeting his eyes.

"Highborn take unnecessary risks?" Scipio asked.

Cassius mentally marked the Highborn down for promotion as a field commander. A Doom Star was a precious military commodity. There were only four of them in the Solar System, and one of those four was still at the Sun-Works Factory under repair. It would be many more months, maybe even another year, before it was operational again. That left them three Doom Stars, two here in Earth orbit and one around Venus.

"We do not take foolish risks," Cassius said. "But it is good for the premen to think that we do."

"Sir?" asked Scipio.

"They will not launch merculite missiles today," said Cassius.

"We found out at Mars how dangerous their proton beams are," Scipio said. "In Eurasia, they have dozens of them. Respectfully, sir, we are much too near Earth's stratosphere."

"Of course we are," Cassius said.

Several Highborn glanced at him sharply.

"I request permission to speak freely, Grand Admiral," Scipio said.

"Permission granted."

That caused eyebrows to loft. Two Highborn traded glances. Cassius mentally marked them down for profile studies. He wondered if their allegiance to him was wavering.

"Why are we much too near the stratosphere, risking serious damage to our Doom Star?" asked Scipio.

"To gauge Social Unity," Cassius said.

"We hold the strategic advantage, sir. We should push that instead of risking our most valuable asset."

"The Doom Stars are not our most valuable asset," Cassius

said.

Scipio blinked at him. "Sir?"

Cassius nodded to himself. Scipio wanted to ask what was, but he was too cautious to do that. He would help Scipio.

"We as Highborn are our most valuable asset," Cassius said. "Our fighting spirit, our aggressiveness and sheer ability gives us the military edge."

"The Doom Stars help, sir."

"Why won't the premen open fire with proton beams?" asked a different Highborn.

"An excellent question," said Cassius. "It is something I'm endeavoring to answer. Now!" he said, signaling Engine Control. "Take us from low-orbit and head fast toward the Atlantic Ocean."

"Should I recall the orbitals?" asked Scipio.

"Tell them to head toward the Pacific Ocean. We will pick them up over North America."

"I'm picking up increased deep-core readings, sir." Scipio looked up. "They're bringing the proton beams online."

"Interesting," said Cassius. His gut began to churn. It made him feel alive. "Strap in, gentlemen. Engine Control, give us emergency speed. Scipio...order an increase in satellite targeting. I want them to rain debris on Eurasia. Since they've brought the protons online, let's give them something to shoot at."

"Enemy sensors are locking onto us, sir," Scipio said.

Cassius's heart-rate increased. The *Julius Caesar* was a huge ship, the biggest in the Solar System. So the premen wanted to frighten him off, did they? Or maybe they thought they could take potshots at his ship. There were personal enemies among the Highborn who would snap at the opportunity to bring him down. If the *Julius Caesar* should take serious damage because of a slip in a routine pass....

"Launch a spread of nuclear missiles," Cassius said in a clam voice. "Use Green Pattern-E. Then begin spraying the upgraded aerosol-gel."

It was a new gel, made specifically to slow proton beams.

A sigh of relief seemed to fill the bridge.

Cassius leaned forward as he studied the holoimages. Ports

opened in the kilometers huge Doom Star. Space-to-land missiles launched toward the planet. Each had a MIRVed nosecone—multiple reentry vehicles. It meant that each missile shot a spread of five nuclear warheads.

He switched settings. The heavy orbitals also launched missiles, but at the floating cylinders, the former farm habitats. Checking range and distances, Cassius quickly calculated debris drop-rates.

"They have battle-level wattage online," Scipio said.

From Eurasia, from Kiev, Berlin and Milan, proton beams stabbed upward at the *Julius Caesar*. The white beams hit the heavy lead-additive aerosol-gels, chewing through them with unbelievable speed.

"Emergency pumping," Scipio growled.

Grand Admiral Cassius leaned back in his command shell, watching the crew. They moved with efficiency, with calm speed. That was another reason he'd dipped so near the stratosphere and over Eurasia. It had been a long time since these warriors had been in space combat. An unused sword became rusty.

"There is a breakthrough," Scipio said.

Cassius returned attention to his holoimages. A weakened proton beam burned through the gels. It struck the Doom Star's outer plating. It wasn't the original plating, but a *collapsium* coating. It was a breakthrough technology, very hard to make. The *Julius Caesar* was presently the only warship with it, a coating micro-microns thick. Collapsium was hard and dense, and similar in nature to the core of a white star. The electrons of an atom were collapsed on the nuclei so the atoms were compressed so they actually touched. Lead in comparison was like a sponge.

The collapsium shielding held long enough for the *Julius Caesar* to begin rotation. No point on the ship received the hellish proton-beam longer than a second. Soon, more gels sprayed, absorbing the beams, giving the huge warship enough time to speed around the Earth's curvature and out of line-of-sight first from Kiev, then Berlin and finally Milan.

"The proton beams are retargeting, sir," Scipio said. The tall Highborn looked up. "They're burning orbitals, sir."

"Point-defense installations are opening up on the surface," a different Highborn said.

"All orbitals are to take evasive action," Cassius said.

"They've already begun do so, sir," said Scipio.

The Grand Admiral nodded. That was the Highborn way, to take matters into your own hands. If a Highborn didn't have the initiative to disregard a foolish order, he wasn't worthy of the exalted status of super soldier. If a Highborn disregarded a wise order, however, he could be shot. A preman might fold under that kind of pressure. A Highborn thrived, exalting on the knife-edge of existence.

"There are new point-defense establishments!" an officer shouted.

"I can hear you quite easily, thank you," Cassius told him.

"There are hits in the Po Valley," Scipio said.

"None on Milan?" asked Cassius.

"It was too heavily defended."

Cassius switched settings on his command shell, which switched his holoimages. A mushroom cloud rose in the Po River Valley. That was prime agricultural land. Good, good, that would hurt them in the belly.

"More nuclear warheads are detonating," Scipio said.

"What percentage made it through their defenses?" asked Cassius.

"Fourteen point three-seven percent," Scipio said. "No, make that fifteen point three."

"So little?" asked Cassius.

"The number of point-defense establishments has dramatically risen."

"Hmm," said Cassius. Yet again, he redirected his holoimage, noting that Felix's two-seater had interposed a drifting habitat between itself and Eurasia. Was the cockerel foolish enough to think he could remain there? Ah, no, the heavy orbital headed for deeper space. Maybe the youth could think after all.

"Begin battle analysis," Cassius told Scipio.

"...Yes, sir," said Scipio.

"Speak your mind."

"Not all the orbitals have escaped the danger zone."

"Notice the nuclear warhead patterns," Cassius said. "Now direct your vectoring—"

"Oh," said Scipio. "Yes, I see, sir. The warheads have affected SU defense, giving our orbitals cover. I will begin the battle analysis."

Cassius switched off his holoimaging. How was it that he could see these things more quickly than other Highborn? Was it merely his superior genes? Or did his intense study of military history have something to do with it? Felix had his chromosomes and he'd received full Academy training. Would Felix be able to see as quickly? It was an interesting question, and one that Cassius planned to study in depth.

20

The raid over Eurasia had repercussions in Highborn High Command. Soon, Cassius found himself under criticism.

Item: He had revealed the existence of collapsium. The axiom concerning a technological advantage was simple. It should remain a secret until a substantial number of units were deployed in order to achieve a strategic victory.

Item: To a lesser degree but with the same logic, the upgraded gel had been demonstrated. Now SU Command realized their proton beams lacked their former punch. They would likely compensate accordingly.

Item: The raid had achieved no appreciable advantage, and Highborn deaths had occurred. The deaths likely heartened the enemy. And even if only minimally, the deaths certainly weakened deployable military strength.

Cassius had weathered each criticism with a repeated counter-argument. Unfortunately, as the Solar System's supreme strategist, he realized that the cumulative effect of the attacks had weakened his position among the Highborn as Grand Admiral.

The counter-argument was simple: the best ones usually were. Social Unity was on the defensive. Pressure had continuously mounted against them. The raid over Eurasia had added more pressure because a) superior technology had foiled the surprise proton-beam attack. And b) nuclear strikes had hit Eurasian food supplies despite the massive addition of point-defense systems. That meant c) nothing Social Unity did could prevent its ultimate demise. This had brought about d) demoralization and likely growing apathy among the SU leadership. In other words, the raid kept the pressure high. Soon, Cassius had predicted, there would be large-scale ruptures within Social Unity. That might well give them the Earth in one fell swoop.

It had been a heated meeting. Cassius now jogged through the corridors and hallways of the *Julius Caesar* to unwind. He wore a sweat suit, with a towel around his thick neck. His iron-colored hair was short and slicked with perspiration. With long, even strides and calm breathing, he'd raced two kilometers already.

He was getting older, but he still credited himself as the most dangerous Highborn alive. Not only was he a strategic genius, but in his opinion, he had few equals and no superiors in hand-to-hand combat. Physically, he feared no entity. It didn't mean he was foolish or took foolish risks.

He saw the monofilament line stretched across the corridor. It was nearly invisible and a quarter-meter off the deckplate. Conceivably, it was meant to sheer through his ankle and deprive him of a foot. The implications were ominous.

Unfortunately, he saw the line too late to halt—he was running too fast through the ship corridor to stop on the spot. So he jumped over the monofilament line. While passing over it, he entered a hyper-state of readiness. Every sense tingled with awareness. His muscles rippled under his skin as his eyes shined with murder-lust. A yearning to kill surged through him as adrenalin hit him like a love-drug.

"Hello, old man."

Cassius spun to his right, toward a viewing port. Through the ballistic glass was pockmarked Luna. There was a big black spot seemingly on the moon. It was the position of the *Genghis Khan* in orbit around it. Stars shined like a blanket of gems in the background.

After noting Luna and the Doom Star, Cassius promptly gave his full attention to the Highborn striding toward him. It was Felix.

Squinting, Cassius interpreted the monofilament line to mean that Felix had been monitoring him and analyzing his patterns. Given Felix's chromosomes, it was possible the cockerel had predicted his run through this very corridor. The look of rage on the young Highborn's face confirmed Cassius's belief that Felix had meant the line to cut off a foot. Maybe as bad, the fool held an old-fashioned sap—a piece of synthi-leather filled with shot. Premen criminals used saps in the underground cities to beat each other to death.

Cassius's options were limited. He noted the hardness of the youth's muscles. They were like steel cables and fresh with youthful vigor. Likely, the cockerel was stronger than he was and quite likely Felix would prove faster.

It was an interesting tactical problem.

Mentally fanning his options like cards, Cassius chose with lightning speed. Suiting thought to action, he put his hands on his hips and laughed contemptuously.

Felix's blue eyes squinted. The young god was the very image of anthropomorphic retribution. He wore combat-training fatigues and armored shoes, giving him yet another hand-to-hand weapon advantage.

"You've meddled in my life once too often, old man," Felix said. "Now I'm going to beat you to death. Then I'm going to shove your carcass through a garbage-chute so they can never revive-to-life a piece of sewage like you."

"You tried to hurt me once before," Cassius said. "Do you remember?"

"I haven't forgotten, old man." Felix took another step closer. "This time you aren't encased in combat armor."

"But you're still as lacking in wit," Cassius said.

Felix spat on the deckplate, and he shook the sap. "You had your chance stranding me out there in the orbital."

"The monofilament line and its strategic placement prove that you can reason at a high level," Cassius said. "Why then do you insist on infantile statements?"

"Do you deny ordering an out-of-sequence launching of my squadron?"

"Why would I deny what is plain on the battle-tapes?" asked Cassius.

"What other rationale could you have for doing that other than trying to engineer my death?" asked Felix.

Cassius shook his head contemptuously. "Your grades were

among the highest in Training Academy history."

"They *were* the highest, old man. Believe me, I checked."

"The records you checked were not complete."

"You can't know that!" snarled Felix. "You're making that up."

"I'm the Grand Admiral. There is nothing about the Highborn—"

"Just answer me this, old man. Why do you want me dead?"

"Come," said Cassius, motioning Felix toward him. "Kill me if you can."

"Oh, I can."

"Because of your combat advantages?" sneered Cassius.

Felix grinned as he hunched his shoulders. "Good try, old man, but no one is talking me from discarding my advantages."

"Good. That is one point in your favor."

"Are you so old and senile that you don't realize I'm about to kill you?" Felix asked.

Cassius leaped, and he shot his left foot out in a flying kick. The sap connected with the foot, instantly numbing it, and Felix twisted in the narrow corridor, allowing Cassius passage. The Grand Admiral landed heavily on his hip and shoulder, and he rolled right, bumping against a bulkhead. An armored shoe whistled past his head, kicking the bristles but missing his skull. With heightened speed, Cassius caught the foot and twisted. Felix grunted, letting himself roll so he smashed against the other bulkhead. Releasing the boy, Cassius jumped to his feet. So did Felix.

"I want you to think," Cassius said. His numbed foot made it hard to maneuver, but he'd make do.

Instead of thinking, Felix chopped. And for the next few seconds they engaged in blows and counter-punches. Each time the sap struck flesh, it deadened muscles or pulped skin and bruised bones. It was then Cassius realized the cockerel was good. Maybe as good as he was at hand-to-hand. With the sap and armored shoes, the young Highborn might even be better. A glance into Felix's eyes showed him the cockerel knew it, too.

"I killed the girl to save your life," Cassius panted.

"What irony then that your nobility is about to get you killed."

"Your talents were wasted in ground combat. It was the reason I moved you into Space Command."

"I liked it where I was, old man. You should have left well enough alone and lived another few years in High Command. Now it's too late for that."

Another flurry of blows produced low-throated grunts, the meaty sounds of fist or sap striking flesh and the crack of ribs.

"That will slow you down, old man."

Despite the pain in his ribs, Cassius grinned, showing blood on his teeth. The blood dripped down from his mashed nose.

Felix's features were equally pulped, although in different areas. Blood welled in his right eye, causing him to paw at it every few seconds.

"You're good, boy," Cassius said.

"I'm going to make you piss blood before you die, old man."

"But you're too foolish sometimes. You need a guiding hand if you're to survive the war."

"Get ready to die," said Felix.

Cassius abruptly turned and ran. The move caught Felix by surprise.

"I knew it!" the young Highborn roared. "You're a coward."

Cassius glanced over his shoulder. The youth gave chase. Running away was ignoble. It was un-Highborn. Yet he was the Grand Admiral for a reason. There were times to retreat. There was an ancient but valuable adage concerning that: *better to run away to live and fight another day*. Not that he planned to run away for long.

Cassius sprinted over the monofilament line, slowed his speed and then roared as he spun around. Felix was hot after him, and the cockerel's eyes widened at the shout. It wasn't fear, but knowledge that the old man was going to fight after all. It was then Felix remembered the monofilament line. Cassius had wondered if he would. Leaping over the line caused Felix to break his stride. Timing that, Cassius leaped, and he put everything into the flying kick. The sap hit, but not powerfully enough. A foot connected against Felix's chest. With a grunt, the youth went backward. Cassius landed on top of him, and his big hands flew to the cockerel's throat. It likely took Felix a second to understand, a critical amount of time in this sort of combat. Then he likely realized the sap was useless now. He dropped it and wrapped his hands around Cassius's throat. They both squeezed, and Cassius found it impossible to breath. His iron-like fingers ground into youthful flesh as he tightened his own throat muscles. Suddenly, it was hard to see. He kept squeezing. Who was winning?

Something snapped. Was it his neck? It hurt like Hades. Cassius blinked repeatedly and vision slowly returned. Felix lay under him, with his neck broken and tongue protruding.

Groaning, Cassius struggled to his feet and to a com-unit. It was time to call medical. He needed to work fast if he was going to save the stupid cockerel from final death. The medics would have to bring Felix back through *Revival* so he could live again.

21

Far from Cassius and the *Julius Caesar*, the weeks blurred as Marten Kluge worked hard. It seemed there was always something going wrong.

The worst was the fusion core. Its outer shell produced a crack, a leak. Before the technicians could fix it, eighteen crewmembers had been irradiated. Marten attempted communication with Fleet HQ. It was then he found that channels were inexplicably blocked.

"It's part of the new directive," Nadia told him later. He'd made her his com-officer. It had meant a lot of technical reading and study for her, which had meant fewer hours alone together for them.

"You mean the directive from Circe?" he asked.

They were in the command center, which looked identical to the one Yakov had used aboard the *Descartes*. There was the same central chair, the main screen and the many cubicles for the officers along the circular wall. Unlike other Jovian warships, however, this one lacked statues. The cyborgs must have removed them when they'd taken over the vessel.

"Circe sent around a memo," Nadia said. She sat in her com-officer cubicle. It was cramped for Nadia, as she was bigger than the average Jovian. "You know Circe prefers the title Sub-Strategist."

"Whatever," Marten said, who stood outside the cubicle.

Nadia looked concerned. "You should try to get along with her better."

"Me?" Marten said.

"She has a high-handed manner," said Nadia. "But she does represent the Jovians. If you anger her too much, she could have you replaced."

"She represents a pain in my rear."

"Don't let her hear you say that."

He nodded, and said, "What's this about the directive? I need to get these sick people off the ship. And I need replacements."

"That part of it has already been taken care of—the replacements."

"Did the Sub-Strategist order it?"

Nodding, Nadia said, "The replacement personnel will be here in ten days."

"That long? I want to be ready to leave in ten days. Who are these new people?"

Nadia turned to her screen, tapping it. A manifest appeared and she scanned it. "Oh," she said.

"What's wrong?"

"There's an arbiter with several more myrmidons coming."

Marten scowled. Just how many myrmidons did Tan plan to pack onto his ship?

"Arbiter Neon—" Nadia was saying.

"What?" Marten said. He leaned into the cubicle and studied the screen. "Can you show me a pic?"

Nadia tapped the screen. An image appeared of Arbiter Neon. It was the white-haired man who had been aboard the dreadnaught.

"I thought he died when the master super-cyborg attacked," Marten muttered.

Nadia did more tapping. "Look at this," she said. "There's a demerit in his profile. It says something about being absent from his post during combat."

Marten laughed sourly and shook his head. "That's all we need. Hmm. Maybe Tan is packing all her unwanted personnel onto my ship."

"She gave you this post because of your experience."

"What she tells me and why she does something can easily be two different things," Marten said. "It doesn't matter now anyway. What I need to know is how I can get permission to communicate with headquarters?"

"You'll need to see the Sub-Strategist for that."

"See her?" asked Marten. "I've been avoiding her."

Nadia shook her head. She wore a military cap. It suited her, especially the way her hair flowed out in the back. None of the Jovians had hair like Nadia. Many of the Jovian women didn't have hair at all.

Thinking about it caused Marten to bend deeper into the cubicle and kiss Nadia on the lips. His wife smiled and stroked his cheek. Marten kissed her again.

"This is most unseemly," Circe said, "and it is further proof of your barbarism."

Marten withdrew from the cubicle as Nadia blushed.

Sub-Strategist Circe stood in the command center with three of her orange-uniformed myrmidons. Today she wore a white gown and black slippers. She was so small, yet she had an exotic way to her, leaving no doubt that she was a woman. Black makeup lined her eyes, highlighting them.

Marten felt Nadia's hand touch his back. Turning, he helped her out of the cubicle.

"I've to decide if it is appropriate for your wife to be in the command center," Circe said. "It distracts you from your duties."

"What distracts me is a lack of communication with headquarters," Marten said. "I need—"

"Your tone is improper." Circe shook her head. "This is most distasteful. I do not wish to reprimand you in front of your sex partner, but I refuse to shirk my duties simply to ease your prickly ego."

"Nadia is my com-officer," Marten said. "And you'd better watch how you speak about her to me. She's my wife, not my sex partner."

The three myrmidons closed in around Circe and eyed Marten.

"False bravado doesn't impress me," Circe said. "I doubt it impresses your sex partner either."

"I'm going to tell you again—" Marten said as Nadia pressed her hand against the small of his back. Her touch made Marten pause, and that made him wonder why Circe annoyed him so easily. Maybe it was her myrmidons. These acted differently toward her than Arbiter Octagon's myrmidons had acted toward him. These myrmidons seemed possessive of Circe, more easily angered. They seemed more eager to attack, and that made him uneasy.

"Sub-Strategist," Marten said.

"This conversation has ended," Circe said. "If you have complaints or requests to make, come to my quarters in three hours. Until then, I shall be otherwise engaged." So saying, Circe turned with a swirl of her gown. She moved regally out of the command center, with her three myrmidons trailing her like dogs.

"What was that all about?" Marten asked. When Nadia didn't answer, Marten turned toward her. She scowled after Circe. Then she turned sharply and stared at him.

"What's wrong?" Marten asked.

Nadia shook her head before saying, "I don't trust that woman."

"Neither do I," said Marten.

"Good," Nadia said.

An officer entered then, asking for Marten's help. There was still much to do to get the meteor-ship ready for the flight to Mars. Marten needed more hours in the workday and less interruptions.

-22-

Returning to her quarters, Circe readied herself for the coming meeting with the barbarian.

He was handsome in a crude way, and he exuded an intelligent ferocity. It was a strange combination, a mixture of myrmidon and Jovian cadet, brain and brawn. Her couplings with the myrmidons were always vigorous, but lacking in wit or grace. A union with a Jovian cadet was intellectually stimulating but left her limply unsatisfied. To experience both sensations at once—it excited her.

Circe removed her white gown.

The myrmidons grew tense, watching her. The dominant male grunted and began to unbuckle his breeches.

"No," she said.

He growled irritably. The others became excited and began to jostle for position. Sometimes she let them wrestle over her, the winner allowed to approach her bed.

"Heel," she said.

The six myrmidons froze, blinking at her.

"Obey," she said, reaching for an obedience rod.

Reluctantly, the six creatures slunk to their shackles. She had trained them well by applying merciless punishment for the slightest infraction.

Using a small thumb, she clicked a button on the rod. Each of their neck-manacles on the wall opened. Each myrmidon in turn rested his neck in a shackle. Clicking the rod again caused the individual shackles to snap shut, locking the brutes in place.

Red silks swathed the room. There were six statues of

aroused men and women. They surrounded a round bed with many cushions. Her favorite statue showed a man on his knees, clutching the thighs of a haughty-eyed woman. The male statue looked submissively up at the female, clearly ready to obey her every dictate. It was the essence of her training to be able to subdue any man, placing him in a state of abject worship.

Circe smiled to herself. Sight of these statues would bewilder Marten Kluge. Tonight, she would subdue him. She would give him pleasure such as few males had ever received. Then she would show him the lash and thus his place in her world. But first, she must prepare.

She lifted her rod and strode naked to the shackled myrmidons. Each stood at attention and grunted hungrily, eyeing her. She smiled, and she lifted a bottle of pheromones, beginning to spray the chemical throughout the room.

Each grunting myrmidon began to thump his hands against the wall, eager to be chosen. Each of them longed to pleasure her tonight.

Circe laughed, delighted at their antics. She'd never released one in this state. She'd never dared. Instead, she began to twirl for them, and dance erotically, driving them to drool and stare at her with glazed lust. Tonight, she would practice the Cleopatra grip on Marten Kluge. But she would leave nothing to chance, oh no.

She sprayed more pheromones as she danced. Then she strode from myrmidon to myrmidon as she buffed her body before them. They pawed for her, and they thrust their hips at her as they tore off their uniforms. She decided then to allow them to watch her couple with the barbarian. It would ignite hatred in each of her creatures for Marten Kluge. If ever the day came that Kluge attempted to free himself from her control, she would release her myrmidons upon him. They would tear him apart.

Twirling to her bed, she made further preparations. The most important was loading a spring-gun. It fired ice slivers that melted in the flesh. These slivers were not normal ice, they were frozen SX-16, a powerful aphrodisiac. Combined with the pheromones and her Aphrodite skills, the barbarian would easily succumb to her control.

Circe ran her small hands down her hips. Once she gained full mastery, she'd make Marten throttle his wife for her. The woman was a cow, a barbaric distraction. She especially hated Nadia's hair. Afterward, Marten would do anything she commanded.

Circe checked her chronometer. Ah, in another hour the proceedings would begin. She shivered, looking forward to the challenge.

23

At the sound of a chime, Marten checked his watch. He was late for his meeting with the Sub-Strategist. Excusing himself from the group, he left the chief mechanic and his workers and hurried down the corridors.

The byways and corridors were narrow, a veritable maze throughout the meteor-ship. Recycled air pulsed everywhere, and clangs, thrums and low murmurs were constant. Marten passed technicians wiring panels and he said hello to his fire-control officer checking laser-coils. After climbing a ladder to a different level, Marten hurried around a corner. He adjusted his uniform and told himself he needed to control his temper better. Nadia was right. Circe was Tan's representative. He needed to learn how to convince the Sub-Strategist, to look past her aloof attitude. There had to be some way to convince her to work together with him instead of battling him at every step.

"Marten—wait!"

Recognizing Omi's voice, Marten halted. "I'm late for a meeting with Circe. I need to hurry."

"You need to hear what I've found first."

There was something troubling in Omi's voice. Then Marten saw Osadar Di. The tall cyborg had trailed Omi. The frowning senso-mask startled him. Marten recalled something about the mask being able to sense its owner's moods and adjust accordingly. How it could do that with a cyborg, he had no idea.

Marten glanced down the corridor toward Circe's chamber.

There were spy-sticks there.

"In here," Marten said, indicating a storage chamber.

With the three of them among coils, auto-welders and construction-foam blowers, it made a tight fit. Osadar took out a sonic-shield, turning it on. The vibration hurt Marten's ears. Listening to it too long would give him a headache.

"I'm late for a meeting with Circe," Marten whispered.

"The crack in the fusion core's outer shell wasn't an accident," Omi said.

"What's that supposed mean?"

"Sabotage," Omi said.

"Do you have proof?" asked Marten.

Osadar slid out a scroll-pad and showed him the evidence. After five minutes of tech-talk and Osadar explaining what she meant by it, Marten realized that they were right.

"The question is now," Marten said, "who do you think did it?"

"I suspect the Sub-Strategist," Osadar said.

"What reason could she have?" Marten asked.

"Delay," said Osadar.

"Why?" Marten asked, as he shook his head.

"Have you studied the manifest of the new personnel?" asked Osadar.

"Yeah," said Marten. "Headquarters is sending an arbiter, more myrmidons and replacement technicians."

"I managed to discover the point of origin of several of the new technicians," Osadar said. "It is Callisto."

Marten frowned. "Has Tan changed her mind about us?"

"Someone has," said Osadar.

Taking the scroll-pad, staring at the names, Marten mulled over the implications.

"You dare not enter the Sub-Strategist's chamber," Osadar said.

"Why not?" asked Marten. "I don't see the connection."

"Given that she sabotaged the core-shell," Osadar said, "shows that she willingly risked the deaths of at least eighteen people. You must ask yourself—after her arrogance toward you—why does she now wish a private meeting in her chamber? The answer is obvious to me. So she can stage an incident and order her myrmidons to kill you."

"Why didn't Tan have me killed when she had the chance?" Marten asked.

"We do not know all the realities of the Chief Strategist's current political position," Osadar said. "Clearly, she feared to have you murdered outright. Now, however, time has passed. A staged incident would allow her to remove you and place one of her people in charge of the warship."

"I don't know," Marten said. "Tan seemed genuine. She also recognized the need for an alliance with everyone else against the cyborgs."

"According to the reports," Osadar said, "this alliance has been achieved. Before, you believed Tan wanted to use your unique experiences with the Highborn, Social Unity and the Martians. It may be that your expertise is no longer required. Therefore, she is free to kill you."

"It's possible," Marten said thoughtfully, "and it might explain why she sent Circe in the first place."

"Kill Circe and the myrmidons," Omi said. "Then kill the new arbiter before he can board."

"That seems harsh," said Marten.

"So does sabotaging the fusion-shell and causing eighteen crewmembers to be poisoned with radiation," Omi said.

Marten rubbed his forehead. The sonic-shield made his brain pound. If all this was true…. He looked up at the others.

"You have reached a solution," Osadar said.

"Maybe," said Marten. "Let me think about it first."

"What about the meeting with Circe?" Omi said.

"Osadar might be right," Marten said. "So I'll let her stew. Yeah," he said with a grin. "I'll make the Sub-Strategist angry enough to come see me."

118

24

Thirteen hours later in a lonely part of the ship, Omi muttered, "Here comes trouble."

Marten looked up.

They were in an outer corridor near a seldom-used docking bay. Several battered patrol boats were attached to the meteor-ship's outer shell. One of the boats had used this emergency bay. Omi had climbed out of the boat and come down here to describe the latest field exercise to Marten. The space marines used thruster-packs to skim around the meteor-ship. Omi still wore his vacc-suit, although minus its helmet. Half the marines were still outside, and would spend another seventeen hours there. Marten wanted them accustomed to spending long hours in their suits, so they wouldn't panic if it happened during combat.

Despite the loneliness of the location, Circe moved toward them. Usually, she remained within the inner ship, seldom venturing into the hollowed-out corridors composed of the asteroid-shell. She wore her sheer gown today, the gauzy one that left little to the imagination. Under the gown, she wore a belt, with a small gun attached to it. The belt accentuated the sway of her hips, which moved in a decidedly un-philosophic manner. Three myrmidons followed.

Marten frowned. Something seemed different about them today. Then he noticed their bloodshot eyes. The myrmidons looked tired, sullen maybe, and a little less aggressive. Once or twice, he thought to see them eye Circe, but it was hard to tell. They hunched their heads like turtles, and constantly glanced about everywhere as if hunting for trouble. Although what they could find in the nearly empty corridor baffled Marten.

"Strange gown for a Sub-Strategist to wear," Marten whispered.

"Nice tight body, though," Omi whispered. "She reminds me of a Sydney hooker, one of the better kind reserved for the hall leaders."

"That sort of thought probably never enters her mind," Marten whispered.

"The way she walks," Omi whispered, "don't count on it."

"Force-Leader Kluge," Circe called, "I would like a word with you."

"Here I am," said Marten.

"In private, if you please," Circe said.

"Omi and I have been through Hell and back," Marten said. "Whatever you have to say to me, you can say in front of him."

"I'm sure your antiquated religious terms make sense to you," Circe said. "But they beg the issue. I need your expertise on a matter and require privacy."

"Sure," said Marten. He'd never heard that before, that she needed help. Maybe he should try to bend a little. "Why don't you order your myrmidons back to your chamber then?"

Circe raised plucked eyebrows, highlighting the black gem seemingly embedded in her forehead. "This is most interesting. My profile on you said barbarian chieftains never admit to fear. Yet now you're exhibiting fright of my protectors."

Marten snorted. "Lady, I've been more afraid than you can possibly imagine. I have no problem admitting it, either. Now if you wish to speak with me privately, then get rid of your myrmidons. I don't like the way they're eyeing me or how their hands keep straying to their knives."

"You have a big gun strapped to your waist," Circe said.

Marten gave a hollow laugh. "I've fought myrmidons before. Gun or not, they're hard to kill."

The lead myrmidon snarled, and took a lurching step toward Marten, passing Circe as he did so. The Sub-Strategist reacted with astonishing quickness and slapped his hand. The myrmidon cringed, backing away, and he whined in a beastly manner. The others glanced at Circe in fear.

120

"Go," she told them. "Return to my chamber. Ready him for punishment by making him assume the manticora position."

The offending myrmidon stood frozen, his bloodshot eyes widening as he stared at her. The other two grimaced uneasily.

Circe raised a hand.

The offending myrmidon whirled around, hurrying away. A half-second later, the other two set off after him.

Marten and Omi traded glances.

"There," Circe said, as she smoothed her gown. "I have rendered myself defenseless before you. Either exhibit your barbarism upon me or send away your bodyguard so we may speak in private."

"What do you want to speak about?" Marten asked.

"I have fulfilled your requirements for a private conversation," Circe said. "Either keep your word or demonstrate your untrustworthiness."

Marten rolled his eyes. "Go on," he told Omi. "I'll hear her out."

Omi hesitated but finally nodded, and he went down the hall toward the engine section.

"Well?" Marten asked.

Circe waited.

"I thought you wanted to speak to me in private," Marten said.

She nodded.

"Look, if you're worried that Omi is coming back...." said Marten.

Circe took several steps closer, and she smiled. "You are unlike Jovian males," she whispered. "You are so strong, so militant and dominant. Do you know that your authority is strangely compelling? I have tried to resist the impulse, but you excite me on some primitive level. It begins here," she said, touching her stomach. "And it wells upward," she said, sliding her hand up between her breasts. "Why does this occur, Force-Leader?"

Marten's mouth opened as he stared at her. He'd never expected such words. She took two small steps toward him. Her eyes, her throat, breasts, the flat belly, her thighs....

"I am deeply attracted to your masculinity," she whispered.

"Wait," Marten said, backing up. "I-I'm married. I have a wife. You shouldn't say these things to me."

"Such a powerful barbarian as you must be capable of multiple engagements," she said. "Surely you can dominate females with…simian ease." Her hand reached toward him.

Then Marten felt a momentary sting on the top of his hand. Jerking his hand back, he saw a tiny mark there. Something seemed to flush up through his arm then, hitting his chest and exploding outward through his body. It particularly struck his groin, seeming to make it swell.

"Ah, Marten Kluge," whispered Circe. Her smile seemed wicked, full of sexual promise.

"You drugged me," Marten said.

"Kiss me," she said. "Feel what true ecstasy is like." Her other hand darted toward him.

At the last moment, he caught her wrist. Her skin seemed to burn like fire. As his groin throbbed, he wanted to yank her near and shower kisses upon her. That gown, the charms beneath—yes, he'd rip off her gown and here in the corridor he'd do her.

"You drugged me," he slurred. He couldn't seem to let that go.

"I can do so much more," she said, and she used her free hand, touching him so he groaned with pleasure. "I can bring you sweet release," she whispered.

While still gripping her wrist, Marten shook his head. Feeling her grope him—suddenly he wanted to use her, to lay with her and have her. But he was married to Nadia. He wasn't supposed to cheat. That was the whole point of marriage.

"Force-Leader," Circe whispered, and she pressed her yearning body against him.

"Drugged," said Marten.

"I've wanted you from the beginning," Circe said.

Marten grinned. Her body, her face—his grip around the trapped wrist tightened as something elemental surged within him. She'd drugged him. Now she sought to use him, to control him in some Callisto fashion. With a savage twist, he bent her wrist around so her clenched palm faced toward the ceiling.

"Oh!" she cried.

He gripped even more fiercely, and her hand opened. There on her ring was a tiny spike. No doubt, she'd meant to stab him with the spike and pump him with even more powerful drugs.

"Let me touch you," she whispered. "Learn what it means to love me."

"Snake," Marten said.

"Embrace me."

Instead, Marten twisted her arm harder. She was so small, so helpless against his strength. He slapped her open hand against her other arm so the tiny spike pricked her flesh.

"No!" she wailed. "What have you done?"

"That's what I want to know," Marten slurred.

This time Circe screamed as Marten twisted her arm. Now with her arm behind her back, Marten forced her down the corridor.

"No, no," she said. There was panic in her voice. "You must inject me with the antidote. I will become an animal soon. This is horrible, a crime against purity, against one of the highest orders of thought."

"We'll see," Marten said. It was hard to think anymore. He wanted to rip off her gown and madly couple with her. Instead, while keeping her hand high against her back, he pulled out a com-unit. He pressed a switch.

"…Yes?" asked Nadia.

"Hurry," Marten said. "I need help. Bring Osadar."

"The antidote!" screamed Circe. "I must have it before you turn me into a creature."

"What's going on?" Nadia asked over the com-unit.

"The Sub-Strategist tried to poison me," Marten said. "Please, Nadia, you must hurry. I need your help more than I ever have."

"I'm coming," Nadia said. "Keep your link open so I can follow the signal."

"Send for the antidote!" Circe wailed. "This can't happen to me."

"You wanted it to happen to me," Marten told her. And he found that he enjoyed holding her wrist like this. Reaching around, he grabbed one of her breasts, squeezing hard.

Circe moaned in pleasure, and she writhed against his hand.

123

With an oath, Marten snatched his hand back. What was he doing? He was married. "You viper," he said. "You drugged me."

"You're only a barbarian, but such a vital and—oh, touch me again. I beg you. I'll do anything for you, Marten Kluge. I must have you. You must take me and do whatever you desire."

Steeling himself, Marten kept marching Circe forward. He had to keep going. If he stopped, there was no telling what would happen.

"…The antidote," Circe whispered.

"What was in your ring?"

"Don't you understand?" she moaned. "The dosage was set for you. I'm so much lighter. This is unprecedented. You mustn't let this happen to me. Please, give me the antidote."

"Keep walking" Marten said.

"Our situation is deteriorating," Osadar said.

It was two days after Sub-Strategist Circe's attempt to poison Marten. She was in medical, strapped down and heavily sedated. The doctor still ran tests, baffled at her inability or unwillingness to engage in communication.

"It's as if an area of her brain has shut down," the doctor had told Marten yesterday. "Or maybe another area is so highly motivated that it controls her thoughts."

"Haven't you learned anything?" Marten remembered asking.

"By accident, I have. When she heard your voice over the ship's intercom, she became tense. Noticing that, I showed her a video shot of you. It induced extreme behavior." The doctor had shaken his head. "I believe she has imprinted on you in a most sexual way. In a word, she desires you above all else. And I think she will do anything to achieve…ah…union with you. With your permission, I would like to run further tests while you're present in the chamber."

Marten had declined. He'd had a hard enough time explaining everything to Nadia.

He presently stood with Osadar outside the fusion core, near the formerly cracked shell. The engine's thrum was heavy so the entire area vibrated. Touching his ribs, Marten could feel them shift. His voice sounded funny here. Dried construction-foam sealed the cracked shell. The foam was a dirty gray color, with intensely white pieces. Technicians with sprayers had poured the foam, which had hardened instantly. The technicians had been experts and had formed blocks, making the wall easier to build.

Osadar moved closer to the dried foam, taking out a Geiger-counter. The clicks sounded ominous, but Osadar declared it good.

"The core is sound then?" Marten asked.

"It is the only factor in our favor," Osadar said.

"That's too pessimistic," Marten said. "The space marines didn't balk."

Yesterday, after too many hours without her, Circe's myrmidons had demanded the return of their mistress. It had been odd speaking with the leader, and it had been a surprise to learn he could use a com-unit. The myrmidon's voice had been so low-pitched and growl-like that Marten had barely understood the man's words. The myrmidon had been a man. Even after the things Marten had seen in Circe's quarters....

The leader had given an ultimatum concerning Circe. Not willing to see what six outraged myrmidons could do, Marten had reached a decision. With Omi and seven of the best space marines, he'd invaded Circe's quarters. The myrmidons could have surrendered. He should have known they never would. One Jovian had died because Marten had insisted they first try to subdue the gene-warped warriors. As the man crumpled to the deckplates, Omi had killed the first myrmidon. The others had died seconds later in a blaze of gunfire. Marten swore his head still rang because of it.

Amid the blood and sprawled bodies, they'd first noticed the sex-statues, the shackles and other various implements.

"Who is the Sub-Strategist?" Marten had asked Omi.

"The sooner we leave Jupiter, the better," had been the Korean's answer.

"You cannot put off Chief Strategist Tan much longer," Osadar said, as she put away her Geiger-counter.

Marten glanced at the tall cyborg. The heavy thrum of the core made her voice sound more normal. What a strange world. Cyborgs, Highborn, Jovian sex fiends pretending to be philosophers—he just wanted a regular life. He wanted a home.

"We can't stay in this system," Marten said.

"Neither can we leave it," Osadar said.

"Why not?" asked Marten.

"We lack enough supplies for a sustained journey."

Marten found it interesting that Osadar didn't suggest they use one of the patrol boats. They'd crossed from Mars to Jupiter in the *Mayflower*. They could go back to Mars in a patrol boat, but it would be highly uncomfortable. No, Osadar's words implied she wanted to remain aboard the meteor-ship. He felt likewise, and he still thought Tan's idea was a good one.

"The rest of our ship's supplies come in a day," Marten said.

"Aboard a military vessel," said Osadar.

"Wrong. It's aboard a liner. You read the orders."

"A conscripted liner full of Chief Strategist Tan's people," Osadar said. "Arbiter Neon and more myrmidons are among them. Without those supplies, our ship will not make it to Mars."

"I've trained our space marines," Marten said. "I've fought with them and understand their capabilities. Taking enemy ships is what I do."

Osadar began to object.

"Remember," said Marten, "I stormed onto the *Bangladesh*. Taking a Jovian liner—" He snapped his fingers.

"We would be branded outlaws for such an act," said Osadar.

"Not if we play it right."

"Chief Strategist Tan—"

"Sent Circe here to do Heaven knows what to me," Marten said. "Okay. Tan made her play. Now it's my turn."

"She will be expecting something like this," said Osadar.

"Tan is a brilliant strategist," Marten agreed. "But she isn't a god. She can't have sent the Sub-Strategist, expecting her to fail. If we act fast and without hesitation, we can storm the liner, take our supplies and be out of the system before they can react."

"I find two flaws with your reasoning," said Osadar. "Tan can always order hunter-killer missiles after us. And our space marines will not commit terrorism against their own government."

"I've heard enough defeatism," Marten said. "Our space marines are from Europa and Ganymede. They have no love for Callisto or Tan's desire to revive the Dictates. Once I show the men the evidence—"

"Dead myrmidons?" asked Osadar.

"Some worry is good," Marten said. "Too much is debilitating. We're in a tight spot. Now we have to fight our way out."

Osadar's senso-mask showed thoughtfulness. "Perhaps that is so. Yes. We have little to lose now. If we die, we die."

"Exactly," said Marten. "Now come on. We have a lot of planning ahead of us."

-26-

Twenty-nine and half hours later, three patrol boats lifted off the half-repaired meteor-ship. The best patrol boat was a battered craft that had survived Carme. Marten piloted it. Each boat had its own problems, and each needed further repairs.

They moved in a triangular formation toward the teardrop-shaped liner. This one was fifty percent larger than the *Thaliana* and it orbited closer to Callisto. New relay stations on the Galilean moon would give it quick contact with the *Erasmus*, which was on the other side of the planetoid. A good third of Marten's people had fought with him aboard the *Erasmus*. No doubt, their positions had been filled with handpicked people beholden to the neo-Dictates.

The patrol boats approached the big liner. The ship's com-officer asked why three boats. The orders had just called for one. Marten talked about his sick personnel. And he added that two of his boats had reactor problems that they couldn't repair on his ship. It was a flimsy lie and the com-officer complained, but she finally gave them clearance.

The boats docked beside huge bays. Big tubes deployed, attaching to the emergency hatches of the boat. Marten and his space marines readied their gyrocs and slugthrowers. Circe's myrmidons had taught him the foolishness of trying to play games. When you fought, you went in to kill and conquer. His instructions to the space marine sergeants had been simple. "Gun down anyone who resists." He didn't like to give that kind of order against a Jovian vessel, but he'd do what he had to.

They sealed their vacc-suits and entered the docking tube. Three space marines could march together at a time in this one.

Marten's stomach seethed as he first climbed the rungs and then floated toward the airlock. He'd taken point. It wasn't the right place for him. The commander was supposed to make decisions, not get in the first gunfights. But this was a commando operation. The first moves were often the critical ones. Smash and grab. He was afraid some of his Jovians might not be willing to smash fast enough.

Why was it always so hard to breathe at times like this? Marten drew his gyroc, wishing his hand would steady out. Then he changed his mind, holstered the gyroc and took out his slugthrower.

"Ready?" he asked over his com-unit.

The many clicks in his headphones told him the answer.

He floated to the airlock. Twenty men at a time could fit in this one, a bulk loading lock.

"Come on," he said quietly, typing in the entrance code. To his relief, the big door rotated open. He floated in and so did the marines behind him. Soon, the door rotated closed. When it clanged, the airlock's speakers burst into life.

"Marten Kluge?" they said.

"Yeah?" asked Marten. He wondered why the man's voice sounded familiar.

"Did the Sub-Strategist give you any messages for me?"

Was this a trick question?

Marten's air-conditioner unit began to blow cool air over his prickly skin as his gut knotted. Had he just led his men into a trap?

"Must I repeat the question?" the man asked.

Marten remembered the voice now. It was Arbiter Neon from the dreadnaught.

"No messages," Marten said, liking this less than ever.

"Ah, I see," said the unseen Neon. "Then I am most sorry to inform you that you will be under arrest when the airlock opens."

Marten glanced back at the space marines packed behind him. He saw the mirrored visors in their helmets and suited men gripping their weapons more tightly. This had to be a trap.

"Why am I to be arrested?" asked Marten, who added a whine to his voice.

"Ah, you are not so arrogant now, are you, barbarian?" Neon said.

The big airlock swished open. Three myrmidons moved forward with stunners and a pair of sonic-manacles. A sneering, white-haired Arbiter Neon stood behind them. His eyes widened in astonishment.

"Lay on the floor now!" shouted Marten, his vacc-suit's speakers at full volume.

"Y-you," Neon stammered.

The myrmidons' hesitation lasted only a second longer. Then they charged, and they died. Arbiter Neon attempted flight and fared no better as a dum-dum bullet blew open his back.

Marten felt sick gunning down a running man. But this wasn't a game. If Neon had escaped—

In the centrifugal-gravity, the space marines trampled past the dead arbiter and the blood splashed on the walls. Marten never halted to mourn. He raced at the head of his commandoes. They had to secure the liner and get the needed supplies to his ship now. He hoped Osadar and Omi's team had been similarly successful. One way or another, he'd find out soon enough.

A miracle occurred. Marten said it was due to their boldness. After capturing the liner, forty-nine hours passed before anyone else learned what they had done.

Living on stims for the next forty-nine hours, allowed Marten and his crew to ferry the needed supplies to the meteor-ship which he had renamed, the *Spartacus*. As a youth, he'd heard an ancient legend about a man by that name. The gladiator-hero had fascinated him. Sometimes, he saw himself as Spartacus, a lone man trying to fight an oppressive system.

The end of the forty-nine hours found Marten in the command center. He sat in his chair, wired, wide-eyed and exhausted. The *Spartacus* was under one-G acceleration, heading away from Callisto and toward distant Mars. First, they would have to leave the Jovian System. Marten knew that might be the most difficult item on the agenda.

"There is an incoming signal," Nadia said from her cubicle. "It's a priority one, with a Seneca clearance."

Marten had been waiting for this. It was the Chief Strategist.

"Put it on the main screen," Marten said. He sat back as Nadia complied, and he knuckled his eyes. There was no use asking for a cup of coffee or taking another stim-shot. As it was, he was too wired.

Tan appeared on the large screen on the wall. She was composed, as her dark eyes peered hard into his. Behind her were several paintings. She wore a stylish red jacket with a large collar. Serene music played in the background. Marten found it irritating.

"I have read a disturbing report concerning you, Force-Leader," Tan said.

Marten waited. Because of the stims, he wanted to laugh and taunt her. His face felt hot, too. He wanted to dig his fingernails against his skin, but resisted the impulse.

This was the delicate moment he'd been dreading. He wondered if it wouldn't have been wiser to rest while the others loaded the *Spartacus*. It wasn't just about him now, or him, Omi and Nadia. This was about his crew. No. This was about the Solar System, and ridding it of the greatest menace mankind had ever faced.

"Do I have your attention, Force-Leader?"

"Fully," he said.

Tan glanced at something just out of sight down by her hands. Her manner hardened as she looked up. "You killed Arbiter Neon and his myrmidons. According to what I have read, you killed Sub-Strategist Circe and her myrmidons."

"Circe is alive," Marten said.

"Yes, her body lingers in a bestial state," said Tan. "But her mind is gone. You as good as killed her."

"Respectfully, Chief Strategist, you're the one who sent her to my ship. What orders did you give that she would attempt such heinous acts?"

Tan's lips became thinner. "I order you to return to Ganymede. There, we shall finish this conversation."

"I am obeying your original orders," Marten said, "and heading to Mars."

"No," said Tan. "I will no longer abide your foolish antics. I hereby relieve you of command. Those of you who hear my voice, and are still loyal, arrest him."

No one moved.

"We are the Jovian warship *Spartacus*," Marten said, who despite his best efforts, grinned at Tan. "I am in command here. My mission is to unite humanity against the cyborgs. Among my crew are people from Mercury, Earth and the Jupiter System. Some here have also fought the cyborgs at Mars."

"I'm not interested in your dogmatic cant," said Tan. "You will relinquish your command or I will have Zeno missiles fired at your ship."

"That is illogical," said Marten.

Tan laughed. It was a short, sharp sound. "You are unhinged, barbarian. Your attempts to ape civilized behavior fools none of your crew. It certainly doesn't fool me. By killing an arbiter, a sub-strategist and willfully destroying myrmidons, you have shown yourself a destructive beast and a chaosist."

Marten leaned forward in his chair. "Listen to me, Tan. Build your Dictates, your philosophic paradise. Run rings around the controllers of Ganymede and Europa and the Helium-3 Barons."

"Are you attempting a dialogue?"

"I'm talking sense," Marten said. "I have a warship heading to Mars. I will follow your directions when they're in the greater good of humanity against the cyborgs."

"You're no philosopher to be able to judge so finely."

"You have a choice," Marten said. "No. I take that back. You don't have a choice. You're too smart, too cagey not to really see what's going on. Okay. Through proxies, you tried to take back this ship. You failed to do it. But what have you really lost?"

"You're a madman, a killer and—"

"Yes!" Marten said. "I'm a killer." He was still feeling guilty about shooting Neon in the back. "A killer is the best kind of human to send at the cyborgs."

"You're not heading to Neptune."

"Not yet," Marten said. "First, we have to stop them."

"You now claim to know the cyborgs' next strategic goal?" Tan asked.

Marten took a deep breath. "I am the Force-Leader of the Jovian warship *Spartacus*. This ship is headed to Mars to help Social Unity. Do you really want to destroy one of mankind's few warships?"

Tan stared at him for several seconds. Finally, she sighed. "You know that I do not."

"I didn't want to kill Neon, but he tried to run," Marten said. "It was either kill him or fail in the greater task. The myrmidons...I don't think they know how to surrender."

"You are correct. It is not coded in their genes."

"Circe took—"

Tan interrupted. "I am not curious about her. You left her aboard the liner, and I have read the report. She pleads now to be allowed to join you. She fiercely wishes to help." The Chief Strategist slowly shook her head. "You are an enigma, Marten Kluge."

"I don't think so."

"For all your barbarism, you are strangely logical at times. You will adhere to my commands?"

"In the common good, yes," Marten said.

"That is an equivocal answer. But I accept it. After all, you killed the cyborg in my quarters. You also successfully...well, never mind now. Go to Mars, and let us see if you can forge an alliance with Social Unity and the Planetary Union."

"I will send you weekly reports," Marten said. "I would also like to know the next reported sighting of cyborgs."

"Never fear," said Tan. "We are searching the void for them. But so far, their agenda has remained hidden to us."

-28-

As the meteor-ship *Spartacus* crossed the emptiness between Jupiter and Mars, Supreme Commander Hawthorne continued his desperate war. He refused to relent against Political Harmony Corps or the Party, as he tightened his grip on Social Unity.

He became leaner, and his shoulders took on a stooped bent. Bags developed under his eyes. A week after he declared North America conquered by the Highborn, a stubborn discoloration entered and remained under his hollowed-out eyes.

There were pockets of resistance in North America, but all reports indicated a major redeployment of the best FEC formations.

Then the Starvation Riots changed in nature and intensity. Underground PHC people joined in several, and nine cities erupted in outright rebellion. The worst offenders were in the Greater Syrian Sector. Aleppo, Beirut and Damascus declared themselves independent soviets.

"It's only a matter of time before they call in the Highborn," Hawthorne told his war council. They met in an underground bunker outside of New Baghdad, with harsh lights overhead.

The hard-eyed field marshals and generals around the conference table waited for his next words. These were his best commanders, culled from every failed front. Two had been snatched out of North America in near-suicide flights. They had shown themselves bitter defenders. Each had personally

136

drawn his or her sidearm on more than one occasion and summarily shot defeatists and disloyalists. There was no surrender with officers like these.

"The three rebelling soviets are an infestation of defeat," said Hawthorne. "They are a cancer in the body politic. If they are allowed to mature, their poison could quickly spread to others and then I foresee chaos of the worst kind. No. I will not allow that to occur. We must quash these so-called independent soviets, and do it quickly and decisively."

"I recommend a thermonuclear solution, sir." The speaker was Field Marshal Baines, formerly in charge of the North American Front. "It's what I'd wish I'd done to Montreal. Three fusion weapons will decapitate the rebellion."

"How will you reestablish control of the cities after that?" Hawthorne asked.

The squat field marshal shook his bald head. "Respectfully sir, there will be no reestablishment of control. You kill rebels. Hit with surface thermonuclear strikes and then use city-busters. The special missile burrows deep before exploding, ensuring massive destruction. We've been developing the idea for use against strategic Highborn cities."

"You mean captured Earth cities?" asked Hawthorne.

"Yes sir, the Free Earth Corps traitors."

"But these aren't FEC-controlled cities," said Hawthorne. "They're in the Greater Syrian Sector, in the heart of Social Unity."

Field Marshal Baines pointed a blunt index finger with his thumb cocked at a ninety-degree angle, as if he was a boy with a make-believe gun. "When I found a defeatist or a coward among my soldiers—" The Field Marshal's gun-hand moved upward as if from recoil. "I killed the offender. It cost me a soldier, but it instilled resolve in the others. It let them know what was in store for anyone who failed in his or her duty. As you pointed out, we can't let this rebellion infest others. Burn them out fast. Drop fusion weapons, and use city-busters on each."

Hawthorne rubbed his eyes. It was a brutal proposal, but it would solve the problem. For a second, he considered it. They had no time for niceties. Their backs were to the wall and this could dissolve the iron in the planet-wide resistance. Then he shook his head. Would he turn on the people? He needed horror. That was true, something to shock and dismay. What kind of—ah, maybe there was another way to dismay these rebels.

"We will strike with speed," Hawthorne said, "but with cybertanks instead of thermonuclear weapons. I've read reports that people run away in terror when they hear the approaching treads of cybertanks."

There was a rustle of uniforms as the field marshals and generals shifted in their seats.

"Yes," Hawthorne said. "I understand your unease. Bringing the cybertanks up out of the cities and onto the surface is a risk. The Highborn might have secretly ringed new laser satellites around us. Those lasers could burn out the tanks. General Manteuffel, you have a comment?"

"Cybertanks are a strategic asset instead of just another tactical battlefield weapon, sir," said Manteuffel, a small, athletic man. He had once helped Hawthorne defeat a cybertank in New Baghdad, allowing the Supreme Commander access to the then ruling Director.

"I'm aware of that," said Hawthorne. "I helped change their designation several years back. I'm willing to gamble, however. I don't believe the Highborn will risk revealing hidden laser emplacements—given they even exist—for the destruction of several squadrons of cybertanks."

"Several squadrons, sir?" asked General Manteuffel.

"I fully appreciate your concern," Hawthorne said. "The cybertanks are potent battlefield weapons of massive capability. In the end, they may be too massive, too potent and too concentrated in destructive ability. They'll draw the enemy's strategic elements onto them. Yet of what use are these strategic weapons if we never use them? No. This is a strategic moment of critical necessity. We must engage the cybertanks."

Hawthorne scanned the frowning field marshals and generals. "I am reminded of Emperor Napoleon Bonaparte at Borodino," he said. "The Emperor of France had invaded Russia. For weeks on end, Napoleon had attempted to catch the main Russian field army and destroy it. Each time he lured them into a trap, they slipped away. Finally, deep in Russia on the road to Moscow, the Russians made a stand at Borodino. There the Russians and French fought a terrible battle. And in the battle came a critical moment. Napoleon's generals begged him to send in the Old Guard. They were his elite soldiers, the bravest veterans in one large formation. Yet they had become a strategic asset to Napoleon, his one trustworthy formation. In the depths of Russia, he feared sending them into battle. He feared that they might take staggering losses and thus he would find himself in the heart of the enemy homeland without a reliable formation left. His very person might become exposed then. So at the Battlefield of Borodino at the critical moment, he held onto the Old Guard. Despite his begging generals who saw the opportunity, Napoleon kept the Old Guard in reserve. He won the battle, but at great cost in French blood. And the surviving Russians escaped in good order. If he had used the strategic asset, he likely would have swept the Russians and won the Campaign of 1812. And he would have likely remained emperor until his death."

Silence filled the war-room. Many of the field marshals and generals looked down at their hands. In the back, a woman stirred, a slim woman in a black jacket and who wore dark sunglasses.

"May I interject a thought, sir?" asked the woman, Security Specialist Cone.

"I require honesty," said Hawthorne.

"The cybertanks are your best security units," said Cone. "The people dread them. I've also worked with General Manteuffel and know he's spent many sleepless nights maneuvering the various cybertanks to the needed locations."

"We situate the tanks with care," Manteuffel said, nodding deferentially to Hawthorne.

Cone's expression never changed. "Many of the cities seethe with unrest. My security teams…the air in many of the cities is charged with explosive tension. I am not a military expert, but I'm certain the removal of cybertanks in certain metropolitan areas could allow the ignition of new rebellions. I'm concerned and wonder from which cities will you take the tanks?"

"That's an interesting question," said Hawthorne. "Which cities do you suggest?"

With an economical move of her right hand, Cone swept dark hair from her forehead. "If I may be blunt, from none of them, sir."

Hawthorne felt the pressure build behind his eyes as he grudgingly accepted Cone's analysis. Yes, he saw the argument and realized its truthfulness. Social Unity was like a balloon squeezed too hard. Soon it had to pop. If it did, mass chaos would grip Eurasia and Africa. The Highborn could walk in as occupation troops. Mankind would forever live as secondary citizens to the Master Race.

The pressure became physically painful so Hawthorne began to nod slowly. "It is a bitter task defending the indefensible. But we will not stop as long as there is breath in our bodies."

He closed his eyes. He was so weary. Worse, he knew that his words just now had sounded pompous. What led dictators to utter such phrases? Hmm. Is this what the Shah of Iran had felt like before he fled from the Ayatollah Khomeini and the chanting mobs? Where could he run? The Shah had died soon after running. Standing and dying seemed infinitely preferable to running and dying like a coward.

Hawthorne's eyes snapped open, and he scanned the field marshals and generals. In several he caught questioning looks. It confirmed in him the desire to die with a gun in his hand, firing at whoever came to take him down. Maybe that was too melodramatic, but it fit his growing certainty that he had two choices, and only two. Hawthorne stood up, his chair scraping the floor behind him. The time for hesitation or timidity was over. Wars led to brutality and to atrocities. And this was the most brutal war in history.

"Field Marshal Baines is correct...up to a point," Hawthorne said, as he nodded at the squat commander. "We shall deploy troops around the cities and demand their surrender. Then we shall obliterate one of them with a rain of nuclear death and with however many city-busters are needed. After that, we shall call on the two remaining cities to surrender. If either fails to comply, we shall destroy the next one. Hopefully, in this manner, we shall save two cities and certainly one. Whatever else happens, however, we will crush this rebellion and return unity to our socially advanced state."

"Have you made a decision on the cybertanks?" asked Cone.

"They will remain where they are," said Hawthorne. "In this instance, the fusion weapons shall be our fist. The deployable troops will merely be the occupiers. Now—to other matters...."

"Sir," said Captain Mune, "I highly recommend you take a different course of action."

Five swift days had produced a change in Hawthorne. His shoulders still stooped and there was a blue tinge in the bags under his eyes, but his heart no longer thudded as if on the verge of a heart attack. It had been a long time since he'd been outdoors under the sun. It was a strange feeling, a good one.

The lanky Supreme Commander stood on the top of his APC. The heavily tracked vehicle was camouflaged green. Instead of benches for infantry, the inside of the armored vehicle held the highest-grade communication equipment on Earth. There were four other vehicles circling Hawthorne. One was a bio-tank with a silver-dome canopy. The other three were carriers. Fifteen bionic soldiers circled the vehicles, facing outward with their gyroc rifles.

The bionic soldiers, the vehicles and Hawthorne were in the hills around Beirut. They were presently parked under tall cedar trees. The wind ruffled the top branches. Below them in the valley by the blue Mediterranean Sea was the rebellious city. Tall buildings and masses of domes and glassy cubes made up the highest level of Beirut. Underground were another twenty-eight levels, holding nearly thirty-one million people.

Hawthorne's heart turned cold then. "This is incredible," he said. He stood on the APC, with hi-powered binoculars glued to his eyes. He scanned the city, at the mass movement in the streets. He saw people, hordes of people moving outward like a swarm of ants.

"I don't know how, sir," said Mune. "But they must know we're here."

Hawthorne lowered the binoculars. His face felt pasty and his heart began to thump. "How...how did they get out?" Then he shook his head. "No one is in control, or not in full control," he said, answering his own question. "It's a rebellion. The people are boiling up out of the lower levels."

This was the chaos he needed to prevent in the rest of Eurasia and Africa. What would happen if the people boiled up out of the cities everywhere?

"We don't have enough troops here, sir," said Mune. "I suggest we move to a more defensible position."

Hawthorne gulped for air as he lifted the binoculars and continued to scan Beirut. Keeping the billions of inhabitants in the kilometer-deep cities made control easier. The physical evidence was down there before him. How many troops would it take to control so much human mass? Sealing off a level *in* the city only took a handful of troops.

A bionic soldier popped his head out of the APC's main hatch. "There is no answer to your ultimatum, sir."

Hawthorne heard the words as he scanned back and forth. Look at all of them! They just marched out of the city. He adjusted the controls, zooming closer. This was laughable. Many held clubs or knives. What did they think they were going to do? Hawthorne cursed softly. They were so skinny, and they wore rags for clothes. Many were shirtless and about half of those he could see lacked shoes. Were all the cities on Earth like this? The idea was shattering, sobering and in the end, sickening.

"Shall I order Field Marshal Baines to repeat the ultimatum, sir?" the bionic soldier asked.

Hawthorne shook his head. Who was he to order nuclear devastation on these desperate people? Even though he kept the binoculars pointed at them, he closed his eyes. He knew then what the Shah of Iran must have felt. To have the force to annihilate and then to feel such pity—it could freeze a man. It could steal his resolve. Stand and fight to the end, bitterly, or run, or surrender to the Highborn.

"I'm killing a city to save Social Unity," Hawthorne said

bleakly.

"This is war, sir," said Captain Mune.

"Is this war?" asked Hawthorne. When no answer was forthcoming, he opened his eyes and lowered the binoculars. The com-soldier and Captain Mune watched him. It was so easy to give advice, to urge a Supreme Commander to give brutal, soul-searing orders. But to be the man who had to give those orders, that was something else altogether.

Why had he insisted on witnessing the operation himself? Being outside felt good, that's true. Is that what they felt down there? He hoped they felt the sun beating down on their faces and the cool kiss of the sea breeze. He hoped they smelled the clean air of Earth at least once. Maybe it was better that so many of them where already out of the levels.

"Order Field Marshal Baines to launch the missiles," Hawthorne whispered.

"You have to come down, sir," Mune said. "Otherwise the flash will burn out your eyes and peel off your skin."

Hawthorne lowered the binoculars until they thumped against his chest. Feeling old, he headed for the hatch. The com-soldier already sat at his station. Hawthorne slid into his seat, turning on his screen. Captain Mune entered and closed the hatch. The main engines purred into life, and Hawthorne lurched in his seat as the tracks outside no doubt churned soil.

"I've sent the order, sir," the com-officer said.

Hawthorne stared at his screen. All those streaming people outside would face the brunt of the missiles.

There! He saw one on his screen. It moved so impossibly fast. The missile zoomed downward. It zoomed toward the cluster of tall buildings, the domes and massive cube-buildings that had been the craze in this part of the world for the last ten years. He could imagine shocked faces looking upward. Would eyes bulge or mouths hang agape? Was there screaming, pushing, shoving and trampling? The missile flashed.

Hawthorne automatically counted the seconds. A thunderous boom crashed against the APC. He grabbed the bars as the shockwave hit. The heavy APC rocked back and forth.

"Halt the vehicle!" shouted Mune.

144

Seconds later, the vehicle's vibrations finally stopped. Hawthorne vaguely realized that he couldn't hear the engines. Multiple thunderous booms sounded now, and soon the APC rocked more violently. How many missiles had he ordered onto Beirut?

A glance at the screen showed nothing but fuzziness. The wash of electromagnetic pulses must be playing havoc with communications.

"Sir!" shouted the com-officer.

"Yes," said Hawthorne, weary beyond life.

"I'm receiving an emergency message."

That made no sense. The EMP blasts—oh, special laser optics probably linked the vehicle with a hardened communications site.

"Are the other two cities surrendering?" Hawthorne asked.

"It's from Mars, sir. At least, it's coded as a Mars Golden Flash."

In took two entire seconds before Hawthorne scowled. "Speak sense," he said.

The bionic com-officer adjusted his screen. "It's a direct message, sir, for your eyes only."

"What about Beirut?" Hawthorne asked. "I'm not interested in Mars right now."

"A Golden Flash, sir," the bionic officer said, swiveling around. "It's from Commodore Blackstone."

"Who?" said Hawthorne.

"The commander of the SU Battlefleet in Mars orbit, sir."

"I know who Blackstone is," said Hawthorne, his voice hardening. "Why's he sending me a message now?"

"That's unknown, sir. Shall I transmit the message?"

Hawthorne stared at the com-officer. With a mental effort, he cleared away the guilt of having just ordered the deaths of millions of people.

"Does the message have a heading?" Hawthorne asked.

"Yes sir. Apparently, it's concerning the cyborgs. The Commodore believes he might have found them."

It took two blinks. Then a cold feeling swept through Hawthorne. He knew then why he'd ordered the thermonuclear weapons. There were worse things than Highborn.

"Hurry man," Hawthorne said, "read it to me."

-30-

Commodore Blackstone stood beside the map-module on the *Vladimir Lenin*. The *Zhukov*-class Battleship was one of four in the Mars System. There were a few other secondary vessels in his truncated fleet, but they were a pittance compared to the ships he'd possessed before facing the Doom Stars.

There was a red glow on the bridge. His officers were at their posts, diligently studying new data.

The hatch opened and Blackstone looked up. Commissar Kursk entered, and the briefest flicker of a smile played on his lips. Kursk was the only happiness he had in the certain knowledge that humanity was doomed.

They had beaten the Highborn. At least, they had made the super-soldiers retreat in their dreadful Doom Stars. For that, Blackstone knew he'd become a legend among the people of Earth. He'd even enjoyed the broadcasts the propagandists had beamed to Mars. It had revived him enough that he'd begun physical training and had regained some of his youthful stamina. Kursk had taken advantage of that in prolonged sexual encounters. That had lasted until news over a year ago had arrived from Jupiter. The story of the planet wrecker…what had that Jovian moon been called? Ah, right—Carme. The moon had changed Blackstone's perceptions, so had the reports of the Highborn blockade tightening around Earth.

There never had been more battleships and no extra missile-ships joining his flotilla. The Supreme Commander had decided to keep a small fleet-in-being between Venus and

Earth. From the rumors he'd heard, it was a deteriorating fleet. One battleship had headed out-system. Instead of stopping at Mars, it had long ago sped for the Saturn System. No one had heard anything from it for over a year.

Blackstone adjusted the map-module. He was a short man, with a newly bio-sculpted face, giving him a younger appearance. The best doctor in the Planetary Union had operated on him. The doctor had sharpened the nose and added authority to his chin. He'd even grafted new hair, which had taken well. Kursk had urged him to make these changes.

"You have news?" asked Kursk.

"It's difficult to see," Blackstone said.

Kursk moved beside him, bumping her hip against his. She was taller and more earnest than he was. He was the more imaginative.

"What am I looking at?" asked Kursk.

"The last readings from the Stalingrad-Seven," he said.

"A probe?" she asked.

Blackstone nodded. The probe had been launched many, many months ago, and it had made a long and silent journey toward Saturn. Several days ago, it had become functional and begun broadcasting data.

"Is that a planet?" Kursk asked.

"For unknown reasons it's blurry," he said. "That's Saturn at extreme magnification."

"Where are its rings?"

Blackstone tapped the map-module, increasing computer magnification of the data. "Run a spectrum-analysis on the interference," he said.

"I already have, sir," said the sensor-officer.

"And?" asked Blackstone.

"A thin aerosol gel," said the sensor-officer.

"Just like the cyborgs did before we attacked the Martian moons," said Kursk.

Blackstone's nostrils expanded. He remembered that tense time, the greatest battle of his life.

"It's not the same," he said. "The scale…."

That was part of his sense of doom, the sheer scale of this war. Mars only had one natural satellite now, one moon.

Planet-busters had cracked Phobos and sent the pieces spinning toward the Red Planet. When the pieces had rained onto the surface, hundreds of thousands of Martians had died. Fierce storms still raged over the planet because of it and made landings and liftoffs difficult. What kind of war was it that changed the natural face of the Solar System? The cyborgs and Highborn had no sense of proportion, no propriety.

Blackstone realized that Kursk was staring at him.

"Do you realize how much gel it would take to block out the rings?" she asked.

Blackstone laughed sharply.

"Wait a minute," said Kursk. "I see some ring there." She pointed at the map-module. "They haven't completely blocked them out. What does this mean?"

Blackstone tapped the map-module, switching the scene. Now the void showed, with a thousand stars in the background.

"Highlight in red," whispered Blackstone.

A tiny object appeared on the module map.

"What is it?" asked Kursk.

"We're still trying to discover that."

"I don't understand. That looks exactly like the object you sent in the file to Hawthorne."

"Yes," said Blackstone.

"How big is it?"

"Our best estimate: a kilometer."

"Do you still think it's made of ice?"

Without answering, Blackstone tapped the module, switching back to the first setting, showing a dim Saturn with wisps of rings.

A Martian-fired probe had discovered the ice-asteroid three days ago. Analysis suggested it had originated in the Saturn System. It presently headed toward the Sun.

A flash occurred on the map-module. Kursk gasped as she threw up her hands. Blackstone ignored her reaction as he glared at the map screen.

"Did you find it this time?" he asked.

"Yes sir," said the sensor-officer, a tense woman, with quick, twitchy hands. Her fingers lacked rings and her name was Quo, Sensor-Officer Quo. "It was definitely an X-ray laser."

"What does that mean?" asked Kursk. "What just occurred?"

"You just witnessed the deliberate destruction of the Stalingrad-Seven probe," Blackstone said.

"From Saturn?" asked Kursk. "The X-ray laser originated from Saturn? I thought the probe was at extreme range."

"Yes," said Blackstone.

"You sent a signal to begin scanning earlier than projected, correct?" asked Kursk.

"I started early," said Blackstone. He had because of the ice-asteroid.

"The distance the laser traveled is quite phenomenal then."

"Not necessarily," said Blackstone. "There could have been a nearby ship—"

"The coincidence of that renders the likelihood impossible."

"Or those in Saturn found the probe some time ago and launched an X-ray laser missile," said Blackstone.

"Again, the coincidence of the timing makes such a thing unlikely."

"Unlikely or not," said Blackstone, "our probe was destroyed."

"We must discover how."

Blackstone made a bleak sound as he glared at the map-module. Ever since he'd received the information about Carme, he'd begun intense scanning sweeps of the Saturn and Uranus Systems. So far, only the Saturn sweeps had brought returns, these meager images. It wasn't always possible to scan Saturn directly, as Mars often passed onto the other side of the Sun as Saturn. Roughly, Mars orbited the Sun every two years. Saturn orbited the Sun about once every thirty years. That meant Mars orbited the Sun fifteen times for every time Saturn orbited it once.

He wouldn't have found the ice-asteroid if the Jovians hadn't initiated talks with Social Unity and the Planetary Union. Because they did, everyone shared data. It was incredibly difficult finding small, dark, cold objects in space. The Solar System was so vast that even Doom Stars were small in relation to the distances.

Searching for relatively small objects in space could be critical for survival. The idea of whipping an asteroid around a gas giant and flinging it at a planet had terrified Blackstone. He couldn't understand why Hawthorne hadn't ordered a greater amount of probes and sweeps of the now silent Outer Planets. Maybe the Supreme Commander had become too Earth-bound in his thinking. Blackstone had definite ideas about how to run a space campaign. He could do it better than Hawthorne was doing, of that he was certain.

"Do you think *cyborgs* burned the probe?" asked Kursk.

"No one has answered us from Saturn for over two years," Blackstone said.

"That doesn't prove the cyborgs conquered the system."

"Given what else we know, yes is does," said Blackstone. "Don't forget about General Fromm."

Kursk scowled. She had shot General Fromm, a cyborg-controlled individual. Fromm had tried to take control of the *Vladimir Lenin* in the most critical phase of the Third Battle for Mars. Learning that cyborgs could and had tampered with normal people…it had been a bitter lesson.

"Can a kilometer-sized ice-asteroid harm Mars?" asked Kursk.

Blackstone laughed sharply.

"What about Earth?" she asked, staring at him. She'd told him before that she hated it when he laughed at her, especially on the bridge. No doubt, he would hear about it tonight. Maybe he'd hear about it all night long.

"The ice-asteroid is extinction-sized," he said. "If it hits the Earth, it means the death of everyone on the planet."

"Bring it up on the module again," she said.

Blackstone complied.

"I doubt the cyborgs would launch a single ice-asteroid at Mars or at the Earth," Kursk said. "We could certainly destroy it before it hit."

"If it's any consolation," Blackstone said, "I believe they've sent more."

"So it must be something else," she said.

Blackstone shook his head. There were other probes headed

to Uranus and still more on the way to Saturn, but they wouldn't reach their destinations for a long time.

"Why spray those gels around so much planetary area?" Kursk asked. "We're talking about a gas giant, not just a tiny terrestrial planet."

"The answer is simple," said Blackstone. "To hide their launching of more planet killers."

"If you're right, they've given themselves away by deploying all those gels. We know how they operate. Surely, they must understand that we wouldn't let ourselves be surprised."

"Everything is a matter of time, distances and size," Blackstone said. "We have spotted one ice-asteroid, and that was almost by chance. It is headed for the Sun, most likely for Earth or Mercury."

"You explained that yesterday," she said.

"We need more data," Blackstone said as he gripped the map-module. "I should have sent more probes months ago."

This informational war at such stellar distances presented difficult problems. One made a move and then waited months for the results. Did the cyborgs want him to rush out toward the approaching ice-asteroid with his fleet? He had no doubt whatsoever that the cyborgs had taken control of the Saturn System. After gleaning everything he could get his hands on about the cyborg assault on Jupiter, it was the obvious conclusion. If he attacked the ice-asteroid, journeying toward it, his battlewagons would be months away from returning to Mars. Was that asteroid a decoy meant to lure his warships out of Mars orbit? Did other hidden asteroids speed toward Mars, hoping to hit and obliterate human life on the Red Planet?

There was a worse possibility. The asteroid could be targeting Earth. Why hadn't he sent more probes? Information was so critical. Unfortunately, the Mars Battlefleet had expended most of its Stalingrad-Seven probes during the fight against the Doom Stars. They only had a few left. With miserly feelings, he'd ordered each one launched. Soon, the Martians would begin construction of large-scale probes. But those would lack certain critical features of a Stalingrad-Seven.

"This means more sleepless nights," said Kursk, sounding

disappointed.

Blackstone hardly noticed. He was mentally computing vectors, fuel-rates and ship tonnages. Space warfare was in large measure a matter of finding the enemy before he struck unexpectedly. Or it was striking him, hoping the enemy hadn't tricked you into a fatal move. The idea of a planet wrecker—it sickened Blackstone to the core of his being. The cyborgs sickened him. They had been like aliens from a different star. He hoped the man or woman or the team of scientists who had invented them roasted in an infernal afterlife. The idea of everyone uniting against them—mankind's only hope was unity against the enemy. Better the Highborn than the cyborgs. It was a shame Social Unity and the Highborn had bled each other so badly. He wondered if the cyborgs had engineered that.

"Where are the other asteroids?" Blackstone muttered to himself. "I have to find them." He knew they were out there. It was a knot in his gut that simply wouldn't go away. The Jovian moon Carme pointed to it. That the cyborgs had tried to make a planet wrecker in the Jupiter System pointed to the possibility they would try that elsewhere. It was time to begin making plans based on that premise.

-31-

The *Spartacus* hurtled through space, journeying the great distance between Jupiter and Mars. The meteor-ship had traveled for over a month now. And it had already gained its highest velocity for the trip. Soon, Marten would order them to begin deceleration.

The speeds gained in the meteor-ship were many times greater than what he'd achieved in the *Mayflower*. The shuttle had lacked fuel for such extended acceleration and deceleration. It was the difference of a warship over a vessel meant to ferry personnel between craft.

"There is a priority message from the Chief Strategist," Nadia said.

Marten sat up, realizing that he'd been dozing. He straightened his uniform, coughed into his hand and nodded to Nadia. Afterward—after listening to Tan's message—he stared at Nadia.

"It's finally happening," she said.

Marten pushed off his chair and floated for the hatch. "Tell Osadar to meet me in the tank," he said.

"Yes Force-Leader," said Nadia.

Despite the nature of Tan's message, Marten grinned at his wife hunched there in her cubicle. She had such beautifully long legs, and the gracefulness of her neck…. He liked being married. He liked—loved—Nadia. Then he recalled Tan's conversation again. The distance from Ganymede was already great enough so the light-speed messages experienced time delays, making normal conversations impossible. They had listened to Tan, begun to speak during some of her pauses, only to quit talking as she resumed her flow of information. A Saturn-originated ice-asteroid sped toward the Sun. It was quite possible that the ice-asteroid was just like Carme. The Saturn System possessed an abundance of moon-sized asteroids. Maybe there weren't as many as in the Jupiter System, but there were enough for the cyborgs' purposes. Had this ice-asteroid gained the needed velocity while circling Saturn many, many times?

Half an hour later, Marten and Osadar floated in the dark of the situation tank. It was a small chamber, formerly Circe's quarters. All the statues and shackles had long ago been swept out of the chamber. In their place was high-tech features looted from the last supply-ship. Holoimages of stars appeared on the walls.

Marten and Osadar worked on the linkage with the patrol boats and downloaded the data sent by the laser-lightguide message by Tan. Two of the patrol boats had lifted off the meteor-ship and moved in opposite directions, until they'd reached exact locations. Big bay doors had opened, exposing delicate sensor equipment toward the Inner Planets. The equipment on the two patrol boats would help the *Spartacus* act as a giant interferometer. Likely, no one expected them to spot what more powerful and closer sensors could. Rather, it would help map the same areas from a different perspective and angle. That data they would beam to a relay Planetary Union satellite orbiting Mars. Something bad had obviously happened in the Saturn System. Something bad was likely going on now that the cyborgs wished hidden.

After the linkages were calibrated, Marten brought up strategic zoom. Saturn, Jupiter, Mars, Earth and the Sun appeared in scale. Saturn was on the other side of the Sun as Jupiter.

The situation placed Earth and Mars on the same side of the Sun as Saturn. It wasn't a one hundred and eighty-degree difference between Jupiter and Saturn, but it meant the *Spartacus* would have to pass the Sun before it reached either Mars or Earth.

It meant their sensors couldn't sweep certain areas, because

155

they couldn't scan through the Sun. Rather, the sweeps took place on either side of the Sun, and at the void behind that.

Marten made a few adjustments with a hand-unit. It awed him, really. The Outer Planets orbited so much more ponderously than the Inner Planets did. In relation to the Outer Planets, the Inner ones rotated around the Sun like tops, going round and round and round. The farther an Outer Planet was from the Sun, the longer its journey took for a complete orbit.

"If we're going to win this war," Marten said, "we need to go on the offensive."

"Do you wish to travel to Saturn?" asked Osadar.

Marten shook his head. The distance was daunting. This journey from Jupiter to Mars was taking long enough. Viewing the planets in strategic zoom showed him something. The Inner Planets formed their own little core, almost their own system. The Outer Planets were each like an oasis in an ocean of vast, incredible nothingness. A journey between stars—it would be a yawning gulf that would take a man's lifetime to cross.

"You can't win a war just defending," said Marten. "We're always reacting to the enemy. We have to make the cyborgs react to us."

"How do you propose to do this?"

"Partly by what we're doing," said Marten. "But more fully, by working together with the Martians and with Social Unity."

"Then where is your complaint?" asked Osadar. "These things begin to occur."

Marten shook his head. "It's the time, I guess, the long stretches where nothing happens. During those times, we wait for the cyborgs to make their next move, their next assault."

"Time has aided us," said Osadar.

"Why do you say that?" asked Marten.

"The cyborgs have moved slowly because the distances are too great for them to move quickly. Each strategic endeavor— each taskforce used—first had to originate at a distant Outer Planet and then ferry over several billion kilometers. On their arrival at the destination, the cyborgs had to survive or die with their limited force, being unable to quickly re-supply it."

"Yeah, that's one way to view it," said Marten.

"It is the correct way," said Osadar. "As a human, I traveled from Jupiter to Saturn and then I journeyed even farther to distant Neptune. Did I ever tell you that I was supposed to pilot the first ice hauler to the Oort Cloud?"

"You might have said something about it once. It was an experimental ship, right?"

Osadar nodded.

"It doesn't matter anymore," Marten said. "I once traveled to a beamship, but that's history."

Osadar rose from where she worked on a holographic imaging unit. She set the sonic-screwdriver on it and stared at Marten.

"Is it broken?" he asked.

"I wonder sometimes," said Osadar. "Maybe the correct action is to take our ship out to Neptune."

"Maybe someday," Marten said. "Yeah," he said, grinning as he envisioned it. "We would go in a giant battle-group with Doom Stars, SU battleships, Martian orbitals and Jovian meteor-ships."

Osadar made a lonely sound. "No. You do not understand. I do not envision fighting the cyborgs at Neptune. Rather, I would search for the old experimental ship, the one the cyborgs invaded. If I could find it, I would modify the ice hauler and turn it into a starship."

"And do what?" asked Marten. "Head to Alpha Centauri?"

"Or go even farther," said Osadar. "I wish to travel beyond the reach of man-made machines. I wish to travel to a place where it would be too far for them to follow. I doubt our ability to defeat the cyborgs. I would like to survive in a world without the constant threat of annihilation."

Marten glanced at Osadar. There was a certain temptation in her idea. But how would they find the ice hauler? Where was it now? "No," he said quietly. "Running isn't the answer."

"It is preferable to death or to the oblivion of being a mindless creature of the cyborgs. If anyone should know that, it is I."

"Sometimes a man is meant to stand and fight. This is our Solar System."

"Not for much longer," Osadar said.

"Yeah? We'll see about that."

-32-

The days passed in tedious scanning and studying the readouts aboard the *Spartacus*. Marten ordered Omi to intensify space marine training, to take the soldiers outside on the meteor-ship's shell. Marten remained in the command center, using the main screen to help study the laboriously gathered data. Everyone in his or her cubicle helped, as did Osadar in the tank.

Marten sipped Jovian coffee as he leaned forward, staring thoughtfully. The ice-asteroid heading fast for the Inner Planets was too much like Carme. They had found little cyborg data in the ruined machines on the tiny Jovian moon, but the action had spoken loudly enough.

The problem finding more data now was that space was vast. It was hard for Marten to grasp the immensity of the Great Dark. AUs, light-years, those were just fancy terms. The human mind couldn't really understand them.

Analogies helped. Take the Earth or Mars and make them the size of a period at the end of a sentence. Then hold the period up in a large room. At the closest approach, Earth and Mars would be four meters away. The tiny speck of Earth with its teeming billions and its clouds, oceans and breathable air orbited through billions of cubic kilometers of empty space. A Doom Star would be like a microbe in an ocean. How did you spot it if it was trying to hide?

Marten took another sip and rubbed his eyes. You found it like this: days and nights of observations. The computer searched for a small glitch against the empty void that would point to movement. That movement might be an enemy vessel or planetoid.

They used thermal scanners, broad-spectrum electromagnetic sensors, neutrino detectors and mass detectors. Hour after hour, they sliced through carefully selected sections of the Great Dark, looking for anomalies.

Normally, an enemy ship emitted radiation, especially if it used a fusion or ion engine. The Great Dark seethed with radiation, however. The radiation came from the Sun and from Jupiter and Saturn. If a black-ice asteroid moved from simple velocity—having gained it around Saturn—then it would emit no radiation and no heat signature.

The Earth's death might have been launched months ago. It was their task to discover if there were more asteroids coming. The lone ice-asteroid suggested that there were more.

"Why would the cyborgs launch such a thing?" Nadia asked.

"They're aliens," Marten said. "They want to eradicate humanity and populate the Solar System with themselves."

"But they originated from humans," Nadia said.

"It's probably what makes them so deadly. If they were just machines—" he shrugged.

"It's so cold, so ruthless."

"Tan should have sent more ships with us," Marten said. He took another sip. "But she couldn't. What if the cyborgs have already launched another attack at Jupiter? There are hardly enough warships left as it is."

"Maybe the cyborgs launched the ice-asteroid to focus our attention on it."

"For what reason?" Marten asked.

"You're the military man," she said. "You tell me what else the cyborgs could do."

Marten frowned at the screen. "What would you say if I ordered the *Spartacus* to change heading?"

"To where?" she asked.

"Neptune."

Everyone in the command center looked up.

Marten was too engrossed in the screen to notice. "What if we went to Neptune and searched for Osadar's ice hauler there?"

"What ship was that?" Nadia asked quietly.

Marten told her about the experimental ship.

"That's interesting," said Nadia. "But wouldn't the cyborgs already have confiscated it and made it part of their Neptune Fleet?"

"Possibly," he said.

"We should run from the asteroid and flee out of the Solar System?" asked the sensor-officer.

"What?" Marten asked. He turned around, and he noticed everyone hanging on his words. He scowled, stared into his coffee cup and shook his head. "It's a stupid idea. You're right," he told Nadia. "The cyborgs would have already converted the ice hauler to their own use. This is the battle, and we'll choose our ground and fight now."

"Where exactly?" asked Nadia.

Marten slotted the coffee cup into a holder on his chair. "That's what we're trying to find out," he said.

-33-

Thirteen days after the initial sighting of the ice-asteroid, Commodore Blackstone of the Mars Battlefleet received an emergency request to report to the bridge of the *Vladimir Lenin*.

He raced out of his quarters as he tucked in his shirt. While riding the lift, he buttoned his uniform. Fitting his cap on snuggly, he strode through the hatch. Commissar Kursk was already there by the map-module. She looked up, and there were lines in her face.

She's getting older...no, she was already older. The strain is getting to her.

"What is it?" Blackstone asked.

Kursk opened her mouth, but no words came. The look in her eyes....

Blackstone felt a cold pit in his stomach. Resolutely, he approached the map-module. Highlighted in red on the screen was a larger object. At least, it was larger than the original ice-asteroid.

"It's a big one," he said.

Kursk shook her head. "That isn't just a single asteroid."

He began to fiddle with the module's controls.

"It's an asteroid-cluster hundreds of thousands of kilometers behind the first asteroid," Kursk said.

Blackstone nodded. He could see that by the readings.

"The cluster is moving faster, however," she said. "The tacticians say the cluster will catch up with the first asteroid."

"When?"

"It isn't *when* but *where*. Oh, Joseph," she said, using his first name. "This is horrible. It's insane."

He heard the bleakness in her voice. He saw it in the lines on her face.

"They'll merge as the cluster nears Earth," she said.

"Give me full magnification," Blackstone said. On the map-module, he watched as the red-highlighted object became many asteroids in close formation. "How many are there?" he asked. This was worse than he'd expected.

"We're working on it. There could be thousands."

"What?" he said.

"There's a possibility that some of those asteroids are really debris fields."

Blackstone adjusted the controls, but couldn't get any better images. Were they using the debris as a mass shield? He shook his head. The debris wasn't as important as the bigger asteroids, many of them.

"They mean to wipe out every living thing on Earth," Blackstone declared.

"The cyborgs are insane," Kursk whispered. "They're inhuman."

"They're aliens," Blackstone said. He tried to envision what this all meant. "Did these objects originate in the Saturn System? Well?" he shouted.

"We're still working on it," the sensor-officer said by her board.

Blackstone leaned against the map-module and found that he was breathing hard. Total annihilation of everything on Earth—the cyborgs meant to smash the most critical planet to Social Unity and the Highborn. This had to be from the cyborgs. The Highborn could have dropped the former farm habitats on Earth if they'd wished for planetary obliteration.

"Prepare a message for Supreme Commander Hawthorne," he said.

"We already have," Kursk said. "What are you going to add?"

Blackstone blinked at the red image on the screen. Had they spotted the asteroid cluster in time? With a start, he began adjusting the controls. There was no telling how little time they had to make the right moves. Weeks from now, the asteroids would approach Earth. If they were going to halt planetary extinction, they had to act now.

-34-

Supreme Commander Hawthorne swam laps in an Olympic-sized pool on the Third Level of New Baghdad. His long arms churned through the water as he fluttered-kicked. Back and forth through the clear water, stroke, stroke, breathe out, turn the head to the side and sip air. He let everything go as he swam through the chlorine-smelling water. The muscles worked and the heart pumped. This was better than stims and allowed him to sleep a solid five hours each night. These days, he couldn't achieve more. He'd lurch awake in bed, his eyes would snap open and he'd be realize his mind was working over a tactical problem or a strategic conundrum. At that point, it was impossible to get back to sleep.

His fingertips brushed the edge of the pool. He curled his long body, turned and brought his feet around. As he began to push off, he heard a shout. The temptation to keep swimming was strong. This was the one time in the day when his problems slid away. Instead, he stopped and treaded in place. Water ran from his hair and he wiped his eyes.

"Sir," said Captain Mune, "the cyborgs are trying to obliterate Earth."

"What?"

Mune began to tell Hawthorne about the asteroids hurtling toward Earth.

-35-

At 8:31 P.M. that same evening, Supreme Commander Hawthorne began an emergency meeting of his Strategic Council. They met in the conference room on Level Three of New Baghdad. Director Juba-Ryder of Egyptian Sector joined Air Marshal Crowfoot of Earth-Air Defense, Security Specialist Cone, Field Marshal Mead of Missile Defense and Field Marshal Baines, Commander-in-Chief of Eurasian Defense.

***

From the Supreme Commander's biocomp transcriptions, File #12:

The meeting opened with a presentation by Colonel Tong of Space Defense. He spoke in an otherwise silent room. Every eye watched the grainy pictures he presented slide by slide. Even Captain Mune watched, momentarily forgetting his preoccupation with protecting the Supreme Commander. Afterward, there were terse questions. Colonel Tong gave the best estimates. Impact time was predicted as minus forty-three days, a little over six weeks from now. Soon thereafter, the Supreme Commander began to speak.

HAWTHORNE: It is difficult to grasp the magnitude of the situation before us. The historians tell us that once dinosaurs ruled the Earth. Then a comet or possibly a stray asteroid struck the Earth. The Age of the Reptile ended with vast

166

hurricanes as hundreds of species perished in something worse than a nuclear winter.

The Jovian information we received about the cyborg assault there almost two years ago I consider critical. This moon Carme, it shows us the cyborgs attempted this once before.

MEAD: Indeed, this is a catastrophic situation. But I fail to grasp this certainty that the cyborgs initiated the attack.

HAWTHORNE: I consider the proof conclusive, but it doesn't matter. The asteroids heading at these unnatural speeds for Earth are all that matters. We must deflect or destroy them.

MEAD: Indeed, the dedicated scanning that allowed us to find these anomalies, these so-called asteroids—

TONG: They are asteroids, sir. Some are debris fields. Some are ice like the first asteroid.

MEAD: Please do not interrupt me, Colonel.

JUBA-RYDER: Is there any possibility the Jovians have fabricated this evidence?

HAWTHORNE: I believe the primary evidence originated with the Planetary Union and then from our own Mars Battlefleet.

TONG: That is correct, sir.

JUBA-RYDER: I find it suspicious that this—what are they called again, these Jovian warships?

TONG: Do you mean the Meteor-ship *Spartacus*?

JUBA-RYDER: Thank you. The meteor-ship's approach to Mars is very suspicious, seeing as it occurs at the same time as these asteroids.

HAWTHORNE: I believe some of the *Spartacus's* scanning data helped the Battlefleet discover the asteroid-cluster. Maybe as important, their sharing of information concerning the cyborg assault on Jupiter gave us reason to scan so thoroughly. I trust the Jovians in this. They fought off the cyborgs and have good reason to fear another attack.

JUBA-RYDER: The Jovians have a treacherous history.

HAWTHORNE: That is inconsequential now. Together with the sharing of information, the donation of the meteor-ship was an act of good faith. Its position may be of use to us.

MEAD: Respectfully, sir, it is too far out for that.

HAWTHORNE: (shakes his head) It isn't only a matter of distance but of speed. They have built up enough velocity to enter the fight.

MEAD: I don't understand that reference, sir. What fight?

HAWTHORNE: Weren't you listening to Colonel Tong's address? The cyborgs converted Carme to a weapon's platform. We must assume the cyborgs have employed the same tactic again. My Social Unity Loyalists, this is a grim situation. The evidence is direct and solid. We face extinction on Earth unless we can deflect or destroy these asteroids. I am ordering Commodore Blackstone to head out to engage the asteroids.

MEAD: Colonel, didn't you say the battleships couldn't reach them?

TONG: (glances at Hawthorne) I did not say *cannot*, but they risk annihilation, and it's doubtful they could stop such a mass.

HAWTHORNE: They must strike the asteroids by launching missiles and using their lasers for long-distance fire. Perhaps as importantly, they will gain critical data on the enemy. There is a negative to this, however. Moving the battleships leaves Mars vulnerable. But at this point, we have no choice and must risk it.

MEAD: What of the Fifth Fleet between Venus and Earth?

HAWTHORNE: This is our last fleet other than the warships at Mars. Fifth Fleet contains two battleships, a missile-ship and some secondary vessels. The warships are reportedly in poor condition and the crews are listless. But they are Social Unity fighters and are armed.

MEAD: Can they intercept the asteroids in time?

TONG: Conditionally, yes.

MEAD: What is the condition?

TONG: The presence of the *Julius Caesar* and the *Genghis Khan* in Earth orbit.

HAWTHORNE: (Pauses, and glances at each of the participants in turn) Now we come to the heart of the matter. The cyborgs are attempting to obliterate Earth. The evidence to my mind is conclusive. The cyborgs mean to crush Social Unity and the Highborn. We must face the facts, as grim as

168

they are. If we consider the islands of Earth and the surrounding territorial waters, the Highborn control a greater surface area of the planet than we do. They cannot wish total annihilation here. Otherwise, they could have already rained the drifting habitats onto the planet.

MEAD: (laughs) The Doom Stars can crush the asteroids for us. Why didn't we see it before? Our problem is solved.

TONG: May I speak, Supreme Commander?

HAWTHORNE: (nods)

TONG: The asteroid tonnage en route suggests the cyborgs can outfight the Doom Stars.

MEAD: How did you arrive at this conclusion?

TONG: It is logical given the cyborg armament history on Carme and the number of asteroids or tonnage en route to Earth.

MEAD: These are not known, *absolute* facts.

TONG: No sir, you are correct. The asteroid tonnage is an estimate. It may be off as much as fifty percent either way. Yet given—

CONE: We must call a truce with the Highborn.

JUBA-RYDER: (stares angrily) Those are seditious words. Supreme Commander, I urge you to enforce your edict of November Third. Anyone suggesting surrender or accommodation with the enemy is to be summarily shot on sight. Your bionic captain could take Cone outside to perform the action.

CONE: With due respect, Director, you are failing to grasp the gravity of the situation. Social Unity is doomed on two fronts. The Highborn are crushing us. Now the cyborgs wish our extinction. There is only one possibility. We must call a truce with the Highborn, attach the Fifth Fleet to the Doom Stars and attack the asteroids. Whatever asteroids fight through them, Earth Defense must destroy with merculite missiles and proton beams.

JUBA-RYDER: I find your words incredible and the idea unsustainable. Surely, you are aware that the Highborn are mass murderers.

CONE: It is better to fight with murderers against those practicing species elimination. The Supreme Commander is correct to tell us that the battle in the Jupiter System points to this truth. The Jovians united with the Highborn and achieved victory over the cyborgs.

CROWFOOT: Will the Highborn see it that way?

HAWTHORNE: That is the question. Specialist Cone speaks too pessimistically concerning the conclusion of our struggle against the Highborn. But I accept the logic of her last statement. If we are to save the Earth, we must unite with the Highborn.

JUBA-RYDER: The genetic supremacists have murdered billions. We cannot possibly trust them.

HAWTHORNE: I never suggested we *trust* them. It may be that our salvation will occur in the fight against the cyborgs. For instance: what if the cyborgs destroy the Doom Stars for us?

CONE: I doubt the Highborn will sacrifice their warships for Earth, at least, not until all our spaceships are destroyed first.

HAWTHORNE: They aren't gods.

CONE: Agreed. But they have proven to be our superiors in every endeavor.

HAWTHORNE: Your words now approach sedition, Security Specialist. Curb them at once.

CONE: (nods)

HAWTHORNE: We have little time left. The asteroids move at outrageous speeds. Therefore, I will attempt to open direct communication with Grand Admiral Cassius. Are there any further comments? No? Director, I see your hand. Do you have anything new to add to your previous objections? If not, please do not waste my time with a reiteration of your qualms.

JUBA-RYDER: (lowers her hand and stares at a spot on the conference table)

HAWTHORNE: Good. Then I declare this meeting adjourned.

36

Grand Admiral Cassius was aboard the *Julius Caesar* in near-Earth orbit over the middle of North America. The Doom Star supplied heavy laser fire against a cybertank charge out of Kansas City. The Tenth and Fifteenth FEC Corps together with the Twenty-Third Jump-Jet Division spearheaded a final assault against this stubborn knot of resistance. The cybertank charge no doubt attempted to blunt the FEC offensive.

Kansas City had been the focal point for the middle North American stronghold. During the conquest of the continent, the Highborn had bypassed Kansas City, covering the approaches with secondary units. The strategy had been classic Blitzkrieg, flowing through weak areas to cut-off and isolate the strongholds. Then they'd besieged the strongholds at their leisure.

"Impressive equipment," said Cassius. He sat in his command shell, examining holoimages of the cybertanks. The one he watched had multiple turrets and independent tracks. It likely weighed well over one hundred tons. The laser beam from the Heavens was red-colored on the holoimage. Unbelievably, the cybertank's armor withstood the laser for several seconds. It even sprayed a cloud of prismatic crystals over itself.

"Amazing," said Cassius.

Then the heavy laser that could fire in a coherent beam an easy one million kilometers burned through the prismatic crystals and punched through the reflective and composite armor. Still, the cybertank launched missiles at nearby FEC troops and chugged thousands of rounds of explosive shells. Wisely, the infantry hugged the ground, staying out-of-sight. Several jet-jump flyers weren't so lucky, but tumbled to the ground as bloody chunks of meat. Then the Doom Star's primary laser destroyed the cybertank, turning the massive vehicle into a mound of slag.

The other cybertanks had already turned around, and roared back toward their underground bunkers.

"It's too late for that," Cassius said. "They should have kept charging, doing what damage they could. Now they will die uselessly. Premen are such fools."

"Your Excellency," said tall Scipio. "I'm receiving a strange message from the premen."

"They wish to surrender, do they?" said Cassius.

"No sir. It isn't from the resistance forces. Sir," said Scipio. "This is a direct message from Supreme Commander Hawthorne of Social Unity."

"Verify that," said Cassius.

"I already have, sir. All indications are this is Hawthorne. Just a minute, sir," said Scipio. "His office is sending us a download."

"Put it into a lone system, unattached to the ship. We don't want them infecting us with a computer virus."

"It's done Your Excellency," said Scipio.

"What does the file say?"

The tall Highborn—Scipio—studied his board. He was silent for a time, his mannerism indicating absorbed interest. Then his bionic hand smashed against his board as he cursed loudly.

It brought Cassius to his feet. In several strides, he was at Scipio's station. "Show me the information."

Scipio turned harsh features toward him. "The war—" He shook his head. "This is beyond reason."

"Show me," said Cassius, as he put a powerful hand on one of Scipio's shoulders, squeezing until the tall Highborn squirmed in probable pain.

Scipio pressed a button and wrenched himself free of the Grand Admiral's grip. He stood and indicated that Cassius sit in his spot.

Cassius did so, and he began to watch video files concerning the ice-asteroid and the larger asteroid-cluster behind it. He received the information in silence, reading the accompanying text many times faster than a preman could absorb such a quantity data.

"Supreme Commander Hawthorne wishes to speak to you," Scipio said.

Cassius stared at the tall Highborn. Scipio's features had turned ashen-colored. The Saturn-originated asteroids, their unnatural speeds, the possibility they were armed as the Jovian moon Carme had been…. The cyborg strategy was obvious. It was ruthless, cold-blooded and brilliant.

With an oath, Cassius surged to his feet. He felt lightheaded. All his plans of Earth conquest—with a violent mental shove, he pushed those plans aside. He was the epitome of Highborn excellence. Quick mental acuity, the ability to shift onto a new strategic axis, those were the marks of Highborn superiority. Hardly aware of what he was doing, Cassius strode to his shell.

"Put Hawthorne through," Cassius heard himself say. "Let's see what this so-called preman genius wishes to tell us."

37

"Shall I order a halt to the primary laser burning out cybertanks?" asked Scipio.

"Negative," said Cassius. "Our attacks in North America have no bearing on Social Unity. North America is our territory now. We are merely destroying rebels."

Cassius settled himself into his large shell. As he'd moved across the bridge, he'd been assessing the Saturn-sent asteroid strike. He breathed deeply, calming himself. Under ordinary conditions, he wouldn't speak with an enemy commander now. Hawthorne had him at a psychological disadvantage. Yes, the Supreme Commander of Premen must have already taken time to ingest the news. This preman was also clever. Cassius mustn't allow himself to forget that. But Hawthorne was still just a preman while Cassius knew himself to be the greatest Highborn of them all. So even though the preman had the psychological advantage, he would engage in direct communication. He accounted it as further evidence of his own genius.

"Ready," said Cassius. He pressed a button on the armrest of his shell.

Before him appeared a holoimage of James Hawthorne's head. The preman had a longer cranium than average, with a high forehead indicating intelligence. There was thinning, sandy-colored hair on top of his head and discolored bags under the man's eyes.

He's tired. The war relentlessly grinds him down. Cassius nodded. How could any preman hope to pit himself against the greatest Highborn without a heavy mental and physical price to pay? To be outmatched in every way—it must be a galling thing. To know that doom and abject defeat was all that awaited him.... Cassius could almost pity Hawthorne. Such a weak emotion was not part of his genetic inheritance, however. Instead, Cassius grinned inwardly. This preman had surely reached the end of his strength. Yes, this last news of the asteroid strike must have crushed his remaining spirit.

"I am Supreme Commander James Hawthorne," the holoimage head said.

He has a firm voice, one filled with authority. Yes, whatever is happening to him, this preman is still used to being obeyed.

Cassius knew it would be so.

"I hope you have read the information we sent you," Hawthorne said.

"I have," said Cassius.

"I trust you understand its significance," said Hawthorne.

Was the Supreme Commander trying to be insulting? Surely, Hawthorne must be aware that Highborn ingested information at five times the rate that a preman could. Why then did Hawthorne speak this way to him? What was the hidden agenda here?

Cassius waited, letting the full force of his powerful personality effect the preman.

"...We have been at war a long time," Hawthorne said. "We have inflicted heavy damage on each other."

Trust a preman to exaggerate. The Highborn had inflicted the heavy damage. The premen had done more in the way of gashing a man's ribs in a knife-fight where the loser drags himself away with his guts in his hands.

"Now, however, our struggle against each other becomes moot," said Hawthorne. "The cyborgs have launched asteroids against both of us, hoping no doubt for our unified extinction."

It was time to let this preman know the true situation. "We Highborn are in no danger," said Cassius. "We can easily ferry our ground troops into space and avoid destruction."

"You would lose the Earth then."

"Only temporarily," said Cassius.

175

"The factories would be destroyed," said Hawthorne, becoming visibly agitated, "as well as the billions of workers needed to run them. Of what use would the hulk of the planet be to you then?"

"Most of the important factories are automated," said Cassius. "We could land afterward, begin the long-term cleansing of the air and rebuild the least-damaged factories."

Hawthorne blinked several times. "Are you saying the asteroid-strike doesn't matter to you?"

"He needs obedience training," a Highborn in the background said.

Cassius motioned the Highborn to silence. He felt likewise, but it was foolish to utter such words in their presence. That was one of the reasons why he was First. He could control his irritation, a point of personal strength. The preman had questioned him as if they were equals. That was terribly insulting. If a preman had spoken to him like this in his presence, Cassius would have killed him. Since, however, this preman represented the billions of unconquered under-men, he could contain his rage.

"Naturally," Cassius said, "I wish the Earth to remain intact."

"Intact?" asked Hawthorne. "What about the billions of human lives at risk?"

"Do you cherish these lives?" asked Cassius.

"Yes," Hawthorne said in a clipped manner.

"Then surrender immediately and I shall save you and the billions of pre…of Earthlings."

Hawthorne shook his head. "You're not in a position to demand our surrender."

Cassius stiffened at the tone.

"You've conquered the islands of Earth and North and South America." Hawthorne stopped abruptly and took a deep breath. Then he took a second one and began to speak more slowly. "Billons of humans depend upon you. There are also millions of men in your FEC armies. Are you willing to flee Earth to save yourselves but let your slaves perish?"

"Save your insults, Supreme Commander, and speak to the issue of your call. Remember, you asked to speak with me, not

176

me to you."

"...You're a brilliant strategist," Hawthorne said shortly. "Your conquests prove that. It is therefore self-evident that you see the strategic ramifications of this attack. No. I cannot believe that you would willingly abandon Earth and let the cyborgs obliterate it. Your greatest industrial base would vanish in a moment. Over time, with the Outer Planets in their grip, the cyborgs would out-produce you and finally hunt you down like vermin."

"I have yet to hear any proposals," Cassius said coldly. If the preman continued with this tone, he would track down the radio signal and send a Hellburner to it. Let them feel the raw power of the Highborn fist.

Hawthorne stared at him. "My proposal is simple. We must pool our resources and deflect the asteroids from Earth."

"What *resources* can you possibly possess in the arena of space combat?" asked Cassius.

"Our Fifth Fleet is intact, as well as the Mars Battlefleet. Those battleships are already accelerating," said Hawthorne. "I am hours away from ordering a missile launch. So you are incorrect in implying Social Unity lacks space armaments."

Cassius closed his eyes and made some mental recalculations. "Hmm," he said, opening his eyes. "It is possible the battleships can have a trifling effect on the asteroids."

"Jupiter has also sent reinforcements," Hawthorne said.

"We've tracked this single Jovian vessel," said Cassius, with a dismissive wave of his hand. "It is a *Thales* meteor-class warship. It can affect nothing."

"Grand Admiral, I understand Highborn arrogance. But the gravity of the situation means that you cannot indulge in your usual vice. We must work together to save the Earth. Anything else is obstinate lunacy."

Cassius felt the blood surge to his face. His thick fingers twitched. He wanted to rip this insulting preman limb from limb. With iron control, he sat motionless, willing the preman to continue speaking.

"Social Unity will fight for humanity's existence," Hawthorne said. "What will the Highborn do? Are you merely killers and conquerors, or can you merge your seething emotions—"

"Silence," Cassius whispered, as he leaned toward the holoimage.

Hawthorne smiled bleakly. "Together, we can possibly save the Earth. Divided, we shall both lose."

"Surrender to us," said Cassius, "and we shall save your simple lives. Then you can survive under Highborn security."

"We will never surrender," Hawthorne said with heat.

"That is a proud boast for a commander who has lost in every front where we attacked."

"Have you forgotten the Mars Campaign?"

"The cyborgs achieved the victory there, not you premen."

Hawthorne dipped his head. The holoimaging was good. Cassius witnessed the sheen of perspiration on the preman's forehead. Was the preman cracking up before him? They were so weak. It was pitiful.

"It is difficult for us to speak together," Hawthorne said slowly. "On my side, I've seen you murder billions. On your side, well, my generalship has foiled you repeatedly. My psychologists tell me this will have caused you to hate me."

Cassius realized abruptly that Hawthorne wasn't cracking up. The preman-genius had iron in him. Maybe it was time to maneuver the preman in a new manner. Yes, he would use the cyborg attack to lure the last SU spaceships into killing range. Hadn't Hawthorne already told him the Mars-based fleet was accelerating toward a near-intercept course? That would open Mars to attack. It might be time to send a Doom Star there and conquer it. Yes, yes, he would destroy the asteroids and the SU warships at one blow.

"For a...Homo sapien," said Cassius, "you are strangely gifted in the strategic art."

Several Highborn on the bridge glanced at him sharply. Tall Scipio nodded, however, with his eyes half-lidded. In that instant, Cassius mentally marked Scipio for highest command.

"I am amazed you would admit such a thing," Hawthorne said.

Cassius shook his head. "We Highborn view reality as it is. It is one of our powers, one of our genetic gifts. Another is the ability to make swift decisions."

"You have changed your mind and have now decided to work together?"

"You are premature," said Cassius. "I have listened to your proposal. I have seen the evidence of this asteroid strike. Now I will ponder the implications."

"Time has become our enemy," said Hawthorne.

Cassius smiled indulgently. "Time is an element, malleable to a strong will. I will asses the information, factoring in time."

"I'll be waiting for your reply," said Hawthorne. "Because I already know that you will be forced to work with me."

"Have a care," said Cassius.

"Your brilliant strategies these past years prove to me that logic governs your actions. Logically, you have no recourse other than to work together with us to save the planet."

"We shall see," said Cassius, impressed by the preman's calm assurance. "For now, Grand Admiral Cassius out."

The holoimage of Hawthorne nodded.

Cassius pressed a switch, and the image faded. Around him, the other Highborn waited in tense expectation.

Cassius took a calming breath. The preman—so that was Supreme Commander Hawthorne. He would have to replay the interview, discovering weakness that Hawthorne would have been unable to hide from a trained eye.

"Hail the *Genghis Khan*," said Cassius. "I wish to hold a conference with Admiral Gaius."

Scipio moved quickly, following Cassius's orders.

-38-

Twenty-seven hours brought an abrupt change to Grand Admiral Cassius's thinking. The change had occurred because of the data pouring in from the giant interferometer near the Sun. The vast sensor array was one of several secret Highborn weapons. The collapsium coating around the *Julius Caesar* was another. There was a third, but it was presently unfinished. When completed, it should give the Highborn the decided technological edge in the coming clinch with the cyborgs of Neptune.

Situated between the Sun and Mercury's orbital path, the giant sensor array of many kilometers turned with ponderous slowness as each component shifted and realigned with the new heading. Then it focused on the asteroid-cluster. Despite the distance, its focusing capability dwarfed anything else turned on the Saturn-launched strike. The Highborn technicians and their premen servitors made critical adjustments. The fuzzy image became clear, and outlines became visible.

Soon, premen servitors counted laser-turret bunkers on individual asteroids. They highlighted massive, crater-sized exhaust ports. These matched known specs from Carme.

The giant sensor array tracked with minute calibrations. Debris fields were counted. Spectrum analysis gave greater precision to the composition of the visible asteroids. The tonnage estimates grew.

Harsh orders emanated from the Sensor-Commander. He wanted more information, complete data on each projectile.

The nature of the cluster, however, foiled him. Too many

180

asteroids blocked those behind them in relation to the giant scanning device.

The Sensor-Commander aligned the laser lightguide system himself with a relay station between Venus and Earth. Then he pressed the transmit button, sending a surge of raw data to Grand Admiral Cassius.

39

Twenty-seven and-a-half hours after Cassius's conversation with Hawthorne found him at his favorite viewing port.

It was on the *Julius Caesar*. Ballistic glass protected him from the vacuum of space. The port was twice his height and four times as wide. The Sun blazed outside, auto-shading within the glass protecting Cassius from the radiation. A circular object floated nearby that was subjectively larger than the Sun. It was the *Genghis Khan*. Below them, but presently out-of-sight, was the Earth. A smaller object half the size of the Moon as seen from Earth floated closer in. It was a farm habitat, slowly rotating as it created centrifugal-gravity.

A portable holoimaging dome sat in the middle of the recreation area. Technicians had set it up an hour ago, clearing away equipment. Heavy bags dangled from the ceiling in one area. In others, were exercise machines, while near the door were mats for wrestling, kickboxing and combat fighting.

Cassius held a controller-unit for the holoimaging dome. He also wore a virtual reality (VR) monocle in his left eye as he studied the data gleaned by the giant interferometer near the Sun. The magnitude of the asteroid-strike awed him.

Some of the asteroids were over thirty kilometers in diameter. Two debris fields were over fifty kilometers wide. The engineering feat of moving asteroid-sized moons out of their orbit around Saturn, bringing them near others like themselves and then whipping them around Saturn as they built up velocity—it was staggering. If this juggernaut of mass hit the Earth…everything living would die, even the cockroaches.

Only microbes and viruses would survive, and even that was questionable. The kinetic energy of the strike would heat the Earth to intolerable levels.

Cassius looked up as motion caught his eye.

Tall Scipio entered the recreation area. He wore an immaculate brown uniform, with a First Class Rifle-Badge clipped to the front.

"Come in here," said Cassius.

Scipio hesitated.

"Is something wrong?" asked Cassius.

"You greatly honor me, Your Excellency. I do not know why, and that troubles me."

"I have my own reasons for bestowing this honor, which should be good enough for you. Essentially, you are here to render opinions and tell me when you think one of my ideas is foolish."

"There are others higher-ranked than me who can do this."

"An obvious truth," said Cassius. "Do not waste my time with it."

Scipio clicked his heels together, and he saluted sharply. "If I am here to render opinions, especially ones you do not want to hear, it is unwise of you to reprimand my first statement."

"Excellent," said Cassius. "I knew I selected you for a reason. Come. Pick up a controller-unit."

Scipio's hesitation lasted a moment longer. Then he strode to the holoimaging dome and picked up one of two other controllers.

"Who else is joining us?" asked Scipio.

"I am," said Admiral Gaius, striding though another door.

He was a classic Highborn, nine-feet tall, broad-shouldered and with a wide face. He moved with arrogant confidence, and was Cassius's closest advisor. He had captained the *Napoleon Bonaparte* in the Third Battle for Mars. Since that Doom Star was presently at the Sun-Works Factory under repair, he ran the *Genghis Khan*. Gaius wore a white uniform, with a Red Galaxy Medal pinned to his chest and an Ultimate Star with its blue ribbon. The bill of his cap was low over his eyes. He had prominent knuckles, with scar tissue over each. Rumors had it that in their teenage years he had given Cassius his single defeat in a fistfight.

Without being asked, Admiral Gaius picked up a controller-unit.

Cassius began clicking his unit. The holoimaging dome hummed with life and began projecting holoimages in the air above it. Earth appeared, with tiny dots around it. Far away down the hall appeared a red cluster.

"The asteroid-strike," said Cassius.

"The more we learn of it, the more daunting the attack appears," said Gaius, as he viewed the red cluster.

"This attack is a monumental effort," said Cassius. "It demands an equally monumental effort on our part to defeat it."

"I suspect we lack the time to do so," said Scipio.

Gaius glanced at him sharply. "You are quick to admit defeat."

Scipio scowled at the deadly insult, but otherwise appeared to hold his temper. "I have poured over the new data," he said. "Projecting it against what we know…the situation is more than grave. With respect, Your Excellency—"

"You please me with your willingness to speak your mind," said Cassius. "And you prove yet again that I am an excellent judge of character. I want you to remember, however that this is a strategy session. Here, you will drop honorifics and speak plainly."

"Yes sir."

Cassius scowled.

"I mean…yes," said Scipio. He examined the control-unit in his hand. He expanded his chest and glanced at Gaius. "I am the last Highborn who would admit defeat," he said. "But it is also true that the parameters are grim. Consider these facts: an impact by a single ten-kilometer asteroid on the Earth would be an extinction-level strike. Given enough velocity, an impact by an object one hundred meters in diameter has been historically devastating. The mass of the Saturn-strike—it boggles the imagination. As I'm sure both of you are aware, for the atmosphere to shield the Earth, an object must be smaller than thirty-five meters. Those smaller objects burn up before impact. Many of the pieces in the debris fields, unfortunately, are much larger than that."

"This is our great test," Cassius said, "the hour that will prove our superiority. The parameters, as you said, are clear and unequivocal. There are only a few tactical methods for stopping the strike. One is to break apart a larger object into many smaller pieces and blow those pieces outward with, say, a thermonuclear charge. That would likely cause the various pieces to change trajectory enough that they would miss the Earth. A second method is to explode several nuclear devices near an asteroid, moving the object with the force of the explosions."

"That would be nuclear pulse propulsion," Scipio said.

"Exactly," said Cassius. "You see my point. The third possibility uses kinetic energy to change an asteroid's course. A spaceship or other object of sufficient mass builds up speed and strikes the asteroid, knocking it off course like two billiard balls. Each of these methods could potentially achieve success."

"Unfortunately," said Scipio, "the sheer mass of the strike suggests we lack the means to successfully achieving this in time."

"What then do you suggest?" Admiral Gaius asked angrily.

Scipio toyed with his control-unit. "There is only one possibility. We go down fighting."

"No!" said Cassius. "To go down fighting means to lose. I don't intend to lose to these cyborgs. We are superior to them and hold critical military assets. Let us enumerate them." He began clicking his controller.

The red dots around the holographic Earth began to pulse, as did another red dot around Venus. "We have three Doom Stars," Cassius said. "These will head out to the asteroid-cluster and do battle with them. We also have the missile complex on Luna, together with the old boosters and shock-trooper equipment on the Sun-Works Factory." With more clicks sounding, the Mercury Factory appeared in red, as did the launch facilities on Luna.

"We'll send a missile strike against the asteroids?" asked Gaius.

"In time," said Cassius.

"We should hit them as far from the Earth as possible," said Gaius. "If we strike the mass near Earth, the planet's gravitational field might pull in some pieces that would otherwise deflect elsewhere."

Cassius hesitated as he lowered his controller-unit. Examining Mercury, Venus, Earth, the approaching red cluster of asteroids and then the admiral and the former com-officer, he grew uneasy.

"You must see what I do," said Gaius. "The farther away from Earth we strike the asteroids the smaller a nudge is needed to deflect them from the planet."

"Where will we find these missiles?" asked Scipio. He clicked his unit. The red cluster of asteroids moved before them as it grew in size. "The mass of projectiles is staggering. The cyborgs have clearly waited until they could build up an unbeatable force."

"I've grown weary of your cowardice," said Gaius. "We are Highborn."

"And Highborn cannot view reality as it is?" asked Scipio.

Gaius strode toward Scipio.

Cassius watched with interest. The tall Highborn intrigued him. If they possessed one fault as super soldiers, it was their tendency toward rashness. Scipio had a rare trait for a Highborn, a touch of caution. On the bridge, it had allowed him to see Hawthorne as dangerous. What Cassius needed to know was if with his caution Scipio still had enough courage.

"You will not utter the word *unbeatable* again," Gaius said, clutching Scipio's forearm.

Scipio wrenched his arm free and took a step back. "You're an admiral of a Doom Star, and thus highly outrank me. But the Grand Admiral has called me to this session to speak my mind. Examine the situation, Admiral. We face a grave threat. It is daunting in the extreme and quite possibly is unbeatable. Yes, I speak the word again."

Gaius growled low in his throat, stepped close and shot a fist at Scipio. The tall Highborn deflected the blow with a smooth karate parry.

"A fancy fighter, eh?" said Gaius. He raised his scarred knuckles and grinned at Scipio. "Defend yourself, boy."

Scipio assumed a classic karate stance. "I have too much respect for us to mouth platitudes and fighting maxims now. Our existence is at stake."

"And that makes you fear, eh boy?" Gaius asked.

Scipio spit on the floor as the fierce vitality of the Highborn blazed in his eyes. "You're an old man, Admiral. You've become senile in your command shell."

Gaius roared as he attacked, wading in with precision blows. Using his longer reach to advantage, Scipio danced around the bull-like admiral, chopping and kicking. Gaius shrugged off the meaty slaps and used his shoulders, upper arms and hips to absorb Scipio's hardest kicks.

"Once I get my hands on you, boy, you're dead," Gaius growled.

"Hitting me doesn't change the truth of our situation," Scipio panted. "We lack the ships and the missiles to destroy or deflect the entire asteroid strike."

"I piss on your truth," said Gaius. "We are Highborn and we will fight our way out of the situation."

"With what means?" asked Scipio.

Gaius rained haymakers. While dancing back and deflecting the nearest shots, Scipio was forced into a corner.

"Now I have you," Gaius wheezed. He lowered his head and shot straight jabs and crosses. Several smashed through Scipio's karate weaves and snapped the Highborn's head back. Then Gaius stepped inside Scipio's guard. With a cunning wrestling move and hold, the two of them smashed against the floor hard. Gaius quickly gained a submission hold around Scipio's neck.

"This is how we'll beat the cyborgs!" Gaius roared, as spittle flew from his lips. He applied terrible pressure. Scipio's face turned red, purple and then white as he struggled to free himself. Not once, did he plead for mercy.

Cassius had seen enough. His old friend was a bull, and fully aroused now. In another few seconds, Gaius would kill Scipio. With a smooth lunge like a fencer, Cassius reached out, touching Gaius's back with a shock rod at full power.

Gaius bellowed, releasing Scipio as he rolled over onto his back.

"Enough of this," said Cassius.

Scipio lay panting on his back, blinking in seeming bewilderment. Gaius glared at him, building up the strength to rise.

"I had to shock you, old friend," said Cassius. "This is a strategy session, not a sparring duel. First, however, I wanted to test our young officer. He has courage and faced you unflinchingly."

"When I get up," whispered Gaius, "I'm going to smash your face into pulp. No one shocks me and gets away with it, not even you."

Cassius shook his head. "We don't have time for that. And now that you're on your back, you should know that the boy— that Scipio—is right. We lack the missiles and the ships to win this fight. So we're going to have to do it another way."

Scipio had been gingerly massaging his throat. Turning his head, he now stared at Cassius.

"I've given this much thought," the Grand Admiral said. "Before we strike the asteroids with nukes, I'm sending Highborn to the cluster."

"What's that mean?" asked Gaius, clenching his teeth as he sat up.

Cassius shook his head. The old bull knew better than to try to sit up so soon. He'd taken the highest-level shock possible. But Gaius was a stubborn fighter, refusing to adjust to pain. Sometimes, one needed that kind of warrior.

"The Praetor once sent shock-troopers to the *Bangladesh*," Cassius said. "I plan to use that tactic here."

"The enemy asteroids have laser-turrets," Scipio wheezed with his injured throat.

"Always with your defeatism," said Gaius.

"You tested him," Cassius said. "Now you will listen to his ideas without insult."

"Bah!" Gaius said. "His manner sickens me."

"We can't all be the fighting Admiral Gaius," said Cassius.

Gaius grunted, nodding after a moment.

"As to these laser turrets," Cassius told Scipio. "It is the reason why I must perfectly coordinate the assault." He turned around and clicked. "Notice the asteroids. They're situated in such a way that those in front block those in back."

Scipio studied the enlarged holoimage, and he soon nodded. "What do you hope the Highborn commandoes to achieve?" he wheezed.

"I have studied the Carme Incident in detail," Cassius said. "Successful landings brought combat troops to the surface, where they defeated the cyborgs. The victors eventually shutdown the asteroid's fusion engines."

"How did you gain this data?" asked Gaius, who climbed to his feet.

"Hawthorne sent it to me."

"How did the Supreme Commander gain it?" asked Gaius, swaying slightly.

"Apparently, the rulers of Jupiter are attempting to unite all premen into a giant confederacy. As part of their endeavor, they are sharing information."

"How does this help us?" asked Gaius.

Cassius turned toward the viewing port, staring at the blazing Sun outside. In this thing, Scipio saw more clearly than Gaius did. The mass of asteroids…. "It is a desperate strategy." Cassius shrugged moodily. "The Highborn commandoes must gain control of as many asteroids as possible. Once this control is achieved, they must fire the engines and redirect the individual projectiles on a new heading. The asteroids that continue on course, those we shall blast with nukes."

Someone gingerly cleared a sore throat. Without turning around to see whom, Cassius asked, "Do you object to the plan, Scipio?"

"I would ask a question."

"Ask," said Cassius.

"How do you know the asteroids still have fuel or that their engines still work?"

"I do not *know*," said Cassius. Silence greeted this revelation. He turned toward the two. Scipio touched his bruised throat. Gaius studiously pinned his fallen Red Galaxy Medal back onto his uniform.

"Hawthorne spoke strategic sense earlier," Cassius said. "We cannot afford to lose the Earth."

Scipio snorted.

189

"An inelegant agreement," said Cassius, "but heart-felt. The Earth is the greatest industrial base in the Solar System. The cyborgs undoubtedly recognize this and have decided to obliterate it, thereby weakening us, possibly beyond recovery."

"The commandoes are a gamble," said Scipio. "The loss of the *Hannibal Barca* to cyborg assault troops during the Third Battle for Mars points to this."

"Yes!" Cassius said. "I gamble. And because I do, I will use everything in my grasp in order to achieve victory. The premen have offered us their vessels. Therefore, I will use them." He laughed. "I will even use the meteor-ship heading to Mars."

"Is it possible that the meteor-ship can be of use?" asked Gaius.

"It's more than possible," said Cassius. "First, however, I must show you the last piece of my strategy. The premen will help us implement it. No doubt, in the absence of the Doom Stars they will attempt treachery. But I will take safeguards, the chief of which is placing you, Scipio, in charge of the new defensive arrangement of Earth."

"What are you talking about?" grumbled Gaius.

Cassius told them, clicking his controller as he showed them the details.

It made Gaius grunt in seeming wonder, and he finally nodded at his old friend. "You've lost none of your guile," he told Cassius.

Scipio grew quiet and his eyes narrowed.

It made Cassius even more certain that he'd chosen the right Highborn to command Earth Defense in his absence. "It is a massive responsibility," he said.

"Why me?" asked Scipio.

"Because I think you're one of the few Highborn who can work with premen."

"Your Excellency?" asked Scipio.

"I watched you on the bridge as I spoke with Hawthorne. Certain of your reactions pleased me. It also showed me this hidden talent of yours that few Highborn possess."

"Doing what you suggest, we risk losing our conquests on Earth," Gaius said.

"Possibly," said Cassius, "but it is unlikely. I will leave Scipio enough space assets to thwart any premen treachery."

"Do you remember their Orion ships of several years back?" asked Gaius.

"Of course," said Cassius.

"They may have more of those ships hidden."

"Of course there are more," said Cassius.

"Have our spies discovered this?"

"I don't need spies to know that," said Cassius. "Logic proves it."

Gaius seemed to think about that. He finally grunted in agreement.

"We have little time to achieve all this," Scipio said thoughtfully.

"True," said Cassius. "But as the Admiral has said, we are the Highborn. And now the Solar System will see what that truly means. This is to be our hour, gentlemen." He thumped his thick chest. "I will speak with their Supreme Commander again, and tell him his part to play."

"I watched a recording of your first meeting," said Gaius. "This Hawthorne is a proud preman. He might object in areas."

"I give that a little less than a ten percent possibility," said Cassius. "No. He will see his chance to regain much of Earth in my offer. Even more importantly, in striving to gain an advantage over us, he will help us more than he otherwise would consider wise."

Gaius looked thoughtful until finally he grinned. "You are a sly fox, Grand Admiral. It is a spectacular plan."

Scipio wasn't as enthusiastic. But he also nodded. "It may work."

"It must work," said Cassius. "Our future rests on the outcome. So as Highborn, we will force events to move in our favor. Now, gentlemen, let us begin in earnest."

40

Several hours later, Hawthorne strode down a gravel path in a park outside a former coalmine. He was in the Joho Mountains of China Sector. Evergreen trees surrounded him, filling the area with pine scent. Captain Mune marched behind at a discrete distance. Other bionic soldiers walked well in front, to the side and in the back.

Hawthorne clasped his hands behind his back. He had spoken with Grand Admiral Cassius again. They had talked about particulars so Hawthorne had a good idea about Cassius's plan. The Highborn was so dreadfully arrogant and yet so piercingly brilliant.

Thinking deeply, Hawthorne now debated with himself. He halted and glanced at the mountain peaks in the distance. Many were capped with snow. Clouds drifted in the sky, while lower down an eagle soared serenely.

Below him underground was the headquarters for Earth Defense. He'd commanded here on the dreadful day the Highborn had dropped their meteors. They had killed a billion people. The weather patterns were still disharmonious because of it, effecting crops negatively.

"Captain Mune," said Hawthorne.

The bionic captain hurried near, the soles of his boots crunching gravel. Mune had saved him near here from PHC killers.

"Look up," said Hawthorne.

Mune did so.

"For the first time in many years, near-Earth space will be

devoid of Doom Stars," Hawthorne said.

"Yes sir."

"I thought I'd be rejoicing over that," said Hawthorne. "Instead, I find myself wishing them luck."

Mune lowered his gaze.

Hawthorne frowned. "I have critical decisions to make, Captain. What I choose...it might mean the death or survival of billions of people on the planet. Do I throw everything in support behind the Highborn to stop the asteroids from annihilating human life? Or do I attempt to practice subterfuge in order to wrest conquered territory from the Highborn?"

Mune shook his head. "I don't know, sir."

"You and I have been together a long time."

"Yes sir."

"You were my jailor once. Do you remember?"

A troubled looked crossed Mune's heavy face. "Lord Director Enkov was a hard man, sir. He...he made me what I am."

"You killed him later," said Hawthorne.

Mune said nothing, but he gave the Supreme Commander a questioning look.

"Do I launch our painstakingly built Orion-ships?" asked Hawthorne. "If so, how many do I send at the asteroids? Should I hold some back to wrest near-orbital space control from the Highborn?"

"Are you asking my opinion, sir?" asked Mune.

"...I suppose I am," Hawthorne said with a tired smile.

"Sir, I watched the meteors fall to Earth that day here. I would not allow you to act then. My sorrow over my actions— I live with that sorrow every day."

"Use everything I have to stop the asteroids?" asked Hawthorne. "Is that what you're saying?"

"We're talking about human extinction, sir."

Hawthorne craned his head, looking straight up. He was a mote in the teeming cauldron of humanity named Earth. In the end, he wasn't that important. Maybe it was time to risk everything. If the asteroids hit...everything else became moot. If they stopped the asteroids, then there was time enough later to resist the Highborn.

Rubbing his forehead, Hawthorne realized that he was tired to the core of his being. He had to throw everything into the fray to try to eke every percentage point he could. The cyborgs would obliterate humanity otherwise.

"Captain," Hawthorne said, "I wonder if you'd be interested in directly helping the outcome."

"Sir?" asked Mune.

"You're the best soldier Social Unity has. Your fellow bionic soldiers...tell me which elite troops we have who are your superiors."

Mune tilted his head. "I've never thought of it that way, sir. I'm not sure I know who those soldiers are."

"I'm afraid I don't either."

"Afraid sir?" asked Mune.

"Afraid," Hawthorne said, as he stared up at the clouds. If Earth was to remain serene like this, he had to act with everything he possessed. Anything else would be egotistical posturing. He'd overthrown other Directors in order to save the Earth. Now he had to risk totally or go down as the man who'd lost humanity its existence.

41

Far away from the Joho Mountains and Earth, a lone meteor-ship hurtled between Jupiter and Mars. It approached the Sun's orbit, trying to get on the other side of it where the Earth, Mars and the asteroid strike were.

Inside in the *Spartacus's* command center, Nadia Kluge said, "Get ready for the transmission."

Marten stood behind his chair, watching the main screen. Jupiter was nearly 750,000,000 kilometers away. At the speed of light, it took a laser lightguide message almost forty-two minutes to reach the ship. A forty-two minute delay was far too long to have any meaningful two-way conversation.

Marten was tense. They had traveled for over eight weeks now. What was going on at Earth? How would the Highborn react to the asteroid strike? The Praetor had helped kill cyborgs. The bastard of a Highborn had given his life to slay the Web-Mind. Would the Highborn sweeping in conquest on Earth feel the same way?

Tan's image appeared on the screen. She wore a white gown with a golden circuit around her forehead. Her eyes appeared glassy and it seemed her head swayed the tiniest bit. In the background waved the Jovian banner of a lidless eye in the middle of a pyramid.

"In the name of the Dictates, I hail the Force-Leader and crew," Tan said softly. "A new adjustment has occurred in the Jovian System. The populaces of Ganymede and Europa agreed to a plebiscite and overwhelming voted me as the new Solon of the Jovian Confederacy. Their faith in my abilities at

195

this critical juncture humbles me. Whatever hesitation I feel accepting the post, I submerge for the good of the all."

"What happened?" cried Marten's weapons-officer.

"Quiet!" snapped Marten. "Let me hear."

"I suspect there is great rejoicing in the *Spartacus*," said Tan. "At this terrible juncture in history, it must bring soothing relief to know that the moons of Jupiter are safe-guarded by my wisdom. Each of us must do his or her part. I have submerged my will in this in order to work ceaselessly toward our safety. Now you in the *Spartacus* must do likewise. You are guardians of great daring and courage. You represent the Jovian people. In the interest of continued human existence, the Jovian Confederacy has agreed to an alliance with the Planetary Union of Mars, with Social Unity and now with the Highborn. After much deliberation, an over-arching strategy has been achieved.

"It will no doubt interest you to know that the *Spartacus* will play a pivotal role in the coming battle."

"What's she talking about?" asked the weapons-officer.

Marten pointed at the officer. "Silence!" he said. Then Marten turned back to the screen.

Small Tan picked up a silver chalice, sipping from it. Smiling at them, she said softly, "After my message, you shall receive strategic data. In a word, you will join in a space marine assault on the asteroids. Marten Kluge is an expert at these sorts of assaults. I point to his attack on the Beamship *Bangladesh* and against the rogue moon Carme."

Marten scowled.

"I am told the over-arching concept originated with Grand Admiral Cassius of the Highborn," Tan said. "As the plan is elegant and economical of force, I have concurred. You are hereby ordered to attack the asteroid-cluster and land space marines on planetoid surfaces, to evict any cyborgs there and gain control of the propulsion systems."

"How are we supposed to reach the asteroids to land on them?" asked Nadia.

"Shhh!" said Marten.

"You will accelerate your ship and pivot around Mars, changing your heading to catch up to the asteroid-cluster," Tan said. "The coordinates will be forthcoming. It is possibly a suicidal mission, and your courage for the good of the whole is hereby noted and applauded. You will not be alone in this assault, but you alone will represent the best of the Jovian Dictates. Given that truth, I implore you to fight with enthusiasm and show the others the greatness of the Dictates. In such a manner, your deaths will not go in vain.

"To the Dictates," said Tan, lifting her chalice in a salute.

The main screen flickered afterward. Her image disappeared, and in its place appeared a pyramid with a lidless eye in the center.

Scowling, Marten slid into his chair. Amidst the silence, he began studying the incoming data.

42

"It's a suicide mission," said Omi.

Marten lay on his back, with his torso shoved inside a panel on a patrol boat. Using a pneumatic-wrench, he adjusted a photon cell. When he was finished, he slid out and sat up.

Omi wore a vacc-suit, with the helmet dangling behind him. They were alone in the patrol boat, which sat secure on the surface of the meteor-ship.

"We're not coming out of this one alive," Omi said.

Marten picked up the grate, shoved it over the panel and switched on the magnetic locks. He grunted as he stood, and he staggered to the pilot's chair. Omi sat in the weapons-officer's seat. They were under heavy and extended acceleration, making movement a chore.

Outside were the *Spartacus's* rocky surfaces and then the glowing blue exhaust of the ship's fusion core. Beyond shined the stars. They headed toward the Sun, but the patrol boat's viewing port was pointed backward.

"This entire assault," said Omi, "it's too jumbled."

"Yeah, I know what you mean."

"Orion-ships from Earth, missiles from the Sun-Works Factory...." Omi shook his head. "It feels scrambled."

"The cyborgs caught everyone napping," said Marten.

"Highborn and Social Unity, they've been tearing out each other's throats for years," Omi said. "Now it turns out we all should have been fighting the cyborgs. Now it may be too late."

Marten switched on the pneumatic-wrench, feeling it hum

198

in his hand. This entire mission…ever since Tan's message, his gut had been tightening. The mission reminded him too much of the Storm Assault Missile fired at the *Bangladesh*. It had seemed soon as if the bulkheads of the *Spartacus* were closing in around him. So he'd grabbed Omi and climbed outside, entering a patrol boat. There were moments he felt like lifting off and just heading away, anywhere without Highborn, cyborgs and crazy political leaders. While sitting Marten switched the pneumatic-wrench on and off repeatedly. Then he switched it off for good and clipped it back to his tool-belt.

"It's a suicide mission," said Omi.

Marten nodded as he stared out of the window into space. "We don't know anything about the asteroids. At least, if anyone knows, they aren't telling us."

"You know the asteroids will be swarming with cyborgs."

Marten glanced at Omi.

"We've learned from our past mistakes," Omi said. "I bet the cyborgs have, too. On Carme, they didn't have enough troops. This time I bet they will."

The churn in Marten's gut grew. Unclipping the pneumatic-wrench, he switched it on. The worst horror of his life had been the ride out to the *Bangladesh* and then storming onto it. He'd never wanted to do something like that again. Yet here he was, accelerating toward death.

"Do we even have a chance?" asked Omi.

"What else can we do?" Marten whispered.

"I've heard about your idea of heading to Neptune."

"Run away?" asked Marten.

"Isn't that better than suicide?"

Marten clipped the pneumatic-wrench back onto his belt. "We've been in a lot of fights, you and me. Others around us die, but we keep going."

Omi became quiet.

"None of the battles we've been in have mattered like this one." Marten clapped his hands. "Everything on Earth dies. Sydney disappears. The islands of Japan burn to a crisp. Korea vanishes. We're fighting for our home-world, Omi."

"The *Spartacus* is our home."

"Is that how the men feel?"

"They're not stupid," Omi said. "They've fought the cyborgs before and know the odds. Everyone understands we were lucky to get off Athena Station alive. Counting force-levels is easy enough. You've seen the number of asteroids, and you can image the number of cyborgs that must be on each. This fight is fatally stacked against us. The cyborgs are making sure they win this time."

"We're fighting for Earth!"

"I understand," said Omi, "but if Earth is doomed, it's doomed."

Marten smacked a fist into the palm of his hand. His gut churned just as much as it ever had, and he hated the feeling. Omi was right. This one had the stink of doom to it, especially their being in a lone ship that was supposed to come up on the enemy's backside. Marten could envision all too well a bank of laser-turrets and a salvo of missiles obliterating the *Spartacus*.

"Tan might have a point about our essential nature," Marten said.

"Meaning?"

"You know how she says we're guardians, fighters. That fighting is what we know and do best. Maybe, however, the smart thing is to turn away. Maybe we should do what the SU Fifth Fleet did. If we hang out here in the void, we might be the last ones to die to the cyborgs. But then what are we living for?"

Omi shrugged. "Do we need a reason?"

"...I need meaning," said Marten. "My life has to count for something."

"Committing suicide gives you meaning?" asked Omi.

Marten shook his head. "Fighting for what I believe in gives me meaning."

Yawning, blocking it with his hand, Omi said, "You keep your meaning. I just want to live so I can eat, drink and bed women."

Marten frowned. He had Nadia to worry about now. That was so beautiful, being with the woman he loved. Maybe he could send her away in an escape pod. As he thought about it, he realized she would never agree to that. The trip from the Sun-Works Factory to Jupiter had scarred her emotionally due to the long-term isolation. She would never willingly make such a long and isolated trip again.

"I need your help," Marten said, as he stared at the stars. "The men respect you."

Omi squinted. "Tell me this. Can we survive?"

"Ultimately, we all die."

"I mean can we defeat the cyborgs."

"…I don't know," Marten said. "I…." He shrugged.

After a time, Omi nodded. He drew his gun, examined it and then shoved it back into the holster. "Let us fight then."

"You're with me?" Marten asked, as he stared at the stars.

Omi turned toward the window. He nodded.

Marten saw that out of the corner of his eye. His gut still churned, but it was good to know that Omi backed him. A man needed friends. There was none better than Omi.

"We've got work to do," Marten said.

"Work," said Omi. "Maybe that's what this is all about."

Marten glanced at Omi.

"Some men repair ships," said Omi. "Some pilot tugs. We're soldiers. So our work is fighting."

"We're guardians like Tan says?" asked Marten.

Omi shrugged. "I don't know nothing about that." He fast-drew his gun. "But I know something about this." He stared at Marten. Then he holstered the gun, put on his helmet and turned toward the hatch.

Far from the *Spartacus* on Luna, Grand Admiral Cassius listened to Senior Tribune Cato. They rode together in a moon-buggy. The vehicle had giant balloon tires and a bubble canopy. If anyone had witnessed their passage, they would have seen the two sitting side-by-side.

The traveled through the Sea of Tranquility. Tiny puffs of moon-dust lifted at the vehicle's passage and slowly drifted back to the surface. The blue-green Earth hung in the distance with nothing but stars beyond. It meant the Sun was behind Luna.

"We have fifty-three percent completed," Cato was saying.

Cassius scowled. "It should be sixty-three percent. You're behind schedule."

Senior Tribune Cato gripped the wheel with gloved hands. Both Highborn wore vacc-suits, with their visors open to reveal their faces. Cato had a burn scar on the right side of his face, with a patch over his eye.

"We're working twenty-four hours a day," Cato said.

"In rotation?" asked Cassius.

"Yes."

Cassius had to restrain the impulse to draw his sidearm and destroy the Senior Tribune. "Listen to me," he said. "Every man is to work twenty-four shifts."

"Grand Admiral?"

"I want those missiles completed in time!" Cassius shouted.

Cato winced at the volume. Then his features contorted angrily. No Highborn liked being yelled at or being berated. He gripped the steering wheel more tightly, and his foot pressed on the accelerator. The moon-buggy churned across the lunar surface, the vehicle swaying more and jolting as it took the small dunes and rocks faster.

In the distance rose a vast missile complex from horizon to horizon. There were thousands of blast-pans and tens of thousands of missiles. It had been built for use against the landing assault on Eurasia. As a secondary measure, it was meant to continue the siege of Earth if ever the Doom Stars were needed elsewhere. There had been long debates about situating the missile facility in near-Earth orbit instead of on Luna. The deciding factors had been Luna's bulk as a permanent platform, its distance from Earth and correspondingly its height in the planet's gravity-well and the proximity of the mining complexes here, aiding in re-supply.

"Have you've studied my timetable?" asked Cassius.

"Yes, but—"

"The cyborgs have achieved strategic surprise against us. Time is now critical. Normally, in a military timetable, there are percentages allowed for errors. We no longer have that luxury. My timetable is precise. You will meet it or face death by hanging."

Cato glared at Cassius. "You threaten me as if I were a dog or one of the sub-species?"

"You have already tested my patience," warned Cassius.

"Twenty-four hour shifts means stim-injections."

"Tell me now: can you can meet my timetable or not?"

"Grand Admiral," said Cato, gesturing angrily. "Extended stim-injections quickly results in mental fatigue. There will be mistakes, more as time progresses—"

"Mistakes are unacceptable," said Cassius.

"Mistakes are inevitable."

"We are Highborn. Highborn achieve. Now you must test your men to the utmost, driving them with stim-injections and forbidding them mental fatigue."

"You ask the impossible," said Cato.

"Is that your final word?"

"Grand Admiral, you must see reason. I have already achieved a miracle. Now you're asking me to do the impossible. Instead of berating me, you should be praising me for what I've done. My men and I have worked incredibly hard."

"Wrong answer," said Cassius. He drew his sidearm, pressed the barrel against the Senior Tribune's head and pulled the trigger. The helmet blew apart in a spray of blood, skull-bone and plastic. One chunk hit the bubble-canopy so hard that the ballistic glass starred.

Cassius shoved the gun onto the dash, grabbed the steering wheel and shouldered the corpse out of the way. In moments, he tromped down on the accelerator. The moon-buggy bounced and churned across the bleak landscape, increasing speed for the giant missile complex.

44

The new Senior Tribune of the Luna Missile Complex assured the Grand Admiral that the men could meet the timetable.

The new Senior Tribune kept glancing at dead Cato, who lay on a slab of metal in an underground garage. The moon-buggy was parked twenty feet away, with the bubble-canopy still open. The gore, congealed blood and brain tissue of the ruined head seemed to fascinate the new Tribune. He'd just learned about his promotion five minutes ago.

"This is critical," said Cassius. "Are you listening?"

The new Senior Tribune tore his gaze from the dead Highborn, looking at Cassius. He nodded quickly.

"You must accelerate the work schedule, but sacrifice nothing in terms of perfection," Cassius said. "Each missile must function to its full potential at the needed moment."

"I understand, Your Excellency. It shall be done."

"Words are unimpressive," said Cassius. "Only deeds interest me."

"I demand that you judge me by my deeds, Your Excellency."

Cassius nodded. "There is no room in Higher Command for failure of any sort. We have five days until launching. Every missile must leave its pad, and each missile must carry its designated cargo, be it soldier or warhead."

The new Senior Tribune saluted smartly. "Then with your permission, Grand Admiral, I must leave you and begin the accelerated work-schedule at once."

"It appears I've chosen the right Highborn," said Cassius.

"Excellence brings rewards," the new Tribune said.

"Perfectly stated," said Cassius. "Now before you leave, show me where I may find the commandoes."

"Do you have a specific commando in mind, Your Excellency?"

"Maniple Leader Felix," Cassius said.

"Do you know his unit number?"

"Troop Six, Battalion Fifty-Seven," said Cassius.

The new Senior Tribune examined a scroll-pad. "It is a penal unit." He sounded surprised.

"It appears you are not intimately familiar with the commandoes."

"We have an infantry specialist, Your Excellency. He can tell you more than I can concerning the commandoes. I specialize...." The Senior Tribune grimaced. "I specialize in completing the assignments given me."

"What was that designation again?" asked Cassius.

With a start, the Senior Tribune thrust the scroll-pad at Cassius. Cassius examined it, nodded and abruptly turned around, heading for his moon-buggy.

45

Cassius sat in a chair before a small wooden table. He was still on Luna, in a bare room. A shock rod lay on the table, the sole object. A single bulb provided light.

The door swished open. A Highborn in battleoid-armor entered. Behind him followed Maniple Leader Felix. The youthful replica of Cassius had changed subtly since that day on the *Julius Caesar*. Rage still burned in his eyes, but his features had become sullen, with a hint of mulishness that hadn't been there before. It was difficult to detect at first, but something vital, a spark of intellect or life force had been drained away. Felix had died, had been injected with Suspend and then he'd been resuscitated. The psychologists claimed he didn't remember his death, but Cassius didn't believe it.

Felix wore titanium-reinforced manacles, effectively trapping his wrists before him. As their eyes met, Felix halted.

"You," said Felix.

Cassius said nothing, he merely watched. It pained him to recognize the resuscitation disease. Some Highborn did better than others when brought back to life. He himself had never died. After studying Felix, it seemed wisest if he never did so.

Lifting the titanium-reinforced manacles, Felix said, "Just how brave are you?"

Cassius clicked a hand-unit. The manacles popped open.

With a snarl, Felix whipped his hands at Cassius, hurling the manacles. Swaying to the side, Cassius dodged them. He'd been expecting that, an elementary maneuver. The manacles clanged against the wall, slid down and hit the floor.

"Wait outside," Cassius told the battleoid-armored Highborn.

The guard never shrugged or bothered with a warning. He simply marched out, slamming the door behind him.

"I could kill you before he entered again," Felix said.

"You tried that once already when you had the advantage. My recommendation is to wait before you attempt it again. Try to gain an absolute advantage."

Felix massaged one of his wrists. He sneered at Cassius. "I've been training hard."

"Good. You're going to need every ounce of your rage and fighting spirit soon."

"You're shooting us at the cyborgs, eh?" Felix spat on the floor. "That's wise, old man. Otherwise, I would have killed you sooner or later."

Cassius leaned forward. "Your fury lacks rationality. We possess similar chromosomes. We are alike in many ways. I…I wish you to excel."

"Is that why you shot my favorite sex object?"

"The premen could have used your girls against you, killing you like an animal."

"Why do you care?"

"I've already stated the reason: our chromosomes."

Felix's eyes widened, and he laughed harshly. "You see me as your father?"

A pang of something beat in Cassius's heart.

"Highborn have no fathers, no mothers," said Felix. "We are alone. It is one of our strengths."

"We are the Highborn, the most superior form of life in existence," said Cassius.

"Do want me to call you father?" Felix jeered.

"I want you to excel," said Cassius.

"Why?" asked Felix, taking a step nearer.

Cassius groped for the right words, and it surprised him that he didn't have them.

Felix's leg muscles tensed.

"Don't do it," Cassius whispered. "You already have a mark against you for attempting to assassinate me. A second mark will bring about your destruction."

"Why do you care?"

"You have the best of genes," Cassius said. "Someday, you may become the Grand Admiral."

Felix roared as he leaped for the table. Cassius was closer, if a touch slower. Snatching the shock rod, he switched it to its highest setting. Then he cracked it across Felix's forehead. With a howl, Felix crashed sideways and collapsed onto the floor.

The door opened as the battleoid-armored guard looked in.

"Get out!" Cassius snarled.

The soldier stepped back, slamming the door shut.

Taking two steps, Cassius crouched beside Felix. "You have courage and you're full of vigor. Those are excellent traits. Now you must learn to use your mind, to think."

"I'm going to kill you someday," Felix whispered.

"First you're going to have to survive the cyborgs."

"You're not getting rid of me that easily."

"I'm glad to hear it," Cassius said. "To survive the cyborgs, you're going to have to kill all of them. Do you think you can do that?"

Felix turned his head. There was something more than mere rage there.

Cassius looked away, and he stood up. He suddenly felt very tired and alone. It was a dull ache.

"Running away, old man?"

"You have the very best genes," Cassius whispered.

"I can't hear you. Why don't you bend your ear near here by my teeth?"

"You must suppress your fury," Cassius said. "For you, indulging your anger will bring eventual madness. You must cultivate your higher reasoning abilities and learn to lean on them."

With a groan, Felix struggled to rise. Old Gaius could have done it, Cassius realized. But Gaius did it through willpower. Felix's mind had been damaged in death or during resuscitation. There had to be a way to fix that.

"Good luck against the cyborgs, my boy."

"I'm not your boy. I'm your death waiting to happen."

The pang of hurt touched Cassius heart again. With a deep

209

breath, he buried that hurt. He steeled himself to the tasks at hand. Then he headed for the door, never once looking back, not even as Felix groaned, fighting to get up.

-46-

Unlike the Highborn in the Luna Missile Complex, Cassius slept an average of five hours a night. It was impossible to go days on end with stims without experiencing mental fatigue. As Grand Admiral, he needed mental acuity.

He presently rowed in a machine, his nine-foot body lathered in sweat. The rowing machine was in his quarters aboard the *Julius Caesar*, one of several personal luxuries. Three days had passed since he'd executed Senior Tribune Cato. It was true he'd asked the impossible from the Highborn. And Cato's objections had been logical. None of that mattered, however.

There had been a particularly effective Marshal of the Soviet Union during World War Two. His name had been Georgi Konstanitinovich Zhukov. He'd been a hard preman and an outstanding general. Partly due to his tireless energy and ruthlessness, the Soviet forces had halted the dreaded German panzers before the gates of Moscow. Even more impressive, Zhukov had carefully husbanded his forces so he could unleash a devastating winter campaign on the exhausted German armies. During the fateful seven months of 1941 and the German blitzkrieg into Russia, Zhukov had been the chief troubleshooter for Dictator Stalin. One of Zhukov's most successful ploys had been to shoot those generals and colonels who failed on the battlefield. The preman had ruthlessly dominated the situation by constantly demanding the impossible from his immediate underlings. Due to their fear of Zhukov, generals found themselves able to achieve feats

211

surpassing their old performance levels.

As Cassius rowed, panting heavily, he was determined to shape reality by the power of his will. Time ticked away as the asteroids sped for Earth. More than ever, he needed strength and fierce will. Then he needed imagination to outthink the cyborgs.

There was a loud *ping* in the room. A red light flashed. The intercom crackled with life. "...Grand Admiral?"

Cassius released the handles and climbed out of the rowing machine. "Give me forty seconds," he said.

"As per your request, the Supreme Commander of the Premen will be online in twenty."

"I require ninety seconds," said Cassius. "Make sure he stays connected."

"Yes sir."

Still breathing heavily, Cassius tore off his clothes, tossing them onto his cot. Then he entered the shower. A hot needlelike spray jetted against his sweaty skin and against scars and old bruises. There was a particularly nasty one on his left shoulder-blade, shiny tissue there showing where a force-blade had once cut him to the bone. He lathered shampoo in his bristly hair and then let the hot water wash it out. Seconds later, he exited the shower, toweled dry and stood before a blower. Cold air caused his skin to prickle. He gasped, and he felt alive. Soon, he put on a shirt, buttoning it fast, and he put a dress jacket over that. He strode to his desk, sat and ran his big fingers through his hair. Facing a video camera, he waited for the seconds to tick away.

"I'm ready," he said.

The screen came to life, and Supreme Commander Hawthorne faced him. There was a bookshelf behind the preman. Cassius mentally made a note to check the titles of those books later, possibly giving him greater insight into the Supreme Commander. Then Hawthorne surprised Cassius by speaking first and immediately to the issue.

"We need to adjust the attack," said Hawthorne.

Cassius practiced calm, staring at the preman. Maybe it would be better to hold these meetings in person. Let the preman feel his presence and the thin specimen would have to deal with physical fear. That might help curb the sub-human's tongue.

"As we've scheduled it," said Hawthorne, "there are too many possibilities for errors, for mistakes at precisely the wrong moment."

"I summoned you for an entirely different reason," Cassius said.

Hawthorne shook his head. "Grand Admiral, we are like two men fighting in a room to the death. Now a pack of wolves has crawled through the windows to kill us both. We have been forced to stand back-to-back and fight together. Otherwise, we shall both die."

"I have no time for analogies."

"Social Unity is one of those men," said Hawthorne. "You Highborn are the other. There is still much hatred between us, much distrust. That hatred and distrust might flare up on the battlefield. Therefore, we must change the parameters in order to forestall such an event. Instead of attacking as a united force and mingling together, I suggest we each accept specific spheres of action. You conquer your sphere and we shall conquer ours."

"Have you forgotten?" asked Cassius. "We attack cyborgs. They will destroy your Homo sapien troops. Then we Highborn shall have to conquer both your sphere and ours. It is better if you Homo sapiens are stiffened with Highborn officers and fighters among you."

"How easily did you conquer North America?" Hawthorne asked.

"No, no, that is the wrong example. In North America, in every battlefield on Earth, Social Unity enjoyed a vast numerical preponderance. Against the cyborgs, we have a limited number of elite units. It is a given that you lack such troops. And that is the nature of my call. The date is late. But I suggest that you allot half your Orion-ships to me. I will fill them with more Highborn commandoes. That will give us a greater margin of superior troops on the asteroids."

"That's out of the question," Hawthorne said.

"The survival of Earth is at stake. What possible reason could you have to object to such a reasonable request?"

"Earthmen will ride the Orion-ships to do battle against our enemy," said Hawthorne. "And instead of fighting under your command, they will fight separately under their own officers."

"Unity of command is a primary principle for victory," said Cassius.

"We are allies," said Hawthorne. "We will fight as equals, not under Highborn dominance. In this, every director, field marshal and general has agreed."

The lowing of cattle, Cassius thought, even as he forced a smile. "Highborn are better soldiers by several factors. You and I have witnessed this on every battlefield. Now under our guidance and protection, you premen—you Homo sapiens will survive longer on the asteroids and therefore do more damage against the cyborgs. Give us half your Orion-ship berths and even more Highborn can reach the asteroids. That will raise the probability of victory by many percentage points."

"Never!" said Hawthorne.

"I fail to grasp your intransigence," said Cassius. "My reasoning is flawless. Why then do you insist on weakening our attack?"

"I'm not weakening anything."

"Replacing Homo sapiens with Highborn will raise the combat value of our limited number of troops," Cassius said. "I know you are a logical person, gifted in strategic sense. You must see this. I know you see it. We're speaking about the survival of Earth, of the billions living here. How then can you—"

"First," said Hawthorne, as he stabbed a finger onto his desk. "I will not allow Highborn on Eurasian soil. Second, none of you shall see our launch sites or examine the inside of our ships. Third, we shall fight for our own survival and not rely solely upon you."

"Supreme Commander, as a collective whole, you Homo sapiens will be providing the Orion-ships. You fashioned those vessels through your labor. Take joy in your craft."

"I ask that you no longer refer to us as *Homo sapiens*," said Hawthorne. "We are men."

Cassius sat back. "Is this an elaborate ploy to attempt subterfuge against us?"

Leaning forward, Hawthorne said, "You are a proud people, Grand Admiral. It is the dominant trait among you."

"Our excellence is our dominant trait."

Hawthorne folded his hands on top of the desk as he looked earnestly at Cassius. "I think the easiest way for you to understand this is pride, human pride, our pride."

"Is that a joke?" asked Cassius.

Hawthorne frowned. "...Grand Admiral, you and I have matched wits for several years now. Surely, you've learned something about me and about humanity, just as I've learned about you and the Highborn. We have our pride, and you must realize by now how stubbornly we can hold to our position."

As much as he hated to do it, Cassius inclined his head. He'd learned that premen could be amazingly foolish in a vast multitude of ways. Here was simply another example. Pride, stubbornness—it would be more accurate to call it bovine dullness and a lack of imagination. He shouldn't have expected more from them, not even from Hawthorne. Perhaps the better plan would be to reconfigure the attack, using the Orion-ships as fodder. He would subtly alter the schedule so the preman vessels absorbed the majority of the cyborg lasers and counter-missiles. Yes, he could already see the best way to do this.

"The size of the asteroid strike is fearsome," Hawthorne was saying. "Earth's survival is questionable. In this hour, we shall fight. We will not stand aside for anyone, least of all for Highborn. Neither shall we fight under anyone but our own."

"Your racial prejudice is a weakness," said Cassius, "lacking any bearing on reality."

"We have fought bravely against you," Hawthorne said. "And we will continue to fight bravely, no matter who comes against us. Will you stand with us in this final hour?"

Cassius attempted another facial gesture of good will. It was time to lull Hawthorne. He would definitely have to reconfigure the attack, setting the Orion-ships to absorb enemy weaponry. It would be the best use of such poor-quality fighting material.

"I see that I must adjust," said Cassius. "What are your exact suggestions?"

"I'll send you the data now," said Hawthorne.

"Yes, excellent," said Cassius. "Begin the transmission."

-47-

Zero hour struck far too soon for Hawthorne's comfort. It found him pacing deep in the control center in the Joho Mountains of China Sector.

Before him were banks of screens and their operators. They showed Orion-ship bunkers in the Eurasian heartland.

Hawthorne fixated on Kazakhstan Sector, on Bunker Ninety-Eight. Around the titanic installation were huge ferroconcrete pillboxes. The point-defense cannons in those pillboxes remained idle today. No one had ever envisioned such a situation as this. Instead, every tactician and strategist assigned to the think-tanks had envisioned the Orion-ships having to fight every inch of the way into space against Highborn missiles, lasers and orbitals.

After glancing around the underground control complex, Hawthorne frowned. He felt naked today, exposed. There were banks of screens and operators, with colonels and generals behind them, watching. In the background were hard-eyed men and women, Cone's security people. They wore black synthi-leather jackets and ear-jacks. Captain Mune and his bionic soldiers were aboard the Orion-ships. It had been a hard decision for Hawthorne. Mune had been with him for so long and had guarded his back so often that now....

Hawthorne knew this was a political risk, and a risk to his personnel security. But the safety of the planet trumped his own. Could Cone's people guard him as effectively as the bionic men had? The answer was no. The better question was: could Cone's people do the job and keep him alive?

Above the whispering around him, Hawthorne heard an operator say, "Bunker Ninety-Eight is opening."

First rubbing his tired eyes, Hawthorne peered at the nearest screen. It showed vast ferroconcrete bays sliding open. Something rose into view from the darkness. He glimpsed the nosecones of various modified attack-craft. Captain Mune was supposed to be in one of those.

"The countdown has begun," said the operator, a red-eyed woman watching her board. "...Three, two, one, zero—we have ignition."

Hawthorne shielded his eyes from the first blast before looking. The great Orion-ship rode a huge, roiling cloud of dust and brightly heated plasma into the air. It was a vast space-vessel, with a mammoth blast-shield of ferroconcrete, steel, construction-foam and titanium. Another nuclear bomb squirted out of its exhaust port. There was a second flash, and it forced the Orion-ship higher yet into the atmosphere.

The blast-shield protected the attack-craft parked on the ship's front. The Orion used nuclear pulse propulsion, with each bomb providing the violent pulse. Nothing humanity had yet devised could lift so much mass, so quickly from Earth.

Hawthorne marveled at the ship. It had been under construction ever since he'd sent the supply fleet to Mars several years ago. If anyone could absorb the punishing liftoff of nuclear bombs, it would be Captain Mune and his men. Glancing at other screens, Hawthorne saw other Orion-ships lifting from their bunkers, seven altogether. These Orion-ships had been part of a two-year-long project to take back near-Earth orbit and possibly capture the Moon. Now the seven giant craft sped toward the stratosphere, smashing their way up out of Earth's gravity so they could reach the asteroids in the coming weeks. These Orion-ships dwarfed those sent on the Mars mission by two hundred percent.

Watching them, Hawthorne felt a lump in his throat. This could be the last SU Fleet ever launched from Earth. If the soldiers in them failed—extinction! Hawthorne straightened and lifted his arm in a crisp salute. "Good luck, Captain Mune," he whispered. "I wish you well...friend."

The bionic soldiers were a secret weapon against the

cyborgs. Hawthorne supposed a person could make the point that Mune was a cyborg. Theoretically, it was true. Mune had mechanical parts and graphite bones in his limbs. But his brain was still pure human, or Homo sapien as the Highborn would say.

An immense flash occurred down the line of screens. Men and women there groaned as they stared at a screen, at the terrific explosion shown. One colonel sobbed.

"What happened?" shouted Hawthorne. He expected the worst: that an Orion-ship had malfunctioned. He strode toward that screen, passing operators in their chairs twisting their heads in that direction.

There was more shouting. It came from the shadows, from the security people in their synthi-leather jackets. They seemed to be responding to the flash shown on the screen. Cone's people drew guns. A woman rapidly spoke into her headset. Other security people clamped a hand over their ear-jacks. Harsh orders tumbled from the security personnel as they ran toward the bank of screens. The security people aimed their guns at everyone. Operators, colonels and generals turned around in surprise at this new development. Then a dozen security people shouted at once for everyone to lie on the floor.

Hawthorne groped for his own sidearm. Was this a coup begun by a surprise flash on a TV screen? Why now and what was its purpose?

"Down, down!" shouted a burly man, motioning with his gun.

"What's the trouble?" asked Hawthorne, as black-clad security people rushed to him and then spun around, facing outward. "Why have you drawn weapons?" Hawthorne said, grabbing a woman, spinning her around to face him.

"That flash on the screen—" she said, sounding frightened.

Hawthorne recognized then that the security people had overreacted. Mune and his men had never done so. The bionic soldiers had been the best guards a Supreme Commander had ever possessed. In their strength, the bionic men had known clam. He realized that he was dearly going to miss Mune.

"At ease!" shouted Hawthorne. "Lower your guns."

The security people glanced uneasily at each other. Several

glanced at Cone, who hurried into the large chamber as she tucked in her shirt.

"Stand down," Cone said.

Only then did the security people begin to holster their weapons and back away into the shadows.

Hawthorne felt coldness stab his chest. The security people hadn't listened to him, but they'd immediately obeyed Cone. She had just become his jailor. Whether the security specialist knew it or not was another matter. He'd have to replace Cone and her people. But with whom? Then he remembered the flash on the screen.

"What happened?" Hawthorne shouted, striding to the offending screen and its operator.

The woman looked up at him ashen-faced, with dark circles around her eyes.

"Speak," said Hawthorne. On the screen, debris rained down from the clouds as smoke billowed upward.

"Orion-ship *Avenger* malfunctioned," the operator whispered. "It exploded. They're…they're all dead, sir."

A colonel on the other side of the operator's chair was weeping silently, with his face pressed against his hands.

Hawthorne gazed at the screen again, understanding now what he saw. *Dead*, all those brave bionic soldiers vaporized into atoms. In the hurry and rush to get everything ready for zero hour, somebody had made one mistake too many. Now Earth's chance for survival had dropped…by however many percentage points that ship represented.

Hawthorne rubbed his eyes. There were so many things to coordinate, to think about, it was breaking him down. It was breaking all of them.

"I wish I'd filled the *Avenger* with Highborn," he said.

Several operators turned and stared at him in shock. One general nodded, however, and even managed a bleak grin.

"Carry on," said Hawthorne. "We can't stop for anyone now, not even for those brave soldiers."

The heavy Orion-ships on screen continued to flash and zoom upward, already leaving the atmosphere as they entered outer space and near-Earth orbit.

As the Orion-ships blasted their way out of the atmosphere, the Highborn Luna Missile Complex fired its first salvo. These were titanic Cohort-7 Missiles, which fired x-rays in the proximity of their enemies. From the hundreds of launch-sites, the missiles rose like stellar sharks, quick, deadly and silent. As the fusion cores propelled the Cohort-7 projectiles, the blue flares appeared as dots against the darkness of space. Those dots accelerated with astonishing speed. Soon enough, they vanished, swallowed by the void.

Orders rang out as the Highborn Senior Tribune watched from his conning tower.

All around him on the moon, other giant HB missiles moved on tracks and onto the still glowing blast-pans. The Senior Tribune laughed as he waited high in the tower. The fatigue of the last several cycles ate at him. It had been so long since he'd laid down his head and closed his eyes. The Highborn leader shook his head now, and his tongue felt thick in his mouth.

"Next wave," he said. "Launch, launch, launch."

Sullen Highborn standing at their stations eyed him. None had slept for days and they were each dangerously exhausted. There was a Highborn term for it: explosive weariness. Many mulishly clicked their controls. One officer suddenly bellowed with rage, drew a gun and began firing into his panel. Plastic and acrylic pieces went flying as loud bangs rapidly followed one after another.

Three other Highborn reacted before the Senior Tribune

was even aware of what occurred. One drew a vibroblade, clicked it so it hummed and hurled it at the berserk. Before the blade could hit the madman, two other Highborn drew their sidearms and emptied their clips into the berserk. He twisted around at the shots, glared at them for a second and then sank with a groan, his gun clattered on the floor.

The Senior Tribune began to tremble, not in fear, but in rage. How dare anyone mar an otherwise perfect liftoff? He was tempted to try resuscitation of the offender in order to use SU tortures on him as punishment.

Then he recalled his purpose. "Launch," he said in a ragged voice.

As smoke drifted from hot gun-barrels, Highborn officers attended to their stations. The Senior Tribune checked his board.

The second salvo of modified missiles began launching. These had taken the most work, the most redesign and refit. Inside them was live ammunition: Highborn space commandoes. These missiles were almost as large as the Cohort-7s.

As the Senior Tribune double-checked the sensors aboard the missiles, a glaring error became obvious. The oxygen-valve settings on a dozen missiles—no, on *twenty* of them, weren't calibrated for heavy thrust. It should have been a simple thing to check beforehand. But these many hectic days on stims and without sleep….

Bending over his com, the Senior Tribune shouted, "Emergency, emergency, the oxygen content will soon approach zero! Don emergency breathing gear and change the settings on the oxygen valves." Then he realized he'd forgotten to turn on the com-system to the missiles. He did so now with a click and repeated his warning.

The commando missiles zoomed out of the Sea of Tranquility, accelerating hard for Venus. As the Senior Tribune checked the responses, he soon discovered that fifteen missiles were dead, or their occupants were. Fifteen missiles—because of a simple single error over a hundred commandoes were dead before the battle had even started. The Senior Tribune banged his forehead against his board until blood began to drip in the light Luna gravity. He badly needed sleep. Oh, he wanted to sleep almost more than he wanted to finish his task. He realized dully that he had to think of a way to hide this fifteen-missile loss from the Grand Admiral.

The Senior Tribune wiped blood from the board and made some quick calculations. No, this couldn't be—oh, wait a minute. He rechecked missile manifests. As his shoulders sagged, he realized that Felix had survived the mishap. The Senior Tribune was aware of the Grand Admiral's strange affinity for the soldier. He'd studied vid shots of the two and had discovered a disturbing likeness between them.

The Senior Tribune straightened. His head throbbed painfully, but that was good. The pain helped him concentrate. Maybe if he were lucky, Cassius would die in the coming battle. Yes, he would hope for luck and the Grand Admiral's violent demise when his Doom Star engaged the cyborgs.

49

"Marten, are you sure this is a good idea?" Nadia asked.

The *Spartacus* accelerated at two-Gs as it traveled across the face of the burning Sun. The meteor-ship had built up tremendous velocity, a speed even greater than the fast-approaching asteroids. Those asteroids sped on a straight collision course for Earth's projected position. It was obvious now that the asteroids had originated in the Saturn System. That was something over 1,400,000,000 kilometers away, nearly twice the distance between Jupiter and Earth. As far as Marten knew, those asteroids had not accelerated since they'd shot out of Saturn's orbit and begun their fatal journey.

"Marten," said Nadia.

They lay on the bed in his Force-Leader's quarters. At two-Gs, both of them needed to practice caution, particularly Marten, or any man for that matter. Each man wore a special cup around his privates. Extended two-Gs for days on end could cause possible rupture.

Marten lay stretched on the bed with his wife. He stroked her face as he lay on the pillow. Gently, the two of them kissed.

"My dearest," he whispered.

"I love you," she said.

He embraced her and they continued to kiss. Soon, carefully, they made love…. Afterward, Marten slept with Nadia.

He dreamed he was back in the Sun-Works Factory, running through the endless corridors. Instead of PHC chasing him, giant Highborn did. He heard Training Master Lycon and the Praetor. They shouted to each other about his coming castration. Just before they rounded a corridor to grab him, cyborgs dropped from somewhere, even though Marten knew it couldn't have been the ceiling. The strange beings dropped, the Highborn appeared and everyone drew guns and began blasting.

Marten woke up with a start. Nadia's head lay on his chest, with her hair sprawled in disarray. He stroked her head and squeezed his eyes closed. What an awful dream. Soon, however, it was going to be reality as Highborn and cyborgs were together again in a confined space. Blowing out his cheeks, Marten listened to the soft thrum of the fusion core.

"Uh, what time is it?" Nadia whispered.

"Shhh," Marten said, touching her cheek.

She looked up into his eyes. He looked back. Then he gazed at her perfect butt and her long legs.

"You beast," she said in a sleepy voice.

"Yeah, that's me."

She turned serious then. "I'm frightened, Marten. We're going to be near Mars soon. Then we have to turn, to shift onto a new heading. I'm not sure the *Spartacus* can take the strain."

"We have to try," he said.

"I've been studying the projected forces. We're hardly anything compared to all the Highborn missiles and Doom Stars."

"I know," said Marten.

"If we fail to show up, no one will miss us."

"Maybe," he said.

"Which is our side again?" she asked.

"I hate Social Unity and I hate the Highborn. But the cyborgs aren't even an option. If the Jovians are to survive, they'll need allies. In this, a man has to choose the lesser of two or three evils. After the war is won, however, I'll go back to fighting Social Unity."

"So first we save Earth?"

"If we can," he said.

She looked up into his eyes. Hers were haunted. "Hold me," she whispered.

He stroked her hair, wondering how this would all turn out.

50

The four *Zhukov*-class battlewagons from Mars approached tactical laser-range with the enemy. They were in a line abreast, with the *Vladimir Lenin* on the subjective left as seen from Earth. A thick prismatic-crystal cloud was between the ship and the asteroids. The P-Cloud protected each battleship, and each taskforce presently moved through velocity alone.

Commodore Blackstone stood at the map-module, with Commissar Kursk across from him. The other officers of the *Vladimir Lenin* sat at their posts, monitoring their boards. Red light bathed the bridge, with quiet noises from communications predominating.

"Why haven't they responded?" asked Blackstone.

Kursk shook her head.

"Our missiles have been in enemy range for almost an hour," he said.

Blackstone adjusted the module's settings. The missiles launched many days ago now neared the front asteroids. The cyborgs had seemingly ignored every rule of space combat, neither building their own prismatic-crystal cloud nor attacking the missiles.

"We'll reach laser-range in ten minutes, sir," said the weapons-officer.

The *Vladimir Lenin* had an effective one hundred thousand kilometer range. Because its targets were asteroids with a precise velocity, a refined targeting technique was being employed.

"Yes," said Blackstone. "Inform the others and ready our

226

mirror."

The weapons-officer bent over his board.

Blackstone touched the map-module.

The four battleships moved on a near-collision course toward the asteroids. Given their present heading, they would pass the asteroids with about seven thousand kilometers to spare. The prismatic-cloud presently glittered in front of the four battleships, acting as a screen in case the cyborgs fired heavy lasers. It also prevented the battleships from directly firing at the asteroids.

Now four large mirrors moved away from the battleships but parallel with the protective cloud. These mirrors had special hardened coating and precise targeting features. Once in position, each tilted at a perfect angle, able to *see* the asteroids because the prismatic crystals were no longer between them and the targets.

The *Vladimir Lenin* began to rotate, so the heavy lasers were pointed at its particular mirror.

"Enemy lasers, sir!" shouted the weapons-officer, a squat Asian man named Wu, noted for his extreme devotion to his weapons.

Commodore Blackstone hunched his shoulders. "Are the lasers firing on us or—"

"Against our missiles, sir!" shouted Wu.

Almost one hundred thousand kilometers separated them from the cyborg taskforce. That meant the information was several nanoseconds old. The missiles launched many days ago were less than nineteen thousand kilometers from the enemy. Surely, the cyborgs lasers could reach farther than that. So why had they waited so long before firing?

"Do you have an estimate of the enemy wattage?" asked Blackstone.

"The readings are coming in now, sir," said Wu.

"...Well?"

"They're similar to our heavy lasers, sir," said Wu.

"Not near Doom Star laser power-levels?" asked Blackstone.

"Negative, sir," said Wu.

"That's something at least," Blackstone whispered to

Kursk. "Give me more data," he told Wu. "What are the other missiles doing?" he asked the missile-officer.

"They're all firing, sir!" shouted Wu.

"What, our missiles?" asked Blackstone.

"I'm sorry, sir. The cyborgs lasers are all firing."

"I want precise data," Blackstone said. "What do you mean by *all*?"

Wu's thick fingers blurred across his screen as he tapped madly. "Twenty heavy lasers, sir," he said a moment later. "No. Make that twenty-two enemy lasers."

"So many?" said Blackstone.

"I'm surprised there aren't more," Wu said. "Given their surface area—"

"Give me power estimates on their fusion cores," Blackstone said. "We need more information and we likely don't have much time to get it."

"We're in laser-range, sir," said Wu.

"Ask the other ships if they're ready to fire."

"I already have, sir. They are."

Blackstone moistened his lips. "Take out enemy laser turrets," he said. "Now!" He made a curt gesture.

As Wu complied, the thrum of the fusion core rose in volume. The *Vladimir Lenin* built up power and pumped it through the laser coils. The concentrated light beamed through the firing tube. That light struck the mirror, the one outside the protection of the prismatic-crystal cloud. Bounced perfectly, the coherent light sped across the one hundred thousand kilometers at the speed of light. It hit a laser-turret on the thirty-kilometer asteroid, the one designated as A. As the *Vladimir Lenin* continued to move toward the asteroids, the asteroids continued to move at Earth. In order to keep the laser focused on the turret, the mirror minutely adjusted throughout the entirety of the beaming.

Now the other heavy lasers from the other three battleships began to beam across the immense distance.

"Have any missiles hit?" asked Blackstone. "I want information, people, and I want it now."

Other devices had moved outside the protection of the cloud, some of them radar dishes and others teleoptic scopes of incredible power. The radar sped to the asteroids at the speed of light, bounced off and sped back just as fast. It took twice as long, however, as directly viewing what occurred through optics.

"Scratch one laser-turret!" shouted Wu, who pumped his fist in the air.

"We can hurt them," Blackstone told Kursk with a grin.

"We haven't gotten to them with the missiles yet," she said. "The missiles hold the nukes, which is the only effective way to nudge the asteroids off course."

"Allow me to enjoy my victory, as small as it is," Blackstone said.

Kursk gripped the map-module so her knuckles whitened. Her intense gaze was fixated on the screen.

"I want—" Blackstone said.

"Enemy lasers!" shouted the defensive-officer. "They're trying a burn-through, sir."

"How many lasers?" snapped Blackstone.

"Sir," the defensive-officer said, "they're focusing ten lasers into a small area."

"Start pumping more crystals!" Blackstone shouted.

"Emergency pumping engaged!" the defensive-officer said. "Sir, at this rate, they'll burn through our P-Cloud in twelve minutes."

"Impossible," said Blackstone.

"Slag the *Leon Trotsky's* mirror, sir," Wu said. "I don't know how, but the cyborgs damaged it."

"We're too heavily outgunned," Kursk whispered.

Blackstone said nothing as he stared at the map-module. The Commissar was right. The cyborgs had too many heavy lasers, and it looked as if they had enough power to fire them for hours. Just as bad, none of the missiles had made it near enough the asteroids to make detonation worthwhile.

"How are we supposed to stop them, sir?" asked Wu.

"What I want to know," Kursk whispered, "is how Hawthorne is going to get any space marines onto those asteroids."

Blackstone swallowed in a dry throat. He had his orders. Hawthorne had ordered him to break off the attack if the cyborgs proved too powerful. Social Unity had to keep a fleet intact, especially if the unthinkable happened and the cyborgs destroyed Earth as a habitable planet. Yet to have traveled out this far and beamed the lasers for less than a minute, and then to turn and run—it was too galling.

"Now they've damaged our mirror, sir," said Wu. "We can't fire at them anymore unless we come out from behind the cloud."

"Or if they burn our cloud away," said the defensive-officer.

Commodore Joseph Blackstone found himself short of breath. The cyborgs had too much concentrated firepower on those asteroids. The big ones possessed greater tonnage than all the Doom Stars, *Zhukov*-class Battleships and missiles combined. How were they supposed to stop the asteroids from smashing into the Earth?

"We must ram them," whispered Kursk.

Blackstone blinked at her. "What?" he whispered.

"We must ram them," she said. She was pale and trembling.

Shaking his head, Blackstone said, "We lack the tonnage to do more than nudge one. You saw the specs. The asteroids have giant exhaust ports. They'll just readjust course."

"We have to do *something*," Kursk said hoarsely.

"Yes!" Blackstone said, and he struck the map-module. "We keep these battleships intact."

"You're running away?"

"I'm saving our fleet—if I can." He knew it might already be too late. The cyborg firepower, it was too much. "Break-off," said Blackstone, "employ schedule three-C."

Several officers swiveled around to stare at him.

"Now!" shouted Blackstone. "We have to get out of range now. There's nothing more we can do today."

"No," whispered Kursk, and there were tears in her eyes.

"Mister," Blackstone told the pilot.

The pilot moved as if shocked, and she began to lay in the new course heading. Meanwhile, orders went out to the other three battlewagons.

"More enemy lasers are firing," the defensive-officer said.

"Our P-Cloud won't last more than a few minutes at this rate."

"Emergency jinking!" shouted Blackstone. "Then each ship is to head to its own destination."

"This is a disgrace," Kursk said, tears freely running down her cheeks.

Had he just consigned billions to their deaths? Blackstone hoped not. He wanted to do more. But the enemy firepower—

"Burn-through in ninety seconds!"

Then everyone aboard the *Vladimir Lenin* was thrown to the left as the big ship began to accelerate toward a new heading.

51

Commodore Blackstone strapped into an acceleration couch as fear boiled in his stomach.

The *Vladimir Lenin*, the *Leon Trotsky* and the other battleships accelerated away at emergency speeds. Each battleship had to contend with its velocity that moved it fast toward the approaching asteroids in a length sense. Because of that velocity, none of the battleships could move away at more than a shallow curve in a width sense. The engagement took place on a three-dimensional battlefield, but in this instance, viewing it as a two-dimensional rectangle problem more accurately portrayed the situation. Human endurance levels, battleship structural design and physics limited the possibility of the various headings. Those were known quantities likely possessed by the cyborgs. They had once been allied with the Mars Battlefleet and were therefore intimately aware of *Zhukov*-class Battleship specs.

Blackstone knew that several factors worked against these grim minuses. The first was distance, the second was time and the third was particle-shielding six-hundred meters thick.

"I'm engaging the computer!" the pilot shouted. "It will use random vectors for emergency jinking. This could get rough."

Blackstone glanced at Kursk. A bruised lump welled on her forehead where she'd struck the map-module. She looked dazed, but she clicked the acceleration straps over her torso. Then she closed her eyes and her head lolled to the side. Blackstone gritted his teeth as the ship veered a different direction by a minimal fraction. Under these speeds, however, the G-force strain caused metallic groans from the heart of the ship.

It was a familiar game from the simulators, but this time it was for real. Blackstone secretly hated the computer auto-piloting his warship. He wanted to make the decisions. But this was a mathematical problem now with precise parameters.

The equation was simple. A laser needed to remain on target in order to burn through it. The thicker and denser a target, the greater amount of time heat needed to drill through it or boil away the substance. The distance between the asteroids and the *Vladimir Lenin*—one hundred thousand kilometers and closing fast—meant that an operator, or cyborg or AI, Blackstone supposed, fired its laser where it believed the object would be several nanoseconds later. The firer had to take into account the asteroid's movement, the battleship's movement and the elapsed time. Therefore, in order to remain on target, a laser-operator needed to adjust the beam constantly. That's why the battleship jinking first one way and then another created difficulties for the enemy lasers, throwing off the beam's calibration hopefully just enough.

Kursk vomited as her skin turned greenish. And the bruise on her forehead thickened as extra blood welled within it.

"We're going to make it," Blackstone told her.

She groaned and threw up again.

"Fight through the nausea," he said. He didn't dare unlatch himself to apply a medkit to her. The constant jinking would throw a person off his feet, slamming him against sharp or heavy objects. "It's for just a little longer," he said.

He didn't watch her response, but checked the monitor before him. He used audio-control, switching to outer cameras. The sight made him grimace.

Heavy lasers had burnt-off particle-shielding. There were black marks on the asteroid-like surface, some deeper than others. On some of the shielding, he saw slagged areas where the lasers had melted the surface into a glassy substance. Fortunately, none of the lasers had made deep impressions yet.

Blackstone frowned. He realized no lasers presently burned into the particle-shield. Could the jinking be that effective?

"Sir," said Wu. "The enemy has changed tactics."

Blackstone brought up Wu's images on his monitor. Then he ordered a close-up and shouted angrily. No enemy lasers beamed at them. Instead—he counted them—twenty-three heavy lasers struck the *Leon Trotsky*. The six-hundred meters of particle-shielding was meant to take heavy fire, but nothing like that. As the lasers beamed across the distance, they chewed away layer after layer of the *Leon Trotsky's* shield. Rocks slagged off. Fused glass bubbled and boiled away, and all the while, the terrible lasers chewed deeper into the shielding.

That was one of his battleships, one of the four left out of a once proud fleet. Blackstone's gut hurt as he thought about the number of warships he used to command. The battle against the Doom Stars, it had cost much too heavily. The cyborgs had been allies then. The cyborgs had reinforced the impulse for Highborn and humans to bleed each other into weakness.

"Re-target enemy turrets!" Blackstone shouted harshly. He was going to save the *Leon Trotsky*. Social Unity couldn't afford any more losses. The alien creatures on the asteroids meant to obliterate humanity—he wanted to murder every one of them.

Blackstone roared an oath as a heavy laser took out a cyborg laser turret. These creatures weren't invincible. It was possible to hurt them. Now he had to kill them, and stop them from pouring that concentrated fire into the *Leon Trotsky*. Then the second enemy turret on Asteroid A burst into uselessness. He saw that through the battleship's teleoptics.

A ragged cheer went up on the bridge. It brought life to Kursk, enough that she wiped the vomit from her mouth.

Then they destroyed a third turret, even as the *Leon Trotsky* took out a fourth.

During that time, the asteroids continued their steady advanced on Earth. And the battleships moved closer to them lengthwise, if desperately trying to put more distance away *width*wise from the asteroids. In that time, the cyborg lasers stripped the last shreds of shielding from the *Leon Trotsky*.

"Captain Jensen," Blackstone said. The monitor wavered, and Jensen appeared on it. She was an older woman with a hawkish nose. Despite her name, she was of Arab descent and wore a green crescent symbol on her cap.

"Deploy your escape pods," Blackstone said, as he watched through a spilt-screen.

One screen showed Captain Jensen shouting orders. The red light flashed on and off on the bridge. The other screen showed the *Leon Trotsky*. The asteroid-like particle-shield had almost completely melted away. In places, Blackstone saw the exposed composite armor underneath the shielding, which was the hull of the battleship. Then the cyborgs lasers struck again.

Blackstone heard shouting. Only vaguely did he realize he was the one shouting. The death of a battleship was a horrible thing to witness. To know he had taken the vessel into combat only made it worse. The lasers struck and burned through the composite armor. In a fantastically short time, the *Leon Trotsky* became twelve separate pieces. Thousands of little bits of debris spilled out of the broken battleship. Some of those bits were crewmembers.

Blackstone felt as if he'd been punched in the gut. He blinked rapidly, and something hardened in him. That battleship had faced Doom Stars and survived, but now it was gone, nothing more than a bitter memory.

"The cyborgs are re-targeting!" shouted Wu.

Blackstone snapped out of his daze as he studied his monitor.

"I loved you," Kursk told him.

Blackstone stared at her. "What?" he said, his mouth bone dry.

"I'm entering a different sub-routine!" the pilot shouted.

The enemy lasers continued to beam. The three battleships attempted to jink out of death, pump more crystals and gels and burn more enemy turrets. As the asteroids zoomed toward Earth, they killed another battleship, slicing it apart as they had the *Leon Trotsky*. Then the full brunt of the cyborg lasers turned on the *Vladimir Lenin*.

Fortunately for Blackstone and his crew, their own emergency acceleration and new sub-routine helped. Even more important was the steady velocity of the asteroids. It meant the Saturn-rocks reached a point where instead of heading toward them they went away. That distance grew rapidly in a length sense, and even more in a width way as the battleships continued to accelerate away from the enemy. Before the lasers completely stripped away the particle-shielding from the ship, the distance grew too great. At the greater distances, the lasers missed more often and hit with lesser power. The laser beams dissipated their coherence. Because of these various factors, Blackstone and his crew survived the first encounter with the asteroids. But before the *Vladimir Lenin* entered another fight, it would need a new six-hundred meter particle-shield.

52

The battle report came in from the defeated Mars Battlefleet at the speed of light. The cyborg lasers, their targeting tactics and lack of prismatic-crystals became well known even on the Meteor-ship *Spartacus*.

"The first round goes to the cyborgs," Osadar said.

Marten and she stood in the think-tank. With the hand-unit, he opened a link with the ship's computer and downloaded the latest information from Chief Strategist Tan. It was dark in the think-tank, with simulated light showing the star fields.

"Now we know exactly what the Highborn plan to do," Marten said.

"It strikes me as overly complicated," said Osadar.

Marten nodded as he switched to strategic zoom. According to Tan, the plan had originated with Grand Admiral Cassius.

Their part was interesting. They had passed the Sun and now sped through the Inner System faster than anyone else did. Their objective was to land on the asteroids. They couldn't do that if they sped straight at the cyborg taskforce head-to-head. The two objects with their velocities as they headed at each other would make landing impossible. Any space marine in a patrol boat trying to land on the surface in those circumstances would be instantly crushed like an insect. Instead of trying to land head-to-head, the *Spartacus* would soon whip around Mars, turn enough and speed toward the asteroids as the asteroids went away from them. The meteor-ship could have accelerated even faster during the trip. But for what they needed to do, they couldn't whip around Mars until the asteroids had passed the Red Planet.

For the Earth and Luna-launched ships and missiles, the problem was similar—at least for those vessels that wished to land on the asteroid surfaces. If they headed straight at the asteroids, none of them would be able to land troops but would smash like two cars in a head-on collision. The angle for Mars was wrong for Earth and Luna-launched vessels. Instead, they headed for Venus. The Saturn-launched asteroids moved almost parallel to the Sun, at least in relation to Earth.

For tactical purposes, the Solar System wasn't just empty space. Planets and gravity were the major terrain features, as it were. Because of the near parallel line of attack from Saturn to Earth—parallel in relation to the Sun—Venus became critical. The Earth and Luna-launched vessels traveling to Venus, would whip around it, turning, and then accelerate on their new heading. They would come at the planet wreckers at an oblique angle. This angle would allow the SU and Highborn vessels to decelerate enough so troops could theoretically land on the surfaces.

It was the gut of the plan.

As Marten examined it, his doubts grew.

"We will have little time to defeat any cyborg occupants, learn how to control the asteroid and then move it out of position enough so it misses Earth," said Osadar.

Marten silently agreed. The Saturn-launched asteroids had gained their initial velocity long ago around the gas giant. That velocity had taken the taskforce across the great gulf between Saturn and the Inner Planets. Roughly, the distance from Saturn to Earth was 1,400,000,000 kilometers. The distance from Mars to Earth was presently nearly 210,000,000 kilometers. In other words, the asteroids had already traveled six-sevenths of their journey, and now time was running out.

A klaxon began to blare.

Marten checked his watch, and he grew queasy. Was it already time?

"Mars approaches," said Osadar.

"It seems we just left it," Marten said.

"Not for me," said Osadar.

"...Do you remember much of what it was like under the Web-Mind's control?" Marten recalled that Osadar had first come to Mars as a full-fledged cyborg.

"Do you recall any of your childhood nightmares?" asked Osadar.

Marten thought about the bad dream he'd had the other day. "They stick with me," he said.

"Yes," said Osadar. Then she made a vague gesture and headed for the hatch. "It is time, Force-Leader."

Marten switched off the think-tank before heading to the control center.

-53-

As the *Spartacus* neared Mars, Grand Admiral Cassius endured heavy acceleration aboard the *Julius Caesar*. His ship and the *Genghis Khan* trailed the Luna-launched missiles and the six Orion-ships from Earth. They fast approached Venus.

Cassius lay in his quarters as he refined the plan. There were so many variables to contend with that the plan absorbed his interest. This was why he'd been created. Some premen gambled for enjoyment. Others rutted. Still others ate gourmet meals. For Cassius, war-planning and its execution was the elixir of life.

He'd been ingesting the information gleaned from the Martian Battlefleet. It had been a pitiful waste of military assets using the battleships like that. One of them could have achieved the data. It also became clear yet again that left to themselves the premen would fall before the cyborgs. This attack on Earth was brilliant, if genocidal madness. To counter it, he'd have to use every ounce of his brilliance.

Cassius rubbed his big hands together. He was under hard acceleration toward the battle of his life. Several of his agendas merged in this fight. He needed to defeat the cyborgs and then smash the remains of Social Unity's pitiful space-forces. Hawthorne's harrying tactic of keeping a fleet-in-being had been making everything more difficult than it needed to be.

After cracking his knuckles, Cassius adjusted his screen. His was the supreme strategic mind in the Solar System. Now was the time to bend every facet and find a slot for it in his schemes.

240

First, the big Cohort-7 Missiles sped at Venus. Behind them followed the Orion-ships and then the commando missiles. The main wave attack would occur after they used Venus as a pivoting post, redirected their heading at an oblique angle toward the asteroids. The *Julius Caesar* and the *Genghis Khan* would follow close behind them, also using the planet.

Secondly, the *Gustavus Adolphus* accelerated toward the asteroids. Behind them accelerated the so-called SU Fifth Fleet with two battleships and a missile-ship. They could theoretically engage the asteroids before the *Julius Caesar* was in range, but Cassius had already forbidden that. The cyborgs had shown the destructive power of concentrated fire. He would do likewise.

Cassius tapped his screen. The cyborgs hadn't deployed any prismatic crystals or gels. That did not necessarily mean the cyborgs didn't have any. He would assume they had crystals and gels and would deploy them at the needed time. It would be a preman mistake to think otherwise.

Hmm, the Jovian meteor-ship neared Mars. It was a small military asset, but it would play its part before the cyborgs eliminated it. Was it worth the designation of third factor? No. It was too puny. Maybe if the Jovians had sent a fleet…but they hadn't. Given this miserliness, it was clear that conquering the Jovian System should prove to be simplicity itself once the cyborg menace was eradicated.

Third then, was Scipio's space defense of Earth. After pivoting around Venus, he would send an inquiry to the Highborn and see how matters stood.

The fourth and final component was the Earth-based defense of proton beams, merculite missiles and Highborn orbitals and laser satellites.

Together, it was an impressive array of military hardware and personnel. The heart of the plan, however, was the Highborn commandoes, whatever the Earth soldiers could perform and the Jovian space marines. Earth would live or die on their collective abilities.

"I can lose this fight," Cassius said.

He scowled, as he hated losing. But it would be a weakness if he couldn't see the real possibility. To that end, he'd ordered every Highborn off-planet and into space. That could mean a possible loss of control of Earth. That would depend in the end on the FEC formations and their loyalty. But if the asteroids made it through everything he could throw at them, he wasn't going to let precious Highborn die. Let the premen cattle do that in their teeming billions.

Scowling more deeply, Cassius shook his head. He did not intend to lose to these aliens freaks from Saturn. How was it possible the cyborgs had conquered Saturn without at least some premen sending out a message of the awful conquest? It showed once again how pathetic premen soldiers really were. Premen were good for rutting and menial labor, nothing else. In the New Order of the coming Solar System, they might not even be good enough for that. Cassius had toyed with the idea of mass geldings. There were too many premen in the Solar System, far too many.

"Grand Admiral."

Cassius looked up, and opened channels with the bridge. "Yes?"

"Venus is near, Your Excellency."

First rubbing his hands, Cassius swung his legs off the acceleration couch. It was time to head to the bridge. "I'm coming," he said. "Carry on."

With a grunt, Cassius stood under the heavy-Gs. Then he slowly headed for the hatch. The battle of his life was fast approaching.

-54-

Marten sat in his badly shaking command chair. Around him, metal screeched in complaint and loud groans occurred that sounded like wounded whales. The vibration of the fusion core became so horrible that his head felt like it was coming part. He sank into the cushions of his chair, forced there by the heavy Gs.

Mars filled the main screen. It had begun as a dot and grown with incredible speed.

No one tried talking, or if he or she did, no one else could hear. Marten endured. Likely, so did everyone else. He didn't even try to turn his head to see how Nadia fared.

The Red Planet filled and then vanished from the screen. He thought about Diaz. He thought about floaters and fighting in the deep valleys of Mars. Most of all, he thought about the nearly hopeless fight inside Mons Olympia. Cyborgs were terrible foes. Diaz had died while fighting them. Omi and he would have become cyborgs except that Osadar had broken her programming.

What chance did they really have on the asteroids? Little to none was the real answer. In the Jovian System, they'd had numbers on their side. How many cyborgs were on the asteroids?

At that moment, the shaking ceased. So did the terrible groaning of the metal of the ship's struts. The vibrations from the fusion core lessened. His head hurt, but he could hear voices again.

"…Marten?"

"I'm here," he said, swiveling his chair.

Nadia stared at him from her cubicle. Pasty-colored, she looked frightened. Everyone in the command center did. He needed to calm them.

"We passed the ordeal," Marten said. "Now let's recheck our equipment. I don't want anything to malfunction so we fail to kick these cyborgs' butts."

One man managed a sickly grin. The others grew more frightened.

Marten swiveled back toward the main screen. He was the Force-Leader, and he was taking them to their deaths. Too bad Yakov wasn't here. He'd know what to say.

Marten tapped an armrest with his fist. Then he surged to his feet. "This is why we came," he said. He turned toward them. "We have allies, the Highborn in case any of you have forgotten. The Praetor helped us defeat the cyborgs on Carme. Now other Highborn will help us kill these cyborgs."

"Do we have a chance?" asked an officer.

"The living always have a chance," Marten said. He wanted to believe that, he really did. But ever since he'd gone over the data from the Mars Battlefleet....

He looked back up at the screen. They'd made it past Mars. Now it was simply a matter of catching up with the cyborg asteroids, landing and fighting for their lives.

The *Spartacus* was under hard deceleration and had been ever since rounding the Red Planet. It was also under greater deceleration than the Highborn's battle-plan called for.

The decision had come easily to Marten. In these types of battles, one didn't want to be the first ship to attack the enemy. He'd been through more than his share of combat to value foolish heroics. There was a time for courage and a time for caution. If he could help it—and he could—he'd slip his space marines onto the asteroids after the first several waves of Highborn and Social Unity soldiers had already tried.

He was speaking quietly to Omi, discussing landing techniques, when Nadia spoke up from her cubicle.

"You have an incoming message from Grand Admiral Cassius," Nadia said.

Marten looked up shocked. Then he swiveled his chair toward the main screen. "Put him on," he said.

Omi stood beside him, with one hand resting on the butt of his gun.

The image of Cassius came online. The big Highborn had bristly iron-colored hair and fierce intensity in his eyes. He wore a military cap and a blue uniform. There was something magnetic about Cassius and something dementedly dangerous. Behind him, other Highborn sat at their stations.

"Who is this?" demanded Cassius.

Marten stiffened at the tone.

"Careful," whispered Omi.

Marten glanced at his friend.

245

"He's in a Doom Star, with the power to destroy us if we anger him," Omi whispered.

"I know that," Marten whispered out of the side of his mouth.

"Just thought you might need a reminder," Omi said.

"Preman, do I have your attention?" Cassius asked coldly.

"I am Force-Leader Marten Kluge of the Meteor-ship *Spartacus*."

"Those are Jovian terms?" asked Cassius.

"We are a Jovian warship."

Cassius leaned toward him. "I know perfectly well what you are. Why are you decelerating so hard?"

A sharp retort came to Marten's lips, but he hesitated. The Grand Admiral seemed many times deadlier than the Praetor or Training Master Lycon.

"Your action smacks of cowardice," said Cassius.

Marten's eyes narrowed. He'd been taking crap from Highborn for far too long. Their arrogance grated just as much now as it ever had.

"Have you fought cyborgs before?" Marten asked.

It was like watching a wild beast. The reaction was swift, the curl of the lip and a minute widening of his eyes. If they'd been in the same room, Marten had no doubt the Grand Admiral would have attacked him.

"You will answer my questions, not bombard me with yours," said Cassius. "Any deviation from that and you risk annihilation once my ship is in range of yours."

"I understand you think of yourself as my genetic superior," Marten said. "But that holds no value with me."

Omi made small, urgent motions, no doubt nonverbally suggesting that Marten watch what he say.

"We have journeyed all the way from Jupiter to aid in your assault against the cyborgs," Marten said. "The least you could do is show some gratitude."

"You are Marten Kluge?" said Cassius.

Marten didn't like the way the Highborn asked that. "I've decelerated harder than you suggested because—"

"I beamed you *orders*," said Cassius, "not suggestions."

"I am in command of a sovereign vessel from the Jovian

Confederation," Marten said. "That makes us allies. It doesn't make me your subordinate."

Cassius had turned his head. He now stared at Marten with greater malevolence than before. "You are a shock trooper and formerly belonged to the Free Earth Corps. You fought in the original Japan Campaign. How did you manage to flee to the Jupiter System?"

"Grand Admiral, that is all history."

"Answer my questions, preman."

"How about you answer mine?" Marten said with heat. "What gives you the right to threaten me and act in such a highhanded manner?"

"I have the ability to obliterate you."

"So might makes right?"

"That is a truism of nature," said Cassius.

"Fine," said Marten. "I left Highborn service because my might proved superior to that of Training Master Lycon."

"You are a fool, preman. Your meteor-ship is of infinitesimal value in the coming battle."

"Then why bother calling us?" snapped Marten.

A chilling smile spread across Cassius's face. "Are you deliberately attempting to goad me into destroying your spaceship?"

"No. I'm just sick of your arrogance, of your highhandedness. We're risking our lives to join this fight. No one has come as far as we have to kill cyborgs and save Earth. Instead of berating us, you should be asking for pointers in how to defeat them. I've fought cyborgs on many occasions. Heck, I've probably faced cyborgs more than any other person in the Solar System has."

"You are delusional," said Cassius.

"I want to land my veteran, cyborg-killing space marines on the asteroids. I'm not going to do that charging in first. I'm a lone ship, while you're hitting them en mass. Fine. My plan is to land after you've softened them enough and gained their attention. From my perspective, that's sound military practice."

Cassius had turned away, perhaps reading from a side-screen again. He now studied Marten anew. "You once stormed onto the Beamship *Bangladesh*."

247

"Yeah, that's right."

"And you fought on Carme."

"These space-landings have become my specialty," Marten said.

Cassius sat motionless as he stared at Marten. "You are a unique preman. I wonder if there has been a miscalculation concerning your abilities." Cassius nodded curtly. "Send me your recommendations for asteroid-storming against cyborgs. If you've gained a tactical insight, I shall glean it from your writings."

"What?" Marten asked.

Cassius checked his chronometer. "You have two hours to transmit me the report. Grand Admiral Cassius out."

The main screen went blank, and after a second, Marten sagged against his chair.

"You're crazy," whispered Omi.

Marten shrugged.

"But for some reason, Highborn like crazy," Omi said. "What are you going to tell him?"

Marten sat up. "Get me Osadar," he told Nadia. To Omi, he said, "Do you realize what this means?"

"That the most powerful Highborn of them all now wants to rip out your throat," Omi said.

"That all our battles against the cyborgs have meaning," Marten said. "We just have to distill the most important aspects. Then the Grand Admiral will likely employ what we've learned to help save Earth."

"Do you know what will happen after that?" Omi asked.

"Victory?"

"Cassius will hunt you down like a dog for killing Training Master Lycon. They never forget, Marten."

"Maybe it's time we never forgot," Marten said. "Where's Osadar?" he shouted at Nadia. "We don't have much time."

"Know what I think?" Omi asked.

Marten shook his head.

"That the Highborn gave you the wrong stamp."

"What's that mean?"

"Back in Australian Sector they stamped a "2" on your hand. It should have been a "1", seeing as you've done more

248

than hit Highborn. You've killed them."

"Now it's time to start killing cyborgs," Marten said. Then he took out a recorder and began to think. He had two hours to write or dictate his report and send it to the Grand Admiral. Before Osadar appeared, he started talking into the recorder.

56

As the *Spartacus* continued its hard deceleration, the cyborgs reacted to the meteor-ship.

Ship's sensors picked up several blips detaching from the main asteroid-pack.

"What are those?" asked Marten.

During some shifts, Nadia doubled as the sensor-operator. "I don't detect any radiation or heat signature from them," she now said.

"What caused the separation?" asked Marten.

Osadar was in the command center, standing at the former arbiter station. "They might have been catapulted off," she said.

"How?" asked Marten.

"By a rail-gun possibly," Osadar said. "Because the vehicles are asteroids, the cyborgs have large surface areas to work with. They might have installed kilometer-long rails."

"They've lit up!" Nadia said.

On the main screen, the blue blips turned bright red, indicating motive power.

"They have fusion cores," said Nadia.

"Torpedoes," said Marten. "How many are there?"

"I'm counting ten," said Nadia. "No, make that twelve. They're big torpedoes, too, with over five times the mass of our patrol boats."

"Say again?" asked Marten.

Nadia's fingers tapped her screen. She nodded shortly. "Five times the mass, Force-Leader. They're huge."

Marten transferred the specs onto the main screen. There was nothing secretive about these torpedoes. The attack used brute power and numbers. Marten shook his head in sudden doubt. This wasn't like ground combat, which he knew to a nicety. This was space war with lengthy time-margins and extreme distances. What he decided now would take hours to unfold. Because of his lack of experience in these matters, throughout the journey he'd been studying ship tactics. The *Spartacus* had point-defense cannons and small counter-missiles. The size of the torpedoes troubled him, however. It did appear as if they were traveling in a pack.

"It's time for our Zeno-missiles," Marten said. The *Spartacus* had a limited number of the big ship-killers. But he didn't think the meteor-ship was going to survive this battle for long. If it reached the asteroid surfaces, the spaceship would have served its purpose.

"How many Zenos do you desire launched?" asked Osadar, who presently acted as the weapons-officer.

Marten had been computing size, likely torpedo armor and spread. "…Six should do it," he said.

"That leaves us with only three Zenos in reserve," said Osadar. "Perhaps you are too generous with your missile expenditure?"

Marten glared at the screen, at the accelerating torpedoes. Maybe he was being too generous. No, this was a matter of weight, armor and numbers, of mathematical formulas. "I'm figuring one Zeno per two enemy torpedoes," he said.

"I only hope the cyborgs do not launch anymore," Osadar said.

"Let's worry about one problem at a time," Marten snapped.

Without another word, Osadar clicked toggles on her board. Soon, the meteor-ship shuddered. It continued to do so as the big missiles launched from the outer surface.

57

The hours passed as the cyborg torpedoes built up velocity. The Zenos continued their advance to combat. Finally, the two sets of projectiles neared proximity. One after another, the Zenos detonated. After the sixth big missile blew its thermonuclear warhead, only two enemy torpedoes survived. One accelerated at half its former speed. The last one homed in on the Meteor-ship *Spartacus*.

"Warm the main laser," Marten said.

The fusion core increased power. On the ship's surface, a large focusing mirror began to move. The calibration took five minutes of careful preparation.

"Fire!" said Marten.

Fusion power surged through the coils. Coherent light flashed through the focusing mirror. A thick beam of laser-light stabbed through the darkness of space. It struck the torpedo. The torpedo jinked out of the path of destructive light. It took another three minutes of calibration and retargeting. Then the laser stabbed again. Again, the torpedo jinked. At the third attempt—

"It detonated!" shouted Nadia.

Marten cursed softly under his breath. But the distance was too great for more than minor x-ray damage. Those x-rays burnt out a point-defense cannon and two space marines who had disobeyed orders and remained on the surface.

"What were they doing out there?" Marten shouted.

"Boredom," said Omi.

"That's two casualties we shouldn't have taken."

"It will be a lesson to the others," Omi said.

"I want that other torpedo," Marten said. Two dead space marines. He had a feeling they were going to miss those two soldiers before this was through.

"The laser is ready," Osadar said.

"Kill it," Marten said.

The laser fired, and the enemy torpedo didn't jink out of the path of killing light. Maybe the blasts from the Zenos earlier had damaged a critical component. Whatever the case, they slagged the last torpedo of the first cyborg salvo.

-58-

Cassius read the shock trooper's report in his wardroom while lying on an acceleration couch. The writing style was simplistic, but certain insights impressed Cassius. For the next hour, he recorded his musings. Then he listened to the musings three times. Afterward, he began to implement a supplement to the invasion tactics of the initial landings.

Marten Kluge…if the impossible happened and the preman survived the asteroid-landings, he was going to have a grueling interview with the Homo sapien. There would be some life-lessons learned, maybe the last things this Marten Kluge would ever experience.

Deciding it was time to close that file and subject in his mind, Cassius concentrated on the approach to the asteroids. On more than one occasion, he'd likened his mind to a computer. He could close a file and open one at will, completely concentrating on the problem or subject at hand. When he closed all the mental files, he went to sleep.

After studying the probable attack sequence, Cassius went to sleep. He awoke six and-a-quarter-hours later to a klaxon. First showering, eating and donning his uniform, he hurried to the bridge. He seethed with impatience and kept clenching and unclenching his fists. This was the battle of his life. This would determine many things.

It was survival of the fittest in a war of extinction. Cassius barked a harsh laugh. Then he strode onto the bridge and entered his shell. He activated his holoimages and began to study the situation. At last, it was the time for truth.

-59-

"It's like a blizzard," Marten said in awe.

It was quiet in the command center as the people watched their screens. The *Spartacus* raced almost directly behind the asteroids, still catching up fast—although not as quickly as before. As seen from the meteor-ship, the first wave of Luna-launched missiles zoomed in at an oblique angle from the left.

Each missile was three times the size of a Zeno. Behind them came another wave, the giant Orion-ships and more missiles. Behind that were the majestic Doom Stars, two of them. The third Doom Star approached from a different angle.

"Look," said Nadia.

An equally thick blizzard of objects detached from the rear asteroids.

"They've gone hot," she said.

On the many screens, the cyborg-torpedoes turned from blue to red.

Time then passed in agonizing slowness, one hour, two. Before the third passed, a quarter of the Luna-launched missiles detonated.

They were x-ray missiles, one of the deadliest in space combat. Each missile's onboard AI targeted a single enemy craft. Then a thermonuclear warhead exploded. The mass of x-rays and gamma rays traveled up special targeting rods. Those rods concentrated the rays into a coherent beam that shot at the various targets. As the rods concentrated the x and gamma rays, the nuclear explosion obliterated its own missile and its various components. The shape-charged warhead ensured that the blast all went ahead, instead of in a ball of force in all directions. This protected the rearward missiles from friendly-fire damage.

"Eighty-three percent devastation," declared Osadar several minutes later.

Marten watched as torpedo after cyborg torpedo went from red, to blue and then often winked away. The x-rays destroyed many torpedoes, but not all of them. Those torpedoes—the surviving cyborg devices—now detonated. They were cruder than the x-ray missiles, and depended upon electromagnetic pulse and heat damage. The Highborn-launched objects were hardened against such attacks, but twenty-seven percent of them succumbed to the cyborg explosions.

Then lasers began to beam from the rearmost asteroids.

"No," Nadia whispered. "They'll destroy the remaining missiles."

"Don't count on it," Marten said.

"How can the Highborn stop it?" Nadia asked.

Her answer came two minutes later. The one-million kilometer-range ultra-lasers of the *Julius Caesar* and the *Genghis Khan* stabbed at the asteroids turrets.

"That's unbelievable," Nadia said.

Another ultra-heavy beam stabbed against the asteroids. It came from the *Gustavus Adolphus*.

The giant lasers took out enemy turret after enemy turret. But they couldn't take them out fast enough to keep the cyborg lasers from obliterating another eighteen percent of the x-ray missiles. Then those sleek objects came into range. There was another mass explosion of thermonuclear warheads. The x-rays and gamma rays targeted the many torpedo launch-sites and laser turrets on the rearmost asteroids.

For a few seconds, masses of lines stabbed on the various screens of the *Spartacus* command center. When the lines disappeared, the vast majority of the rearward-facing cyborg turrets were dead.

The expenditure of hardware and firepower left a pall of silence aboard the meteor-ship. There had never been anything like this in the Jupiter System, not in such quantity.

"What happens next?" asked Nadia.

Marten swallowed, and said quietly. "Now it's up to the Orion-ships."

-60-

In Attack-craft Seventeen that rode the Orion-ship Delta with countless other vessels, the klaxon wailed its alarm. There wasn't any need for the warning, as Captain Mune and his bionic soldiers were already strapped into their crash seats.

"This is going to be fun," the unseen pilot said, speaking through their headphones. She piloted Attack-craft Seventeen. If the big Orion-ship made it close enough to the asteroids, the attack-ship would detach with the others to attempt a landing.

Mune double-checked his straps. Then he went over his vacc-suit's seals and lastly he rechecked his pod of weaponry. The space inside the attack-craft was cramped, the air close and the heavy-Gs constant.

"I've giving you visual," the attack-craft pilot said.

A monitor above the prone couches snapped into life. It meant little to Captain Mune, just masses of stars. He missed Earth. He missed the normal gravity, the heat of the Sun on his skin and he missed the constant vigilance of guarding the most important man in the Solar System. But he was meant to serve in whatever capacity was most needed. Long ago, that had meant painful surgery and retraining with enhanced strength and speed. He'd taken a battery of tests once. It had satisfied highly suspicious people on his loyalty and willingness to serve.

"Here we go," the pilot said.

The Gs switched directions. To Mune, it felt as if a car sat on his chest, making breathing difficult.

The unseen, overly-cheery pilot of the attack-craft was an

unmodified human. Only the cargo was bionic.

Now the sudden thuds began again that meant nuclear bombs exploding as fuel. Their Orion mother-ship decelerated. If they didn't decelerate, they'd hit the asteroids too hard and crush the attack-craft.

"How long is this going to last?" asked one of the men.

Mune shrugged. He had no idea.

"Who decided the order of the advance?" asked another soldier.

"We live to serve," Mune said. It had become his creed, and he'd found comfort in it. Hawthorne was the only man he knew who could defeat the Highborn and now these genocidal cyborgs. To help Hawthorne and to save Earth, he'd volunteered for the mission.

"In case you're wondering," the pilot said into their headphones, "that little dot there is our destination."

A blue circle appeared around a dot fractionally brighter than the stars around it.

"If the Orion-ship is turned around so it can decelerate, how can we see the dot?" asked a soldier

"Rearward facing cameras," the pilot said. "Are there any other bright questions?"

A massive explosion occurred to the left in the screen. It filled the monitor with intense white light. Some of the soldiers near Mune shouted in alarm. He flinched, and to his surprise, he found himself trembling.

"What was that?" a soldier shouted.

"Scratch one of our Orion-ships, good buddies," the pilot said, her voice sounding strained for the first time.

"Lasers?" asked Mune.

"Not a chance," said the pilot, "not against an Orion blast-shield. That was a whale of a torpedo."

Another huge explosion and fiery white light filled the monitor.

The pilot cursed loudly in their headphones, letting them know it was another lost Orion-ship.

"We should have stayed on Earth," a soldier said.

"We serve here," said Mune. He wasn't aware of it, but his face was contorted into a horrible grimace.

"Give us just a few more minutes, you freaking machines," the pilot hissed.

The next few minutes saw blooms of orange explosions in the distance. There were stabbing red rays and a thick column of sparkling light. The small dot had expanded now into the greatest thing in the void, about something fist-sized as seen on the monitor.

"We're going to detach," the pilot said.

A sudden jolt caused Mune to shift heavily to his left.

"We did it!" the pilot whooped. "Now we have a chance. Are you boys ready?"

"Ready," Mune said hoarsely.

"Then hang on," the pilot said. "We're going in."

"Grim," said Omi.

Marten was bent forward in his seat. He had been watching the battle, with an elbow on a knee and his fist clenched. The cyborgs had destroyed two Orion-ships before the attack-craft could detach. Then attack-craft from four big Orion-ships spayed outward like shotgun pellets.

Omi's comment came from the fate of the four surviving Orion-ships. After launching their attack-craft, the big nuclear-bomb-powered vessels accelerated once again. They accelerated faster than at any time in the journey. A torpedo took out another one. But the three surviving ships crashed into asteroids.

"People piloted those," Marten whispered.

"Better than being captured by cyborgs and turned into one," said Omi.

Now the Orion-launched attack-craft decelerated, attempting to land and unload their soldiers. On too many asteroids, however, point-defense cannons opened up, and counter-missiles rose up to destroy the landing craft.

"It's all suicide," said Omi.

Even though he knew he should try to remain calm, Marten couldn't tear his eyes from the screen. The ultra-lasers from the Doom Stars still smashed into the asteroids. And now another mass wave of HB missiles came up.

Marten squinted. With an effort of will, he uncurled his fingers and moved toggles. He wanted to know what kind of missiles those were. The information startled him, although he knew it shouldn't. "Those hold Highborn commandoes," he whispered.

"Huh?" asked Omi.

"The next wave," said Marten, "the new missiles. They're filled with Highborn shock-troopers."

"Great. After that mass expenditure of cyborg-hardware, at least a few of them should get through to the asteroids."

Marten glanced sharply at Omi.

"Trouble?" asked the Korean.

Marten glared at the main screen. "The self-centered hypocrite, he planned for this."

"Who did?" asked Omi. "What are you talking about?"

"The order of attack," Marten said. "This is Grand Admiral Cassius's plan. Do you remember he berated me for slowing down?"

"Sure I remember."

"He engineered it this way," Marten said.

Omi gave him a blank look.

"He sent the Orion-ships in first to take the hits," Marten said. "He used them to absorb damage so his precious Highborn wouldn't take any scratches."

Omi's features hardened. "He was trying to use us."

"It's time we changed that," Marten said.

"How?"

"Yeah, that's going to be the trick," said Marten.

-62-

As Hawthorne looked up, small Colonel Manteuffel entered the underground Joho office. The officer wore a gun and a grim expression.

"Cone wishes to speak with you, sir," Manteuffel said.

"Have you enlisted the other officers yet?" asked Hawthorne.

"I have. But Cone, sir, she's angry, and I think more than a little worried." Manteuffel hesitated.

Hawthorne had been watching the space battle through the monitor on his desk. This was a cramped room, lacking windows because it was underground. The recycled air was too cold and felt too much like a morgue.

"In your estimation," Hawthorne said, "is Cone worried enough to do something rash?"

"I'm not a security expert, sir."

"You'd better become one, Colonel, and quickly."

"Why me, sir?" asked Manteuffel. "I still don't understand. I'm a cybertank expert."

These past days, Hawthorne had made some swift and critical security changes. Cone remained underground here in the Joho Command Bunker. But her people no longer guarded anything. In fact, they were no longer her people, as Hawthorne had stripped her of authority. Colonel Manteuffel was now the Chief of Hawthorne's Personal Security. Manteuffel's people were all higher-grade officers, and daily practiced at a firing range to gain needed proficiency.

"The easy answer is that I trust you," Hawthorne said.

263

"Because of what happened with the cybertank several years ago?"

"That's right," Hawthorne said. "You were with me in the bleak days. You risked everything then because you believed in me and in my plan. I want true believers around me, people I can implicitly trust, and who make wise decisions."

"I'll do my best, sir."

"What does Cone have to say to me?" asked Hawthorne.

"It's concerning the Free Earth Corps."

Hawthorne sat back, picking up a smooth metallic ball. Rolling it in his palm, he wondered what was the correct course of action. After watching the space battle and the destruction of the Orion-ships, he realized that Cassius was too clever for him. It wasn't only the order of the landings, but the use of the Doom Stars. It was obvious now that Cassius meant to stand back and beam the asteroids with the ultra-heavy lasers. The Grand Admiral wasn't going to risk his super-ships. The Fifth Fleet remained with the *Gustavus Adolphus*. If the battleships wished to fight, they'd have to close in and likely face destruction. If the battleships remained where they were, after the fight with the asteroids, those SU warships would be hostage to the Doom Star.

"I have to strike before Cassius does," Hawthorne said.

"Sir?" asked Manteuffel.

"But if I strike too soon, Cassius might decide to let the asteroids hit Earth."

"I'm not sure what you're talking about," Manteuffel said.

"No? Well, let Cone in. Then you stand in the corner over there and listen to our conversation. Afterward, I'm sure you'll understand. Oh, by the way, make sure she'd unarmed."

"Yes sir," Manteuffel said, saluting, striding for the door.

Ex-Security Specialist Cone entered the office with Manteuffel. She reminded Hawthorne of Blanche-Aster's bodyguard clone. Today, Cone had taken off her dark sunglasses. Her pale eyes seemed eerie, and her sharp features added to the affect. There was something frighteningly effective about Cone. It was the chief reason Hawthorne had originally selected her.

She sat in the chair across from the desk, her synthi-leather jacket crinkling.

Opening a lower drawer enough so he could see the shiny pistol there, Hawthorne wondered how good Manteuffel's pat-down had been. Cone was dangerous. Once more, Hawthorne missed Captain Mune. It had been a mistake letting him go on the mission. It had been a mistake sending all the bionic soldiers. Too many of them had died in the space-battle, never getting the chance to prove themselves as ground fighters.

"Earth-to-space traffic has increased again in the Highborn-controlled territories," Hawthorne said.

Cone nodded carefully.

"These liftoffs had little to do with the former farming habitats," Hawthorne said.

"The Highborn are fleeing Earth?" asked Cone.

First glancing at Manteuffel, Hawthorne asked, "How did you learn this?"

"I didn't. It's a guess."

"It's a good guess," Hawthorne said. "To the best of our knowledge, yes, this is the case. The Highborn are fleeing

Earth."

"It makes sense," said Cone.

"Perhaps," said Hawthorne. "It might also be a mistake on their part."

"Not if the asteroids hit Earth."

"No, obviously not then," Hawthorne said. "But let us suppose for the moment the asteroids don't hit Earth."

"In that case," said Cone, "with all the Highborn in space it's time to appeal to the Free Earth Corps left on Earth."

"Are you suggesting I give them all free pardons?" asked Hawthorne.

Cone shook her head.

"…Well?" asked Hawthorne. "What do you suggest?"

"Sir," said Cone, "I'm not sure it's in my best interest anymore to give you advice."

"And why would that be?" asked Hawthorne.

"You already know why."

Manteuffel took a step toward Cone.

Hawthorne ignored the colonel, watching Cone instead. "Suppose you tell me just the same."

"I've lost your trust," said Cone. "Now, if I give you advice that sounds too devious, your distrust of me will grow accordingly. It might lead me to the firing squad."

"This is nothing personal between us," Hawthorne said. "I just don't like jailors."

Cone pursed her lips. "You acted swiftly against me, sir. It was a lesson in commando and coup operations. If you're going to beat the Highborn that way, you'll to need to strike before they do. The Highborn are frighteningly good. But their arrogance is their weak point. They will know the perfect moment to strike, and act accordingly. You are gifted at these sorts of calculations. Try to think like a Highborn, see what they see, and then strike just a little too soon. In that manner, you might possibly catch them by surprise the first time. But you're only going to get one chance to surprise them. So you have to make it count."

"If you were attempting to change their allegiance, what would you offer the Free Earth Corps?"

"More than what they already have," said Cone. "Let them

keep their formations and give them governmental control of the areas they already possess."

"I'd have set up a competing government."

"You'll have gained allies and weakened the Highborn accordingly," said Cone.

"Why won't the Highborn simply bombard the planet themselves then?" Hawthorne asked.

"Because they'll have a greater task to complete," Cone said.

"Being?"

"The destruction of the Neptune and Saturn Systems," Cone said.

"I doubt they'd agree with you."

"They're realists. They'll have Mercury and most of Venus. Social Unity will have Earth, and the Planetary Union will control Mars."

"How would you approach the FEC people?"

Cone smiled coldly.

First setting the metal ball into a felt container, Hawthorne said, "I'm adjusting your position from ex-Security Specialist to FEC coordinator."

"Meaning what?"

Hawthorne pushed a scroll-pad across the desk. "Meaning you begin negotiations with the various FEC formations."

Tilting her head, Cone examined Hawthorne. Then she picked up the scroll-pad. "These numbers here only represent a quarter of my former people."

"Which I'm sure is more than you thought I'd give you," said Hawthorne.

"Yes," admitted Cone. "I expected to be shot."

The frankness of the admission startled Hawthorne. "I don't like to shoot useful people. I don't like to shoot anyone, but I particularly hate to waste someone like you. Will you accept the new position?"

"I don't have much choice."

"Give me a straight answer," said Hawthorne.

"Yes, I accept," said Cone.

Hawthorne nodded. He'd have to keep a close watch of her. He trusted Cone less now than before. "Do you have any questions?"

Cone shook her head.

"Good luck," said Hawthorne, standing. Cone stood too. They shook hands across the desk. She had a firm grip. Then the former Security Specialist took her leave.

Sighing, Hawthorne turned to Manteuffel. "That's the problem, Colonel. The truly effective people are always the most dangerous." He sank into his chair and turned back to the screen. "What do I do with the Fifth Fleet? I wish I knew the answer to that."

"Sir?"

"War isn't only about winning, but about winning the peace that comes afterward."

"Don't we first have to win the war before worrying about the peace?" asked Manteuffel.

"That's what makes this such a difficult decision. How you win the war—if you can—will determine much of the peace. For instance, if we destroy the asteroids but lose all our spaceships, it puts us at a severe disadvantage against the Highborn."

"What if we fail to use our spaceships well enough and the asteroids destroy life on Earth?" Manteuffel asked.

"Ah," said Hawthorne. "Now you're beginning to understand my dilemma. And that's what makes Cassius so dangerous. I think he's better at these calculations than anyone else is."

"Maybe what we need is luck, sir," Manteuffel said.

"Luck is for fools and madmen. No, what we need is to make the right decisions." Hawthorne stared at the monitor and began to rub his forehead. What should he do with the Fifth Fleet? He needed to decide soon, because no decision was still a decision. What should he do? Why couldn't he make his choice?

-64-

"Time's running out for Earth," Marten said.

Nadia sat beside him in a patrol boat, which was parked on the surface of the meteor-ship. Nadia was in the patrol boat's pilot's chair and wore an armored vacc-suit like everyone else. Her visor was open and her pretty features were strained.

As the space fighting continued, the asteroids reached the halfway point between Mars and Earth. All the commando missiles had either perished or disgorged their cargos. EMP blasts, hard radiation, x-rays, gamma rays, lasers—radio communications with others had become nearly impossible. Maybe as bad, the sensors picked up little more than harsh static.

"Are you ready?" Marten asked.

A red light flashed on Nadia's board. She groaned fearfully.

The patrol boat had a direct link to the *Spartacus's* controls. No one remained aboard the meteor-ship. They'd all crammed into the patrol boats that so far were still parked on the *Spartacus's* outer shell, on the side farthest from the asteroids. In the end, mass made the best shield against lasers and against the big cyborg torpedoes.

Marten adjusted the controls of his screen. Their targeted asteroid was ten kilometers in diameter. It was deeper in the field and thus partly shielded by bigger asteroids. It still had lasers turrets and now several torpedoes lifted from it, accelerating for the *Spartacus*.

"Osadar!" Marten shouted, using a tight-link to a different

patrol boat.

"I see them," Osadar said. "And I'm launching."

Even through the patrol boat, Marten felt the *Spartacus* shudder. It meant Zenos had blasted off the meteor-ship. The *Spartacus* decelerated, slowing its velocity as the asteroid loomed ever closer. The patrol boats still lacked enough thrust and fuel to decelerate hard enough to land. If the *Spartacus* died too soon....

"We should have decelerated before this," Nadia whispered.

"Not a chance," Marten said. "It would have left us exposed too long."

Behind him in the patrol boat, space marines rustled as they adjusted their armored suits. Each vacc-suit was composed of articulated metal and ceramic-plate armor. A rigid, biphase carbide-ceramic corselet protected the torso, while articulated plates of BPC covered the arms and legs. Weapons clacked, boots shuffled and men breathed too heavily.

Through the tight-link, Osadar cursed.

Marten studied his board. Another flock of torpedoes zoomed toward them from deeper in the asteroids. How many cyborgs had toiled like ants to achieve those launches? In Marten's opinion, there were simply too many asteroids to capture and redirect and too little time in which to do it.

"Light up the defenses," said Marten.

Osadar in her patrol boat controlled some of the meteor-ship's functions. Nadia controlled others and Omi the remaining aboard his patrol boat.

On his screen, Marten watched. The *Spartacus's* point-defense cannons began to adjust as they targeted torpedoes. Each fired depleted uranium pellets. In the background, Marten saw the Zenos' exhausts as the missiles sped at the torpedoes. Then a huge stabbing beam struck from a million-kilometers away. The beam hit a torpedo, destroying it.

"Highborn sensors must be better than ours," Osadar said.

Marten tried to swallow in a dry throat. This was the worst part—the approach to landing. He wished he were anywhere but here. The cyborgs were living murder. The number of asteroids—there were seventeen of them if you counted the two debris fields as two loosely-packed asteroids. Seventeen objects, each large enough to bring extinction to Earth. How were they supposed to deflect them in time?

Another torpedo disintegrated in the beam of the Highborn laser. Then a smaller cyborg missile exploded, filling the vacuum with a powerful electromagnetic pulse.

"I've lost visual," Omi said over the tight-link.

"I never should have brought you into this," Marten told Nadia.

She was too busy with her board to respond. Now a second ultra-heavy laser flashed to their aid.

At that moment, a terrific jolt shook everyone in the patrol boat.

"What happened?" Omi asked over the tight-link.

"Here comes another torpedo," Osadar said. "Prepare to detach."

"It's too soon," Omi said.

Then Marten saw it on his screen. A black-as-sin torpedo sped at the *Spartacus*. A big laser flashed near the torpedo, missing it. Three point-defense pellets hit, tearing holes but failing to stop the monstrosity. Then the torpedo went nova. Through the patrol boat's heavily-tinted window of ballistic glass, the intense flash hurt Marten's eyeballs and put splotches in his vision. The terrific jolt of the shock-blast made Marten's teeth rattle until he clamped them together. Twenty seconds later, a second explosion dwarfed the first. All around Marten, the boat's bulkheads rattled uncontrollably and groaned in metallic complaint.

Outside, a jagged and growing crack splintered the meteor-ship's shell. Oxygen sheeted upward as the inner ship spewed its precious air. A wobbling patrol boat fired thrusters, fighting to escape the *Spartacus's* destruction.

"Launch!" someone screamed.

In a daze, Marten saw Nadia. She slapped buttons. Then Gs thrust him lower into his crash-seat. They were lifting off the dying ship.

It was a Hell-ride to the asteroid. The patrol boat's auto-cannons fired constantly. Anti-missiles bloomed around them. And the lunar-like surface grew larger. Then a patrol boat to their left exploded.

Marten tried to open channels with the others. Because they'd lifted off the meteor-ship, he'd lost the tight-links and had to rely solely on radio transmissions. Harsh static played in his ears. With a shake of his head, Marten decided to ignore the others for now as he studied the growing asteroid. It had a crater-sized exhaust-port, which was a huge cavity making it like a massive cave. Near the port—

"Laser turret!" shouted Marten.

Whether the cyborgs had saved it as an ace card or maybe had made fast repairs was impossible to know. The critical thing was that a beam erupted from it, lancing straight at them.

Nadia yanked the controls. Gs forced everyone to the left as the patrol boat banked sharply. Decoy chaff spewed. The beam struck, and one of the stubby, wing-like projections disappeared in a slag of hot metal, taking two auto-cannons with it.

The beam lanced again, and now it cooked decoy chaff.

The last launch of a counter-missile made the patrol boat shudder. Blips on Marten's screen showed that other patrol-boats had fired missiles. For a moment, he heard Osadar's voice. The patrol boat banked hard in a different direction as Nadia ejected an electronic counter-measure pod. Its single purpose was to emit dummy patrol-boat signals.

The laser turret beamed again. The right side of their patrol boat turned red and some of that side melted away. Hot globs of metal cooked seven space marines in their armor.

Marten shouted obscenities as he struck his board in helpless rage.

Then a patrol-boat-launched missile exploded against the laser turret. The armored turret absorbed the effect as it lost mass. Two more hit as depleted uranium pellets hammered it, gouging and blowing away armor. As the beam stabbed again, taking out a counter-measure pod, a last missile destroyed the turret.

By now, the lunar-like surface filled half of Marten's screen. "There," he said, pointing at a computer-generated map with his stylus. "Is everyone seeing this?"

Like the others, Marten's visor was down and his HUD on. There were domes on the surface, three of them in a cluster. There were also many burnt turrets, slagged point-defense cannons and empty torpedo bays. As Osadar had once predicted, a long rail system had been laid on the surface. Some of the rail-line was twisted and melted in places. A Doom Star laser must have done that.

"Can we land?" asked Marten.

Nadia's gloved hands worked over the controls. "Maybe," she said. "The enemy laser took out our—"

"Don't give me excuses," Marten snapped. "Just get us down."

Nadia's silver-colored visor turned sharply toward him.

"Get us down, honey," he said. "But do it fast."

She turned back to her controls as the space marines in their crash-seats watched the window or the laser-opened section of the boat.

-66-

Marten used the last outer camera, turning it. Behind them, three patrol boats each burned a long exhaust plume. They each decelerated the last amount, which would hopefully allow them a soft landing.

"Nadia," he said.

"I don't dare push the engine any harder," she said, as she pointed at her board.

Marten saw it. The coils were overheating and in the danger zone, far in the red. The patrol boat's engine could easily explode. He computed their thrust and ran the probabilities of surviving a landing at this speed.

"You have to push it," he told Nadia. "Otherwise, none of us will survive the crash landing."

"I've spotted cyborgs," Osadar said over the com-link. As she spoke, her patrol boat's auto-cannons fired.

On the asteroid's surface appeared tiny bright lights.

"What's that?" Marten said.

Then his sensors picked up the objects. Shoulder-launched missiles zoomed at them.

Nadia punched a button. "That's the last of the decoy chaff," she said.

Marten couldn't tear his eyes off the screen. The missiles—two veered toward the chaff. The last hit them, exploded and the patrol boat had another new hole, with three more deaths, this time from shrapnel.

"Push the engine to its limit!" Marten shouted. His eyes were glued to the screen, watching for more bright dots on the

274

surface. Had Osadar's auto-cannons killed those cyborgs?

The patrol boat began to vibrate, and the vibration increased steadily. So did the size of the asteroid, at least their view of it. The other asteroids were kilometers away now.

Then their ten-kilometer asteroid, the one designated as E, became their world. Marten viewed lunar-like hills, ancient impact craters and stardust. How long had this stellar object orbited Saturn before the cyborgs had ripped it out of orbit? The vibrating became unbearable, making it impossible to focus his eyes. Marten didn't know it, but if there had been air in the main compartment, his eardrums would have burst from the sound. But because vacuum didn't carry sound waves, those noises never affected him or any of the space marines.

The hills loomed bigger and they became more jagged. The patrol boat vibrated madly so Marten had to grip his seat. Then a single mountain became everything, and Nadia achieved the impossible. Instead of crashing against the hill, she landed their wounded boat and shut off the tortured engine. Stardust billowed upward, surrounding them, and then it slowly began to settle.

They'd reached Asteroid E. Now they had to kill the cyborgs, find the asteroid's controls and engage its engines if they could.

-67-

Climbing down the hill was hard work in the negligible gravity. The hundreds of hours of practice on the *Spartacus's* outer shell gave Marten and the others their only chance. If they jumped too high, they would reach the asteroid's escape velocity and simply keep drifting out into space.

The space marines were tethered together in groups of three, the line attached to their belts. Nadia was tethered to Marten, and Kleon was attached to Nadia.

"You have one task," Marten told Kleon, a space marine from Europa. "Keep Nadia alive." She'd tried to complain, but Marten hadn't listened.

Most of the space marines carried IMLs, the Infantry Missile Launcher. Each of those held a new and improved Cognitive missile. The rest carried gyroc rifles or lugged extra ammunition and missiles. The armored vacc-suits were just like those they'd used in the Jovian System. None of the suits had thruster-packs. The weight saved allowed each marine to carry more ammo.

The survivors reformed into three platoons and moved down the hill. They looked like big insects, an infestation of bipedal cockroaches with weapons ready and helmet sensors sweeping everywhere.

"Overhead," said Nadia. She carried a bigger sensor-unit, one of Marten's tactical improvements.

Marten looked where Nadia pointed. Three patrol boats zoomed surface-ward for a landing.

"They're bunched too close together," Marten said.

"No!" shouted Nadia.

From the other side of their hill, bright objects accelerated up at the patrol boats.

"Cyborgs!" a space marine shouted.

The bright objects were shoulder-launched missiles. A flock of them zoomed at the patrol boats. Dots of light appeared on the patrol boats, auto-cannons firing. Then the missile-flock struck the lead patrol boat. It quit decelerating as the thrusters abruptly stopped, and it seemed to leap ahead of the last two boats. Its heading would take it past the asteroid.

Marten closed his eyes. When he opened them, he said, "Up the hill and over. We have to take out the cyborgs."

"I killed them," Omi said from his patrol boat. He must have meant with auto-cannon fire.

Marten stared at the last two boats coming in. They floated now, it seemed, and they came toward him.

"Follow my signal down," Nadia said, as she adjusted the controls on her box.

"Roger," said Omi.

"Three boat-loads of space marines," Marten said. "I hope it's enough to conquer this asteroid."

Then the last patrol boats off the Meteor-ship *Spartacus* began to settle at the bottom of their hill.

-68-

The three domes were in the center of a shallow crater two kilometers in diameter. Marten had taken pictures of it during their descent. Ringing the crater were burnt-out laser turrets. The torpedo bays were between the turrets and domes.

Marten, Nadia and Kleon crawled up the outer slope of the crater. Above them shined the stars and the bleakness of the Great Dark. Marten fought the impulse to jump to the top of the slope. Instead, he continued to walk in the soft stardust. At each footstep, dust slowly puffed upward.

"We should have brought thruster-packs," said Kleon.

"We have what we have," Marten said. "Now lower your transmission strength. We don't want the cyborgs monitoring us."

Soon, Marten flattened himself on the slope. He eased up the final distance and peered over the crater. Ancient rocks, a few boulders and smaller pitted craters dotted the plain before them. Across the plain stood the three low domes. The domes were situated more on the Earth-facing side of Asteroid E. Therefore, they were out of the line-of-sight of the Doom Stars' lasers.

Nadia crawled beside Marten as she set down her sensor box.

"Turn that on, and the cyborgs are going to know we're here," said Kleon, through the com-link.

"They already know," said Marten. "Ping them," he told Nadia. "And be ready to slide down the slope."

First adjusting the sensor-box, Nadia flipped a switch. Then she crouched lower down the slope, with her arms reaching upward to the box.

Marten used his helmet's zoom feature. The three domes seemed to leap forward. There were rotating antenna dishes on top of the domes. Now ports slid open on the sides. There were flashes from those ports.

"Slide down!" shouted Marten. He pushed himself and wriggled madly down the slope.

Nadia pulled the box toward her.

"Leave it!" Marten roared.

She obeyed, and the three of them crawled. Seconds later, the top of the slope exploded. Kleon flew backward, and the line tethered between him and Nadia snapped tight, jerking her off her feet after him. A second later, Marten tumbled after Nadia. Marten clawed the ground. He was terrified they'd all be knocked upward and that they'd drift into space. As the line jerked again, pulling him off the ground, Marten gripped the edge of a boulder. His hands tightened and he strained to keep his grip. It slipped. He bellowed and clawed for a purchase, barely finding one. With grim determination, he clung to the boulder. In a moment, the intense pressure pulling him spaceward ceased. He looked up. Kleon was obviously dead, his helmet shattered.

"Cut him loose," Marten said.

Nadia floated above him, with Kleon's corpse even higher than she was.

"Nadia," Marten said as calmly as he could. "You have to cut him loose. Kleon is dead."

With a groan, she drew a vibroblade from her belt and cut the tether.

"Good," Marten said. He began to drag her down to the surface.

"We've got cyborgs coming!" shouted Omi.

"Stay here," Marten told Nadia. He barely remembered to unhook his tether to her. Then he crawled up the slope.

On either side of his former position, space marines were crouched at the crater lip. Marten eased into position twenty meters from where the cyborg missile had struck. Using his helmet's zoom, Marten scanned the domes and then the plain between them and him. His gut clenched as he saw twenty, no, twenty-three cyborgs charging toward them. The cyborgs used their trademark glide, moving four to five times faster in the nearly weightless environment than a human could do.

"Twenty-three of the aliens," Omi said.

"Twenty-three cyborgs," corrected Osadar.

"Sure," Omi said.

Marten studied the enemy. Each cyborg carried a bulky backpack, with a line from it to his laser-carbine. Twenty-three of them were coming. Under normal circumstances, a cyborg was worth ten space marines. They were therefore badly outnumbered using that counting system.

More space marines crawled to the lip of the slope. Many settled their IMLs, aiming at the approaching cyborgs.

"Hold your fire," Marten said.

"Isn't this the perfect opportunity?" asked a space marine. "Our Cognitive missiles can easily take them out at this range."

"Wrong," Marten said. "The distance is far enough to give the cyborgs time to sight and fire their lasers, taking down our missiles."

"They can't be that good," the space marine said.

"They are that good," said Omi.

"Beside," Marten said. "They're sure to have other anti-missile ammunition in the domes. Think of the domes as heavy support stations."

"Do we run for it?" asked Osadar.

"Negative," Marten said. "We use our missiles, just not right away."

"Ports are opening in the domes," Omi called.

Marten waited two heartbeats before he shouted, "Down, down, down, crawl down from the lip!"

Most of the space marines listened. They had learned in a hard school that Marten Kluge had good instincts. Unfortunately, not all of them listened in time. Small cyborg missiles from the domes blew away two marines, and sent another two space-borne.

"Help us!" shouted a marine, as he failed his arms and legs, slowly drifting higher after the corpse that had jerked him into orbit. Tied to him was another flailing marine.

"Use filament line!" Marten shouted. "Shoot it to him. Hurry!"

Before anyone could uncoil filament line, another missile streaked into view, exploding and killing the two drifting marines.

"We're dead men!" a marine wailed through the headphones.

"Shut up," Marten ordered. "We're far from dead. If we're going to save Earth, we have to keep our heads, marine."

"How do you defeat the invincible?" another space marine asked.

"First, by realizing that no one is invincible," Marten said. "Second, by playing to our strengths. Omi, I want you set up fire-control teams. When you see those missiles coming, use antipersonnel gyroc rounds."

"Got it," said Omi, "shrapnel defense."

"Right," said Marten, afraid the cyborgs might send airburst missiles and end the fight before it could really get started.

"Ports are opening in the domes," said Osadar. "They're launching more missiles."

281

Omi raised his gyroc rifle. So did twenty other marines. "Look at your HUD's," Omi said. "Fire into your vector—now!"

Rocket-propelled shells leapt out of the gyroc rifles. A nanosecond later, the shells' mini-engines ignited. They flew at the cyborg missiles, exploded and sprayed antipersonnel shrapnel into the missiles' flight paths. Some of the cyborg missiles exploded. Others crashed onto their side of the crater-slope, hitting like duds.

During that time, the twenty-three cyborgs gliding toward them rapidly closed the distance. Now red laser beams began to flash. A space marine visor slagged into a glob of ballistic glass. In other places on the lip, stardust melted into a dirty-colored glaze.

"Ready your Cognitive missiles," Marten said, who lay out-of-sight of the cyborgs on his side of the slope.

"We're losing too many men," a space marine cried.

"We'll lose more before this is through," Marten said. "Now do as I say." He crawled to the crater-lip and peered onto the plain. A cyborg about three hundred meters away swung his head around and lifted the carbine into position. Marten slammed himself prone onto the stardust. It puffed around him. He flipped a switch, heard the ping of lock-on, pulled the trigger and felt the blast of the missile whooshing away. Immediately, he ducked behind the crater-lip. A beam cut through the ground where he'd just been.

On top of the slope, other space marines were doing likewise.

"Now switch to gyrocs," Marten said. He counted to five, and crawled back up. Many cyborgs lay sprawled in death. Too many—more than a dozen—kept gliding toward the slope, fast.

The surviving space marines opened up with gyroc fire, while lasers stabbed back. More space marines died. All the cyborgs then perished under the withering volley.

"Get under cover," said Marten.

Most of the space marines knew what to do now. Three more didn't, and they paid with their lives as missiles from the domes killed them.

"We're losing too many men," Omi said a few moments

later as he lay beside Marten.

Marten's air-conditioner-unit blew cold against his face. He was breathing hard, and he saw the still corpses on their side of the slope.

"We can't win like this," Omi added.

Nadia crawled near, entering into the two-way with them. "We have to reach the domes," she said. "Otherwise...."

"We'll never reach the domes on our own," Omi said. "The cyborg missiles will cut us down if we try to charge across the plain. We need space support."

"And how do we get that?" asked Nadia.

"We don't," said Marten.

"Then we're finished," said Omi.

"No," Marten said. "There's another way."

"What is it?" asked Omi.

Marten told him.

It took an hour to reach the huge exhaust crater.

"I don't like this," Osadar said, while standing beside Marten. They looked down at the massive cavity that sank into the guts of the asteroid. "All the cyborgs have to do is turn on the engine and burn us to death."

"That's right," said Marten.

"Why won't they it?" Osadar asked.

"We're taking a risk," Marten said. "But it's certain death to march across the crater-plain to the domes. Our only other choice is to reenter the patrol boats and fly our way to the domes."

"That would be suicide," Osadar said.

"Can you think of anything better than this then?"

"I cannot."

"Should we do nothing?" Marten asked.

"That is not logical."

"So this is the only rational choice we have," Marten said.

"We never really had a chance," Osadar said.

"Yeah," said Marten. "I've heard you say that for a long time now, but we're still here. These big rocks are still heading for Earth. So I can't dither all day talking to you. Are you coming?"

The tall cyborg took her time answering. Finally, her voice crackled over his headphones. "Lead the way, Marten Kluge."

Gripping his gyroc rifle, Marten began the descent into the massive exhaust-port.

It was dark inside the long exhaust tunnel that extended deep into the asteroid. Space marines used infrared to see where they were going. The sides of the rocky surfaces were coated with high-grade photon-fiber.

"I don't like this," Omi said.

The photon-fiber produced an odd *bounce* in the radio transmissions. It sounded to Marten as if Omi were a million kilometers away.

"If you feel a thrum," Osadar said, "it will mean that death is seconds away."

"Thank you for the update," Marten said. "Now let's move, people. Since we don't have to worry about flying off the asteroid anymore, I want all of you to run. Watch your heads, though. I don't want any of you to crack your helmet."

Suiting words to action, Marten began to take long, loping leaps. He glanced back, and saw the many red forms that indicated space marines. Then he concentrated on what he was doing. The exhaust tunnel was huge, like an immense cavern. When the mighty fusion engine had been going, it must have sent an exhaust plume an easy one hundred kilometers behind the asteroid.

"What was that?" Omi asked.

Marten had felt the sudden vibration too. Did that mean the cyborgs had turned on the fusion core?

"Faster," he said. And now Marten moved. He'd spacewalked early as a lad on the Sun-Works Factory. It was something that felt natural. Osadar kept up with him and so did

Omi and a few other space marines. The others fell back, as they weren't as good at this.

Back in the Jovian System fifteen months ago, he'd studied Carme Moon for weeks. Marten recalled its exhaust-port and tube. There had been repair hatches in that asteroid's exhaust-port. He was hoping for the same thing in this one, as his plan was predicated upon it.

The vibration in the tunnel grew.

"They must be starting up the fusion core," Osadar said.

"We know they can't start it right away," Marten said. "And it's likely been off for a long time. I'm counting on that."

"Hope is futile once they turn on the core," Osadar said.

The exhaust-tube changed now. It was no longer simply bored-out asteroid with photon-fiber coating. The chamber possessed the same polymer as one used in a warship's exhaust-tubes.

"What if the repair hatches are locked?" asked Osadar.

"Keep a sharp lookout," Marten said. He'd been using his HUD and reading a Carme Moon file.

"There!" Omi shouted. "I see a hatch."

The growing vibration made Marten leap harder. If the fusion core started while Nadia and the slower space marines were still in the tube….

Osadar landed near the repair hatch. She walked to and tried it, but the hatch remained closed.

A space marine cursed profusely. "There's no way she's strong enough to force that hatch. The thing was made to take the pressure of—"

"I didn't see this," Osadar said. She turned something in the hatch.

On Marten's infrared HUD, the hatch opened into blazing red heat.

"We have to pass the coils," Osadar told them. "They're on and it's hot in there."

"Don't talk," Marten said. "Go, go, go!"

72

"Cyborgs!" a space marine shouted.

Marten threw himself onto the floor amid the huge coils that glowed red with energy. There were rows upon rows of the giant coils. Each stood six meters high and was thirteen meters across. They pulsed with power and emitted intense heat.

Sweat trickled down Marten's neck as his air-conditioning unit thrummed overtime. There was screaming in his headphones, and coils blew apart.

Marten crawled as sweat slid from his back and across his ribs. He fired his weapon. So did space marines near him. The flashing gyroc rounds blew apart cyborgs, smashed coils and spilled laser-fluid from the bulky packs on the enemies' backs. Electrical discharges made it nearly impossible to see and jammed the helmet's sensors. In this vast coil-chamber, the Cognitive missiles were useless. It was head-to-head fighting with gyroc rifles, vibroblades and shock grenades.

Using his elbows and knees, Marten kept crawling across the floor. Communications were jammed in this chamber. It was just training, warrior-instinct and fighting skills.

A cyborg stood up and aimed its laser at Marten. As the cyborg did, a jagged piece of shrapnel cut into its chest-plate. The titanium-reinforced arms and legs went rigid. The carbine slowly dropped to the floor.

From his prone position, Marten pumped three APEX rounds into the cyborg, blowing it backward each time. Then he crawled to the fused machine-man and felt his nape hairs stand on end as the thing's head turned toward him. Marten shoved his rifle barrel against the head and blew it to pieces.

This was a horrible place to fight. A cyborg could be hiding behind any of a hundred giant coils. The baking heat, the lack of sensor-data and the frightening bolts writhing everywhere, even into the ceiling so tiles and chunks of plasti-steel rained down, made this a nightmare. Snatches of words or phrases occasionally broke through the static in his headphones.

"Advance!" shouted Marten.

There wasn't anything refined or clever about the tactics. It was like two wrestlers grunting on the floor, trying to choke the other one to death using brute strength.

A cyborg jumped before Marten. Its laser-beam burned a good meter above his prone body. There was a scream in Marten's headphones. He had no idea what had just happened. He didn't really care. He just lifted his gyroc and fired. But the cyborg jumped fast behind a coil. The gyroc round whooshed past the thing's former position and exploded against a coil farther back. The coil emitted bolts like sparks, and Marten rolled wildly out of the way, barely avoiding the energy-bolts as they hit the floor like lightening from some god's hand.

Gripping his rifle with manic strength, Marten cursed and jumped to his feet. Always do the unexpected with cyborgs. It was something he'd learned the hard way. They were logic wizards, and had incredible computing ability. Marten leaped at the coil the cyborg had used. The cyborg took that moment to roll around the edge, aim its carbine at the floor where Marten would have been, and adjusted with insect-like speed as it spotted Marten coming down from a high leap.

Three APEX (Armor-Piercing EXplosive) shells spewed from the rifle. They penetrated the cyborg's armor and blasted the thing apart. As it tumbled backward, Marten landed, pumping three more rounds into it. Through bitter lessons, Marten had learned to make triple-certain a cyborg was in pieces before he declared it dead.

Terrible explosions began to occur throughout the coil chamber. There didn't seem to be any rationality as to why one area blew and another didn't. Space marines were fried. Cyborgs melted.

"Get out here!" Marten shouted. "Get outside!"

He had no idea if anyone heard him. As his suit's air-conditioner unit thrummed, as the chamber became an intense red wall of heat and flame, Marten loped in almost zero gravity. The sweat poured down his body now, and the air burned down his throat, almost too hot to breathe.

He spied a heavy door. A cyborg set up a plasma-cannon there. Other charging space marines shot madly, and the cyborg went down.

The vacc-suit's functions were approaching critical. Marten blinked, and blinked again as sweat stung his eyes. He wasn't sure what happened next. There were gaps in his consciousness. Then he loped over the dead cyborg and shoved his shoulder against the heavy door, slowly opening it to another compartment in the asteroid's vast engine complex.

73

The coil chamber was murder, a gauntlet of death that halved the number of Jovian space marines. Marten and Omi dragged out heat-fatigued men from the hellhole. Then coils in the middle of the chamber began to explode.

"Shut the door," said Osadar.

"Nadia!" cried Marten. "I haven't seen Nadia."

Osadar shoved Marten away as more coils erupted in the vast chamber. With cyborg strength and speed, she slammed the heavy door shut and engaged the locks.

Marten's last vision was of a space marine on the floor, raising his arm for aid and the door closing on his last hope. Then explosions caused the hall to tremble, and the door buckled and seemed as if it would blow into them. But it held.

As if in a dream, Marten turned toward Osadar. He was aware of the rifle in his hands, and he contemplated aiming it at the cyborg.

"We would have all died if Osadar hadn't done that," Omi said.

Marten's tongue was thick in his mouth. "Nadia," he whispered. Had that been her raising her arm to plead with him to help her? He never should have brought her to this nightmare. He—

"Sound off," Omi said through the headphones. "Let's see who made it. First Platoon, begin."

"Thebes here," said the Group-Leader.

"Jason."

"Cleon."

"Marten, where are you?"

That was Nadia's voice. Marten's arms went limp as he looked around. "Nadia," he said, using his override function. "Raise your arm."

In the back of a group of space marines, Nadia raised her arm. Her vacc-suit was black and one of the lines had torn free. But she was alive.

As the others continued to sound off, Marten waded through a group of marines and clutched Nadia's gloved hand.

"You're alive," he said.

She nodded her helmeted head.

"What do we do now?" A half moment later, someone strong turned Marten around. The armored speaker was tall. It was Osadar. "What do we do now?" she asked again.

Marten had to think about it. Nadia was alive. To keep her alive, he had to kill all the cyborgs. "Right," he said. "We made it through the exhaust. Now its time to come out of here like the Japanese did to us. Do you remember?"

"Japan?" asked Osadar.

"That's right," Marten said. "You weren't with us then. It was Stick and Turbo during the Japan Campaign."

"What do we do here on Asteroid E?" asked Osadar.

"We make like rats," Marten said. Nadia was alive. It was time to keep fighting. "Right," Marten said. "Here's the next step."

74

Everyone checked his weapons, taking out damaged parts and fitting in replacement pieces. Then they reloaded as Omi paired depleted squads together. Sometimes only one member of a squad had survived. This was gruesome, bitter work.

"We've made it this far," Marten told them. "And we've killed cyborgs. There can't be that many left."

He had no idea if that was true or not, but it was good for morale if the men believed it. They'd lost over half the space marines who had made it onto the asteroid. If you counted all the space marines and ship personnel who had made the journey from Jupiter, less than a third had survived this far.

They used stairwells, avoiding lifts, and climbed for the domes. These were the veterans from the cyborg assault in the Jovian System. They'd fought the melded machine-men before and survived, some of them more than once. They'd absorbed Marten's refined tactics and had trained religiously before and during the trip here. Each knew what to do. Few panicked anymore, and each had his own method for dealing with the aliens from Neptune, in this instance from Saturn, too.

Marten signaled by pumping a gloved fist. He stood near the hatch that by the specs in his HUD said led into the first dome. Then he raised his index finger and made a circular motion. These were Highborn-taught signals that Marten had learned in his shock trooper days in the Sun-Works Factory.

Omi and three other space marines crouched nearby. Each gripped a grenade cluster.

Marten hardened his resolve, braced himself against Osadar

and shoved open the hatch. Then Omi and the others lunged forward, hurling their grenade clusters into the room. Flashes occurred, one right after the other.

With a ragged cry, Marten sprang through, his gyroc firing. The room held screens, monitors and a vast computer array. There were clear bubbles with layered tissues of programmed brain-mass in them. Marten counted seven. All around were computer-banks, cryogenic-units and medical facilities. Tubes pulsed with red liquid. Green gels shifted in the bubbles and tiny rays beamed back and forth from odd antenna.

Marten's trigger finger moved four times before his brain registered the thought: *This is a Web-Mind*. Even as he realized it, the bubbles shattered and brain-mass exploded outward. Then other space marines added to the mayhem, blowing away computer banks and medical units.

It was a glorious moment, and it made Marten grin harshly. He grinned even as he realized that this moment had been dearly paid for in human blood and agony. He hoped the vile mass of brain-tissue felt pain. He hoped it hurt like hell.

-75-

Marten, Nadia and Omi sat in a control room in the third dome. Dead cyborgs lay scattered on the floor. A window showed the asteroid's bleak surface of crater-plain and the star-field above. The room held breathable air.

With a hiss, Marten unsealed his helmet, rotated it off the locks and lifted it from his head. The room reeked of burnt electronics. But Marten didn't care. He scratched his nose and rubbed tired eyes.

Nadia and Omi acted similarly. Nadia had dark circles around her eyes. A cut on Omi's forehead dripped blood into one of his brows.

"We did it," Omi whispered. "We took our asteroid."

"Maybe," Marten said. "We haven't checked everywhere. There may be some cyborgs hiding."

Omi shook his head. "They attacked when it might have been better for them to wait for us. I think they've thrown every cyborg into the fray."

Nadia stood up, moved near and half-collapsed into Marten's arms. He kissed her salty lips as she wept silently.

"I thought I was going to die," she whispered.

"We all did," said Marten. He hugged her. It was difficult with her armored vacc-suit. Their pieces clanged against each other. He was overjoyed she was alive. If she'd died…what would have been the point of all this?

"It's time," a tinny voice crackled from each of their helmet's headphones.

Marten lifted a hand-unit. "What was that?" he asked.

"The fusion core is online," said Osadar.

"What about the damaged coils?" Marten asked.

"There are some secondary banks," said Osadar. "I've already rerouted."

"You should send a message to the Highborn," Nadia said. "Otherwise, they might bombard the asteroid if we move it without first announcing it."

"I don't agree," said Marten. "By moving the asteroid, we show we won. And I don't like the idea about broadcasting our victory."

"Why not?" asked Omi.

"Maybe the cyborgs will send torpedoes from the other asteroids," Marten said.

"They'll more likely do that once we're moving," Omi said.

"But at least the asteroid will be moving by then," said Marten. "That's the point."

"What do we do after that?" asked Omi. "Ride the asteroid to its new heading?"

"You know the answer," Marten said. "Once our asteroid is safely headed to a new destination, we climb into the patrol boats and storm another asteroid."

"We don't have enough space marines left for that," Omi said. "Look how many we lost capturing this one."

"We'll have to coordinate with others," Marten said.

"Has anyone else won?" asked Omi.

"If we did it, Highborn should have been able to," Marten said.

"We tackled a small asteroid," Nadia said. "They hit the big ones."

"It is time," Osadar radioed.

Desperately wanting nothing more than to sleep, Marten stood up just the same. Then he approached the asteroid's primary controls. Mankind's future rested on their ability to decipher cyborg routing.

Captain Mune witnessed it from a nearby asteroid, the one designated as D. Grand Admiral Cassius watched from the *Julius Caesar* as he sat in his shell, examining holoimages. Supreme Commander Hawthorne saw it on the screens deep in the Joho Mountains.

Asteroid E rotated as huge jets flared. Seventeen minutes later, a flicker appeared in the giant, crater-sized exhaust-port. Then a vast plume erupted from the asteroid. It lengthened to over one hundred kilometers. With the thrust, Asteroid E so very slowly began to change its heading and velocity. Given enough time on this new vector, it would glide past the Earth and no longer impact with the third planet from the Sun.

Unfortunately, it was only one asteroid out of seventeen, and time was fast running out.

As the battle raged on the asteroids speeding for Earth, Hawthorne accepted a fateful call from Cone.

She was in the Japanese Home Islands, Highborn-controlled territory. During these past few days, Cone and her teams had made contact with Free Earth Corps people. Now she called with interesting information, and spoke via a tight-link security beam to Hawthorne in his office in the Joho Command Bunker.

***

CONE: I'm afraid I must keep this short, sir. My expert has established the fact of nearly constant enemy surveillance of my whereabouts and communications. The FEC soldiers and their loyalty monitors are nervous.

HAWTHORNE: Are you in immediate jeopardy?

CONE: Every minute I'm here. The islands are heavily militarized, full of military police and secret service personnel. The first runs loyalty checks on the soldiers and the second searches for spies and saboteurs.

HAWTHORNE: Perhaps we should try to establish contact with the security services.

CONE: The FEC soldiers don't recommend it.

HAWTHORNE: Why not?

CONE: Sir, my expert has assured me I'm clean of listening devices—for the moment. But the tails will close in soon and likely frisk us more thoroughly. This will be my only call from the islands where I can guarantee a tight link.

HAWTHORNE: I understand. What do you have for me?

CONE: As I said, the FEC soldiers are nervous. Everything is in turmoil and the Highborn have left Earth as we surmised. I can fully substantiate that now. The soldiers I've spoken to are certain the asteroids will strike the planet. Why otherwise would the Highborn have completely evacuated Earth?

HAWTHORNE: And these soldiers are willing to turn?

CONE: (pauses) They're sensitive to terminology. Perhaps it's their long association with the super soldiers. They bristle at the idea of disloyalty to the Highborn or any idea that they've betrayed Earth through their hostilities.

HAWTHORNE: What is it they think they've done?

CONE: Become the best soldiers in the world.

HAWTHORNE: Do they think they're better than the Highborn?

CONE: They're proud of their military achievements and constantly point to their victories in North America.

HAWTHORNE: Don't they realize that space superiority and Highborn insertions into critical battles allowed them these victories?

CONE: They're proud, sir. And they think of these victories as coming from their sweat, blood and military acumen.

HAWTHORNE: So they don't understand that they're traitors to everything they used to hold dear?

CONE: Enemy propaganda has brainwashed their thinking.

HAWTHORNE: I think I understand. The ancient French Foreign Legion used to achieve the same results with their recruits.

CONE: I'm unfamiliar with this legion.

HAWTHORNE: It doesn't matter now. You're on a tight schedule and wish to let me know something critical, I presume.

CONE: I've found several colonels willing to meet with you, sir.

HAWTHORNE: I'd hoped to speak with generals and preferably with a field marshal or two.

CONE: There are no FEC generals or field marshals.

HAWTHORNE: Before they left the planet, did the

298

Highborn order them shot?

CONE: It is my understanding that there have never been any FEC generals or field marshals.

HAWTHORNE: Explain that.

CONE: It is simple political cunning, maybe military cunning, too. Highborn officers command all division-level or larger FEC formations. Therefore, the highest slot a man can aspire to is colonel.

HAWTHORNE: What about staff officers?

CONE: Excuse me, sir?

HAWTHORNE: Surely, there must be chief of staffs of general grade.

CONE: No man is higher-ranked than colonel. That's been made clear to me on several occasions.

HAWTHORNE: Who controls the various FEC divisions and armies now that the Highborn have fled?

CONE: As I said, sir, with the Highborn evacuation there's great unrest among the FEC soldiers.

HAWTHORNE: That will make everything much harder. I'd hoped to win a charismatic general to our side and have him bring over other FEC personnel.

CONE: I read your brief, sir. And I think I've found your man.

HAWTHORNE: A colonel?

CONE: Two colonels, sir. One is Colonel McLeod of the Twenty-second Jump-Jet Battalion. He's the most highly decorated FEC soldier on Earth. Originally, he's from Australian Sector. He's a fire-breather, as they say here. And he's angry at the Highborn.

HAWTHORNE: That they fled Earth at this critical hour?

CONE: That they failed to take him. He spoke about his spilled blood on three different continents. Colonel McLeod believes himself betrayed.

HAWTHORNE: (laughs grimly) Is he delusional?

CONE: He's enraged at the idea of dying helplessly, and he wants revenge. I think Colonel McLeod may be your man, sir.

HAWTHORNE: You spoke about another colonel.

CONE: I'll have to cut this short, sir. My expert says security people are already cordoning off the area.

HAWTHORNE: Yes, yes, hurry then.

CONE: Colonel Naga is a panzer officer, a tank-man. He enlisted after the Japan Campaign and he has driven from the tip of South America to Hudson Bay in Manitoba Sector. His men are fanatically loyal to him. He believes himself worthy of higher command, and he hungers for power. If you offered him political control of North or South America, I believe you'd win him over.

HAWTHORNE: These two are the only—

CONE: Excuse me, sir. I must run or risk execution. Are you willing to meet these two? They insist on a face-to-face meeting.

HAWTHORNE: Where?

CONE: I suggest along the coast of Korean Sector.

HAWTHORNE: Yes, agreed. Where exactly do you suggest?

CONE: (panting) On the Pyongyang beachhead at twelve hundred hours. We will arrive via hovercraft.

HAWTHORNE: I'll be waiting. Hawthorne out.

-78-

Early next morning, Hawthorne left the Joho Mountains in a two-seater attack-jet. The pilot flew nap-of-the-Earth, roaring over trees, valleys and low hills. At times, Hawthorne twisted around and watched the highest leaves rustle from the jet's wash. The trip was tiring, with everything soon blurring below him.

The Highborn laser satellites had headed out to space to do battle with the approaching asteroids. But Hawthorne wasn't taking any chances. He trusted the Highborn to act with ruthless cunning, keeping something in low orbit to hit when the right moment came.

Toward the end of the trip as they flashed over the Liaotung Mountains, Hawthorne pressed his nose against the canopy's glass. Orange flowers blossomed on the hillsides. They were beautiful. The idea that cyborg-sent asteroids would soon crash into Earth and burn everything in an end-of-the-world holocaust made him nauseous. That he'd had anything to do with originally summoning these aliens made it a hundred times worse. Were the Highborn to blame for that? They're the ones who'd started the rebellion.

Highborn, cyborgs, plunging asteroids—madness gripped the Solar System. Now he was rushing to meet traitors to humanity, outlaws who had cast their lot with mankind's nightmare. Had the fools only realized now that they were bootlicking slaves to genetic supremacists? How could he trust such people?

Hawthorne sat back as the jet whooshed over a mountain,

301

zooming toward a river in the distance. He couldn't trust them. He didn't even trust Cone. Maybe the only people he'd ever really trusted were Captain Mune and his bionic soldiers. Most of them were already dead from trying to storm stellar death.

Gazing up at the sky, Hawthorne wondered how they fared. He wondered if Mune was even alive.

"We're near our destination, sir," the pilot said.

"Yes, thank you," Hawthorne said. Two FEC colonels, two traitors, two ambitious climbers wanted to speak with him face-to-face. For the sake of Earth, for the sake of humanity's future, he would deal with them. But if he ever trusted them, he hoped he'd die a crushing death beneath the steel treads of a cybertank.

Waves lapped onto the sandy beach, throwing up swirling foam and a tangled cluster of rubber-like plants.

Hawthorne stood on a grassy dune ninety meters back from the beach. Beside him, Manteuffel spoke into a com-unit. Snipers with scopes lay everywhere and out of sight. Jump-jets waited ten kilometers inland, ready to come screaming into action, firing cannons and missiles.

"There, sir," Manteuffel said, pointing.

Hawthorne nodded. He'd been watching the speck out at sea. It had steadily grown larger. The speck represented a hovercraft, which had left Japan and sped up the southern side of the Korean Peninsula.

"You're too exposed here, sir," Manteuffel said.

"I sent Cone, not suicide troops," Hawthorne said.

"The Highborn have used hypnotically-motivated soldiers before. This may be a trap."

Hawthorne glanced at the worried Manteuffel. The wind tugged at the small officer's tunic and he kept brushing his watering, narrowed eyes. For a fact, it was chilly on the beach. The salty tang, however, was a joy compared to the recycled air of the Joho Complex. It was even better-smelling as he considered that this might be the last time he'd ever see the ocean.

"Caution is wise," Hawthorne told Manteuffel. "But sometimes too much fear becomes paralyzing. The end of the world is near. Taking a chance or two...." Hawthorne shrugged.

"I've never known you as a fatalist, sir."

"The war has worn me down," Hawthorne said. He considered that, and he turned to Manteuffel. "Do you know that Napoleon said a general only has a few years for fighting? Then his time is over. Napoleon went on to prove his adage, showing in his later years that his fine grasp of the art of war had slipped. I wonder sometimes if my time has passed."

"If not you, who sir?" asked Manteuffel.

Hawthorne smiled sadly. "It would be a nice fantasy to think myself irreplaceable. Many leaders have thought of themselves like that. They were each wrong. If I pass, another will rise up to take my place."

Manteuffel frowned thoughtfully.

Soon, the hovercraft roared toward the beach. It was a loud vehicle, protected by composite armor and outfitted with a cannon, two torpedo-launchers and three heavy machine-gun mounts. A battalion flag snapped from the top of a long antenna, while slanted glass windows showed where the hovercraft's operator stayed. The machine roared toward them as it blew spray and foam across the water.

"It's heading straight at us, sir," Manteuffel shouted in warning.

Hawthorne's legs tightened. He wanted to hurl himself to the grass. But that would be too undignified. Then he wondered if he'd become too proud. Wouldn't it be wiser to throw himself prone and survive, then keep his pride, stand and die? But if this were a test of his mettle and the outcome would determine if the colonels betrayed their masters—

Before Hawthorne could convince himself to hit the ground, the hovercraft rose up on a cushion of air and then whined less as it settled onto the sand. A few moments later, a hatch opened and three people jumped onto the sand.

They trudged toward him. Hawthorne recognized Cone in her black jacket and sunglasses. The big man beside her must be McLeod. He had wild red hair, a mass of freckles and likely possessed a Viking heritage. Even in combat fatigues, the man looked as if he should be captaining a dragon-boat of old. The other one must be Colonel Naga. He was slim, with black hair that almost seemed purple. Dangling from his neck was a pair of goggles.

Soon, Cone raised her hand and shouted a greeting.

Hawthorne waited, watching as McLeod and Naga glanced at each other. Cone spoke to them. McLeod laughed loudly and nodded. Naga glanced back at the hovercraft.

"Stay here," Hawthorne said.

"Sir, I don't recommend this," Manteuffel said.

As he strode down the grassy dune, Hawthorne smiled to himself. Those had been Captain Mune's favorite words. It brought a pang of nostalgia. Now there had been a bodyguard.

The sand crunched under the soles of his shoes. In moments, he met the trio in the middle of the sandy beach.

Cone introduced him, and then introduced the colonels to Hawthorne. Holding out his hand, Hawthorne shook each of theirs. McLeod had a crushing grip, and seemed compelled to try to break bones by squeezing. The blue eyes showed exactly what McLeod was doing: sizing up the Supreme Commander of Social Unity. Naga bowed slightly at the waist. He had dark hooded eyes like a snake, revealing nothing of his thoughts.

They spoke a few pleasantries. Then McLeod glanced around. "I don't see any soldiers. Do you think you can take Colonel Naga and me?"

"More importantly," Hawthorne said, "do you think we can take Earth back from the Highborn?"

McLeod put his ham-like hands on his hips and laughed. "What happened in North and South America, there's your answer, man."

"If you don't think we can defeat the Highborn, why are you here?" Hawthorne asked.

"The Highborn left me to die," McLeod said. "Me! There isn't a better soldier on the planet. I left pieces of my flesh on three different continents for them. You'd think they'd be grateful."

"Are you grateful when a dog injures itself protecting your house?"

"You watch your mouth, Hawthorne." Colonel McLeod glanced around, and he smirked openly at Hawthorne. "Two steps and I can snap your neck before any of your hidden security teams can do squat."

"What would that gain you?" asked Hawthorne.

"It would be as good a way to die as any," McLeod said.

"What would be a good way to live?" asked Hawthorne.

"If the asteroids strike Earth," Colonel Naga said in a quiet but authoritative voice, "what does any of this matter?"

"That we die free," Hawthorne said.

"I am free," said Naga.

Hawthorne shook his head. "You two are just a pair of subhumans to the most bigoted individuals the Earth has ever seen. To the Highborn, you are dogs. That they've spent your blood recklessly ought to prove it to you."

"Your soldiers have died in greater numbers than ours," McLeod said.

"Our soldiers have died to keep their freedom and their planet. What have your men died for?"

"Glory," said McLeod.

"How does glory feed your family?" asked Hawthorne. "How does glory keep humanity free?"

"The Highborn have deserted us," Colonel Naga told McLeod.

"They're highhanded blokes, no doubt about that," McLeod said, scowling. "I'd like to stick it in their arses before I'm burned to a crisp. What do you have in mind, Supreme Commander?"

"That you stand with us against them," Hawthorne said. "They're highhanded, as you said. They're arrogant and spit on all of us. I'm tired of it, and I suspect you're tired of it, too."

"You are said to possess the entire FEC roster," Naga said. "Political Harmony Corps desires to march each of us before a brick wall and shoot us."

"I've de-fanged Political Harmony Corps," Hawthorne said. "If you join us, I'll delete the lists."

"…And?" asked Naga.

"And the Free Earth Corps can keep the territories it has conquered," Hawthorne said. "I'm also willing to recognize you as the highest authority in North America."

"I'd want South America," McLeod said. "There are some pretty women in those sectors."

"Can each of you sway his men?" asked Hawthorne.

306

McLeod snapped his meaty fingers. Naga made another faint bow.

"What about other officers, other colonels?" Hawthorne asked.

"There is much anger," Naga said. "But there is also much fear. How do you propose to defeat the Highborn?"

"I'm not proposing anything fancy," Hawthorne said. "But I am offering you the chance to rejoin Social Unity and help us kill the genetic supremacists who dare to act like gods among us."

"They left me to die," McLeod said. "I can't ever forget that. I don't care a whit about Social Unity or your brotherhood of humanity propaganda. But I do want to kill the Highborn and teach them their mistake. They shouldn't have abandoned Earth or the soldiers who fought so long and hard for them."

"What guarantees do you have that I will gain North America?" Naga asked quietly.

"My word," said Hawthorne.

"A word easily broken to those you consider traitors," Naga said.

"Did you see me flee when you drove the hovercraft at me?" asked Hawthorne.

"You stood your ground like a soldier," McLeod said begrudgingly.

"What is your point?" asked Naga.

"A man is a man, and he keeps his word."

"Quaintly stated," Naga said. "But it does have validity. Yes, I am ready to fight the Highborn. But there are others in FEC who will not join our unity."

"We've our work cut out for us," Hawthorne said. "You two gentlemen are the kernel toward uniting the Free Earth Corps and Social Unity. Therefore, you two should reap the lion's share of the reward."

"Will the Earth survive?" asked Naga.

Hawthorne glanced up at the clouds. So did the others. "That is still being decided," Hawthorne said.

-80-

Aboard the *Julius Caesar*, Grand Admiral Cassius seethed with pride and elation. With a victorious shout, he leaped from his command shell.

Highborn officers glanced at him. Their eyes radiated intensity as their muscled chests swelled and their biceps repeatedly flexed, making their uniformed sleeves ripple.

"We are the Highborn!" Cassius shouted, slapping his thick chest. "From primordial days, to antiquity, to medieval times, to the Age of Reason—all the way to our modern era, none have possessed our greatness. We crush those who dare to take a stand against us." As he spoke, Cassius raised his large right hand and curled his fingers into a fist, shaking it and snarling another savage laugh.

"The premen proved too puny for us," Cassius told his officers. "Therefore, the universe threw up a tougher challenge—the cyborgs. They are hideous creatures, as much machine as flesh, coldly rational and soulless. Their powered strength almost matches our reckless vitality. But they lack our iron will, our relentless need to dominate. Thinking circuitry tireless, they have forgotten that an exalted spirit can fire a warrior to divine acts of glory."

"Look!" roared Cassius, pointing at his holoimages. "Marvel at what our strength has achieved in such a short time."

The other Highborn rose to their feet. Like kingly lions, they approached the expanded holoimages. They grinned and laughed aggressively.

Cassius put his hands on his hips and exuded in the achievement of the first phase. His heart swelled with thumping pride. Did the cyborgs think to smash the jewel of Earth? Well, they would have to think again.

Seventeen asteroids or debris-clusters appeared as holoimages. The rearmost five asteroids showed something else—incredibly long exhaust plumes that disappeared into the bridge's bulkheads.

"We attacked five asteroids," Cassius said. "We successfully stormed each and conquered each, ripping them out of weak titanium hands."

"The cyborgs are filth," a Highborn said.

"They are genocidal freaks," said a second.

"We have put our boots on their armored torsos," spoke a third.

"What about the other twelve asteroids?" another asked. "We still have to deal with them."

Everyone on the bridge turned and stared at the speaker, an older Beta Highborn, a mere seven feet tall. The Beta Highborn scowled as he hunched his head. Stubbornly, he said, "Those twelve are still headed for Earth. And they will soon hit the planet."

"Ah, Marcus Maximus," said Cassius.

The other Highborn chuckled. *Maximus* was Marcus's nickname, a slur on his inferior size and status. Cassius kept him on the bridge as a reminder that first there had been the Beta Highborn, a weaker subset of a superior breed. Marcus worked hard to maintain his rank, and he provided moments of amusement such as this because he lacked the raw power of a completed Highborn.

"Five isn't even one third of the asteroid-strike," Marcus said.

"Tell me, *Maximus*, what waits in our bays?"

Marcus Maximus's head hunched just a little more as his scowl deepened, putting lines in his rugged features. "The bays hold armored shuttles, Grand Admiral," Marcus said.

"And?" prompted Cassius.

"In the shuttles await Highborn commandoes."

Cassius grinned. The five long plumes showed that on each

captured asteroid the fusion cores worked. The plan moved according to schedule.

At that moment, a red flash winked among the holoimages.

"Back to your stations," Cassius said. "We have a fight to finish."

As the others returned to their posts, Cassius strode to his shell and reentered it, strapping in. He opened channels, having recognizing the call sign of Admiral Gaius. The Admiral's holoimage appeared, showing his white uniform, Red Galaxy Medal and the short bill of his cap low over his eyes.

"There's possible trouble," Gaius said.

Cassius raised his eyebrows.

"The preman on D have monitored signals from the other asteroids," said Gaius, "from the cyborg-controlled rocks."

"And these cyborg rocks show...what?" asked Cassius.

"Interior explosions," Gaius said, "likely of the fusion cores."

The fierce joy and exaltation drained from Cassius.

"Given their mass and nearness to Earth," Gaius said, "it will take many outer explosions to nudge those asteroids off course."

Cassius thoughts were in turmoil and now flashed from item to item. Perhaps there had been a miscalculation. Or maybe the sequencing of the accelerating asteroids—he snapped forward. "Which captured asteroid first employed the cyborg-engines?"

"...I believe it was Asteroid E," Gaius said.

"The Jovians," whispered Cassius. His eyes narrowed. Marten Kluge led them, the ex-shock trooper.

"Do you suspect treachery?" asked Gaius.

Cassius stabbed a button. "Attention, Admiral Gaius of the *Genghis Khan*, Admiral Octavian of the *Gustavus Adolphus* and Vice-Admiral Mandela of the SU Fifth Fleet, report at once for a four-way."

CASSIUS: By destroying each asteroid's fusion core, the cyborgs have locked their rocks on a collision course for Earth. Fear obviously motivates them, as they recognize our ability to storm and capture the individual asteroids. They have sabotaged our ability to reroute the remainder of the planet wreckers.

OCTAVIAN: This means their asteroids cannot deviate from their course.

CASSIUS: Your tone indicates you believe that is beneficial to us.

OCTAVIAN: Yes! They can no longer maneuver in any fashion.

CASSIUS: At this late date, that is a limited asset.

OCTAVIAN: Yet it is something we must take into account. Like a good judo expert, we must use their maneuvers against them.

CASSIUS: (shaking his head) Time now operates against us. We shall therefore bore straight into their formation, obliterate all offensive capabilities and storm each asteroid. Afterward, we shall use nuclear pulse propulsion to deflect the planet wreckers from Earth.

MANDELA: Please forgive the interruption, Grand Admiral. But what do these landings gain us now? Earlier, we landed to take over the controls and reroute the asteroid through their own motive power.

GAIUS: Do not waste our time stating the obvious, preman.

MANDELA: I-I object to that term, Admiral.

CASSIUS: (to Gaius) *Preman* is a pejorative word and benefits none of us here. We shall need every vessel and nuclear weapon in our arsenals. Vice-Admiral Mandela, we must clear each asteroid in order to place precisely what will now be nuclear pulse propulsion, as I've stated. Some asteroids may also contain more nuclear bombs, which we need to find. What I now need from you, are the warheads from every one of your remaining missiles. They will be more beneficial to us as propulsion units than in their limited combat capabilities as SU weaponry.

MANDELA: That will only leave us with our lasers, which are shorter-ranged than yours. How, therefore, do you propose that we—

CASSIUS: We lack the time to engage in debating rituals. Our object remains the same. The methods have changed slightly. Perhaps you are unused to this, Vice-Admiral, but we Highborn adjust to new situations with fantastic speed. It is one of our many superiorities. The *Julius Caesar* will lead the attack. After shuttling us the warheads, the Fifth Fleet will follow in the rear, keeping a Doom Star between each of its ships and the enemy. Admirals, are there any questions?

MANDELA: I would like to point out—

CASSIUS: I'm sorry, *Vice*-Admiral, I was speaking to the Admirals of the Doom Stars. You already have your orders. Now remain silent until we have configured the exact attack sequence. Well, Highborn, do you have anything further to add?

GAIUS: We're wasting time. We must attack.

OCTAVIAN: Attack!

CASSIUS: It shall be so.

-82-

Cassis gave the orders. The mighty *Julius Caesar* began to accelerate toward the asteroids. Behind it by several thousand kilometers followed the *Genghis Khan* and now the *Adolphus Gustavus*, which had matched velocity and heading with its fellow Doom Stars. Farther behind came the two battleships and missile-ship comprising the SU Fifth Fleet.

Cassius used his time configuring shuttle attack sequencing. It was an elementary tactical problem. He needed to obliterate whatever offensive space-weaponry the cyborgs had managed to keep after the first phase. Then he needed to bring the Doom Stars in close, decelerate and launch the shuttles in a wave assault. The less time the shuttles spent in open space, the less chance any surviving cyborg weaponry had in destroying them. Highborn were precious, a limited commodity in the sea of premen and growing cyborg populations. After a short but intense flight, the shuttles would land and disgorge battleoid-armored Highborn. Cassius had studied the data of the first-phase and now configured optimal combat ratios in order to sweep each asteroid as quickly as possible. He also read critical reports, refining tactical procedures versus cyborg infantry.

While halfway to the asteroids, the chief bridge officer spoke up. "There's a message from Asteroid E, Your Excellency."

Cassius clicked pause on a battle report. The nature of the asteroid-strike—its suicidal quality—seemed to have affected the cyborgs troops. According to several accounts, the cyborgs

313

used what he had come to mentally term as *banzai charges* to try to kill the invaders before they could establish themselves on the asteroids.

While blinking, Cassius shut his interest on the tactics of asteroid capturing. He concentrated on the officer's words. Asteroid E…. "Is it Marten Kluge calling?" he asked.

"I don't know the speaker's name, Grand Admiral."

Cassius scowled.

"All premen look alike to me," the chief bridge officer explained. His name was Sulla. Three red chevrons braided his right sleeve. He oiled his face and exuded a bright intensity— what Highborn termed a warrior's *glow* or *shine*. Sulla was an open Ultraist, believing in premen extermination. The Ultraists spoke about purity to the Race, an elimination of the premen infection. They worried about the possible seepage of the weak emotions of mercy, kindness and humility from too much contact with the bleating subhumans.

Sulla told Cassius, "I find it difficult to distinguish male premen from the females. They are each equally soft and both exhibit extreme submissiveness in a superior's presence."

"Inability to distinguish premen can lead to possible misjudgment," Cassius said. "You must retrain yourself and learn the art."

"You might as well ask me to distinguish one rabbit from the next," Sulla said.

"I have not *asked*," said Cassius in a dangerous tone.

Sulla's oiled features became taut. Curtly, he inclined his head. "Is there a mnemonic trick to this *art*?"

"Indeed," said Cassius. "Search for an obvious defect such as an abnormally large nose, a crinkled forehead or ears canted at a right angle. Such defects abound among the subhumans, often pointing to the genetic weaknesses in them. Despite these faults, it is critical to be able to tell important premen apart."

"*Important* premen, Your Excellency?"

"Do not let your zealousness confuse the issue. Despite their puny size and stunted intellects, some of them like this Kluge have rabid tendencies. They bite at the most inopportune times. Consider, even a fly can distract a Highborn driving a vehicle enough to cause an accident."

314

"Such a Highborn deserves death," Sulla said. "It weeds out the weak and thereby purifies the Race."

"Pray you are never ill among your Ultraist brethren," Cassius said. "Now connect me with the speaker."

A glowering Sulla complied.

Before Cassius appeared a bristle-haired preman with stubborn features. The Grand Admiral recognized Marten Kluge. As a holoimage, the preman stared at him with insolence.

"I thought you might want to know," Marten said. "The lead asteroids are rotating."

"You found this out how?" asked Cassius.

"Just as you would," Marten said, "through sensors."

"Insolence," hissed Sulla. Several other Highborn turned from their boards to watch the exchange.

Hiding his irritation with Kluge and his bridge-crew, Cassius said, "It was my understanding that the cyborgs had dismantled each asteroid's fusion core."

"So that's what was happening," Marten said. "Nadia read some strange sensor—"

"If the cores have been dismantled," Cassius said, "how are the asteroids managing this rotation?"

"I have no idea," Marten said. "In fact, it doesn't matter how, just that it's happening."

"You should punish the preman," Sulla said.

Cassius muted the holoimage and cast a cold eye on Sulla. This was a delicate balancing act. One must never accede to an inferior's demands. Yet he couldn't let Kluge speak to him this way. The bridge-crew observed, and they reported almost everything in time to others.

"You must learn that premen are tools," Cassius said. "Ultraist creed would deprive us of these tools at this critical juncture in the war."

"We must live or die on our own abilities," Sulla said. "To rely on others implies weakness in our own strength."

Cassius laughed and shook his head, making Sulla bristle. "You wear a battleoid-suit into combat. It amplifies your strength. Likewise, you marshal weaker premen into a force to multiply power. Our strength allows us to do this. Yet you are

315

correct about Kluge. He has irritated me once too often. I will capture and strenuously retrain him so the preman learns his place."

"Better to kill him," Sulla said.

"I would rather make him suffer," Cassius said, "and turn a rebellious tool into an efficient instrument. Now attend to your tasks." Not waiting to see if Sulla obeyed him, Cassius switched off mute. He asked Kluge, "In your estimation, why are the asteroids rotating?"

"I don't know for sure. But it's my guess that most of the enemy lasers and torpedo-bays are aimed primarily in one direction. Those in the back were aimed back. Those in front—"

"Were aimed in front," Cassius finished. Despite his insolence, the preman was clever. This was going to be a bigger fight than he'd anticipated.

"The rotation shows me they don't like your Doom Stars coming in," Marten added.

Trust a preman to state the obvious. Hmm. He needed to increase the assault forces, to use the troops already landed on the first five asteroids. "Are any of your patrol boats operational?" Cassius asked.

An evasive look swept over Kluge's features. "They're pretty beat up," he said.

How crude their attempts to dissemble. Premen were like children in their simplicity. "You must board your least damaged boat and await my signal."

"I not sure we have enough space marines left to take another asteroid," Marten said.

Sulla slapped his panel.

Cassius refused to let either Sulla or Kluge irritate him further. Still, it was unimaginable that a subhuman should speak to him this way, and in front of his bridge-crew. Premen had endless examples of Highborn superiority and should know by now how to snap to obedience at the slightest order. Kluge—when the time came, he would retrain the subhuman harshly.

"You will join in the assault or face punishment," Cassius said.

316

Marten glanced away, and there were muffled sounds. Likely, someone off-screen spoke to the preman. When Marten faced him again, a hooded look had transformed the subhuman's features. The cleverness had taken an ugly turn, giving Kluge the look of a liar.

"We await your orders," Marten said.

Cassius bared his teeth. The blatant subterfuge didn't fool him. But there would be time enough to deal with Kluge. Now he needed to concentrate on the rotating asteroids. It appeared as if he was going to have to fight his way to the Saturn-launched planet wreckers. He'd have to fight and guard his shuttles in order to keep Highborn causalities to a minimum.

Asteroid E continued to accelerate out of the asteroid-pack. In the control room of the first dome, Marten watched Nadia at her sensor board.

Osadar stepped away from her station to stand beside Marten. Despite the fusion-generated power blasting out of the crater-sized exhaust-port, the G-forces were slight. The asteroid's mass saw to that.

"Logically, we are in danger," Osadar said.

"From the Highborn or the cyborgs?" asked Marten.

"...Both," said Osadar.

"We don't have the people or the hardware to take another asteroid," Marten said. "But we might be able to hold onto the one we have. What do you think is going to happen next?"

"The most logical move," Osadar said. "The cyborgs will beam our dome, destroying our controls and possibly disabling our fusion core."

"Maybe," said Marten. He was still thinking about the Grand Admiral. The Highborn frightened him. There was something grimly effective about Cassius. The Highborn possessed a driving force that had managed to radiate through the communications.

"As a Web-Mind," Osadar said, "I would beam this asteroid into submission."

"Marten," Nadia said. Her voice was thick with worry. "The cyborgs are beaming—"

Marten shoulders tightened. Was he about to die? Was Osadar correct?

318

"—The cyborgs are beaming the Doom Stars," Nadia finished saying.

Marten hurried to Nadia's board. The captured asteroids, the five, accelerated at a gentle angle away from the tight formation of the remaining twelve. That had exposed the inner asteroids, making them the rearmost ones now. The debris-fields acted as shields for some of them. From other asteroids with a line-of-sight shot, it seemed as if a hundred lasers lanced out, striking the lead Doom Star, the *Julius Caesar*. The vast warship was ahead of the other two by one thousand kilometers. It used a debris-field as a shield from four asteroids, boring in toward the others like a sonic drill. Marten knew why. The *Julius Caesar* wanted to launch its shuttles from close range.

"Where its shielding cloud?" asked Marten. He didn't know why Cassius had refrained from normal space-combat procedures.

"The battle is over," Osadar said in gloom. "The Doom Star lacks even the slightest particle shield, and it has inexplicably forgotten to spray any gels or crystals. How could the Highborn be so reckless as to charge the asteroids like that?"

"Look," Nadia said. "The Highborn are striking back." She adjusted her controls. "The wattage expended by the ultra-laser—it's amazing."

For the next thirty seconds, Marten, Osadar and Nadia watched the cyborgs pour concentrated laser-fire against the *Julius Caesar*. Impossibly, the outer armor held. It should have already melted in spots.

"What's going on?" Marten finally asked.

Osadar's head swiveled with cyborg speed. "Run an analysis please."

"On what?" a bewildered Nadia asked.

"On the composition of the *Julius Caesar's* outer plating," Osadar said.

Nadia's fingers clicked on her board. She frowned at the readings and finally looked up. "This doesn't make sense."

"What doesn't?" asked Marten.

"The plating…it's like collapsed star matter," Nadia said. "I've never seen anything like it."

-84-

From his command shell aboard the *Julius Caesar*, Grand Admiral Cassius rapped out orders. It was hard to shout over the thrum of the fusion core and the beaming ultra-laser. Every time the laser fired, the thrum increased to an ear-piercing whine.

That was the secret to the long-range laser. Power, massive amounts of power pumped through the system. To gain that power, one needed large engines and coils. It was why each Doom Star was so vast. Frankly, he thought the cyborgs should have installed ultra-lasers on their asteroids. But that would have taken much longer than installing regular combat beams. And there was secret technology needed for the one-million-kilometer-ranged lasers.

Cassius studied the holoimages. He clapped his hands over his ears—the whine, the noise penetrated his shell's buffering. The laser shot from the holoimage of the *Julius Caesar*. It struck against Asteroid C, down into a deeper than usual impact-crater. The wide beam lighted on the cyborg turret there. The array of focusing mirrors, pumping station, coil-chambers and armored-plating heated to intolerable levels. At the same time, the turret's beam fired through the Highborn ultra-laser, producing a strange radiance of wavering color. Then one mirror melted into a molten lump, dripping onto the lunar-like surface. Gas began to radiate into a feeble cloud. Before the turret slagged into an indecipherable mound, the Highborn laser retargeted elsewhere, having destroyed its prey.

The battle had turned into a maelstrom of beams, torpedoes

and cyborg troop-pods. The enemy was trying to recapture the five asteroids. It surprised Cassius the cyborgs had saved so much weaponry and not employed it during the first phase of the battle. But it wasn't going to save the aliens, this desperate fighting. The cyborg lasers struck his collapsium-coated ship, the only one in the Highborn fleet. It was their fatal error—one he'd worked to achieve. Given this window of opportunity, Cassius continued to strike.

The ultra-powerful beam from each Doom Star destroyed one enemy laser-turret after another. Most kills took less than a minute. More time was taken retargeting. Though Highborn efficiency, Cassius destroyed the enemy's offensive capabilities. It was one of the reasons he'd driven straight into their vitals. A laser beam increased its deadliness the shorter its range. So this close the million-kilometer-ranged laser became an annihilating beam of fearsome destructiveness.

Yet there was a risk. Not even collapsium could long sustain the concentrated attack of a hundred lasers. The breakthrough technology had been difficult to make and was incredibly dense. The plating on the *Julius Caesar* was only a micro-micron thick, but it had greater mass than the normal six-hundred-meter thick particle shield of a *Zhukov*-class Battleship. The electrons of an atom had been collapsed on the nuclei so the atoms were compressed. The atoms touched, producing a substance that made lead in comparison seem like a sponge.

The *Julius Caesar* rotated slightly every several seconds, timing its firing of the giant laser. No enemy beam remained on one spot long. Even so, the collapsium weakened under the prolonged mass-attack. The plating grew red and then black in places. The blackness thickened so it appeared as a light-absorbing spot of nullity. During that time, the Doom Stars beamed with immunity, destroying whatever the lasers touched. Then cyborg lasers began to slip through the weakened collapsium. It wasn't a complete breakthrough, but occasional beams firing through null-spots. For those seconds, the various beams burned into the composite armor underneath. Once through that, the coherent-light struck highly-polished reflex plating. The initial bounce off the reflex gave the *Julius*

Caesar yet more time. The ultra-lasers continued to rave with annihilation.

Then the impossible occurred.

"Your Excellency," Sulla told Cassius. "There's damage to the forward coil-banks. I'm also reporting strikes in the number five shuttle-bay."

Cassius absorbed the message as he glared at the holoimages before him. Those images swirled in a kaleidoscope of movement. It seemed as if space between the Doom Stars and the asteroids was alive with life, with mechanical corpuscles, many containing a deadly virus of gun-toting death. There were beams, torpedoes, counter-missiles, point-defense-shot depleted-uranium pellets, energized sand clouds, hot plasma globules and cyborg troop-pods.

"Enemy pods are gaining on our five asteroids!" Sulla shouted.

Images and words washed over Cassius's senses, and they would have surely swamped a lesser personage. A ruthless adherence to his victory conditions guided Cassius and helped him see the correct solution in moments of crisis.

"I see the troop-pods," Cassius said, speaking in a calm voice. It was one of his powers to be able to do so at a time like this. "Continue with the laser-turret destruction."

The *Julius Caesar* rotated slightly, beamed, destroyed, retargeted, rotated again and shot its laser at yet another hapless turret. Cassius thought to himself that it was hard to defeat advanced technology married to Highborn valor and resolution. The collapsium with the ultra-laser…it spelled victory.

"The enemy lasers are retargeting, Your Excellency!"

Cassius shifted in his shell. He'd hoped the cyborgs weren't that smart or quick. All he needed was another ten minutes to slag every enemy turret in sight. He'd deal later with the asteroids hiding behind the debris-cluster. The *Genghis Khan* and the *Gustavus Adolphus* had remained well behind the *Julius Caesar* for a reason. It was a calculated risk bringing those Doom Stars so near the enemy. Their armor could not long sustain the enemy lasers at this range. If they were to defend themselves, they would need to pump out prismatic crystals and heavy lead-additive gels. But if they did that, they would be unable to fire their lasers, which he needed in order to finish the fight. The cyborgs might well cripple the *Julius Caesar* otherwise.

Tilting his head, studying the data, Cassius knew that this was the moment of decision. This is what made a commander into a legend or turned him into a loser. The weight of the decision pressed upon Cassius as the squeeze to his heart made his wide face pale. Forty-three percent of the enemy laser-turrets had already been destroyed. Did he gamble with the heart of Highborn power? Every second he hesitated was fraught with risk. He parted his lips to issue the order to spray the protective clouds.

"No," he whispered.

This was the fatal moment of time, of the Solar System. The asteroids represented Earth's death. Earth was the great industrial basin. With it and the Sun-Works Factory, the Highborn could out-produce the cyborgs. Without Earth, it became a grim possibility that the cyborgs would out-build them. The cyborgs would then likely send a vast stream of material in a deadly war of attrition the Highborn couldn't win.

The decision tested him. Cassius knew that. Bold words were meaningless now. It was just his naked soul riding on the outcome of battle.

With effort, he tore his mind from the possibilities and forced himself to take a deep breath. Then he exhaled as hard as he could, expelling the air from his lungs. This time, he sucked air so oxygen seeped to the farthest reaches of his tissues, and he held his breath.

"I am Grand Admiral Cassius of the Highborn," he whispered, letting the breath go. Color returned to his cheeks. Once more, he studied the holoimages, wondering what the next few minutes would bring.

"Here they come!" shouted Nadia.

Marten stood behind her. He wore his armored vacc-suit. Behind him, the dome was packed with space marines in theirs suits gripping weaponry.

The mass-meter of Nadia's board indicated shuttle-sized vessels. Five had made it through the blizzard of spewing lasers and radioactive death to reach Asteroid E. Five cyborg troop-pods!

"They're heading straight for us," Nadia said.

Marten saw them on her board, oval-shaped vessels coming nearer and nearer.

Nadia twisted around and looked up at Marten. "If those five troop-pods are full of cyborgs, we're badly outnumbered."

"I know," Marten whispered, as he hefted his gyroc rifle. They were going to face more cyborgs. There was no way, by no stretch of the imagination and hard fighting, that his space marines could defeat five troop-pods of cyborgs. The trick, he'd learned long ago, was to change the rules. A barehanded man facing a cyborg had no chance. A man toting a gun versus a carbine-carrying cyborg would lose almost every time, but there was a possibility of winning. A man encased in a tank against a tank-driving cyborg would up his odds tenfold.

"Now," Marten whispered. "Send it now."

On the board, the five troop-pods began their approach to landing. They drifted over the crater and neared the three domes. All the asteroid's laser-turrets were destroyed. Marten might have sent out men with Cognitive missiles, but the troop-pods had weaponry to take out such a force.

Nadia pressed a switch on her board. It sent a weak signal, a three-sequence pulse.

Marten turned to the space marines. "This is it, boys. It is do or die time again." He raised the gyroc rifle over his head. "Death to the cyborgs."

Metallic sounds were made as the space marines raised their gyrocs and IMLs. Then they roared as one," Death to the cyborgs!" Afterward, visors clicked shut and armored suits clanged as the men headed for the airlocks.

-86-

Osadar Di received the three-pulse signal. She sat at the controls of the least damaged patrol boat. The Jovian spacecraft had never been designed as a space-marine shuttle. That was a secondary purpose. The patrol boats were space-attack craft. Jovian military theory called for them to fight in three-boat formations.

When Nadia had first picked up the approaching troop-pods on her sensors, Marten had made a quick decision. Osadar and a few others had re-crossed the crater-plain and returned to the patrol boats. The men had scourged the more damaged boats for the remaining cannon shells and missiles. These they'd loaded into the good boat.

"Strap in," Osadar said. Long ago, in her days as a human, she'd trained as a Jovian fighter pilot. Now she was a fighter pilot again, ready to fly her most important mission.

"Ready?" she asked the men.

They gave her the thumbs-up sign, one instituted by Marten Kluge.

Osadar flipped switches. The engine roared into life. She revved it, and with a lurch, she lifted off the lunar-like surface.

Marten peered around the edge of the dome at the troop-pods floating down for a landing. The stars glittered behind them. The oval-shaped craft had stubby anti-personnel guns along the sides. If needed, those guns would fire masses of exploding pellets. The pods no longer floated, but moved down in controlled, jerky bursts. Assaulting a small asteroid like this with its almost nonexistent gravity was delicate work. Unfortunately, the cyborg pilots seemed up to the task.

Encased in his armored vacc-suit, Marten desperately wanted to scratch his nose. Why had no one ever designed a nose or face-scratching suit? He twitched his nose as he leaned against the dome and watched the troop-pods. They had skids on the bottom of the oval craft. As he waited, he wondered if the cyborgs cared that ultimately they were on a suicide mission. Was there some way to break cyborg programming, the way Osadar had broken hers? That seemed like the most cost-effective way to defeat the cyborgs, turning their soldiers the way cyborgs turned ordinary people into aliens.

A space marine stepped past Marten and slid his Cognitive missile around the dome, aiming up at the nearest troop-pod.

"What are you doing?" Marten said, grabbing the missile-tip and yanking it down. "You might accidentally achieve lock-on. That will ping on a troop-pod's sensors and alert the cyborgs."

The space marine backed farther behind the dome.

The five troop-pods came down in a strict formation. They were almost to the surface, with stardust beginning to swirl upward in a cloud. The top of the cloud began to hide them.

"There," Omi said.

Hearing that through his headphones, Marten swiveled around. He followed Omi's pointing finger. Low on the horizon flashed movement. In a second, a Jovian patrol boat reached the crater-lip. It zoomed upward and swooped down on the five troop-pods easing into the billowing cloud.

"She's firing!" Omi shouted.

It looked like sparks on the patrol boat's wings. Bigger blooms were the ignition of missiles.

One troop-pod began to drift. Another blossomed in an explosion, showering metal and machine parts. Something flashed past Marten and plowed into the soil, sending up a puff of stardust. On the third and fourth troop-pods, the stubby anti-personnel tubes moved upward and pellets sprayed in shotgun-like blasts. But Osadar had already passed the pods and began a long banking maneuver so she could come back at them. As that occurred, hatches opened on the troop-pods. One after another, cyborgs jumped, and thruster-packs expelled hydrogen-spray as they began to descend individually.

This was the most vulnerable moment in a space-landing assault. It's what Marten had hoped would occur.

"Kill them!" he shouted.

Space marines hurried past him. More, he knew, came around from the other side of the dome. Jovians sank onto one knee and raised their infantry missile launchers. Others went prone. A few stood. In moments, a flock of Cognitives zoomed at the remaining troop-pods and at individually exposed cyborgs. Marten knelt, raised his gyroc and sent up one rocket-shell after another. He fired, reloaded and continued firing. Nearby, Omi did the same thing.

In the patrol boat, Osadar passed again, destroying the last functional troop-pod and dozens of thruster-pack-spewing cyborgs. Those cyborgs used laser-carbines. But as they fired, their unattended thruster-packs often took them in the wrong direction. It was far from a turkey-shoot. Cyborgs had uncanny reflexes and abilities. But with surprise and the patrol boat, the odds now lay with the Jovians.

"It looks like we're going to hold our asteroid," Omi said as he reloaded.

Marten grunted, even as his rifle pinged with lock-on. On his HUD, a dot centered on a red silhouette of a floating cyborg. Marten fired an APEX shell. The hardened round struck the cyborg and exploded, killing the target.

"What's troubling you?" asked Omi.

Marten looked over at his friend. He'd been watching the dead cyborg drift into space. "*We're* winning," he said. "But how are the others doing?"

-88-

The space battle raged as the *Julius Caesar* bored into the asteroids. Behind it by over one thousand kilometers, the *Genghis Khan* and *Gustavus Adolphus* followed.

From his command shell, Grand Admiral Cassius watched the nearest debris-cluster. He'd given orders so the *Julius Caesar* continued to use the cluster as a shield from the last cyborg asteroids. A grim thought kept beating in his brain, however. He wanted to take his ship past the debris-cluster to entice the cyborgs to turn all their beams onto the *Julius Caesar*. He wasn't sure how much longer the *Gustavus Adolphus* could survive the laser pounding. He had to kill the enemy lasers before they gravely injured a Doom Star.

By what quirk fate had chosen the *Gustavus* instead of the *Genghis Khan* Cassius had no idea. Cyborg lasers continued to beam en masse against the targeted Doom Star.

"He's pumping crystals," Sulla said.

Cassius held himself rock-still. This was a matter of timing now. Admiral Octavian had just disobeyed a direct order. He'd better succeed.

"His laser has gone offline," said Sulla.

"Why did he do that?" said Cassius, asking himself the question more than desiring an answer from others.

"There's an incoming message," Sulla said.

Cassius ignored it as he studied the situation. Doom Stars could pump crystals and gels at a fantastic rate. Ports had opened on the *Gustavus Adolphus* as it spewed. The growing crystal-cloud blocked Octavian's laser against the still-firing

330

asteroid turrets.

"I hope you've chosen correctly," Cassius whispered. It was a Highborn's prerogative to disregard orders. But if the officer chose poorly, it meant disgrace and likely death by hanging. In Octavian's place, Cassius would have continued to attack instead of choosing to defend and let others do his fighting for him.

Cyborg lasers chewed through the growing cloud. The *Julius Caesar* and *Genghis Khan* sought out the enemy beam turrets, destroying them as fast as they could. Seconds turned into minutes as time ticked by.

Sulla's oily-bright face turned toward him. "Your Excellency!"

"I see it," Cassius whispered.

Three lasers cut a hole in the prismatic-crystal cloud. Another beamed and sliced through the *Gustavus Adolphus's* nearly nonexistent composite armor. It must have been the perfect spot, or the worst. The reflex shielding behind didn't hold, and the cyborg laser remained on target for far too long. The deadly laser—the terrible offending beam—burned through a shuttle bay. It continued to drill and smashed through a coolant tank, living quarters, medical facilities, the edge of a coil-chamber and into the meld reactor to the fusion core. That started explosions, and those explosions wrecked vital inner components of the ship. Highborn died in mobs from shrapnel, heat and meld-poisoning and soon from vacuum-exposure.

"Destroy that laser!" Cassius shouted.

"Retargeting," said Sulla, his big hands roving over his board.

Time ticked by, and growing explosions added to the wounding of the *Gustavus Adolphus*. Big shuttle-bay doors opened. One after another in a stream, shuttles accelerated out of the stricken warship. Meanwhile, the ultra-lasers of the two sound Doom Stars hunted and destroyed the final enemy laser turrets.

Watching the battle unfold put a worm of doubt into Cassius's stomach. Torpedoes in waves now accelerated out of the nearest debris-cluster. It meant the torpedoes had been carefully weaving their way through the debris-field. That implied individual cyborgs piloted the one-way craft. Those torpedoes burned hard for the *Gustavus Adolphus* many hundreds of kilometers beyond them.

"That's it, Your Excellency," Sulla said. "Except for the ones behind the debris-fields, we've silenced the enemy beams."

Cassius hardly knew what he said in response. Destroying torpedoes, seeing them burn, absorbed his attention. More kept coming. How many torpedoes did these cyborgs have? Time, distance, velocity and power-levels—that's all Cassius could compute now.

"The last Highborn shuttles have escaped the *Gustavus Adolphus*," Sulla said some time later.

Prismatic crystals like wisps of cloud drifted before the mighty vessel. The warship's great beam fired, highlighting a cyborg torpedo before disintegrating it. Point-defense cannons fired as the last missiles launched from torn ports.

From in his shell, Cassius swallowed uneasily. The *Gustavus Adolphus* was like a great wounded beast. It was too tired, too drained of blood to sidestep death barreling down at it. That death came as schools of cyborg torpedoes, missiles and point-defense-cannon-shells converged on the ship. The *Julius Caesar* and *Genghis Khan* were using every weapon they had, trying to defend the stricken Doom Star. But now it was too little, too late. The cyborgs simply had too much. They should have used this mass earlier. Why had they saved so much hardware? The mass of destructive weaponry was simply too heavy to completely halt.

"No," Cassius whispered. He watched on a *zoomed* portion of his holoimages.

A huge torpedo smashed through the weakened composite armor and drilled its way deep into the Doom Star. It exploded with a nuclear fireball in the guts of the warship. Another torpedo struck as the electromagnetic pulse of the thermonuclear warhead washed outward. An emergency device caused the second torpedo to explode before the EMP blast disabled its systems.

Disbelieving, Cassius watched as a great section of armor blew away from the *Gustavus Adolphus* as blast holes appeared elsewhere. This part of the fight was over. The Doom Star was dead, as was every Highborn that had remained onboard to fire the ship's weaponry to the end.

-89-

Chief Coordinator of Earth Defense Scipio read the news with alarm.

The tall Highborn with the prosthetic hand stood before a large screen. It took up an entire wall of the largest room in the former laser satellite. The satellite had once orbited Earth. It was torus-shaped. As the satellite traveled through built-up velocity, the torus rotated, creating centrifugal-gravity.

"There's no more they can do."

Scipio barely heard the words of the Social Unity Earthling beside him. To him, the woman was tiny, barely five and half feet tall. She'd coordinated the SU premen, the *Earthlings* as Scipio tried to call them in his mind. Those Earthlings from Eurasia and Africa had brought engine-machinery and helped install them. Tens of thousands of Earthlings had helped the Highborn repair the least-damaged habitats orbiting Earth. Once, those habitats had contained algae pools and bacteria tanks.

Instead of drifting uselessly in orbit, Scipio had coordinated the repairs and sent the habitats toward the asteroids. As slow as they were, they'd built-up speed. The critical aspect of each was its mass. As constructs, the habitats were huge, many greater in bulk than a Doom Star, although none had as much mass.

Scipio still couldn't believe the *Gustavus Adolphus* had been destroyed. The Highborn were down to three Doom Stars, one at the Sun-Works Factory under repairs. Once, they had possessed five of the giant warships.

"The Grand Admiral can do no more," the woman said.

"You are correct," said Scipio.

On the wall, the asteroids less than three days away from impact against the Earth appeared as red images.

Cassius had sent the grim message. The Doom Stars had used every nuclear weapon in their cargo-holds. Scouring the captured asteroids—all fifteen of them—the Highborn had found more nukes and used them, too. Highborn had maneuvered some of those nuclear bombs deep into the debris-fields before detonating them. Most of the debris, the rocks, had blown outward, enough that eighty-seven percent of the mass no longer constituted a threat against Earth. That still left a critical thirteen percent of the debris-fields. Other nuclear explosions had deflected smaller asteroids. A few of the biggest nukes had been sunk into the center of the monster silicon-based rocks and detonated. Those asteroids had splintered and separated into pieces, a few of those pieces were still on a collision course for Earth. There were seven major objects left and the lesser remains of the former debris-fields and asteroid-smashed debris. One of the seven major objects was a giant, thirty-kilometers in diameter. The Doom Stars, Orion-ships, Highborn commandoes and SU warships had done all they could. Now it was Scipio's turn.

"We needed to refit more habitats," the SU woman said. "We simply didn't have enough time."

"We shall see," Scipio said.

"Have you read the data?" she demanded.

Scipio frowned. The preman, the SU Earthling, acted too familiarly with him. Any other Highborn would have slapped her into obedience. It was such a trying task working with premen.

"Do not query me," Scipio told her.

"I'm sorry," the woman said, as she cringed. "I didn't mean any offense."

Scipio squinted at the wall, at the red images representing the seven major objects and debris. Blue dots were the advancing habitats, eight of them.

Curtly, he nodded. It was time to put in the final coordinates and drive the habitats against the asteroids. The question that plagued him was this. How many should he send at each? Or should he send all of the habitats at the four biggest rocks and ignore the rest? Let the Earthlings use their merculite missiles and proton beams on the remainder. What was the best decision?

Scipio touched his prosthetic hand. It was better to be certain with a few. If the Earth were to survive, let its occupants defend it. Otherwise…maybe the planet and the premen weren't worthy of life.

90

With iron control, Cassius held his brooding in check as he stood on the bridge of the *Julius Caesar*. Efficiently, his officers went about their tasks. Toggles clicked, uniforms rustled and images flickered on the screens.

Since the *Gustavus Adolphus's* destruction, Cassius had grown weary of his holoimages. He presently watched over Sulla's shoulder. The Ultraist's screen showed a nearly futile picture. Two Doom Stars stayed ahead of the two biggest asteroids headed for Earth. The warships alternately beamed their heavy lasers at the largest object. They sliced off surface-areas one tiny section at a time. It was tedious work, and both lasers had entered the danger zone more than once before being shut down for cooling.

"We must save Earth," Cassius declared.

None of the officers turned toward him.

Cassius straightened, and he held a retort in check. He'd said that too many times already. He knew it, but the words kept bubbling out of him. They had to save Earth, or the war against the cyborgs was lost.

Closing his eyes, Cassius witnessed the *Gustavus Adolphus's* obliteration yet again in his memory. He'd risked, and he'd lost the gamble. Now he might lose Earth. He might lose the industrial capacity of billions of premen laboring for the New Order of Highborn supremacy.

"I refuse to despair," Cassius whispered. He glanced at his officers. Their bearing told him he'd lost status in their eyes. Might he lose his rank, as well?

Moving deliberately, Cassius entered his shell. He must remain calm. He must act as he'd done hundreds of times before. Any deviation in his behavior could trigger their aggression against him. The battle wasn't over and Earth might yet survive the attack. The asteroids rushed to meet the slow-moving but still accelerating habitats. Social Unity possessed proton beams and merculite missiles. There was still hope.

Turning on the holoimages, forcing himself to study them, Cassius saw the remaining shuttles collecting the surviving Highborn commandoes off the various asteroids. Many had died in the assaults. But more premen dead lay slain on the Saturn-launched planet wreckers. The Jovians—

"Marten Kluge," Cassius whispered. He needed a diversion, something to do to take his mind off losing a Doom Star. He needed to relax in order to keep his mind sharp enough to keep his high command. The Jovian-captured asteroid continued to accelerate away from its former heading. Kluge had refused the order to space here in a patrol boat. Perhaps the subhuman understood all too well the punishments that awaited him here. But Kluge's refusal wasn't going to save him. Even now, three Highborn shuttles raced after the rogue asteroid. The Highborn commandoes had orders to capture Kluge and bring him to the *Julius Caesar*. Thinking about that helped divert Cassius. That in turn helped deflect his brooding.

This was the final round in the genocidal asteroid-strike. While he was alive, he would dominate the Highborn and through them the universe.

91

"We can't pull the same trick against the Highborn," Osadar said.

"So we accept defeat?" Omi asked.

"No," said Marten. The three of them played cards in a storage locker. Boxes were stacked in the corners. Plastic barrels of water made a wall on one side. They'd taken down the top barrels and made the table with it. Smaller boxes were the chairs. The worn cards were from Mars, stored in Omi's pocket.

"No," Marten said. "You take off and leave the asteroid. It's me they want."

"They want all of us," Omi said.

Marten grinned tiredly. "You saw a replay of the message. Cassius all but gloated about the things he was going to teach a mulish preman like me."

"You have an odd ability," Osadar said. "It is uncanny how easily you anger those in charge."

"Yeah," said Marten. "It's because I like to be my own man. My mistake, I guess."

"It is immaterial," said Osadar. "With the successful strike against Earth, the cyborgs will have clinched victory."

"Nothing's clinched yet," Marten said hotly.

Osadar glanced at Omi and shrugged. "He is incurable," she said.

"I want you to leave," Marten said, as he stared at his cards. He had two aces, a ten of clubs, a two of diamonds and a Joker. "Take Nadia with you."

Omi laid his cards on the table—on the plastic water barrels. "No one is running out on you. One: the shuttles will overtake our patrol boats and we have no ammo left. Two: you're our Force-Leader. We stand or die with you, Marten. Accept it."

Marten looked away as his heart beat rapidly. He didn't deserve friends like this. He was spent and it told on his emotions. He rubbed his eye as he thought about his friends staying to die with him. There was a speck in it, that's all. He kept telling himself that until he stood up. "I'm not going to meekly surrender."

"No one thought you were," Omi said.

"Okay," Marten said. "I just wanted to get that straight."

92

Marten, Nadia and Omi were the only ones in the main room of the first dome. His wife sat at the sensor board.

Marten stared out of the big window. It showed the crater-plain and the stars overhead. If he looked hard enough, Earth was the biggest dot to his subjective left. How long ago had it been since he'd left Earth? Stick, Turbo…Hall-Leader Quirn…Molly, all old memories. He'd left as a slave of the Highborn, one of their decorated, chosen pets. Now he was a Force-Leader of free men. Now he had to keep his people free of the shackle-bearing, castrating Highborn.

Squinting, Marten studied the bright dot. The idea that he rode a world-killing asteroid seemed unbelievable. He had done his best to save Earth, deflecting one of seventeen planet wreckers. If more meteor-ships had joined him, he could have stopped more. He kept trying to think of something profound to say regarding billions of dead people. He shook his head, hating cyborgs and Highborn. Social Unity didn't look so bad now in comparison. He still loathed the rampant, deadening socialism, but it wasn't annihilation. If everyone on Earth died, if Social Unity perished as a force, it meant the supremacists and aliens would win. One represented eternal slavery for humanity. The other meant extinction.

"Two of the shuttles are braking, and they're not going to land," Nadia informed them.

Marten turned and studied his wife's long dark hair. She'd tied it in a ponytail. He liked it that way. It let him kiss her neck more easily.

"The third shuttle is moving in," Nadia said. "They're hailing us." She turned as a light on her board blinked yellow. Her eyes were red-rimmed with fear. "What should I do?"

"Open channels," Marten said in a rough voice.

Nadia did, and an arrogant Highborn appeared on the screen. He had the signature wide face, the square chin and chiseled features, the stark-white coloring. Some of his dark, pelt-like hair had been shaved away. Worse, half of his face was covered in a more human tone of a plasti-flesh bandage. The rawness of his skin around the bandage showed that his face had taken bad burn damage or cyborg laser-fire. Marten supposed that was the same thing. The fierceness shining from the Highborn's good eye showed that the soldier hadn't taken any painkillers. They were all mad, all hyped-up on their quest as supermen.

"I recognize you," the Highborn said.

"I'm Marten Kluge."

Irritation flashed across the damaged face. "Since I've already stated I recognize you, there was no need to tell me your name," the Highborn said. He held up a big hand as Marten began to speak. "I am aware of your habits. It is the reason we have been given our mission. Do you know what that mission is, preman?"

"Why don't you tell me?" Marten asked.

"You are to return with me to the *Julius Caesar*."

"Is that right?"

The Highborn bared his teeth. They were big and strong-looking.

That triggered something in Marten. He leaned closer to the screen, minutely examining the Highborn. "You look familiar to me," he said. "Have we met before?"

"Your insolence is making this difficult," the Highborn said. "Premen should learn better manners and keep their mouth closed until personally addressed."

Marten snapped his fingers. "You look just like the Grand Admiral. Are you his son?"

The Highborn snarled an oath and must have grasped his communication device, for this thumbs appeared on the image. "I am Felix of the Ninth *Iron* Cohort. Know that the Grand

Admiral and I share the same chromosomes. In his mania, Cassius shot my favorite sex object, exiled me into space and killed me once. Then he packed me into a missile as a living warhead and launched me in a suicide mission against the cyborgs. I survived that, but gained this," Felix said, indicating the plasti-flesh on half of his face. The Highborn breathed heavily so his nostrils flared. "Now Cassius will learn what it means to have made an enemy of me."

Marten glanced at Omi and raised an eyebrow.

The stoic Korean shook his head.

"Are you going to gain the Grand Admiral's favor by bringing me in?" Marten asked.

"You stupid preman," Felix snarled. "Are you truly that slow-witted? No. I am declaring my independence from the Grand Admiral and his tyranny. His ineptitude has cost us Earth. I mean to see him ousted from power and hanged by the neck. In the interim, I, and those who think like me, will use your asteroid as a base. Since the Grand Admiral despises you, I will give you a choice. Remain among us for a time or leave in your spacecraft, if you possess any. It is more than an irritating subhuman deserves. But I feel that doing this will anger the Grand Admiral. Well, preman, what is your choice?"

"Can you give me a few minutes to think about it?" Marten asked.

"No!" Felix said. "Decide this instant. Speaking to you is a burden I'd rather not have to practice a second time."

"We'll leave," Marten said.

"Felix of the Ninth *Iron* Cohort out," the Highborn said.

"How do you know he's telling us the truth?" Nadia whispered.

"I've rubbed shoulders with them for a long time, honey. This one is crazy like Sigmir. I know the look. But I bet he's honest." Marten turned to Omi. "Get the men. It's time we left while the getting's good."

"Go where?" asked Omi.

"We'll decide that once we lift off," Marten said. "Maybe if we're lucky, we can land on Earth."

Omi nodded and headed for the hatch.

-93-

In the former laser satellite that monitored the eight habitats, tall Scipio kept flexing his prosthetic hand. Why did it hurt at times like this? That didn't make sense. He lacked pain-sensory equipment and none of the skin was raw. It was ghost-pain, imaginary. Yet even though he knew all that, the metal hand throbbed dully and made it difficult to concentrate. Not that he needed to concentrate now. Everything was set.

Scipio stood before the wall showing the first targeted asteroid. It was the outer one of the two biggest, at least outer in relation to Earth. The wall showed the asteroid in detail, particularly its frozen *cryovolcano* or ice volcano.

The cryovolcano fascinated Scipio. It meant that much of this asteroid was icy. Ordinary volcanoes spewed molten rock. A cryovolcano erupted water, ammonia or methane and was known as *cryomagma* or ice-volcanic melt. The energy to form the eruptions usually came from tidal forces—the tug and pull of gravity from larger objects that twisted the asteroid's center. It was doubtful there had been any eruptions during the asteroid's journey from Saturn. No, the cryovolcano would likely never have another eruption again. Unless he could nudge the asteroid out of the way, it would end its existence as it smashed into Earth and obliterated life.

While flexing his bionic hand, trying to ease the imaginary pain, Scipio sat down at his desk. It was clean and minimalist. Using his real hand, his fleshy one, he began to change settings. The test of his work would begin in an hour. He would succeed and possibly save a world, or he would fail and

344

condemn billions to death.

He was ready…. But why did his inhuman hand have to hurt so much?

94

As Scipio watched on his wall, the asteroid with the cryovolcano approached the blue-green world. If anyone had been left alive on it, he or she would have seen the third planet as Luna-sized from Earth.

The line of former farm habitats—gently accelerated these past days—moved like giant billiard balls. They approached in silence and in near formation. That had been Scipio's greatest decision. Should he work on one habitat at a time and send it alone at the asteroids? Or should he work on all of them and launch them together? He'd chosen a third way, working on eight at a time. Because of a thousand problems and delays, these were the only eight he'd been able to fix enough to blast out of Earth-orbit.

From hundreds of thousands of kilometers away, Scipio witnessed the first event. A cylindrical-shaped habitat plowed into the asteroid. Metal crumpled at the impact and then burst apart, flying in many directions. The hit caused trembling to shake crystals loose on the cryovolcano ten kilometers from the impact-point. The second habitat caused greater trembling. Unfortunately, the habitat's mass was a pittance compared to the asteroid. Fortunately, another came in a line, hitting, crumpling and flying apart.

At the third strike, the combined jolts caused the cryovolcano to crack, shatter and burst apart. Giant sections tumbled down onto the icy plain or flew off into space. Each strike had deflected the asteroid a little. The trick, the point of this exercise, was to move it enough that Earth's gravity wouldn't pull the object down upon itself. If these strikes had occurred even two days ago, it could have easily moved the asteroid far enough off course. Now, it was going to be dicey. It would have been good to hit this asteroid with another object, but those were on other intercept courses. The targeting decisions had been made a day ago. The mass of the habitats, their velocity and the relative weakness of the engines meant it was impossible to redirect them now.

Scipio faced the wall as Supreme Commander James Hawthorne appeared on it. The Earthling sat at a desk, with his hands folded on top.

"The habitats have struck," Scipio said. "My projections say that four of the asteroids will not hit the planet, but will pass between the Earth and the Moon."

Hawthorne nodded solemnly. He had discolored bags under his eyes.

"There are three major asteroids still coming," Scipio said. "And there is much debris, enough to annihilate life on your planet."

"We've been monitoring their progress," Hawthorne said in a raw voice.

Scipio tried to refrain, but he had to know. "Can you stop the barrage and save Earth?"

"We're about to find out," Hawthorne said. His chair scraped back as he rose to feet and gave the Party salute. "Long live Social Unity!" Hawthorne shouted. Then the connection ended abruptly, as if planned.

What did all that signify? Scipio ignored his throbbing bionic hand. One thing he'd learned while working with these premen: they were more technologically cunning than he'd ever given them credit for. Maybe conquering and ruling them wasn't going to be as easy as the Grand Admiral believed. If there was anything left to conquer, that was.

On Earth and deep underground in the Joho Mountains, Supreme Commander Hawthorne shrugged on his jacket. His fingers felt stiff as he buttoned it. He was so tired. He felt like an old man and his eyes burned from reading endless reports.

The probabilities and projections—

Hawthorne sagged into his chair, opened a bottom drawer and took out a small flask of old Scottish whiskey. Unscrewing the cap, he put it to his lips and threw back his head. The liquid slid down his throat, and it burned. Then warmth burst in his stomach and moved throughout his body. It made him shiver. Waiting a moment, he did it again. He was thinking about a third slug, when someone rapped at his door.

Screwing on the cap, he put the flask in the drawer. Then he hesitated. Maybe he should keep it with him. A second knock occurred, more insistent this time. With a clunk, Hawthorne dropped the flask and slammed the drawer closed.

"Enter," he said.

Manteuffel opened the door, sticking in his head. "Cone would like a word with you, sir."

Hawthorne blinked several times before the words registered. He nodded as he straightened his tie.

Frowning, Manteuffel hesitated before he asked, "Sir, are you well?"

"No," said Hawthorne. "I'm sick with worry, with fear that we're all about to die."

"But the merculites, the proton beams," Manteuffel said. "The news sites all declare an easy victory."

349

"The probabilities and projections were altered for publication," Hawthorne whispered. "They were propaganda lies."

"What was that, sir?" asked Manteuffel.

"Nothing," Hawthorne said. He wanted another sip of whiskey, a long one. He flattened his hands on the desk instead, spreading his fingers. "Let her in."

Manteuffel nodded, withdrew and then followed Cone into the room. She moved briskly to a chair before the desk. Then she glanced at Manteuffel, who had taken his place in a corner.

"You wished to see me?" asked Hawthorne.

Cone took off her sunglasses. Her pale eyes added to her beauty. If only she could smile occasionally. She was like an ice queen. Hawthorne suspected her smile might transform her.

"Colonel Naga is having second thoughts," Cone said.

It was difficult for Hawthorne to wrap his thoughts around the FEC traitors today.

"Naga says his men and tanks will be exposed to the asteroid-strike if they move today," Cone said. "They'll be on the surface."

"It's why he'll take everyone by surprise," Hawthorne said.

"I know that," Cone said. "But we're not the ones who are going to be on the surface. He is."

"What can I do about it?" Hawthorne asked, irritation entering his voice.

"Talk to him," said Cone.

Hawthorne frowned at his spread fingers. Slowly, he shook his head. "I don't have the strength. I'm going to need it all for the battle against the asteroids."

"Then empower me," Cone said.

Hawthorne looked up as Manteuffel cleared his throat. Cone stared at him with those pale eyes. They hid her thoughts, but he recognized her thirst for power. How he envied Cone her relative youth. Was his time for command over?

"Empower how?" Hawthorne asked.

"Reinstate me as your Security Specialist," she said.

Manteuffel tried to signal him with his eyes, but Hawthorne ignored the man.

"This is the moment to strike, sir," Cone said. "I can

motivate Colonel Naga, but I'll need a position of authority to do it."

"Very well," said Hawthorne.

Manteuffel shook his head.

Hawthorne took out a scroll-pad and began to tap in the needed electronic-work. Doing it gave him energy. This was a risk. But the Earth needed hard, ambitious people. It might not survive the next twenty-four hours. If it did, then their window for retaking the planet from the vacant Highborn would be small indeed. Now was the time for energetic climbers to strike. Now was the moment for someone like Cone.

"There," Hawthorne said, as he stood. "You're back in, Security Specialist."

Cone stood too. "You won't regret this, sir."

He already did, but the die was cast.

97

Aboard the *Julius Caesar*, Cassius gave the order. The two Doom Stars pulled away laterally from the final planet wreckers.

From in his command shell, Cassius closed his eyes. Despite his vast reservoir of energy, he was tired. He'd pushed the crews of both ships. They'd fired the ultra-lasers for so long that key components had gone critical. Cassius had also used up almost every shell of the point-defense cannons, blowing up the larger pieces of debris.

With a lurch and the snapping open of his eyes, he hailed the Sun-Works Factory through his communications. The fight against the cyborg-launched objects was nearly over. He had to be ready for whatever happened afterward. That meant a *total* re-supply of the Doom Stars, including point-defense cannon shells, missiles, reflex plating, collapsium slabs, coils, meld-synapses and key laser parts. It might be time to head for the Sun-Works Factory for a major overhaul. He doubted the war would give him that luxury.

Cracking his knuckles, laying back, Cassius allowed himself a moment of introspection. For him, that meant checking his mental files, opening them and seeing if matters had occurred how he'd desired. Hmm. Yes. He needed to send a call to the Luna Missile Complex. The Senior Tribune there should face a review board. Maybe that would be a good place to transfer Sulla, upgrade him off the *Julius Caesar*.

It occurred to Cassius then that he'd never received a confirmation from the Highborn sent to Kluge's asteroid.

"Sulla," he said. "Who was the officer in charge of the Asteroid-E pickup?"

Sulla swiveled to a different console, tapped on the screen and said a moment later, "First Maniple-Leader Felix of Ninth *Iron* Cohort, Commandoes."

Cassius felt several things at once. The first was the oddness of the tone from Sulla. So he watched the Ultraist. The Highborn turned toward him, glancing at him too carefully, with too much calculation.

"You have something to add to the report?" asked Cassius.

It might have been his imagination, but Sulla's mouth seemed to twitch. The oily, shiny face held inner gloating.

Cassius felt something else, too. Felix of his chromosomes had gone to collect Kluge. That didn't seem like a chance assignment. His enemies among the Highborn must have engineered it, hoping for something to occur that would further mar his image as Grand Admiral.

"Has the Maniple-Leader returned yet?" asked Cassius.

"Felix landed long ago," Sulla said.

The longing to unbuckle from his shell was nearly overpowering. Cassius wanted to beat Sulla's face into bloody pulp. The tone and implications—this was the next thing to insubordination. Yet the Grand Admiral hesitated. It wasn't fear of Sulla, but a grim understanding that his rank was under jeopardy. He needed to react with care.

Cassis asked, "In which shuttle-bay did he land?"

Sulla took his time answering. "Oh, the Maniple-Leader never arrived here. I misunderstood you, Your Excellency. I meant he landed on Asteroid E."

"The Maniple-Leader has captured Marten Kluge?"

"I can hail him and find out," Sulla said.

"No," Cassius said. "Return to your tasks."

Sulla opened his mouth, maybe to say more. Then he smirked and returned to his controls.

Although he shivered convulsively, Cassius otherwise kept a tight reign on his rage. Sulla must die soon, but he couldn't kill him on the bridge. No, he must do this subtly. His secret enemies among the Highborn, those who craved the highest command for themselves, must sense blood from his wounding, from losing the *Gustavus Adolphus*. He must maneuver with extreme delicacy now in order to keep his leadership and his life.

Twisting around in his shell, he opened a private channel. Asteroid E was far away, although not yet beyond range of the ultra-laser. That laser was now down, however, certain burned-out components being replaced or under repair. Cassius watched a small screen as he practiced a calming technique. There was a time for rage and a time for stalking prey.

A face-burned Highborn appeared on the screen. It was Felix, and it looked as if his left eye was gone.

"This is Grand Admiral—"

"I know who you are," Felix said.

Cassius pursed his lips. "Have you returned to the *Julius Caesar?*"

"In time, I might."

Lightheadedness made it difficult to think. Cassius shook off the weakness as he concentrated on the hatred shining in Felix's single good eye. The boy had gone rogue. He could see that now. There would be no saving of his chromosomes. He should have seen it sooner, but in this, a paternal feeling had blinded him.

"Where is Marten Kluge?" asked Cassius.

"Gone," said Felix.

"You disobeyed a direct order?" Cassius asked.

"Someday, I'm going to kill you," Felix said.

Instead of arguing, instead of using verbal trickery to discover more, Cassius cut the connection. Why his chest felt so hollow, he had no idea. In a mental fog, a haze, he unbuckled, exited the shell and left the bridge as he strode down the corridors.

It was some time later that Cassius found himself in his quarters, strapped into an acceleration couch. He had no idea how he'd gotten here. A com-link was open and Sulla was telling him…that it was time.

Time for what?

At that moment, the ship engaged its huge engines. A thrumming tremble caused his couch to shake as the noise levels rose. Then a ten-G-burst deceleration slammed Cassius against his couch. That cleared his mind, and he turned on an outer video.

The *Julius Caesar* and the *Genghis Khan* sharply pulled away from the asteroids headed for Earth. The blue-green ball was huge now, less than a quarter-of-a-day away at these speeds.

The three zooming asteroids and the mass of debris surrounding them kept on a straight collision course for the planet. Much of the debris could theoretically cause billions to die if they hit.

Aboard the *Julius Caesar*, Cassius began to plot. He wanted to tame Kluge, and he would someday in a brutal fashion, but he had bigger problems to tackle now. Felix— Cassius shook his head. He'd worry about Felix later. Now he had to hold onto his supreme station. His position was gravely weakened if his own bridge crew maneuvered behind his back.

He judged his odds for survival as Grand Admiral. They were bad. His only chance was if the Earth survived the asteroids. Then he had to strike first and strike hard. He had to outmaneuver his hidden enemies. If the cyborg-objects annihilated premen-existence on the homeworld, his challengers would likely pull him down like dogs ravaging a de-fanged lion.

He had a moment to wonder if Kluge was responsible for Felix's rebellion. Cassius snarled, vowing to capture Kluge someday and turn him into a docile and obedient beast.

Then another high-G burst slammed him against the couch, slowing the warship so it could soon enter near-Earth orbit.

355

98

Deep in the Joho Command Bunker, Hawthorne watched the Doom Stars decelerate. He, along with everyone else monitoring near-orbital space on the screens, knew the moment had come.

"Open channels with Vice-Admiral Mandela," Hawthorne said.

Soon, a black-skinned man with curly-white hair appeared before Hawthorne's sight. The man had large eyes, a stern expression and a badly rumpled uniform.

"Use the approaching asteroids as shields," Hawthorne said, forgoing pleasantries. "Flee from the Highborn while you have the opportunity. Whether the rocks hit the Earth or not, use the planet as an even bigger shield. Keep yourself from those ultra-lasers. You must keep your fleet intact."

Mandela blinked in seeming bewilderment. "W-we're practically weaponless," he finally stammered.

"Do as ordered," Hawthorne told him. "Social Unity is going to need that fleet."

Mandela hesitated before saying: "The Highborn will disapprove of such actions."

What had happened to the man? Once, Mandela had been tough. Maybe the years drifting between Venus and Earth had taken a psychological toll on him. Maybe working under the Highborn had sapped whatever had remained of his will. It was time to shove some steel into the man.

"Vice-Admiral Mandela," said Hawthorne, "will you obey my lawfully given order?"

356

Mandela tried to stare Hawthorne down, at least the Supreme Commander felt like the Vice-Admiral did. Then Mandela glanced right and left. Likely, he studied his bridge crew. The old man seemed to wilt in his chair.

"Your plan is risky," Mandela whispered.

"I need that fleet intact and away from the Highborn," Hawthorne said. "I need spaceships so I have something to threaten them with later."

"Supreme Commander—"

"If you cannot obey me, Vice-Admiral, I will relieve you of command and order you shot."

Mandela scowled. Hawthorne took that as a good sign. The old man still had some will left. Then the Vice-Admiral nodded. "I have my orders, sir. Is there anything else you want to tell me?"

"Yes," Hawthorne said. "Good luck."

"Thank you, sir. I'll need it."

99

The SU Fifth Fleet—two battleships and a missile-ship—accelerated. Cassius watched it on his images. The *Julius Caesar* and the *Genghis Khan* continued to slow down. Between them, the asteroids and debris zooming at Earth acted as a screen.

Cassius hailed Vice-Admiral Mandela and soon spoke to him screen-to-screen.

"Where do you go in such a hurry?" asked Cassius.

"I have my orders, Grand Admiral," Mandela said, as he stood before his chair. The preman seemed nervous. "It has been a pleasure fighting under your inspired leadership. I hope we can fight together again and destroy the cyborg menace."

"Help us stop these objects," Cassius said.

"I'm afraid we need more military stores to do that."

"Ah," said Cassius, "I see. If you decelerate, we shall re-supply you."

"That's a generous offer, Grand Admiral. But I cannot. I've been given my orders straight from Supreme Commander Hawthorne of Social Unity. I dare not disobey him."

Cassius adjusted the transmission. Everything was turning against him at once. Did the universe mean to test his greatness to the limit? Somewhere, he needed events to move in *his* favor. Cassius scowled. A superior man *forced* events to move in his favor. The preman Vice-Admiral seemed badly frightened about something. It was time to play on his worst fears.

"What if I said that I shall fire on your ships unless you

358

decelerate?" said Cassius.

Mandela glanced about as if for moral support. There was whispering around him, maybe directed at him. Mandela nodded and took a tentative step forward. "Speaking theoretically, sir, it would mean our alliance was at an end."

"Ah," said Cassius, "speaking theoretically. Go then, preman. I grant you leave." The ultra-lasers were still under repairs. He would never forget this preman's treachery, however. After he had fought so hard for them, they acted like ingrates and ran away.

Hours passed. In time, the three SU warships accelerated far away from the asteroids.

From Earth, the first salvo of merculite missiles ignited off the blast-pans and headed for the stratosphere, rising to do battle with the mass of potential kinetic death to every living organism on the planet.

Cassius watched the lone planet, and he wished in that moment he possessed the ancient premen superstition of a belief in God. He would have liked to ask someone to help him for a change. But if God was real, He kept silent. God had never spoken to the Grand Admiral of the Highborn. Therefore, because he was alone, Cassius desperately hoped the dice of fate rolled in his favor. He needed the Earth intact, and then he needed to outmaneuver his Highborn enemies.

100

Supreme Commander James Hawthorne stood with his hands clasped behind his back. Deep underground in the Joho Mountain Bunker, he watched the screens. Around him, officers and operators murmured among themselves. It had been calculated that the planet wreckers would likely smash into South America. They had to stop that. The many screens showed many different things.

In Bavaria Sector, giant ferroconcrete bays opened. Slowly, giant merculite missiles appeared. Seconds ticked by. The image shook as one after another, the merculite missiles began to lift off. Yellow flames burned behind them as they moved slowly and then quickly accelerated to escape-velocity and faster.

Another screen showed the outskirts of Kiev, the flowing wheat fields with their critical food growth. A giant tube poked out of the main proton generating station. The tube aimed into the heavens. Below it underground and out of sight, the city's deep-core mine supplied power. Then a milky-colored beam lanced into the sky.

Other proton beams flashed. More merculite missiles flew. On other screens, cannons began to spew defensive shells. Highborn orbitals flew up from North and South America. Everything Earth possessed in way of space-defense exploded, beamed or kinetic-force smashed against the incoming asteroids and the masses of meteor-debris.

The rocky chunks of matter launched long-ago in the Saturn System now approached near-Earth orbit. The long journey was almost over. They had passed through vast reaches of empty space and survived ultra-lasers, Highborn-fashioned nukes, ricocheting habitats and magnetic-induced shoves. The cyborg trajectory calculations had proved flawless. Now these objects headed straight for South America at immense velocity.

Sirens wailed in the Joho Bunker. Warning bells rang. Men and women stood up as they watched the possible end of life on Earth.

The proton beams were devastating, consuming the smaller objects one after another. The merculite missiles held upgraded warheads. They nudged the big asteroids, and finally caused them to crack, splinter and burst apart. All the while, however, the objects came closer, closer.

A big chunk of the former fifteen-kilometer rock stubbornly shrugged off a nuclear missile. It had a solid nickel-iron core. A proton beam washed it and burned away mass, but the nickel-iron took time to destroy. The object obliterated a cylindrical habitat maneuvered into its path, sending a spray of metal toward Earth.

"Sir!" a woman shouted.

"I see it," said Hawthorne. "What's its mass?"

"It's just under four kilometers in diameter," a man said. "If it keeps on this course, it will hit in upper South America."

"That ought to keep Colonel Naga happy," Hawthorne whispered.

"Sir?" the man asked.

Hawthorne shoulders slumped. "Never mind," he said.

On the screen, more objects kept coming. Some smashed through other habitats, a few of the smaller meteors deflected from the atmosphere.

"Milan has gone offline!" a woman moaned.

"There's a deep-core burst in Cape Town. They pushed too hard."

"Help us!" Hawthorne shouted, as he threw up his hands and implored the Unknown One.

"Here it comes," a woman said. "Nothing can stop it now."

-101-

There were various objects under thirty-five meters. Each burned through the upper atmosphere. The first one became visible to the naked eye at one hundred and five kilometers high. Air friction began to heat the rocky object. Gasses burned off the meteor and the denser air turned it white hot. The increasing friction and heat caused the Saturn-rock to break apart into seven different pieces. Those burned faster, creating a glowing tail visible in the daylight to those craning and watching the doom of Earth. Because of its rocky nature, this object burned up at fifty-seven kilometers above the surface.

The other small meteors also burned up in the atmosphere.

There came one big object, the nickel-iron asteroid slightly under four-kilometers in diameter. Its velocity had taken it from Saturn to its destiny here over South America. It appeared at one hundred and five kilometers above the surface, smashing down through the thin atmosphere. Soon, gasses boiled off the increasing heated object. A gigantic tail appeared and remained like a jet's exhaust as a streak of grim finality. Still the massive object sped down. At seventy kilometers from the surface, it blazed at four thousand degrees Fahrenheit. At fifty-five kilometers, the ear-splitting booms began. It roared and blazed like a projectile from Hell as it headed for the Amazon Basin in Brazil Sector. At twenty-two kilometers, it cast a shadow on the surface like a targeting dot.

Soon thereafter, the terrible asteroid struck the surface of the Earth, releasing incredible kinetic energy. A circular shock wave of obliterating proportions flattened everything for half the continent. Trees, buildings and even mountains blew down, apart and often into the air. Earthquakes shook the planet. Billions of tons of debris billowed upward in a vast cloud that dwarfed anything ever seen on Planet Earth.

In South America, moments after impact and continuing in a ripple-like wave, over five billion people died in the crumbling underground cities. Billions more were going to die as the planet entered a new era of weather patterns and cycle of seasons.

The cyborgs had made their annihilating mark, creating the hugest crater on Earth. Likely, it would become a new lake in the middle of South America. The cyborgs had also achieved a first: the greatest single death toll of any one particular action.

Some time later in the Joho Mountain Bunker, Hawthorne slowly picked himself off the floor.

"What happened?" someone asked nearby.

Hawthorne worked his mouth, but no words issued. His mind was numb.

"Sir!" a man shouted. It was Manteuffel. The small ex-cybertank colonel sat at a communications board. Blood leaked from Manteuffel's nose. "Sir, Grand Admiral Cassius of the Highborn is hailing you."

Hawthorne limped near the screen. On it, he saw Cassius and the proud manner of the Highborn leader.

"I'm glad you're alive," Cassius said. "Our Doom Stars shall reach near-Earth orbit soon and assist you in any way we can."

All Hawthorne could do was stare at the Grand Admiral.

"They hit South America," Cassius said. "I doubt much lives there now. You're lucky none of the pieces hit the oceans and created tidal waves."

Hawthorne frowned, trying to absorb the thoughts.

"Earth is going to be a harsh place to live," the Highborn said.

"Death," Hawthorne said. His mouth was dry. So was his heart.

"Excuse me, Supreme Commander?" asked Cassius. "What did you say?"

"Death to the cyborgs," Hawthorne whispered.

"Yes, it is time for a real alliance," Cassius said, nodding. "Through these past weeks, we've seen that we can work together. And we've learned to trust each other."

Hawthorne stared at the Grand Admiral, believing nothing the Highborn said.

"You need us," Cassius said. "And we need to concentrate on the real enemy before the cyborgs obliterate us both."

Hawthorne's head swayed as the idea struck home. Likely everyone in South America and maybe even Central America was dead because the cyborgs had launched asteroids at Earth. What he saw from some satellite cams....

Was it possible to trust the Highborn? Earth couldn't survive a second strike like this.

"We must unite," Cassius said.

It felt like there were cobwebs in his mind. Hawthorne tried to think. He said, "You are the Highborn and we're premen. Can we work together without you trying to dominate us?"

"I'm the only chance you have," Cassius said. "Agree to a real alliance, and I can hold my position as Grand Admiral. Believe me, Supreme Commander, there are officers among us who wish your species' destruction. I do not agree with them. If nothing else, this strike shows that we don't have the time to subjugate or annihilate you. We must turn our effort against the cyborgs, or risk total defeat."

"I have work to do," Hawthorne said. "The world needs me now. Maybe we can speak again later."

Cassius lurched closer until his face filled the screen. "Listen to me, Hawthorne. You just lost billions of your fellow humans. If you want to save the rest, you need me so together we can kill these genocidal cyborgs."

Hawthorne stared into those feral eyes. Cassius was the Highborn Grand Admiral. The Highborn could change course with amazing speed and decision. Did Cassius see something new after this strike? Maybe Social Unity no longer had a choice. South America—

"Yes," Hawthorne whispered, "a true alliance. Together, let us kill the cyborgs."

Two Jovian patrol boats headed for Earth. In the first one, Marten sat at the controls with Omi. It was packed within the spaceship.

"Well?" Omi asked.

"The cloud movement is crazy," Marten said. He scanned Earth with a long-distance telescope. "But the indicators—"

"I have an incoming message," Nadia said.

"From Earth?" asked Marten.

Surprised, Nadia looked up. "It's from their Supreme Commander."

"Put him on," said Marten. A tired man with hollowed-out eyes appeared on the screen.

"I'm Supreme Commander James Hawthorne of Social Unity. My com-officers tell me that your designation is Jovian."

"Yes," said Marten.

"Does the alliance still hold?"

"It does."

"Good," said Hawthorne. "It's time we humans began to truly work together before the Highborn and cyborgs annihilate us."

"That's what I think," said Marten. "But Grand Admiral Cassius might not see it that way."

"I'm sure you have an interesting story...."

"I'm Force-Leader Marten Kluge."

Hawthorne nodded curtly. "Well, Force-Leader, I'd like you to rendezvous with our warships. We need to mass what little strength we have. Then you and I need to talk face-to-face."

Marten chest tightened. Earth, Social Unity—he nodded. "That sounds like a good idea. Do you have the coordinates of your warships?"

"I'll have one of my officers give them to you. I look forward to our meeting."

"As do I, sir."

"I would talk more, Force-Leader, but I have much to do. The Earth—" Hawthorne eyes tightened. "It's time we humans banded together…before we're extinct."

"I agree, sir. It's time we went on the offensive."

"I like your attitude, Kluge. Do all Jovians think like you?"

"…not yet," said Marten. "But the war isn't over."

"No," Hawthorne said. "For me, this war has just begun."

The End

13084188R00206

Printed in Great Britain
by Amazon.co.uk, Ltd.,
Marston Gate.